Wah-say-lan

Wah-say-lan

A Tale of the Iroquois in the American Revolution

JAMES HERBERT SMITH

PLAIDSWEDE PUBLISHING
Concord, New Hampshire

Designed and composed in Warnock Pro
at Hobblebush Books, Brookline, New Hampshire
(www.hobblebush.com)

Cover art by Bill Tyers

Printed in the United States of America

ISBN 978-0-9840650-2-8
Library of Congress Control Number: 2009938360

Published by:

PLAIDSWEDE PUBLISHING
P.O. Box 269 · Concord, New Hampshire 03302-0269
www.plaidswede.com

FOR ANNE GREENE,

WHO WAS THERE WHEN IT COUNTED.

AND FOR JACKY SMITH,

WHO WAS ALWAYS THERE.

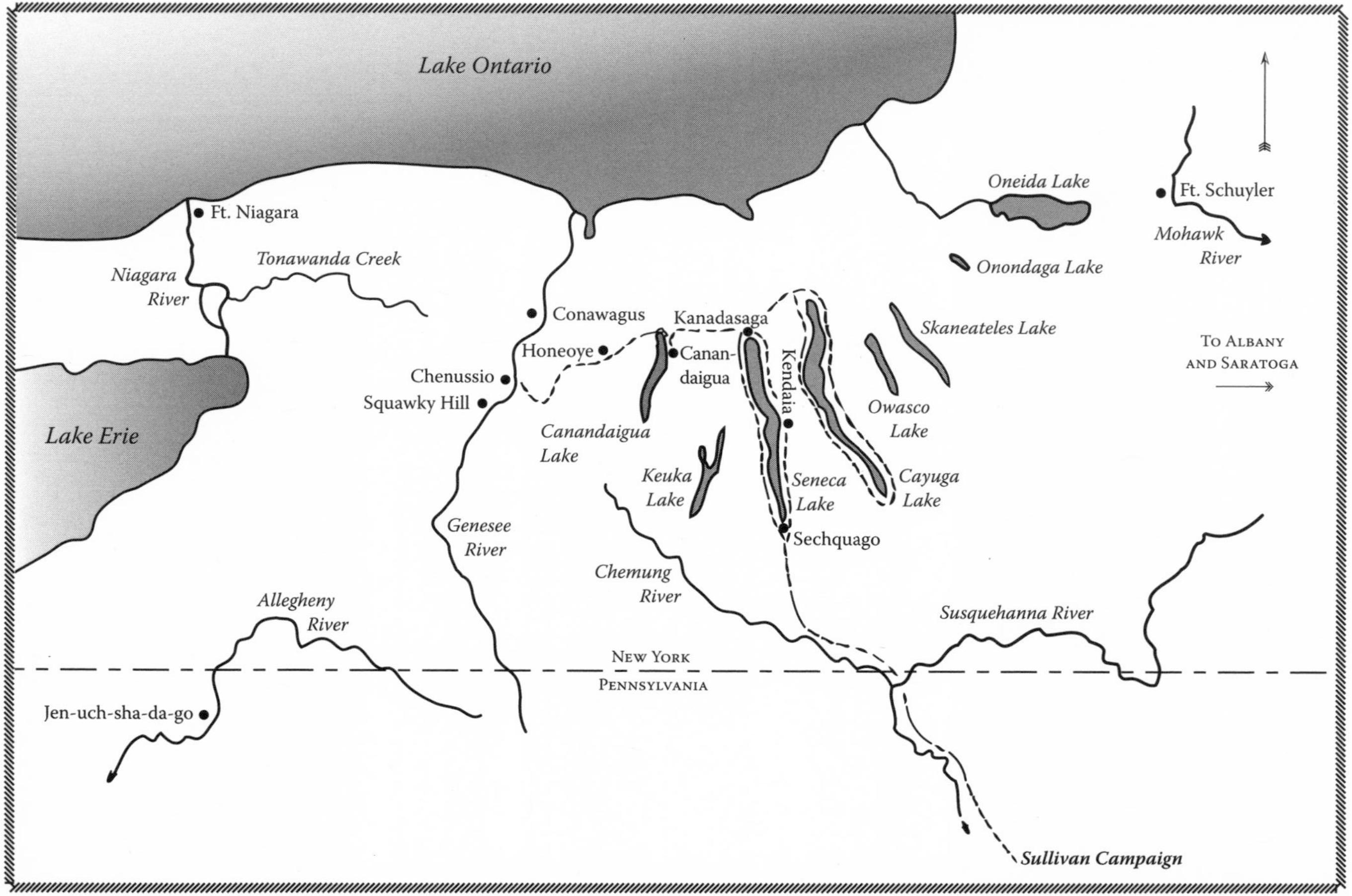
Lake Ontario
Ft. Niagara
Tonawanda Creek
Niagara River
Lake Erie
Conawagus
Honeoye
Chenussio
Squawky Hill
Kanadasaga
Canan-daigua
Canandaigua Lake
Keuka Lake
Kendaia
Seneca Lake
Sechquago
Cayuga Lake
Owasco Lake
Skaneateles Lake
Onondaga Lake
Oneida Lake
Ft. Schuyler
Mohawk River
To Albany and Saratoga
Genesee River
Chemung River
Allegheny River
Susquehanna River
New York
Pennsylvania
Jen-uch-sha-da-go
Sullivan Campaign

A. SMITH

CONTENTS

Part I ◈ The Attack

Part II ◈ The Trek South

Part III ◈ Surrender

STORYTELLING

Having fictional characters interact with real people is the essence of historical fiction. Wah-say-lan and Freeman Trentham/Jamwesaw, though he is based on a real slave in Wallingford, Conn., who joined the Continental Army, are wholly the author's creation. Mary Angel is loosely based on the historical Mary Jemison, who was adopted by the Seneca at about this time.

The historical figures—Cornplanter, Red Jacket, Joseph Brant, Thomas Jefferson, Benjamin Franklin, George Washington, the Marquis de Lafayette and others—at times speak their actual words, though the place or time they said things may have been changed.

During the Sullivan campaign against the Iroquois in 1779 there was a skirmish at Newtown, near the Chemung River, that is alluded to in this novel. The Seneca war chief Cornplanter called for a stand at Canandaigua. Now, more than two centuries later, he gets that battle in this book.

In some parts of the book, particularly after the surrender of Lord Cornwallis, time is shortened for the purposes of the story.

ACKNOWLEDGMENTS

First and foremost I thank my publisher, George Geers, who took a risk on a first novel; and my editor, Glenn Richter, who cajoled, bludgeoned and otherwise moved me to make the story better. Thank you to Jacky Smith, for reading every word at least twice; and to Barbara Ann Davis and Stephanie Smith for their sense of storytelling and critical eyes. Also to Diane Szymaszek for her points of view challenging mine; and to Sarah and Rebecca Flinn for listening to various readings. I am indebted to Reid MacCluggage and Steve Smith for their early and continued support through ten years of researching and writing this novel; and to Andy Smith for his fine map of Iroquois country. Linda Daniels took great care in reading the manuscript and making good suggestions to improve the storytelling. I thank the Canandaigua Lake people who, either with purpose or perhaps unknowingly, incubated this story: Ann, James A. and Bill Smith; Susan Hastings Lunt and Clark Hastings; Herb, Leslie, Jack, David and James H. Hutchinson; Dan Dowling; Andy Conine; Fred and Mary Harrington; and most especially, the Zornow family: Margaret, Ted, Margaret Mary, Teddy, Carol, Betsy and Fran.

Wah-say-lan

Part I

THE ATTACK

◈ CHAPTER 1 ◈

The Island

The blue water was calm. The sun sparkled behind the thick forest, shooting streams of golden light through the intertwined oak and hemlock branches. As always, the beach was still shaded in the early morning before the sun would rise above the tree line. The young Seneca woman made her way from the longhouse. She stopped to put a few dried branches on the embers of the fire, then continued to the water's edge as she did every summer morning.

Wah-say-lan thought of her youth and took time to celebrate in her mind how her life stretched before her. She marveled to herself as she walked that she lived in a beautiful, ancient place where her people had lived back beyond memory, and how her own young life rejuvenated the long history of the Seneca dating back through generations of women just like her who swam in these same waters.

Only a few women in the village had stirred. Her cousin, Tun-weh, was already knee deep. Ripples surrounded her as she waded out farther.

"Wait, Tun-weh, I am right behind you," said Wah-say-lan as she stepped out of her deerskin robe and felt the fresh, cool lake water lick around her feet and ankles. All her life, through seventeen summers, Wah-say-lan had looked forward to her morning swim.

Her cousin, who was three years younger, turned and waited.

Tun-weh would much rather swim with Wah-say-lan. In fact, she would rather be with Wah-say-lan no matter what they were doing. Tun-weh's tall, intelligent cousin always made everything right, every circumstance better.

Tun-weh, like every other woman in the village, was shorter than her cousin and not nearly as beautiful. She loved Wah-say-lan but envied her full breasts, her long, sinewy legs, her deep, knowing eyes and the set of her smile. It was as if Wah-say-lan could not frown. And she strode always gracefully and with a purpose to her gait.

"I am glad you are here today," said Wah-say-lan, reaching out and touching her shoulder. "Let's swim for the island. I need to feel my body toss off the night."

They waded a few more steps, then dove in. The two young Indian women surrendered to the clear water, delighting in the sensation of the lake carrying them, buoying their lithe bodies as they swam toward the island. Their mothers had swum, as had their grandmothers and *their* grandmothers, out to the little island and back before breakfast. Its northern shore lay flat on the water. A hardwood and pine forest covered the ground as it rose gently to higher ridges at the southern end.

Seneca women who had a man did not do this. Once they were with a man of the village, they could bathe in the morning, but the swim to the island was a luxury left behind along with their virginity. Many wondered why the beautiful Wah-say-lan had not chosen her mate. Only her little cousin was brave enough to ask. "When I am ready," Wah-say-lan said. "When I am ready."

Tun-weh struggled to keep pace but her arms, though sturdy and strong, simply could not match the long strokes Wah-say-lan made through the water, propelling her body with great speed.

The shore of the island was just like that of the lake—gray shale rounded into small, flat pieces by eons of lapping waves. Hold it between thumb and forefinger and a flick of the wrist could send a piece skimming across the top of the lake the Indians called Canandaigua.

"You see how the shale bounces and stays afloat as long as it keeps moving," said the older woman to the younger, picking up and skipping a stone. "That is like us. Once we stand still, we stagnate, we might as well sink."

Tun-weh looked at her cousin in awe. No one else talked to her in these ways. It was always get the wood, watch the baby, start the fire. Seneca women were held in high esteem and given positions of honor and authority among the people, but the tribal ways were strict and the division of tasks rigid. So Tun-weh cherished free moments like this with Wah-say-lan, sitting naked on the beach of the island and listening to her thoughts.

When she was alone, Wah-say-lan would gather the best pieces of shale she could find, the most perfectly round ones, the smoothest ones. She would not choose jagged pieces or any with scratches on them. When she had a good pile, sometimes as many as twenty, she would pick up one, examine it, whisper a little something to it like "have a good adventure" and flick it across the lake's surface. She loved counting the number of splashes each made and watching how each splash sent out small ripples, making a line of ever-expanding tiny circular waves. She wouldn't skip the next piece until the ripples of the last one had faded. Somehow the endless supply of shale reassured her of life's timelessness on her lake.

This morning, though, Tun-weh turned her thoughts to troubling matters. The youngster brought it up reluctantly because she knew the subject riled her older friend.

"I saw some Red Coats yesterday," she confided. "I was picking blueberries and saw them with their long rifles talking in the clearing with Pundatha and others on the council."

"I do not want to hear about Red Coats right now, Tun-weh. Tell me later," Wah-say-lan said with finality.

Tun-weh tossed back and lay flat on the beach. "Look, the sun comes almost to the treetops. We should get back. Mother will be angry that I have not helped with the baby."

"You go ahead. I will catch up," responded Wah-say-lan. She

watched her younger companion dive into the water. Wah-say-lan loved being alone on the island. It was even better watching the sun set over the green hills to the west, but this moment will do, she thought, as the sun rose and bathed her body in the new day. Why did Tun-weh have to bring up the smelly Red Coats and their white-wigged officers marching through her woods? They get the war council all worked up and the men start their belligerent ways that lead only to bloodshed among her people.

"I do not need a Seneca man to be my own, only to run off whenever the British come and whisper treachery in his ears," she thought.

◈ CHAPTER 2 ◈

Freeman Trentham

At that moment, along the trail five miles to the east, a musket ball whizzed by Freeman Trentham's head. The "clap-varom" of several muskets being fired sounded through the forest.

"Halt! Take cover!" hollered Capt. Israel Stone.

He led a scouting party ahead of Gen. John Sullivan's army, sent by George Washington to break the British and Iroquois alliance.

The British were beginning to learn that warfare in the wilderness was not fought in straight lines. Though the royal officers still preferred their disciplined columns, the Six Nations of the Iroquois—Mohawk, Oneida, Onondaga, Cayuga, Tuscarora, and the farthest west, the Seneca—had shown them it was no way to win in North America. Overcoming their sense of chivalry, British Red Coats adapted to ambush as a military strategy in the woods.

"Good thing they haven't learned to shoot straight," thought Trentham as he jumped behind the trunk of a thick white pine. But he also knew that if the shots came from in front, chances are Iroquois warriors could be sneaking up behind. He wasn't sure why they decided to fight with the British. All he knew was that a charging warrior with his tomahawk held high was a sight he never wished for in life.

"Fix your circle!" shouted Capt. Stone. "Close it in!"

Trentham saw some of the others dash toward a stand of hemlocks about 30 yards to the south. He knew he had to get there, but the scene sent shivers through his taut body. His mind reeled back to what had happened under some other tall trees, far away and long ago.

The shooting and the screaming erupted at the same time. One mother scooped up her baby and ran for the forest. More firing of long guns. The infant flew out of her arms. Both were hit and slammed lifeless to the thick African grass. Men tossed nets over the scattering people. Trentham and his mother and all the other mothers and their children were captured.

They were tied together and marched two days to the seashore, where they were forced onto a huge, dark sailing vessel. The black captives were pushed down into its bowels and chained to rough wooden posts, joining others already in chains.

That was ten years, half his lifetime ago, yet the memory had never faded. Dozens of Africans squeezed into the hold of the stinking ship, his mother pushed away from him so that he had to strain his chains to get a glimpse of her beautiful but now tortured face. Gruff men with pale skin came and took her up out of the dark hole. If she resisted, they would beat her and spit on her and tear her blouse. Each time they brought her back, she held her head down and would not look at her son or any of the defeated black men chained in the hold.

◆ CHAPTER 3 ◆

Wah-say-lan's Bow

Wah-say-lan did not hear the shooting five miles away as she walked the narrow, pine-needled path from the island's shore toward the clearing in its center. There she reached into a hollowed-out oak tree and pulled out the buckskin pouch holding a shirt and long pants she had made to hide here with her bow and quiver of arrows. She had watched the men of her village make their bows from the branches of the shagbark hickory. She had watched carefully how they attached sharp flint points to the tops of their arrows. She could accompany a hunting party and help skin the slain deer, but, like the other women, she could not shoot. So she made her own bow and her own arrows and she learned to shoot true here on the island.

The women of the Iroquois Confederacy could help construct the great longhouses of elm, and prepare the elm bark for their canoes. The women were in many ways equal partners in the ancient rules of the Confederacy formed so long ago by Hiawatha and Dekanawidah, the Peacemaker. Along with making baskets and clothing and planting and cultivating corn, beans and squash, the women of one of the world's earliest democracies were considered the heirs. Family names were those of the women. They were empowered to admonish and correct the chiefs of the council. When a vacancy occurred, the women of the council chose the successor. These rules, set countless summers before, were part of what made the Iroquois the strongest of all Indian nations.

Iroquois women were not warriors and did not hunt. Wah-say-lan longed to hunt. "If I can skin a deer, why can't I bring one down with my own arrow?" she pondered as she stepped into her clothes and then placed an arrow on the bowstring. She pulled it back to her chin. It flew at its target and hit the birch sapling right where she had aimed. Wah-say-lan knew her aim was good and she knew she could take the elusive white-tailed deer. It was an honor to kill the deer for your sustenance and warmth. The meat carried the Seneca through the hard winters; the deerskins clothed the Seneca from foot to head. But Wah-say-lan had not yet dared to bring her bow to the mainland. The village council would punish her, just as they had punished her grandmother, Lan-lu-seh.

She was ostracized for breaking the confederation rules. Lan-lu-seh's husband had broken his leg chasing a bear. It was bad luck for her family and meant other families had to share their meat and their fish from the lake. Lan-lu-seh did not like to accept the food from others and so snuck into the forest with her husband's bow. She had not even taken a shot when a hunting party returning to the village found her with the weapon.

Her granddaughter was determined not to be caught, but Wah-say-lan was just as determined to know how to fend for herself. She knew she was as good as any man among the Seneca. She pulled another arrow from her quiver and aimed at the knot chest-high on the oak well beyond the birch. She let the arrow fly and again it found its target.

As she pulled the arrow back on the bowstring, her thoughts jumped back to when as a child she found a curved stick and immediately made it her weapon. It was after her seventh winter and she had heard the stories around the council fire of how a small boy and girl were the only ones left in the original Seneca village after the legendary serpent had devoured everyone else. According to the hallowed, ancient stories, the little boy slew the monster with a magic bow and arrow.

She remembered pretending that she was the little girl and at the last minute the boy stumbled and it was she who released the lethal arrow, killing the beast. With her curved stick she was shooting off magic arrows when her father came around the longhouse.

She remembered his calm voice: "My Wah-say-lan, what are you doing?"

The little girl was startled, but composed herself. "Why, Daddy, I am killing the serpent who ate our people. I am saving the Seneca! The little boy fell, I had to do it."

The big and strong Lan-lu-rah stifled a laugh but said to her firmly, "Young girls need to plant the crops. They do not shoot arrows. Now give me that bow—I mean stick—and go to the fields with your mother."

She saw herself reluctantly handing over her weapon and running down the path. She thought to herself, "It was not the last time my father had to remind me of tribal rules and customs." She pulled one more arrow from her quiver and shot it into the notch next to the last one. "That little girl has grown to be a good shot with the bow and arrow," she said to herself as she walked to the trees and pulled her arrows out, placing them back in her quiver.

◈ CHAPTER 4 ◈

Trentham Eats Alone

Freeman Trentham shook off the memory of his capture 10 years ago and moved toward the stand of hemlocks where Capt. Stone was gathering his men. Francis Herndon was running a few feet ahead of him and stopped, then crumpled to the ground, an arrow sticking out of his head. Freeman hit the ground. He looked into Herndon's open but unseeing eyes.

The soldier had been no friend of Trentham's. He was one of many of Sullivan's men who refused to eat at the same table with Trentham. "Niggers don't sit at our table," Herndon once said as Trentham brought his rations from the campfire.

"Never," added Cpl. Alan Richswill. "Never, nigger, do you eat with us."

Trentham ate alone that day and many days. He was in the Continental Army fighting in the cause of liberty for a very personal reason. If he fought, his master would have to grant him his freedom at the end of the war.

As he lay looking into Herndon's dead eyes, Trentham felt only pity for the man. But then he said to himself, "You don't have to worry where I eat my meals anymore," and the pity dissolved. There was no time for feelings anyway. The Seneca and the Red Coats were still firing. He had to get to the trees with Stone and the others.

Trentham was tall, over six feet. He carried his rugged frame topped by wide, squared shoulders always upright, refusing the bowed posture of most slaves. He grabbed Herndon's musket and powder horn, uncoiled in a grand leap and loped in his long strides for the cover of the next big tree. When he made it to the stand of hemlocks, Stone was counting his men and the Red Coats were still firing. Their Seneca allies were closing in from the south.

"Sir, Herndon didn't make it," said Freeman Trentham.

"Either did Prichard," said a soldier.

Capt. Stone counted nine men left of his scouting party. "Keep the circle. Ready your bayonets," he said. "We'll get out of this."

Trentham wasn't at all sure of that. It was the first time on the long trek west that so few of them had faced an enemy they couldn't see. He hunkered down between two towering pines, their tops swaying in the morning breeze. His mind shot back to his last sight of his mother.

The ship, after endless, gut-wrenching days and nights of sailing from West Africa, came into a harbor with wooden structures larger than the 10-year-old boy had ever imagined. The gruff men who had taken his mother so many times came down and pushed all the slaves out of the hold. They marched onto docks where many white-skinned men in strange clothes stood watching. Soon one man was talking swiftly and pointing to the Africans. Other white men nodded and shot their hands in the air and shouted odd words.

Groups of Africans were herded to wagons pulled by large brown animals bigger than wildebeests but without horns. Slaves were tied to the wagons and carted off. The young boy was frightened beyond belief. He saw his mother down the dock and ran toward her, but a rough hand cuffed him and knocked him down. Then another man took his mother, two other African women and several men and shoved them onto a wagon. The man who grabbed his mother was speaking in loud, harsh words. The boy listened but could not comprehend. He held one sound in his mind and said it over to himself—"Jefferson. Jefferson." The large animals pulled the wagon away. His mother kept looking back at him until they turned behind the huge building and out of sight.

The African boy did not know what to do or what to think. He tried to say he was dreaming and that he would soon wake up at his parents' side, his father ready to show him how to hunt on the high plains above their village.

Then he was lifted to his feet and put on a wagon with two other young boys and a young girl. They were from other tribes. He did not know them, did not know their language. Noah Willington took a whip and snapped the horses into motion. It was a ride of many days.

Trentham did not know then that it was Baltimore where the slave ship had sailed to, or that his new home would be in a place called Connecticut, or that the year was called 1769. Willington gave him the name Trentham after the ship's captain and called him boy until he reached what they believed was his 18th year. He then became Freeman in an irony the slave did not like, but he could not choose his own name.

The officer's orders snapped Trentham back to the fight he was facing. "We'll have to make a break for it," the captain said. "There's too many of them."

He ordered Cpl. Richswill to take three men including Trentham and head due east. "Stay in a line but keep 30 feet apart. Don't stop until you reach Sullivan's column. I will take the rest of the men southeast. Good luck. Now head out."

"Nigger, you go first," growled Richswill.

Freeman Trentham rushed ahead, the others followed. An arrow flew close over his head. Another got the last man in the back. That left just the corporal, Trentham and one other trying to get back to Sullivan's army some 10 miles away. Stone and his small contingent were making their way southeast.

Richswill's group had run only a couple hundred yards when they saw a line of Seneca braves circling south. Somehow the Indians hadn't detected them and the corporal whispered, "Let's go."

"No, sir, wait one minute. They always have one man . . ."

"Lousy nigger, I said let's go," and the corporal ran ahead. As he ran past a large boulder, a brave jumped out and threw him to the ground. The Indian lifted his tomahawk as Trentham, on the run, rammed his bayonet into the warrior's back. The tomahawk fell to the ground. In a spasm, the Indian leaped up, turned and gazed at the black man, then fell in a heap.

"Run!" said Trentham, picking up the dazed Richswill. He pushed him ahead and they ran through the forest without looking back.

◈ CHAPTER 5 ◈

Captured

Wah-say-lan carefully folded her clothes back into the pouch and placed it and her bow and arrows back in the hollow tree. She walked to the big rock at the island's south end. She stood for a moment looking at the expanse of water stretching southward. Canandaigua Lake lies in a narrow, green valley. A canoe can cross the lake quickly east to west, but it would take half a day to paddle its full length. Its deep water provided trout, bass, perch, pickerel and other fish for her people.

Wah-say-lan dove into the clear water and swam toward the village. She thought how strong her grandmother was to try to feed her family when her husband couldn't. She thought of Lan-lu-seh diving off the same rock and swimming back to the village. When she gave birth to Wah-say-lan's father, few white men had ever seen Canandaigua. But now there were many and the Seneca were trying to determine how to protect their homeland.

The young Seneca was composed in front of others, but inside there were times when she had many questions. Where did these white men come from? Why don't they go back? How can I make them go away? But she had no answers.

At noon the village council met. She sat just outside the circle around the fire, behind her mother, Wah-say-han. Her father,

Lan-lu-rah, was speaking. The British made white man names for many Indians. They called her father Bear Hunter. She could speak their English language, but she refused to let them call her anything but Wah-say-lan.

The sachem, Pundatha, listened as the brave told of the skirmish that morning. Two Red Coats had died, one Seneca was bayoneted, but several continentals had lost their lives. They prayed for the soul of the slain Seneca, Rah-weh-un, who had grown up in the village with Wah-say-lan and who died with honor defending his people. At sunset they would bury him on the sacred bluff above their lake.

"We captured the two running like dogs," said Lan-lu-rah, and he pointed to Cpl. Richswill and Freeman Trentham, lashed to a post in the sun a few yards from the lakeshore. "Another with them took a tomahawk in his heart. The wolves will feast tonight and thank the Seneca," said Lan-lu-rah.

Wah-say-lan could not help but stare at the black-skinned prisoner. She had never seen an African and wondered what the gods had done to put him among the white man. She also knew the prisoners were doomed.

Pundatha declared, "One will die today, one when the sun rises."

"But wait," said Maj. John Butler, the British officer who had led the fight against the rebels' scouting party. "We could trade these men for ours taken prisoner. The Blue Coat army is not far from these men."

"Sullivan's Blue Coats burn Iroquois villages," replied Pundatha. "All across Iroquois lands, even with the British with us, the continentals burn our villages. These men must pay!" said the sachem.

"Pundatha, listen, if we meet with Sullivan and have these men, maybe your village will be spared," the officer said.

The Seneca sachem was silent for several moments. "I will think on it tonight. I will decide when the sun rises over Canandaigua. Tonight we will feed the Blue Coats. Tomorrow they may die."

◈ CHAPTER 6 ◈

Washington in Connecticut

Three years earlier, Freeman Trentham was showing Noah Willington's young daughter her addition and subtraction tables when the Rev. Samuel Andrews knocked on the door.

"Come in, Reverend," said Mr. Willington. "To what do we owe this honor of your visit?"

"Thank you, Noah. It is always a pleasure to join you. I cannot, however, stay. The selectmen have asked me to inform you that Gen. Washington will be here this evening. He has left Boston and travels to defend New-York. He will be dining at the church hall and, of course, your presence is requested."

"Wonderful. Gen. Washington has seen the British out of Boston," said Willington.

"Yes, but it appears their ships are headed for New-York," said the town's Anglican minister. Andrews served the Church of England, but he had lived most of his life in Connecticut Colony. To some in the small village of just a few hundred families, he took the call to liberty to extremes.

"The commander-in-chief is stopping again in Wallingford just for the overnight rest. He will be off at daybreak. His light cavalry brigade is with him. As short as his stay is, I nevertheless intend to raise the slavery question with him," warned the good reverend.

Willington glanced nervously at Trentham, bent over the board correcting Beatrice on her numbers.

"There's more talk of a document on independence and freedom from the King," the minister continued. "How can we enslave fellow human beings whilst we also declare that freedom is a God-given right?"

"Now Samuel, we have been over this before and I beg of you to keep your voice down in front of my young servant," whispered Willington while showing the minister to the door. They stepped outside and the merchant went on: "Do not forget that there are more than a hundred men and women in bondage in this community and you do not make friends of patriots when you bring this matter up."

"Precisely. The hypocrisy, sir, ought to be obvious," Andrews insisted.

"Reverend, do not forget that Gen. Washington is from Virginia. His farm is worked by perhaps 300 slaves. He is commanding our Continental Army and you must show the proper respect!" the townsman shot back, losing his patience.

"Mr. Willington, I must be off to bring invitations to the others. If the general is to lead us to independence, even a Virginian needs to consider our oppression of Negroes. But I shall make my points this evening to our commander with all due respect," he said and walked down Center Street to spread the word of the coming visitor.

Willington could not understand how the selectmen put up with the young clergyman. "He is a troublemaker," he thought. "He cares more about slaves than independence."

As he walked down the street, Andrews thought Willington was a puzzle. "He's one of the few citizens who actually educated a slave and yet, really, bondage seems not to be on his conscience."

Freeman Trentham was not concentrating on math. He had heard the exchange but was careful to show no reaction. He resolved to find a way to be in the church, or at least as near as he could get, at dinnertime.

"That's enough ciphering today, Beatrice. Freeman, it is time to harvest firewood," the master said brusquely. The slave would much rather stack wood than tutor the little girl. She loved telling him what to do in a haughty tone that Freeman knew he could do nothing about. "If she were my own child, she'd understand respect for elders," he thought, but immediately dismissed the idea of bringing a child into slavery.

Later that afternoon, as Trentham brought a load of cut logs from the woods, he saw the commotion. Washington was riding into town at the head of his entourage of officers. Connecticut's own Gen. Israel Putnam, who had shown great bravery at Boston's Breed's Hill, rode beside Washington. Nearly a hundred cavalrymen were mounted in the column.

"Freeman," his master said, "leave that wood. Get over to the church. Several boys are standing down the brigade's horses. Haul a load of feed and help secure the mounts for the night."

"Yes, sir, Mr. Willington," he said, delighted at his good fortune. He pushed the cart to the woodpile and grabbed the feed basket.

As soldiers pitched their tents, a handful of Wallingford slaves helped string ropes along a stand of white birches to tether the horses. Freeman Trentham scooped healthy portions of oats and corn kernels onto the ground in front of the tired and hungry animals. The brigade had made 50 miles that day over the rough inland route, avoiding the better-traveled Post Road along the coast. In three days Washington had made the half-way point to New-York.

"When you're done there, boy, take this bucket and fetch water for these horses," said a gruff, blue-coated sergeant.

Willington's slave looked at the soldier for a moment, then answered quietly, "Yes, sir. The river, the Quinnipiac River, isn't too far. I'll take two buckets."

As he walked to the place where he was allowed to fish, he thought back to his boyhood in West Africa when he could roam at will, when he and the other boys of his village explored the forests endlessly. Freedom was not something he took for granted back then. He didn't think of it. Freedom was simply a natural fact of his life. Now, in the late spring of 1776 in Connecticut Colony, on this land where Indians once roamed freely, he is as tethered as the horses he just fed.

He remembered the cruel day on the docks of Baltimore when angry men pushed his mother onto a wagon and drove her out of sight. He remembered their strange language and said again that one word—"Jefferson."

"Where is she?" Trentham asked himself. "Where is my beautiful mother? Where did they take her?" His heart pounded as he carried the buckets of water. He ached because he missed her and because he did not know if she was dead or alive.

The Rev. Andrews' wife Mildred walked by and brought Trentham out of his bad memories and back to his constant goal—to plan, however he could, to find his mother.

"Ma'am, might'en I help serve the dinner?" he asked.

"Why Freeman, I shall ask. We certainly do need some help with all these fine officers here," she said and walked on to the church hall, where Washington's command staff was politely accepting goblets of wine as they gathered for dinner. The town's merchants, largest landowners, and Selectmen were greeting their visitors warmly.

The scent of roasted venison and beef rose from the kitchen as the First Selectman urged everyone to take their seats.

"Gentlemen, gentlemen, our good Rev. Samuel Andrews, graduate of Yale College, our spiritual guide here since 1769, would like to thank our Lord for our bounty and our evening together," he shouted.

Everyone waited for Washington to move to the head table.

As the general sat down, the reverend rose and spoke. "Gen. Washington, Gen. Putnam, and officers of our Continental Army, we heartily welcome you to Wallingford and we applaud your victory in casting the King's men from Boston. Your bravery and skill are to be commended and now we know you must face further peril in the defense of New-York.

"We are honored you saw fit to choose our humble village for a respite in your march to fight for liberty," he said.

He asked them all to bow their heads. "May the Lord show us the way from under the oppression of a monarch across the wide ocean . . . "

"Gawa," Freeman Trentham said to himself, as he carved ribs onto platters. "Ocean means gawa. The big gawa," he thought to himself in the way he tried to hang on to the language of his childhood. He could now speak and write English flawlessly, but he would spend time each day talking to himself in his native West African language. The results were some hybrids of English and African words: big gawa for the wide expanse of water he was forced across. He would envision conversations with his father and with his mother. Then he would question, where was his father the day he was captured? Why didn't he come and save him?

Washington had risen to his full 6 feet, 2 inches, taller than everyone present, except Freeman Trentham.

"We are in the midst of a perilous fight. When I was given this commission, I did not think this fight could be anything but a new beginning, a break from the past. Gentlemen, I can inform you, in fact I am anxious and proud to inform you that our efforts cannot and will not be anything but a full rising to a free and independent nation. We cannot battle the King's armies and expect to continue as colonies of the Crown, tied like slaves to a faraway master. The Continental Congress has appointed a committee, headed by Mr. Adams of Massachusetts, to draw up a document to declare our independence from the British Empire."

The general paused. The room was hushed.

"We Americans shall proclaim our new nation based not on the rule of a despot, but on the will of the people," he declared.

The men of Wallingford, Connecticut, rose at once with huzzahs and hear! hears!

Washington went on: "John Adams is joined by Dr. Franklin and Connecticut's own Roger Sherman, Gen. Putnam's good friend. And

I am most proud to say, that also appointed to this crucial committee is my fellow Virginian, the young Thomas Jefferson."

Freeman Trentham heard the name and nearly dropped the platter of ribs he was carrying. His knees felt weak. He stopped, steadied himself, tried to show no emotion, but whispered to himself. "Jefferson. The young Thomas Jefferson. Fellow Virginian." It had been seven years, nearly half his life, since he had heard the word. "Jefferson of Virginia," Trentham said to himself again.

"Freeman, these officers are hungry. Let's go now," Mrs. Willington whispered just behind him, herself carrying a large platter. Her mission at the moment was to serve dinner. She was not listening to Washington speak of independence from Great Britain.

Trentham delivered his steaming meat but he kept alert, listened to every word.

Those assembled in Wallingford revered Dr. Franklin, were awed by John Adams and his cousin, Samuel, of Boston, but they had never heard of Thomas Jefferson. First Selectman Elihu Yale stood up next to Washington and said, "Mr. Adams will surely bring forth a fine document on liberty from King George. We do not know, sir, your Thomas Jefferson, but we know our Mr. Sherman, who has championed freedom and independence even before those first shots at Lexington and Concord."

The Rev. Andrews saw his moment. "With all due respect, Gen. Washington," he said while rising from his chair again. "If we talk of liberty and freedom from oppressive Kings, liberty that God and nature have granted mankind, how then do we justify detaining in captivity a part of our fellow creatures? Two years ago the General Assembly of this colony abolished the trade in African slaves. Is it not time to let those we oppress go free?"

Stunned that the cleric had such gall, Noah Willington rose to silence him but caught Washington's stare and waited worriedly for the general to speak. Willington, Yale and Washington were all standing and staring back at the minister. Washington began slowly, in measured tones.

"Sir, first comes the freedom of nations. God willing, we will establish a new nation based on the will of a free people rather than the rule of a monarch. Then the people will codify the liberties in our nation. I might add, unlike your New England mercantile economy, Virginia and the colonies of the Southern part, the Carolinas, Georgia, our livelihood is based on farming and the labor for more than a century of the unfortunate African race."

The Rev. Andrews, principled yet practical, sure of himself as a man who knows he is right, nodded and smiled and asked the commander-in-chief to consider his suggestion in another way. "Gen. Washington, you lead us to the future on a foundation of freedom. We value it deeply, so how dare we proclaim it whilst we keep so many in bondage? Have we not heard, sir, the British offers of freedom to any Negroes who join their side in the present war? Might I suggest, sir, as you recruit men to fight for our victory, can we not also send those we hold in bondage into battle with the promise of freedom upon victory?"

"My good reverend," Washington replied, "these matters have been discussed at the highest levels in military command . . ."

The minister persisted. "Again, with all due respect, general, begging your indulgence, perhaps individual slave holders could decide to send a bondsman to your forces with the promise of freedom after he has shown bravery on the field of battle. After we have defeated the oppressor and established our independence."

Washington raised his hand and, in a firm voice with a tone of finality, said, "This, Rev. Andrews, is a decision not for the military. I shall tell you it is my fondest desire to see some plan adopted by which slavery may be abolished, but I shall also warn that officers do and will dread the inclusion of ignorant slaves in their ranks. This is a decision for the Continental Congress, which appointed me to this post." He sat down, making it clear he felt this line of discussion concluded.

Willington, inwardly seething at Andrews' impertinence, meant to silence the minister. "Thank you, Rev. Andrews, for your enlightened thinking. I'm sure you will address a correspondence to the Congress on this issue. And now we must all please enjoy this feast and thank again Gen. Washington for honoring us with his presence. To the officers of the Continental Army, drink up and eat hearty for we know that tomorrow onward you must go to the defense of the patriot cause."

Trentham's thoughts were racing. Freedom will be to join this army, an army that might need to move to Virginia. He knew vaguely of Virginia. He always listened when Willington discussed issues with other Wallingford leaders. Schooled by Willington in order to assist in the business, Trentham was allowed to read the Connecticut Courant and other periodicals circulated in the small community. But, until this night, he had not heard the word "Jefferson" since the day he lost his mother. Now he knew of a Thomas Jefferson in Virginia.

The Continental Congress did not need to wait for a letter from Rev. Andrews. Alarmed by British tactics and always fearful of slave rebellion, the Congress sent orders to Washington and disseminated proclamations that slaveholders could, instead of sending a son to the militia or to the Army, substitute an able-bodied slave. If the slave performed his duties, he could gain his freedom at the conclusion of hostilities and the Congress would reimburse the slave owner.

Willington had always planned to send his son the 15 miles to Yale College in New Haven to be educated as a lawyer. Not only would his son help carry on the family business, but now that the colonies were on the path to nationhood, his son's legal training would put him in good stead to lead the former colonies into statehood.

When the day came, several weeks later, it was not hard for Willington to convince Trentham to join the Connecticut militia. Washington was calling for troops to defend New-York. A battle was imminent on Long Island.

"Yes, sir, I believe I can be helpful in the army," said Freeman Trentham.

◈ CHAPTER 7 ◈

A Prisoner Meets Wah-say-lan

Trentham towered over Richswill, a short, barrel-chested man. The 20-year-old slave was thinking of the Revolution he was fighting with this man, fighting for independence and freedom. Then he saw her coming toward them. She walked so gracefully, with such nobility. Her long black hair framed an angelic face. He could not help the stirrings inside him. Trentham nearly lost his breath. His mind stopped thinking. He just stared as she came nearer.

Wah-say-lan held a bowl and raised a wooden spoon.

"You must eat," she said to them in English and raised warm venison broth to Richswill's mouth. He refused the offer. She brought the spoon to Trentham, who received the warmth of the nourishment.

"Where do you come from?" he heard the woman ask. She touched his arm. "What is this skin?"

Freeman Trentham stared back. He felt her touch. He was entranced by her beauty.

"Where are you from, continental?" Wah-say-lan asked again.

Trentham thought about Africa but answered Connecticut.

"The land of the Mohegan," she said. "Do white men have black skin in Connecticut?"

Trentham could not help but smile. "Do white men have black skin," he quietly repeated. "No. I am a slave of the white man," he said.

"A slave? Slaves as warriors? The whites have odd ways. But what of your skin?" She touched him again. "Where do the white man's slaves get black skin?"

Trentham took more soup. He could not keep pace with his thoughts about this Seneca Indian woman before him. He wanted to ask where she got such big, dark eyes, why she grew so tall, why she asked such frank questions.

Wah-say-lan did not think them frank. They were her questions. So she asked them. She expected answers.

Trentham found himself saying, "I came from across the big gawa—the ocean—as a child, captured and sold to white men," he said. "All my people have black or brown skin just as your people have darker skin. The white slave traders took my mother. I have not seen her since. They say she might be in Virginia, a slave to Thomas Jefferson."

"Quiet, nigger!" ordered the corporal.

Wah-say-lan asked Richswill, "Where is his mother?"

The corporal looked away.

"Wah-say-lan, Wah-say-lan! It is time for the burial!" hollered Tun-weh, coming from the longhouses.

"Did not your people across the big gawa fight the white slave traders?" Wah-say-lan asked Freeman Trentham.

"We fought, but I was a boy," he said. He did not want her to leave. He forgot he was lashed to a post. He forgot he was in a war.

When she walked away to join the people of her village for the burial of the brave Trentham had killed, he watched her purposeful movement until she was out of sight. His knees were weak, his chest was pounding. He had never felt like that before. It had nothing to do with his capture and everything to do with the woman he had just met.

The rawhide lashed to the post cut into his ankles and he remembered his predicament. His wrists were tied behind his back, but not as tightly.

As the Seneca went off to the burial ceremony, Freeman went

over her words, remembering how they sounded, listening to her voice over and over in his mind. It reminded him of the gentle lapping, the soothing ebb and flow of small waves on a lakeshore. Her voice was inquisitive yet calm, frank but not frantic. She wanted answers but did not demand them.

No one had ever asked him such questions. She reminded him he was not of the white man. Noah Willington had educated him to help in the family grain and mill business in Wallingford, Connecticut. Trentham had learned the English language, their numbers, their calendar, even their Congregational religion. He not only weighed and loaded grain, he had learned so well that he tutored Willington's young daughter. Still, though, he was a slave and would remain a slave until the war's end. The end required the defeat of the British and their allies, the Iroquois.

His thoughts turned to the words of George Washington, words he had read in the Connecticut Courant three years ago; he had read them over and over again until he could not forget them. The General Orders of the Commander of the army in 1776: "Let us therefore show the whole world that a free man, contending for liberty on his own ground, is superior to any slavish mercenary on earth."

How true, Trentham had said when he read those words. "A free man contending for liberty on his own ground" was the phrase he repeated to himself. He had not chosen this ground. He was put here. But it was his life and he would live it free if he could.

Just before the battle for Long Island, Freeman had been close enough to hear Gen. Washington address the Continental Army. The commander had turned to an aide and said, "If Thomas Jefferson can write the Declaration of Independence, then I can try to find the words to inspire these men who have offered their lives for our noble cause."

He mounted his black steed, stood high in the stirrups and raised his voice: "Men of the Continental Army! Listen! The time is now near at hand, which must determine whether Americans are to be free men or slaves."

Washington had paused as Trentham and hundreds of others moved closer. He began again: "The fate of unborn millions will now depend, under God, on the courage and conduct of this army. Our cruel and unrelenting enemy leaves us only the choice to conquer or die."

"Free men or slaves," Freeman Trentham whispered to himself, amazed that he could recall so much of Washington's speech. "George Washington is a good leader," Trentham thought. For some reason he thought of Noah Willington, the man who had made sure his slave could read and write. "But even that was not my own free choice. It was a demand from master to slave," mused Trentham.

Night had come. The rawhide hurt his ankles, but his mind sped as he peered skyward at a canopy of countless stars.

"To conquer or die," thought Trentham. "Conquer or die. I will not die here. I will not die yet," he told himself. He rubbed the rope up and down on the post. He pulled at his wrists. He said to himself over and over: "Jefferson, Jefferson, he wrote the great document, Jefferson." Through the night the black man rubbed and pulled and twisted until his wrists bled. But finally he could sense some slackening.

Then one strand snapped. He pulled hard and his hands were free. He reached down and found the knot holding the rope around his ankles and soon had it undone. Freeman looked at Cpl. Richswill, who was sleeping. His head hung to one side.

"Free men or slaves—conquer or die," said Trentham to himself. "How many times in one day do I save this lout? Leave him and he'll die a cruel death. Good. He deserves it. I'd be better off without him. He's trouble. Then again, he could be useful."

The Big Dipper had traversed the sky and it was about to sink below the horizon, just then turning from dark black to a lighter gray. He would have to act fast. He started to untie the corporal's feet.

"No!" Richswill yelled, and Trentham jumped up and clasped his palm across the man's mouth.

"It's me, corporal. Be still!" said the slave.

Richswill did as commanded, then whispered, "Hurry, the dawn comes."

When Trentham had freed the corporal, they both ran away from the village but Freeman grabbed Richswill and said, "Stop. The best way is the lake."

The corporal didn't argue. In the lightening sky the two men swam west. Before dawn they pulled themselves onto the island. "This will do for now," said Cpl. Richswill, and they hustled across the shale and into some bushes as the first rays of sun streamed through the forest. Over the water they heard yells and knew the Seneca had discovered their escape.

◈ CHAPTER 8 ◈

A Dream

Wah-say-lan had not slept well. She could not get the black man out of her mind. She smiled at how he had said, "I came from across the big gawa." She thought of how he had explained his black skin by talking of her skin. She dreamed of him touching her arm the way she had touched his and she realized she had never before dreamed of a man's touch. "Yet I dream of this man," she whispered to herself.

She heard the hollering and rushed out. When she saw the post without the prisoners, she thought Pundatha had decided on an early execution. No, she said to herself, he must not die. She would not let that happen, she thought, and then instantly asked herself, "Why would I not want the continentals killed? These soldiers have come to burn my village and kill my people. These white men have come to where they have not been invited. But he is not a white man."

Braves running in different directions interrupted her thoughts and she knew the two had escaped. She forgot to ask him his name, she thought, and then wondered why she was thinking that.

"Oh, my mind is clouded," she said to herself. "And they will stop me from leaving if I don't go right now."

She slipped out of her robe and waded into the lake, carefully pushing off without a splash, and swam for her island. She was enough a creature of habit that her morning swim was almost a necessity. “I need to think about my thoughts,” she mused as she swam. The tall black soldier must be a strong swimmer, she thought, picturing him not lashed to a post but stroking freely through the water. Her own body shivered at the image.

“I will be quick. What if they are captured? Maybe I shouldn’t go all the way to the island,” she thought.

CHAPTER 9

"Hold Still, Wench"

Pundatha brought his braves together and deployed parties to head south along the lake's shore and east back toward Sullivan's army. "They could not have gone north through the village. South and east. Go on foot and canoe. Check all the coves," he said.

Cpl. Richswill loathed being alone with a slave, a slave who had somehow freed them from certain death. "Why did Herndon take the arrow and not this slave?" he thought.

They watched from the thickets as several canoes a half-mile away headed south along the shore of the calm waters. "Go scout this island. How big is it? How far to the west shore? What food is there here? Bring back something to eat. Are there stones suitable for a weapon? Go look and report back," Richswill ordered Freeman Trentham.

As the corporal watched from his hiding place, he saw a solitary figure swimming toward him. He looked to see if it was really just one. Instinctively he sought out a stick or rocks. He had no gun or knife, but he had the element of surprise. As Wah-say-lan swam closer to the island, Richswill realized it was the woman who offered food last night.

Wah-say-lan had looked back twice and knew the braves were still searching. She would go back if the soldiers were captured in order to—to what? She thought again. To argue for the black man's life, she decided, even though she was not sure why. She kicked up her speed for the island. She wanted to sit on the beach and think as the sun rose over the trees to the east.

"Why would they send a woman out here?" he thought, then smiled to himself. "Nothing like a morning treat," and checked again to see if anyone else was swimming behind her. She was alone.

Trentham scouted through the trees and kept an eye on the canoes. When he was sure they were sticking to the east shore, he headed for the center of the island and came upon a large patch of blueberries. Quickly he filled his pockets with the ripe berries and worked his way toward a clearing. A large white oak stood alone with a hollowed-out trunk.

Wah-say-lan waded up on the shale beach. She picked up a piece and skipped it across the top of the water, watching how it bounced across the lake, slowed and sank. She sat at the water's edge and let the water drip off her naked body.

Richswill could not believe the sight he was seeing. He fidgeted with his crotch. He never thought an Indian could be so attractive. Her father must have been white, he thought. No matter. He checked across the lake again and saw only two canoes heading off in the distance, southward. He crept toward the naked Seneca woman.

Freeman Trentham put his hand on the large oak. He peered inside the gash in the trunk and wondered how nature had provided such a shelter. Then he saw the bow and arrows and the pouch. He could not believe the luck. He took the bow and set the string. He felt the power of the weapon in the tension of the taut sinew. Trentham slung the pouch and quiver over his shoulder, carried the bow with an arrow at the ready, and headed to check the west shore of the island.

Richswill ran the few feet from the bushes across the shale. He grabbed Wah-say-lan from behind. She did not scream as he tugged her backward across the beach. She pulled at the dirty white hands that were violating her breasts. She knew immediately it was the man who had shouted, "Shut up, nigger!" the night before when he was tethered to the post.

Richswill pushed her down and tried to get on top. Wah-say-lan heaved him over. He was taken aback by her strength but grabbed her around the neck and started squeezing. He jabbed his knee into her stomach and pushed her over. She fought back, slamming the side of her hand repeatedly into his side.

"Where is the black man? Why just one?" she thought. "How do I do this?" Just then something hit hard against her head. She felt her muscles go loose and saw the rock in his raised hand. She grabbed his arm and stopped a second blow. Blood was oozing onto her black hair. Her eyes were losing focus.

Richswill threw his leg over her body and pushed her back down. Wah-say-lan was on her back. He pushed between her legs and held her arms with his hands.

"Hold still, you nasty wench," she heard him say as he released one of her arms to pull at his pants. She could not raise her arm. He plunged between her spread thighs.

"No!" she shouted, and strained and pulled and found the strength to hit him hard across his mouth. He responded with a fist smashing into her lips. She flailed and squirmed and fought without thinking. She would not let this stinking white man have her. She would sooner die.

When Freeman Trentham first noticed the commotion, he crouched down and crept toward it. When he saw Richswill on top of an Indian, Trentham quickly looked around for others. Then he saw the long black hair and long graceful arms and knew it was her. He dashed toward the two struggling on the ground.

"Nigger!" shouted Richswill. "Hold her down. You'll get your turn. Hold her arms."

Trentham was horrified. "Sir! She is a woman. We do not fight women. Let her go!"

"Get over here and hold her, I told you!"

Wah-say-lan struggled with fury. She did not hear their words. She did not remember it was the black man. She knew only that there were now two of them.

"Sir, let her go!" Trentham repeated, stepping back and fingering the bow.

Richswill hit her again across the mouth and slammed his fist into her right temple. She went limp. He bounced up on his knees and spread her thighs again.

"Now we'll see, you Seneca devil!"

They were his last words. The arrow hit him in the middle of his chest. He looked up at Trentham, back at the arrow. He struggled to his feet and staggered toward the slave. Richswill fell forward. As he hit the ground, the arrow stuck out through his back. He did not move.

"You lousy bastard," Trentham said aloud. "You deserved a slower, more terrible death."

◈ CHAPTER 10 ◈

Search Party

Trentham saw the blood in Wah-say-lan's hair and a thin red line running from her mouth down her neck. He knelt down and straightened her long legs, put his left arm under her knees, his right arm under her back and carried her into the lake. He walked out waist deep and gently lowered her legs into the water. He cupped his palm, scooped up the cool water and patted the blood away from her mouth. He did the same over her head and washed the blood from her hair. He dipped her whole body in and gently brushed away dirt and mud from her smooth skin. He carried her back, reached down for the pouch and walked back to the clearing, laying her on the thick bed of pine needles.

Trentham pulled out the clothes and put the shirt over her head, her arms into the sleeves. Then he pulled the buckskin trousers up over her legs. She had not stirred. He held her head in his lap and caressed her long black hair.

Her breathing was steady. He felt she would be all right. The sun was fully above the pine trees to the east. Canandaigua Lake was blue and calm. He sat there wondering how his life had brought him to this little island in the middle of a lake in the wilderness. Freeman Trentham had been captured as a child, forced across the Atlantic Ocean, separated from his mother, hauled up the east coast of North

America into slavery, then as a young man started fighting for his freedom in this white man's war. Caught in the middle is this young woman he is holding in his lap.

He tried to examine his feelings for her, the most powerful attraction he had ever felt. He did not even know her name. He had heard the young girl holler to her and call her Wah-say-something, but who is she? He found himself concluding that the mind cannot analyze the heart. He could hold her forever, he thought. He was in love with no explanation other than it was true.

Then her hands moved. Wah-say-lan's eyes blinked open. She gazed up into his handsome black face. Instantly she sprang to her feet, then wobbled. He caught her and eased her back to the pine needles. She drew her legs up and braced her hands against the ground.

"Easy," he whispered. "Take it easy. He hit you hard."

She grimaced and choked, "Where is he?"

Freeman pointed back toward the beach. "He won't be bothering you, or anyone else." Then showed her the bow.

She fingered the buckskin sleeves of her shirt. "How did . . ."

"I found them with the bow. You needed clothing . . ."

She did not blush. She looked straight into his eyes. "He was on top of me. I fought . . ."

"I saw. He won't do it again."

She crossed her legs in front of her. She felt like curling into the fetal position, but she didn't dare. She thought of that man between her legs, of his fist slamming into her lips. She recoiled and hunkered her arms tight around her.

"He can't hurt you anymore," said the black man.

Wah-say-lan kept her gaze down. She was shamed. She should have been able to kill that white man. If only she had killed him. If only she had her father's knife, she would have enjoyed sticking it in his ribs. The filthy white man. No Iroquois would ever force himself on a woman. Iroquois men respected women. White men are pigs, she thought.

Freeman Trentham knew she was far away. He also knew he was a half-mile away from capture with a woman of their village. But he sensed her devastation.

"That soldier had no right," he said to her quietly, tentatively. "He can't hurt you again."

She started. His voice was soothing but it was still a man's voice. But not a white man, she thought. Not a filthy pig. She hesitated, then whispered, still with her head staring at the ground, "I do not know your name."

He smiled and said, as softly as he could, "You are Wah-say of the Seneca."

"I am Wah-say-lan, daughter of Lan-lu-rah and Wah-say-han of the Seneca of the Iroquois Nation," she said, her voice stronger and taking on the smooth, confident cadence of the night before. "You do not act like a slave."

"I have been a slave most of my life," he said. "Now I am a soldier in Washington's army for freedom and independence."

She sat silent, then said again, "What is your name?"

"They call me Freeman Trentham."

"What do you call you?"

"They do not know my name is Jamwesaw, son of Jamleman and Andoogagow of the Hitu people. They never asked. They told me I am Freeman Trentham."

The black man and the Indian woman sat facing each other on her island. He reached out and touched her hand. She took his and held it and again marveled at the strong, unfamiliar feelings she had for him. She told herself, "It was not this man who attacked me. This man saved me. This man stirs my heart like no other man ever has."

She said to him, "Thank you. I owe you my life."

He took her other hand, and moved closer. Their knees touched. Their dark eyes met and they did not move for several moments. He found himself saying to her, "I want to always save your life. I want you always to be with me."

Then, over her shoulder, he saw two canoes heading for the island.

She did not know the words to respond. She had spoken English when she had to all her life, but some of the feelings she could express to herself only in Seneca. She did not know this man, but she knew she did not want him to go away. Then she saw his expression, turned toward the lake, and saw the braves paddling for the island.

Her mind raced. They will kill him. She is in men's clothing. He has her bow. No one knows it is hers, but they will ask where he got it.

"Come," she said, grabbing the pouch. "Bring the bow and arrows. Stay down."

She led him to the west side of the island. "Step carefully. Do not disturb the shale. Good. Into the water. Farther. Swim. Follow me," she said. The island's terrain rose swiftly to a bluff. They swam toward it.

"Come. Quick," she whispered. "See the boulder jutting out. Just before, we must dive under. There is an opening. We will come up inside. Stay with me. Give me the quiver and arrows. Don't lose the bow. Come, Jamwesaw!"

No one had called him that in 10 years. He dove, following her, and they came up in a dark space. She lifted herself onto a ledge and told him to give her the bow. Then he pulled himself up next to her. A tiny shaft of light leaked in from a crack far above their heads. Their eyes adjusted and he asked her to say his name again.

"Shh! Quiet," she whispered but repeated his name, "Jamwesaw."

The Seneca found Richswill's body. They scoured the island looking for Trentham. She heard them say he must have swum for the western shore. She surprised herself and found her head seeking his shoulder.

He put his arm around her and held her. He remembered the blueberries in his pockets and offered her some. They both were famished and sat there in the semi-darkness eating berries in silence.

"Where did he come from?" she was thinking to herself. "Why is he here? Why now? But here he is. Yesterday he wasn't. Now he is. Now I have my head on his shoulder. Yesterday I did not know such a man existed. Today I cannot stop touching him. Where will he go? I don't want him to go, but how can he stay?"

She was forming the thought that he could wear her clothes and she could swim back to her village naked, as she always had. She could tell them she had swum north and then back. She and Trentham could meet in secret and make plans. But they had no time for plans.

◈ CHAPTER 11 ◈

To Battle

The shooting began and the search party quickly left the island for the village. Trentham had nearly forgotten that Sullivan's army was heading this way. It would have been too late to save him, but not to carry out the orders to rout the Iroquois and burn their crops and villages.

Capt. Stone and one of his men had managed to get back to the main column. His report put Sullivan on the alert for resistance, but did not stop his inexorable advance through the wilderness. Crossing Pennsylvania and up the Susquehanna River in the summer of 1779, his army had swept north and westward, killing Indians and burning villages. In a skirmish on the Chemung River at Newtown he had routed 600 Indians and British troops with just three dead Americans and 39 wounded. By September his 3,000 men were marching north along the shore of Seneca Lake and then west toward Canandaigua—60 miles of setting fire to a half-dozen Indian villages and acres upon acres of corn and other crops. At Kendaia it took hundreds of men half the day to chop down apple, cherry and pear orchards. At the large town of Kanadasaga at the north end of Seneca Lake, the Iroquois were first going to stand and fight, but fell back as Sullivan's troops appeared sooner than expected, with massive force.

Pvt. Trentham had been among those ordered to torch the 30 longhouses at the edge of the lake. "This just isn't right," the former slave had said to himself, "making war against women and children. What does this have to do with freedom and independence? Where will all these people live as the winter approaches?"

Now, at Canandaigua, Pundatha had 100 braves with Maj. Butler's 100 British Rangers. Butler's pleadings for reinforcements from Canada had gone unheeded. Sullivan marched with his thousands. Their first volleys a mile from the Canandaigua village brought down several British soldiers. Butler called for ordered retreat, establishing a defense among a jagged line of rocks and boulders just a few hundred yards from the Seneca longhouses. Pundatha sent his braves out to meet the Continental Army.

Trentham turned to Wah-say-lan. "It is Sullivan's army. It is a large army," he said.

"Come," she said, and dove under. She came up, swam to shore and ran to the east side of the island. He was right behind her.

"I must go back. My family will need me," she said to him.

"You will not win. There are too many," he said, "but I will not let you go alone."

"It is my turn to save your life. You stay here. I will come back, but I cannot wear these men's clothes in my village. You cannot wear the Blue Coat clothes. These are for you. They were always for you. They were waiting for you to find them," said Wah-say-lan.

She slipped out of them and told him to put them on. He took his clothes off and they both stood there, young, beautiful and pulled toward each other. He embraced her. She clung to him. They held each other without moving. They felt their bodies were one, but she pulled away.

"I will be back," she said and ran into the lake.

He watched her swim and heard the muskets' retort and he knew he would not stay. He pulled on the deerskin pants she had made and then the shirt. They fit a tad tightly. He hugged himself, and thought how they had just clothed Wah-say-lan. He waited until he saw her get almost to the shore.

He swam slowly and watched her run into the village. He recalled Washington's words "conquer or die" and then he recalled Jefferson's Declaration: "when it becomes necessary for one people to dissolve the political bands which have connected them with another." Trentham changed the one word he always did when he ran the phrase over in his head: "when it becomes necessary for one *person,*" he thought, "to dissolve the political bands."

"I am dissolving my bands, Master Jefferson," he said out loud. "My pursuit of happiness is not with your war for independence."

◈ CHAPTER 12 ◈

The Battle of Canandaigua

Trentham swam north, trying to form a plan, and glided under a clump of willows overhanging the water at the edge of the village.

Though there were always a few young braves who liked to watch Wah-say-lan come out of the water each morning, no one noticed her this time. Pundatha had directed all the warriors to defensive positions. Wah-say-lan threw on her clothes. Her mother, her mother's sister and Tun-weh were packing pouches and putting extra clothes on the babies and children. They were too busy to ask her where she had been.

"Go to the last longhouse and bring the dried meat and fish. Bring as much as you can carry," her mother said to her. Wah-say-lan nodded, but on the way out stooped quickly for her father's hunting knife, and took his second bow. Outside, she grabbed someone's quiver of arrows. She ran toward the musket fire.

No one paid her any attention. She came to the line of boulders and saw several Red Coats lying on the forest floor, bleeding. She headed north in back of the line and glimpsed her father leading a party of warriors out into the forest. She saw smoke rise in front of them and almost immediately the sound of the muskets.

Lan-lu-rah fell, as did several others. Blue Coats ran for them, bayonets fixed. The other warriors yelled and ran with their tomahawks raised. Hand to hand they struggled, but the Blue Coats kept coming. Wah-say-lan set her string and pulled an arrow from the quiver. She saw her father get up and lean against a tree and saw the soldier run at him. She let the arrow fly and he slumped a few feet in front of the wounded Indian.

Lan-lu-rah turned and saw his daughter with the bow. She swore he smiled before the musket ball struck his heart and sent him reeling back. She ran to him as braves and Blue Coats fought around her. She knelt and held his head.

"There are too many. Save your mother," he said and died in her hands. She kissed his forehead and ran back toward the village.

Three men with muskets were running for her. One fired and a pine limb broke above her head. She reached a small rise, swirled around with bow drawn. They stopped; one got an arrow through his neck. She pulled another from her quiver and hit the next soldier in the thigh as he ran for cover. He fell with a yelp. With her father's words ringing in her ears, she drew his hunting knife and ran for the continental soldier who was pulling himself for cover. She was on him and slit his throat, blood spurting on the ground. He was dead in seconds. The third man was gone.

Wah-say-lan ran for the village. She saw Red Coats with raised hands and continentals marching them to the east. Pundatha was drawing his warriors in a tighter circle around the longhouses. Women and children were rushing to get into the canoes. She ran over and found her mother, who was herding several young children into the center of a large elm-bark canoe.

"Mother, you are to paddle this canoe, in the front. I will find Tun-weh for the back. She knows how to handle a full canoe."

"Tun-weh is with the baby in the longhouse. Tell her to come now," the Seneca woman responded with calm. Wah-say-lan found her young cousin, picked up the baby and said, "Tun-weh, come now. We need you to paddle the big canoe. My mother is in the front. Get the children to the west side of the lake."

Tun-weh followed her. The baby was placed in the boat. With

Tun-weh in the back, Wah-say-lan touched her shoulder, smiled, and said, "I will see you on the other side. Take them over the hill to the valley with the falls. We will meet there," and she shoved the boat into the water. A dozen were already heading across Canandaigua Lake. Soon 40 more were pushing off, with Seneca women paddling their children to safety.

Wah-say-lan heard Pundatha say the center was holding but Blue Coats were coming in from the north. She took her bow and hurried that way, following several braves, all of whom she knew; many were her age.

Past the last longhouse and up the path along the lake, they ran into a fusillade of musket fire. Two fell. The others drew their tomahawks and charged where the smoke rose. A horde of continentals came out with bayonets fixed. A second volley from behind and more Seneca fell. Wah-say-lan aimed an arrow at the lead soldier. He fell and another arrow hit the man next to him. The braves met bayonets with tomahawks.

One Blue Coat stood and raised his musket at the woman with the bow. From behind, Trentham jumped him. They rolled on the ground, but he grabbed the weapon and smashed the man's head in. Another was charging Wah-say-lan. She drew her father's knife. Trentham aimed and shot him in the back.

He rushed to her. "It is lost. You must come this way."

"But the fight goes on," she said. To the south, longhouses were burning. The canoes were past the island. They saw Pundatha wade into the water. He signaled his braves and waved them by. They swam westward. Then more and a few more. Some 70 men and their chief were swimming for their lives.

"They will fight another day," Trentham said, and grabbed her hand. "We cannot do more right now. I need you with me. I need you." He pulled her toward the water.

"No!" she screamed. "These pigs cannot take my home!"

"Wah-say-lan, look in the lake. Who is in the lake? Your chief.

Your chief is saying to go across the lake. He knows you cannot win today. There will be more days," Trentham pleaded with her.

"Give me your knife, we need to swim west now." He was pulling her arm.

She looked at him. She looked at her burning village. She looked once more at her father's body under a tree. She sheathed the knife and walked into the water with Trentham. They swam.

Wah-say-lan's tears came. She could not stop them. She dove under water and her tears mixed with Canandaigua's water, but still she cried.

Then she said, "We cannot swim with my people. Go north, Jamwesaw, swim north."

They swam away from the fleeing Seneca. Sullivan's troops rushed to the water's edge, firing at the Indians. But they did not pursue them. Other Blue Coats were setting the longhouses on fire.

No one noticed two figures swimming west and north. Freeman Trentham and Wah-say-lan were silent as they went.

As he watched the Indians swim for their lives, a scene from Wallingford crept into Trentham's mind. He was one of more than a hundred slaves in the small Connecticut community. Maybe it was trust, maybe it was his master knowing he could bring fish back to the table, but he was allowed to frequently carry his fishing pole to the little river that flowed south toward New Haven. There he met the Quinnipiac, who had lived along the river for centuries. But in the 100 years since Wallingford's founding, more and more of the tribe's land had been taken or sold; only a few remained.

Fish Carrier of the Quinnipiac showed Trentham the deeper holes in the stream where the big fish could be found. The two soon competed for the biggest trout; sometimes even a sturgeon could be hooked.

The Indian had told the slave of the Quinnipiac Chief Momaugin, who greeted the white man in 1638 as they sailed into the harbor and the tribe's main village. The Quinnipiac were never great in number, Fish Carrier told his black friend, but they lived peacefully on the river for generation after generation, avoiding the wars the Pequot and other Connecticut tribes fought against the encroaching white man.

One day as Trentham headed to their fishing spot, Fish Carrier, with his wife and two young sons, came along the path carrying all of their belongings.

"The Quinnipiac are no more," he said. "The farms of the white people fill our hunting grounds. My people have gone. Some left a few days ago. My wife and I will take our sons north. The Tunxis people, I hear, can still hunt in their forest. Good-bye, my friend."

Trentham hugged Fish Carrier and watched the family walk away. They were the last Indians in Wallingford, Connecticut. The Quinnipiac had dispersed and disappeared.

The black man shivered as he swam next to the brave and beautiful Wah-say-lan.

◈ CHAPTER 13 ◈

Jamwesaw's Boots

Pundatha, chief of the Seneca village on Canandaigua Lake for two decades, longer than Wah-say-lan had lived, turned in the water as he swam and looked back at his home. Smoke filled the air. Orange flames brought his longhouses crashing to the ground. Soldiers massed on the shoreline. Yet the chief felt proud and he felt brave. He remembered the stories of his grandfather's time, 90 years earlier, when the French from Canada came to Seneca country to burn and kill. Then his forefathers outsmarted the white man by abandoning the village and hiding out with the Cayuga people, miles away. The French and their Huron allies burned the village and the acres of corn. They cut down the apple and cherry trees. But they found no Iroquois. When he heard the stories as a child of how the Seneca had fooled the French and stayed strong, he did not disagree with the strategy, but he thought he himself would fight the invaders. And so, in his time, and with the great war chief Cornplanter's urging, he made a stand. His braves killed many white invaders. His women and children were safe in canoes. The men he lost will go to the Sky World with courage in their hearts, thought Pundatha. He asked his departed brethren to send their courage to him as he gathered up his people to get ready for what was still to come in this war against the American rebels.

Tun-weh was nearing the western shore of the lake and she could see the village women already pulling canoes up off the shore and into the thick forest. She was still paddling hard, but her thoughts were of the glimpse she had caught of Wah-say-lan stringing a bow and aiming an arrow. At her friend's waist she had seen the big hunting knife and Tun-weh knew Wah-say-lan was not busy carrying food as her mother had requested.

"How can one woman be so beautiful, so smart and also so brave?" Tun-weh pondered. "When she touched me on the shoulder and said she would see me across the lake, she smiled calmly and her touch was love itself and I knew at that moment the baby and I would be safe. I want to see her when this canoe hits shore. I want her to be there waiting for me, but I fear that we won't see Wah-say-lan again this day."

The late afternoon sun still made the water sparkle. Given the violence of the battle just finished, the deaths of many Americans, British and Seneca, the water seemed oddly calm. But then the waters of Canandaigua are often smooth, with the high green hills cupping the lake on both sides as if Mother Earth herself held it in her hands. The Continental Army had accomplished a classic frontal attack with flanking actions to the north and south, encircling the Seneca village. They had expected an easy fight and a quick surrender. But Canandaigua Lake not only sustained the Indians with an endless supply of fish and water, it also was their escape route when they needed one. The lake served the Seneca in all ways.

The young Seneca warrior Ban-er-man-jah was bleeding from his right arm into the water. A soldier had rushed at him with his bayonet, but in one sweeping motion with his tomahawk the brave had brushed the weapon aside and smashed the soldier's forehead in two. Ban-er-man-jah was 17, born a few days after Wah-say-lan.

He said to Deh-wan-guh, swimming next to him, "Did you see Wah-say-lan avenge her father?"

"What do you mean?" Deh-wan-guh asked.

"You did not see Wah-say-lan hit the man with an arrow and then rush him with the knife and cut his throat?"

"You must be having war nightmares already, Ban-er-man-jah. Wah-say-lan is different. She has always been strange, but she is not a warrior," Deh-wan-guh said.

"I saw her. Her father saw her as he lay dying. She slit the throat of the man who slew her father," said Ban-er-man-jah. "Then a Blue Coat was on me with his bayonet, and when I looked again she was gone."

"You always look for Wah-say-lan," his friend said. "Do not let your thoughts wander. When we get to the western shore we will have much to do. The American Army will come again. We are still many; look at all the Seneca swimming right now. But what is our next move? Where do we go to fight again?"

Ban-er-man-jah heard, but he could not get the young Seneca woman out of his thoughts. Ever since they were young children he had admired her, but she never noticed.

Wah-say-lan had two men on her mind and Ban-er-man-jah, the boy she grew up with, was not one of them. Freeman Trentham was right next to her as she swam with him away from her tribe. She could not shake the image of her father dying in her arms. At the same time, she was truly bothered thinking about Trentham's boots. "How will he run in the forest?" she asked herself and then asked, "but why am I worried about boots? My village is burned, my father is dead, my mother and my people are fleeing an invading army and I am worrying about boots. Boots for a man I met last night. The man who saved my life on the island this morning. The man who pulled me out of the battle when I was not ready to go and probably saved my life again—twice in the same day."

She stopped and treaded water. "Jamwesaw, what about your boots!"

She shocked him out of his own deep thoughts. The sound of his African name alone was so new to him. Her voice, too, was new, but somehow he felt he had heard it his whole life. He loved her voice, so clear and smooth. But just now there was an edge to it.

"What about your boots?" she asked again.

"I cannot swim across this big lake in boots," he said.

"But what will you do? What if we must run?" she asked.

"I spent half my life barefoot. Do not worry, Wah-say-lan, I know how to get around without boots. Are you all right?" And he wondered why she focused on such a small thing.

"We must go north. You can't meet my people today. We must go somewhere and talk. And our clothes are wet. We will have to build a fire and dry them. But do we dare have a fire? And what of when our clothes are drying?" her large brown eyes dropped.

Trentham pondered all these tiny little things and her concern over them. He thought they were no more than pebbles on a path to a deeper understanding they both needed about their future and about each other. He also felt these questions were the doors to more important answers. He decided that the momentous convulsions in both their lives in the past 24 hours could not be addressed without first talking of boots and fires and drying clothes.

"Wah-say-lan, look at me." He smiled. "We will go deep into the forest and build a fire. Sullivan's army will not come today, maybe not even tomorrow. And then they must march around the lake. We will build a fire and dry our clothes. Remember I put clothes on you this morning after . . . after I killed the corporal on the island. Before you swam back to your people we stood with each other without clothes. We will hang our clothes near the fire and it will dry them and it will warm our bodies and I will hold you and I will warm your body. And we will talk."

She held the image of them standing naked together and how they had touched each other. Seneca are not ashamed of their bodies, yet with Trentham that moment on the island she had felt at once modest and exhilarated. She tried to hold the sweet, brief moment in her mind as more questions poured forth: "You wore my buckskins from my hollow tree and I said they were always meant for you, but probably they are too small for you, and the lake and the drying fire will probably shrink them, and what will we do then?" she asked.

Trentham worried about her, but just then his feet hit bottom. They had been swimming steadily and were only a few yards from shore a good two miles north from where the Seneca were pulling their canoes up. He grabbed her hand. "Come," he said. "Do not talk, just show me through your woods."

She took his hand. She was glad to hear him tell her what to do. She did not like to be told what to do. But right then, her mind was racing, her father's face was in her thoughts—"there are too many, save your mother" he had told her—and now this black man, yesterday's prisoner, was telling her to show him her woods. She squeezed his hand tightly as they ran into the forest.

◈ CHAPTER 14 ◈

Regrouping

When Pundatha came up on the western shore, he walked into the trees where he knew his people were gathering. When they saw him come with his tomahawk in his belt, his four eagle feathers still in his dark hair, his broad tawny chest, his strong muscular legs unscathed, the small knots of men and women quieted and waited for him to speak.

"We lost many brave warriors, but so are there many dead Blue Coats. Look around, you can see more than half our people are here. We have stopped the continentals. They have not defeated us. We have saved our children. We will send messengers to Red Jacket and Cornplanter on the great river Genesee and tell them of what happened here and how the Ancient One gave us courage to stop the white general Sullivan. We have given the Seneca Nation time to prepare to deal with him again. What we will do now, for this night, is walk over the hill to where the water falls into the valley. Sullivan's army cannot get there and we will have a council fire and wait to hear back from our people on the Genesee."

Tun-weh whispered to Wah-say-han, "The valley with the falls. That is where Wah-say-lan told me she would meet us."

"She did?" her mother responded.

"Yes, Wah-say-lan sees things clearly. She knows what to do," said the young Tun-weh, picking up her baby brother and hugging him.

The Seneca of Canandaigua gathered up what gear and provisions they had thrown into the canoes. They carried packs of supplies and spare weapons and started walking up the steep hill guarding their lake.

◆ CHAPTER 15 ◆

Their First Night

Farther north, the terrain was an easier slope of oak and pine forest. After a mile, Wah-say-lan and Trentham came to an outcropping under an enormous hemlock.

"I have been to this spot," said Wah-say-lan. "I will make a fire and set poles for the clothes. We don't have a deerskin or a blanket. We don't have anything . . ."

"Except each other," said Trentham, and he put his face close to hers. He whispered, "You will make a good fire. It will dry our clothes." He put his cheek against hers, his right arm around her waist. She pressed against him.

"My thoughts are pushing against each other. My mind is like many blue jays squawking and fighting in one tree, each trying to find his place on a branch and shoving the other aside," she said. "I do not know which thought comes first and which second."

He took her knife from her belt. "See what you remembered . . ."

"It is my father's," she said, accepting it from his hand.

"It is his gift to you. It is his thanks to you for helping your people," said Trentham. "I am going to gather pine needles for a fine bed. You make a good fire and set the poles." He put his hand on her cheek and then his other hand on her other cheek. He held her face gently and gazed on her beauty and he said, "Wah-say-lan, you have survived this day for a reason. You have helped your people. You have been courageous. Tomorrow you will do more. Today, tonight, it is time to rest."

His hands were warm, and when he touched her and spoke to her, she knew this man was part of her future. She said nothing. She held up her knife and slipped away to go about her tasks.

She found long pine branches fallen on the ground and carried a few to two gray boulders that tilted against each other, forming a shallow shelter. Crusty circles of gray-green lichen hugged the rocks. She angled the branches into crevices and they became crossbars. Just under them she gathered twigs and pine needles into a pile at the opening and pulled the flints she always carried from a deep pocket in her wet clothes. She knew September nights could be chilly. With just a few strikes a spark caught and she had the campfire going, then went to gather more firewood.

"This is so familiar," she mused as a picture shot through her mind of the two boulders and her father starting a fire in the very same spot. She remembered her mother holding her hand as a small child. They were walking under these same tall pines and she remembered the little girl who was so excited to be discovering new places with her parents. Yes, she had climbed that tallest hemlock to the left of the little cave. Her father had encouraged her to go as high as she could and to tell him what she could see. She climbed and climbed and as she got higher she was amazed how such a great tree could sway in the breeze. "Father, I can feel the wind," she had called out. She remembered what he called back: "It is kissing your face and whispering the secrets of the air to you."

Little Wah-say-lan listened, but the wind must be kissing more than whispering, she thought, and the view of her lake a mile to the east glistening in the sun sent her scampering higher for a better look. Near the top she stopped and gazed across at the longhouses in their village on the eastern shore. It looked so peaceful, she remembered thinking, and she felt so protected and hidden at the top of the evergreen tree.

Trentham walked by with an armload of soft pine needles and Wah-say-lan told him, “I remember now, my father and mother brought me here many years ago. He started a campfire in the very spot I just chose. We cooked a rabbit. My mother sprinkled herbs on the meat. It was a good supper. As the sun set, we crossed the lake and watched the moon rise in the south where the hills touch the stars. I fell asleep in the canoe.”

“What a fine story,” said Trentham. “I wish we had a rabbit, but at least we will be cushioned. I will spread these under the boulders and your fire will keep us warm.”

He was anxious to sit with her and listen to her, but he wanted it to be as cozy as possible. He saw her crossbars and took off his still-damp buckskin shirt. He draped it across her pine branch and could feel the warmth of the flames reach toward it.

“I will be right back,” he said and went to gather more bedding.

She started a bit and caught herself marveling at his strong back, broad shoulders introducing well-defined biceps. She rushed over to him and wrapped her arms around his neck and held him tight. He could have stayed that way for hours, but just then he spied a movement on the ground. Slowly, a fat brown snake angled toward some brush.

“Wah-say-lan,” he whispered, “let me take your knife.”

He lifted it from her belt and he warned her not to move. “I see supper,” he said.

In a dash, he grabbed the creature. It instinctively coiled back. Freeman Trentham shot his left hand up around the snake’s neck and pushed it to the ground. It wriggled madly but in two quick slices its head was severed. He turned with it and smiled.

“Oh, I am hungry,” said Wah-say-lan. “The meat is so sweet. It is such a treat. And it is big enough to give us two new belts.”

She took it from him and sliced it lengthwise to skin it. Then she shivered as she watched the knife do its work. She saw the very same weapon stuck in the soldier’s neck. She saw her father’s face in her arms. Trentham was off gathering pine needles. He did not see the tears well up in her eyes, or her body heave in sobs of sorrow.

"Oh my father. Oh my father. The wind never whispered to me that you would be gone so soon." She knelt and dropped her head to her chest. It ached with an emptiness she had not felt before. Wah-say-lan let her tears fall down her neck.

After several silent moments, she said, "At least the man who shot you paid for it with his own life. I must try to stay busy."

She uncurled and stood on her long legs, stepped out of her clothes and draped them next to Trentham's. She added more wood and felt its heat rise to warm the buckskin. The young Seneca woman knelt back down and skinned the snake. She cut the meat into pieces and pierced them with sticks. She quickly fashioned a spit and set the meat to cook. It sizzled above the flames, its tangy scent wafting in the air. She hung the skin on a low branch of the great hemlock and felt the fine, smooth surface, tracing the darker brown lines along the lighter brown of the animal that would now give them sustenance. She thanked its spirit and told it the first belt she makes will be for this wonderful man who was coming her way with another armload of natural bedding.

He had fern leaves, too, and spread the last bunch of pine needles as close to the fire as he dared. He covered that part with the ferns to protect the bed from sparks. He watched in joy as Wah-say-lan came to him. They said nothing for a long while, sitting with their arms around each other and staring at the fire as it cooked their supper.

His nakedness stirred her. She rubbed his dark-skinned arm up and down. She put her arm against his and said quietly, "Are these two different arms to be one? Will your body become one with mine? Where did you come from? Yesterday when I swam to the island with Tun-weh and we skipped shale, I did not know of you. Now you are here. Why? You came with an army to fight my people. Now you sit with me and you tell me you will never leave. How did you get here?"

The young soldier from Washington's army did not answer right away. He had been thinking the same things but he wanted to ease into such a conversation. He smiled broadly, "I thought you were wondering if my feet were all right?" and laughed.

Her lips could not help but smile and she reached down and caressed his feet. "You are strong everywhere, Jamwesaw."

"You are my love, but I know you are my hungry love. You tell me a snake is a treat," he said and handed her a piece on its stick.

Soon their serendipitous meal was nearly gone. As he reached for the last pieces, she took them and set them aside.

"They will be good for the morning," she said.

She lay back on the thick cushion of fragrant pine needles. She always loved their scent, and soon exhaustion swept over her.

"I want you, Jamwesaw, and I will say to you I have never been with a man. And I want you . . ."

He stretched his body next to hers and held her face close. He kissed her forehead and her cheeks and drew her breasts into him. He held tight and knew he wanted to hold her tight forever. He sensed her exhaustion and thought back to her fighting his former comrades-in-arms. He held the image of her aiming her bow, of her standing and fighting for her village. He thought of what she just said and of what she had done a few hours earlier. What an understatement, he mused to himself: "I have never been with a man," and what a time to have to deal with something so, so new to her. She had never been in a battle, either. He resolved that this day must end quietly for this girl.

Before he could say "Shh," he saw her eyes close and felt her gentle breathing. He knew he would be with her every night for the rest of his life, however long that may be.

◈ CHAPTER 16 ◈

Bad Dreams

Wah-say-lan saw the panther inch toward her in her dream. She stood with her bow and arrows and thought, how strange. She hadn't seen a panther in years. It still crept toward her. She pulled an arrow and was ready to let it fly, but noticed that it already had a wound in the back of its neck.

The light brown panther still came at her and then it staggered. Blood spurted from another wound in its side. It fell and rolled over, looked up at Wah-say-lan and said, "There are too many, save yourself." Then the panther disappeared into the ground. Booming sounds came from the woods behind it and the trees shouted, "Too many! Too many!"

Wah-say-lan ran and came to a clearing. A mother black bear was crouched over its lifeless cub. The mother shook the baby with her paw, but the cub did not respond. The black bear stood and said to Wah-say-lan, "There are too many." It wandered away out of her sight. The baby sank into the earth.

In her dream she saw herself holding her father's bloody body in her arms. "Save your mother," he said, and died.

In his dream Freeman Trentham pointed the arrow at Cpl. Richswill and said, "Sir, we do not fight women."

The corporal spat and spread his prey's legs.

"Sir, let her go," Freeman said in his dream. He fired the bow and missed. The corporal raped the young woman as Freeman watched, frozen in his steps. The corporal finished and then went over and slammed the black soldier against a tree. He tied Freeman up and told him, "Dirty nigger. You know what we do to deserters—you'd just as soon wish the Iroquois had captured you. Nigger deserter."

Richswill went and pulled Trentham's arrow out of the ground and was about to jam it through the young Indian woman's heart when Trentham screamed, "No!"

Wah-say-lan jolted up from their pine needle bed. Trentham was sitting up straight, sweat covering his body in the chilly night. She hugged him and brought him close. She rolled over on top of him and kissed him on his mouth. With natural ease she spread her legs so that the inside of her thighs pressed against the outside of his. Trentham tried to shake off his dream and succumb to her movements. She could feel his hardness, reached down and guided it to where she wanted it. She could not help but think, in her firm grip, "Is there nowhere this man is not strong?"

But his rape dream would not go away. He held her as tightly as he could and said, "I want you. But my dream was bad. I want you when my dreams are good."

The wounded lion reappeared in her mind's eye. She slackened and said, "Loving you after bad dreams, you are right, it is not the right thing to do. When you and I are one, it will not be in the middle of bad dreams." She got up and put more wood on the ebbing fire. She felt their clothes warm and dry and slipped her shirt on. She handed him his and he pulled her back down. He put the shirt over them both. They lay on their sides and gazed into each other's eyes.

"Sleep, my love," he said.

◈ CHAPTER 17 ◈

"Cornplanter Must Know"

In the morning the chief of the Canandaigua Seneca called a council fire. Pundatha was stoic but grief-stricken that not all of his chiefs had survived yesterday's battle. His oldest friend, the father of Wah-say-lan, he missed most.

"It was our friend Lan-lu-rah who brought the two prisoners in, the one with the black skin and the other," began the chief after nine of the 12 council members were seated around the fire. "When Sullivan's army attacked, he defended the northern approach to our village and held it so that our women had time to load the canoes with supplies and come here for safety. Some say his daughter Wah-say-lan was with him when he died. Neither are here now and we will wait to see if Wah-say-lan will find us."

Tun-weh knew she could not speak up at a council fire, but she again whispered to her cousin's mother, "She will be here."

"We will send two scouting parties out today," Pundatha continued. "One will run with our message to Cornplanter at Conawagus on the great Genesee River. Our War Chief had said we must make a stand at Canandaigua. Sullivan's army of thousands of soldiers marched for two moons burning our villages. He has destroyed 40 of our towns and sent our people scurrying for safety. So many of our towns have only a few braves. They could not stand against such an army. Many had to retreat. Our Canandaigua was the place to stop the man George Washington sent to destroy us. Sullivan has many dead to bury. He will not find us here in the valley with the falls. A large army cannot get here. But we must go to the westward path and keep his movements in view. And we must go to Cornplanter and tell him of our success. Cornplanter must know that we hurt Sullivan but that he probably will keep heading for the Genesee."

Next to the famed Mohawk Chief Joseph Brant, Cornplanter of the Seneca was the most trusted war leader of the Iroquois Confederacy. He lived in the western territory of the Seneca Nation, the "keepers of the western door" for the Six Nations. His village of Conawagus was on the Genesee River, which flows north into Lake Ontario, Canada's border with the 13 rebellious British colonies.

Canandaigua was the largest Seneca village between the Cayuga people on the east and Cornplanter's town on the west. Nearly 300 Seneca lived at Canandaigua, including 100 warriors. Pundatha now counted 86. He sent 20 to watch for advance elements of Sullivan's army and to search for any surviving British allies. He believed that the wily Maj. Butler must have found a way to escape and fight another day. He sent six west to take the news to Cornplanter and the other Seneca war chiefs. So he had 60 men to help the women build a temporary home in this secluded valley in this third year of war against the American rebels. He sat with his council and they talked of how long their people had lived on this land, fished Canandaigua Lake and ruled over their territory.

"Our ancestors have been here since before memory," he said. "The old stories reach back to that time when our ancestors stopped traveling. It was when they grew the three sisters: corn, beans and squash. In the east they became our brothers the Cayuga. And here in these lands and on our Chosen Place of Canandaigua Lake, the Seneca became the strong arm of the Iroquois Nation in the west, much like our brothers the Mohawk in the east."

Pundatha wanted to reassure his people after yesterday's encounter. He took time to go over what had made the Seneca strong. "Our women are entrusted to name the chiefs. They also decide which prisoners die and which will join us. We have found our tribe to be stronger when others choose to join us. Choosing chiefs and choosing who can join us are important decisions. Our women saved our children yesterday. Our women grow our crops, weave our baskets, make the pottery, cook what we eat, cure the deer hides for our clothing, prepare our vegetables and fruits from the orchards for winter storage. Our women are as important to our future as our braves who hunt and fish and fight our enemies."

"Hiawatha and the Peacemaker, Dekanawidah, brought the five nations together in the long ago times at the great council fire at Onondaga," Pundatha continued the familiar tale. "Forty-nine chiefs sit on the Confederacy council when it meets on the shores of Onondaga Lake. When it is time to make new tribal chiefs, our women will do so as they always have. They will decide which three Canandaigua Seneca warriors will join the council fire as sachems."

Tun-weh was too young to be on the women's council, but she stayed close to Wah-say-han and the other council members. Someday Tun-weh would be making the same decisions.

◈ CHAPTER 18 ◈

"White Man's Writings Are Lies"

Wah-say-lan awoke with Freeman Trentham at her side. She studied him and she searched her heart. "How could I love a man I barely know?" she asked herself. "He saved my life; is that why I love him? He says I am his love. He loves me, so am I just trying to respond in kind? Many men have wanted me. The beautiful young Ban-er-man-jah is a good man. But until Jamwesaw was tied to that stake, until he escaped—how I don't know—but until then, no other man has made me feel the way I do. But is that love?"

Trentham stirred, opened his eyes and saw her face. His heart jumped and he rose to greet her. He had never known love. In fact, in Wallingford, Connecticut, as a slave, he didn't have normal personal relationships. He could tutor his master's child, but his one friend, Fish Carrier, had walked out of his life and into oblivion. Here in the wilderness, beyond the civilized world of slave and master, Freeman Trentham did not *know* he was in love. In New England he *knew* he was a slave. Love wasn't something to know, he thought, it was something to feel, something to fill your whole being. He had never felt it before and he did not want to lose it.

He decided to speak to her of simple things this morning. "A swim in the lake would feel good, but let's not risk running into any soldiers who may have found a canoe or two. I saw a small stream just over that rise. Come, we will freshen our faces and have a good drink," he said.

He stood and slipped his shirt over his head. "There, see. You were right. It was made for me." He pulled the deerskin pants off the crossbar. They were a tad shorter, but so what, he said, and smiled at her.

Wah-say-lan pulled on her leggings and slipped into her moccasins, remembering again that her man was barefoot.

"The clothes I made do fit you and it makes me happy. But I do not think my moccasins could fit."

"Do not worry. I will be fine."

At the stream she told him she knew her people were only a short distance away. "We have no choice, Jamwesaw. You must come with me. You cannot go back to the army. Maybe you could join the Red Coats, but we don't know their fate."

"I have no intention of leaving you," he said.

After eating the leftover snake, she again thanked its spirit, rolled its skin carefully and put it in her pocket. She sheathed her knife. Trentham checked the ashes and surveyed once more their first bed. They walked south through the forest, the terrain getting steeper as they went.

She stopped and said, "You need to know that my people must choose to let someone join our village. If not, the person is tortured so his spirit will ease the suffering spirit of a slain Seneca. You were our prisoner and no one will know how you saved me after your escape."

"They will listen to you, Wah-say-lan, won't they?" he asked.

"Yes, they will listen and then decide."

"Didn't the Iroquois adopt the entire Tuscarora tribe to become the Six Nations?" he asked.

"Yes, and we became stronger because of it. My people have adopted whites and other Indians, but my people have never seen a man with black skin who came across the big gawa from Africa."

She ducked behind a tree, pulling him with her. She put her finger to her lips. "Do not move," she whispered.

Then he saw them walking along a low ridge, the party Pundatha had sent to scout Sullivan's army. Twenty warriors went by. In that time Wah-say-lan was absolutely motionless.

When the forest had swallowed them up and she could no longer hear a sound, she said, "I would not have had much of a chance explaining us to that group. They have vengeance in their step."

Trentham remained silent.

"Jamwesaw, at the village, or rather where they are now probably building a village, it is the women's council who will decide your fate. My mother is on the council and she will make sure they hear me."

What turns his life has taken, he thought as they walked. Captured in Africa, enslaved in America, torn from his mother as a boy. He could not remember making a decision in his life. All his decisions were made for him. Even his request to fight in Washington's army was decided by his master, Noah Willington. The promise to slaves who fought was freedom when victory was achieved.

Now he had made his first big choice in his young life, but even that must be approved by a council. He chose to be with Wah-say-lan and to live as a Seneca with her and her people—if they will let him.

In another sense it was not his choice, his logical choice. His heart made it for him. His heart chose and he was walking with her, following his heart. He could not imagine not being with her. He had a hard time grasping the intensity of his feelings toward her. It was as if a larger force, the opposite of the yoke of slavery, but a guiding force, brought him to Wah-say-lan.

The hill leveled and they could see Canandaigua Lake. He took her hand and stopped. They stood in the morning silence and admired the majestic view. The lake stretched to the southern horizon, disappearing in the green hills folding into each other under a bright blue sky. They could see the island and a few miles beyond to the north end of the lake where Sullivan's army would have to go in its destructive march against the Iroquois. Smoke still rose from where her village had been, a mile away across the lake. They could see small figures milling about.

"I do not have words for them," she said. "My people have been here long before any white man came across the big gawa in their sailing boats. Now they think they can steal our world away from us—just like they stole your mother."

Her words jabbed at his heart. He saw his mother chained to the wagon, being hauled off into slavery. And he thought of Connecticut and the Quinnipiac Indians. He did not speak of them to Wah-say-lan.

He knew the Iroquois as a large and strong confederacy, the most powerful Indians he had heard of, but obviously without the numbers to hold back Americans who want to move into and rule over this beautiful country. Already the confederacy has been broken, with the Oneida and the Tuscarora fighting with the rebels against the British. Perhaps the Mohawk, Onondaga, Cayuga and Seneca can put up a long struggle, but it almost does not matter for the Iroquois who wins, the British or the Americans.

Trentham turned this over in his mind as they walked. Though the British seem more benign to the red man, like the Americans they will expand their culture into this territory. Both will infringe on the Indian way of life. Wah-say-lan has grown up in a world that her grandmother would not have envisioned. She does not yet understand that her fight is a futile fight, that the Seneca could face the same fate as the Quinnipiac. Trentham knew Wah-say-lan's life would not be as the Seneca had always lived. Whatever his chances were of freedom as a black man in a white world, they had now changed: he was a black man among Indians with a troubled future. He wanted to help her however he could, but first he had to be accepted.

He came to realize that if his mother is held by Americans, then it is perhaps their enemies who can help free her. He turned to Wah-say-lan and said, "If your people know I must fight American rebels to free my own mother, maybe that will help them welcome me into your village. I believe she is a slave of the American Thomas Jefferson."

"Tell me more of this Jefferson," she said.

Jamwesaw was silent a few moments, putting his thoughts in order about the patriot leader. "They say Thomas Jefferson is a tall man and handsome. That he is brave and has a smart mind. He wrote a great document telling why they fight the British and their King."

Wah-say-lan interrupted, "All the white man's writing is lies. Pundatha has shown me writings they call treaties. The white man does not write true things. They put their words down in writing as promises, but they do not keep them."

"Jefferson's document is not a treaty," he said. "They call it a declaration of independence from the King across the big gawa. Jefferson wrote down that all men are created equal and must have liberty."

"That is not true. No Indians are equal to the Iroquois. All other Indians honor the Six Nations of the Iroquois. If Jefferson believes what he wrote down, then why does he keep slaves? Is that equal? You see, Jamwesaw, the white man tells lies in his documents."

The black man again marveled at the young woman before him. "Americans believe those words," he said. "You show me they are false, but I have heard even George Washington, their great war chief, say that such words in Jefferson's document are why they war against the British.

"And the Seneca, Jamwesaw. Didn't you tell me it was this Washington who sent the soldiers who burned my village and killed my father?" she said.

"Yes, that is true, as it is true that Washington sent me to you," he said.

They stood and looked out over Canandaigua Lake. Wah-say-lan thought about Jamwesaw and what he might do to this Jefferson should he ever find him. The man Jefferson kept tugging at her thoughts. She felt she wanted to meet him. She wanted to ask him what he meant by liberty. The Seneca have always been free. Would this man who writes about liberty understand about Iroquois freedom?

She turned to her man. "They sent soldiers to kill my people and burn everything we have. But Pundatha right now is building another village. They cannot destroy us, Jamwesaw. Come. It is time for you to see."

◈ CHAPTER 19 ◈

Jamwesaw Meets Pundatha

Tun-weh was digging a pit to line with elm bark for storing corn and squash. Others were cutting and hauling young saplings to set and bend for the roof of a new longhouse. The 14-year-old girl, on the verge of Seneca womanhood, was thinking which warriors her elders would choose for chiefs. "Who could possibly replace the strong and wise Lan-lu-rah, father of my cousin?" thought Tun-weh. Ban-er-man-jah would be my first choice, she thought. And then she saw her coming down the hill past the falls. Tun-weh shouted and ran toward her. "Wah-say-lan! Wah-say-lan! You have come . . ."

She stopped still when she saw the black man. She tried to grasp that the man was in Seneca clothes, but wasn't he the prisoner captured by Wah-say-lan's father? She could not help it, though, and surged toward her friend, wrapping her arms around her and burying her head in her breasts.

"You have come, you have come," she said.

"And you are already busy, I see," said Wah-say-lan with great calm. "You, Tun-weh, the strong future of our people."

Her young cousin grinned and beamed at her words.

"This is Jamwesaw. I want to introduce him to Pundatha and the women elders."

Tun-weh glanced at him, then turned and ran, saying, "I will find them."

Soon the chief stood before Wah-say-lan, his best friend's daughter. Others gathered, her mother among them.

Wah-say-lan stood erect. She was a woman of calm confidence; but here and now she told herself to be careful.

"Pundatha, you know this man with me was our prisoner who escaped. I have found him. He wants no more to be in the Continental Army. He wants to join the Seneca."

"He is your prisoner?" asked the chief. "I was told you took up the hatchet in the fight yesterday."

"He is not my prisoner. He saved my life. His name is Jamwesaw from Africa across the great water. I went looking for my father during the fight. I found him wounded and then he was shot again while lying on the ground. I killed the man who killed him."

"Where is the other soldier we captured with this man?"

Wah-say-lan was trying to avoid certain details but also to answer directly. "He is dead. Jamwesaw killed him. Jamwesaw also saved me after my father was killed. He pulled me from the fight. I did not want to leave the fight. I wanted to kill more Blue Coats. He pulled me from the fight and showed me our canoes were crossing the lake."

"How do you know this man killed the other?

"I saw him. The man had me and Jamwesaw shot an arrow into his heart."

Pundatha turned to Freeman Trentham and said to him in English, "Where did you get a bow and arrow and where did you get Seneca clothes?"

"I will address Pundatha, the Canandaigua chief, with respect. I will tell you that after I broke from the post I was fortunate to come upon the bow and quiver of arrows, and these clothes. Cpl. Richswill was captured with me. He is a man who hated me. I was a slave and many of the white soldiers hated me and did not want to fight with me. We got away but he wished to be away from me. Later, Wah-say-lan was fighting him and I killed the corporal. I found deerskin clothes and wore them instead of my army uniform."

Pundatha listened carefully. He knew there was more to this tale and he sensed this would be a story told for many years. He loved Wah-say-lan like a daughter, but he knew he must follow the aged ways of his people. He said, "Wah-say-lan, you say he is not your prisoner. But he was our prisoner and now you bring him to us again. What do you want our people to do with him?"

She paused, then said slowly, "I want our people to adopt him and I want him for my husband."

"One thing at a time," said the chief, taken aback. "This is for the women's council. They will sit and consider this."

◈ CHAPTER 20 ◈

The Women's Council

The entire village had heard the news. Pundatha asked the women's council to meet immediately. All work stopped as the 12 women of the council sat in a circle around the campfire.

Wah-say-lan sat inside the circle. Freeman Trentham stood outside, surrounded by braves.

Her mother began with a question. "Did not your father bring this man in as a prisoner? Did he not say this man killed Rah-weh-un with his bayonet?

"Yes," her daughter answered.

"Should we not take this man's life to pay for Rah-weh-un, a strong young man you grew up with you in our village?"

"Jamwesaw has paid twice for Rah-weh-un's bravery. Jamwesaw has killed at least two soldiers and saved my life."

"Now he has killed two soldiers! Why does that make him worthy to be a Seneca brave? You say you want to marry a man of black skin! Why would a Seneca woman not marry a Seneca man? Why would you marry a slave of the white man?" Wah-say-lan's mother was becoming exasperated.

Mary Angel spoke up. She was one of the older women at Canandaigua and was known as Mary Angel because that was her name when her parents were killed in a raid on a white settlement and she was taken 35 years earlier as a 15-year-old girl. She grew up a Seneca. She learned the old ways, especially the ways of medicine and herbs. Mary Angel always had a way about her. She knew things sometimes before they happened. She was a respected medicine woman and healer.

She said to Wah-say-lan, "I knew your grandmother. She was a strong woman. She took a bow to hunt the deer when her man broke his leg. I know you have always asked about your grandmother. I know you swim to the island nearly every morning like your grandmother did when she was young."

Wah-say-lan knew Mary Angel would elicit the whole story. She shot a worried look over at Trentham.

"This man found your bow and quiver of arrows, didn't he?" the old woman said. "He and the other escaped to the island. When you swam there yesterday, this man had to make a choice. He chose you—a wise choice. What was the corporal doing that the black man had to choose?"

"He was trying to rape me. He told Jamwesaw to hold me down and he could have his turn too. You are right, Mary Angel. Jamwesaw had my bow. He found it in my hiding place. His first arrow killed the dirty corporal," Wah-say-lan said in a near whisper. She did not want to revisit that episode.

"And the clothes. They were your clothes," said the medicine woman.

"Yes. I hid them in the tree with my bow."

Wah-say-lan continued: "I was hurt. The filthy pig hit me with a rock on the side of my head. Jamwesaw saved me. Later we heard the shooting and I told him I must go. I told him to wait for me on the island, that I would be back. I told him to wear the buckskin clothes I made—I said they were meant for him, that they always were meant for him. I knew that to be true when I told him."

"But he did not wait for you."

"No. In the battle, after I killed the soldier who killed my father, another soldier came after me. Jamwesaw came out of nowhere and killed him. The brave Pundatha was waving our warriors into the water. Jamwesaw grabbed me and made me swim with him. I did not dare swim with him over to our people. We went northward. We had a campfire last night. He killed a snake with my father's knife and we thanked the snake's spirit for a good meal. We talked into the night."

"And now you want to marry this black man?" asked Mary Angel.

"You are a white woman, Mary Angel, and you married a Seneca. You are among our leaders, among the women I have respected all the summers and winters of my life. The women I have looked up to. Yes, I revere my grandmother. She was brave. She could do all the things women do—have babies, skin deer—and she thought she needed to shoot deer. She lived long and always did what the village needed and brought many new Seneca into the world. Today we are threatened as never before. The American rebels will not stop until they can have our lands. We must stop them. How can we honor all of our people who came before us, if we all do not do everything we can to save our way of life, the way it has been for hundreds of summers, from before memory? Hiawatha and the Peacemaker told us from the shores of Onondaga that we must multiply and be strong. That we must be united to fight our enemies and keep the peace among us. Our great ancestors have always brought others into our nation if they chose to be Iroquois and honor our ways. We brought you, Mary Angel, into our village and you have made it better for all."

Wah-say-lan swept her hand around the circle of women and addressed them: "My women of the council, Mary Angel's wisdom is well known. Her healing power has saved our children. Jamwesaw of Africa has already killed our enemies and saved my life. He is a wise and strong man. He is my man. He was meant to be my man. The Earth Holder, our Ancient One, led him here to our land and he has found me and he wants to be with me and my people."

Trentham listened in awe. He did not know her words spoken in the Seneca language, but he burst with pride at the way she spoke and how they listened. He forgot he was in danger. He wanted to touch her and hold her, but he could not move.

Wah-say-lan was worried. She spoke as best she could. She surprised herself doubly when she heard herself say, "He is my man." She knew she had to be clear and strong, but she also knew she had doubts about her love.

The council thanked Wah-say-lan for her words and then dismissed her. The warriors would not let her near Trentham. She went and stood with Tun-weh. Her young friend grabbed her hand and held it tight.

"I have never heard such a story," she whispered to Wah-say-lan. "How is it that you always amaze me? Do not leave, Wah-say-lan. I do not know how I could get on without you."

Her older cousin put her arm around Tun-weh's shoulders. She rubbed the back of her neck with her hand and whispered back, "Do not worry, little one. We will be together."

Pundatha waved her over to him. She walks regally, he thought. She is her father's daughter.

"The black people are slaves of the whites. How did this happen?" he asked her.

"Jamwesaw and his mother and many women and children of their tribe were captured and sold to white men who brought them over the great water in their sailing ships. As a boy Jamwesaw was taken to the land where the Mohegan live on the river. His mother was sold away from him. Jamwesaw told me the only word he remembered as his mother was carted off was 'Jefferson.' He said he later learned that Jefferson is a white chief like Washington."

"Monticello," said Pundatha.

"Monti-what?" asked Wah-say-lan.

"Monticello. Jefferson, one of the white chiefs, he lives in a place they call Monticello. It is near the end of the warriors' trail. Near the Cherokee people far to the south," he said. "Many summers ago, before you were born, we had a treaty with the whites that said they cannot move beyond the warriors' trail. Jefferson built his home very close to the treaty line."

Mary Angel announced that the council had made a decision. She stood in the circle as all gathered close. Wah-say-lan bit her lip. A breeze stirred her long black hair. She tossed it back with her hand and thought she should have braided it that morning. "Why, right now, am I thinking of braided hair?" she said to herself. She caught her mother smiling at her and knew it had gone well.

"We will adopt Jamwesaw of Africa," said Mary Angel. "Today he will work at whatever he is told to do. There is much to do. There is also food that must be gotten. At sunrise tomorrow Jamwesaw will take bows and arrows and he will take Wah-say-lan and they will go hunt and they will bring back the meat we must have for the winter. When they get back, if they still want to be married, we will perform the ceremony. If they do not want to be married, Jamwesaw still may join the warriors of the Canandaigua Seneca and help us in our battles with Washington's army. And so it is spoken and so it is done," the old woman said.

She spoke with her accustomed authority, yet she had private doubts. Wah-say-lan was still so young. How could she know she wants to be with this stranger for all time? She says they are in love, but with everything that is happening—war, a lost village, building a new village, her father slain before her own eyes—is she thinking clearly? Yes, she has seen young people fall in love. She herself, an adopted Seneca, understands learning new ways and being in love. This Jamwesaw turned it upside down. He apparently fell in love before understanding the ways of the Seneca people. Still, she knows love can happen in an instant. She has seen it happen before. All Mary could do was convince the other women of the council to send them out together again, alone. Perhaps, she thought, in those days and nights, Wah-say-lan can sort out her true feelings.

Ban-er-man-jah put his hand on Freeman Trentham's shoulder and looked into his eyes. "It is an honor to be a Seneca warrior. Now you must live up to that honor. It is hard to live with a strong woman like Wah-say-lan. She is different. She is separate. You must live up to the honor of being with her or you will answer to me," he said.

"I will honor her and I will honor her father's memory, I promise you," said Trentham. He walked over and took Wah-say-lan's hands. They held their gaze. She kissed his cheek.

"I will see you at sunrise," she said. "I will bring you a new belt and I will make you a fine pair of moccasins."

He went off with braves to cut young saplings for longhouses.

◈ CHAPTER 21 ◈

Wah-say-lan Makes Moccasins

Wah-say-lan went over to her mother. They hugged. The mother had done what she could for her daughter but she could no longer hold back her own tears. "He is gone. Your father is gone. I will not see my husband again."

"Your husband was noble. He held my hand in the battle. I will tell you his last words. With his last breath he said, 'Save your mother.' I did not save you. Tun-weh saved you and the baby. I avenged my father's killing, but I did not get to do what he told me. I knew Tun-weh could paddle your canoe, but my mind was on killing, not saving. I would have been killed if it were not for Jamwesaw. His slave name is Freeman Trentham, but I do not call him by a slave name. His mother in Africa named him Jamwesaw. That is his name again. Thank you, Mother, for accepting him. Last night we stayed at a place that you and my father had taken me when I was a young girl. I built a fire on the spot you and he built a fire. I believe Sky Woman, who gave birth to the twins, led me with Jamwesaw to that place. You will see he is a good man and will be good to Lan-lu-rah's daughter," said Wah-say-lan.

"Do you mean the place with the giant hemlock and the two boulders that make a shelter? Your father and I went there many times. Over the years I knew there would be a day when he would not come back. I knew, but still it stings. I see the sky and the clouds and, like a cloud, he has moved along, leaving me with an empty sky. When I see the stars at night and he is not by my side, the stars will not shine as they always did. But I have lived long and I know my man has joined the Ancient One in the Sky World and our people of long ago. I hope you know your man. I married your father after knowing him for many years. You are marrying a man you just met. I know that can happen. But do you know your heart speaks the truth about this man who comes from the other side of the great water?" her mother asked.

"I have the thoughts but they are scrambled. I told the council some things but I cannot put all my thoughts into words for you right now, Mother. I need some time. I need to work with my hands, then I will try to explain to you my feelings. I need to make some moccasins; do you have any skins?"

Then Wah-say-lan made an instant decision. She had handled herself well in front of the women's council, but here she was alone with her mother. "Yes, my thoughts are scrambled, Mother. But please, can you tell me about loving my father. Love is not thoughts. It is feelings, right? It was not your brain that told you to be with him, it was inside you somewhere, is that right? My thoughts are scrambled, but inside me I feel stirrings for this man that I have never felt before."

Her mother paused and took her only daughter's hand. "Yes, Wah-say-lan, it is inside you, in here, and that is good that you can feel it. Now I will get you a skin so you can make your man what he needs."

She went to the supplies that Tun-weh had carried to the canoe. She handed Wah-say-lan the deerskin and thorn needles and twine. "This is from the last deer your father took. It will make a good pair of moccasins," said the woman who only yesterday became a widow.

Wah-say-lan kissed her mother tenderly on the cheek. She took the skin and walked off alone to do her work. She decided first she must make the moccasins from her father's deerskin. Then she would fashion the snakeskin into a belt for Jamwesaw. She laid the skin on a rock in the sun for more drying. She took her knife, her father's knife, and started to cut the deerskin. She performed with precision. Wah-say-lan did all women's work with ease and often with pleasure. She loved most the harvest, picking the ears from the rows and rows of corn and carrying them in the large baskets back for storage and for that day's soup. She was taller than all the women and had no trouble reaching even the highest ears on the highest stalks. Making clothes was a task she also enjoyed. She never told anyone, but she took extra care with her own clothes. Something inside her said the clothes she wore should reflect her beauty. This was a curious characteristic, she thought, and it would be brazen to say such a thing. Seneca people do not boast and vanity is not acceptable, she knew. Nonetheless, she smiled to herself when she made her own clothes.

But now she concentrated on Jamwesaw. She envisioned his feet and cut the skin for them. She folded the first piece over, fur to the inside, and stitched up the front then the back. She folded over the top, inserting twine for tying the moccasins tightly. With a smaller needle she sewed the flap. She held it up and thought how he will like it. She finished the other and was anxious to present them to him.

Wah-say-lan took her knife to the snakeskin and scraped away the remaining pieces of flesh. She set it back on the rock in the direct sun and thought how it would look around Jamwesaw's waist. She remembered marveling yesterday when he took off his shirt to let it dry what a strong body he had. And she remembered climbing on top of him last night and wanting him. It excited her thinking of it and she asked herself, "Why have I not had the same excitement over other men? Why did it not even enter my mind to lie with another, to offer my body to a man? I am a woman, yet I did not have a woman's yearning—until now, until him. But I do not know him. What do I know? I know he is beautiful and brave and strong. I know he can grab a large snake and kill it instantly. I know he is gentle and that he cared for me and cleaned me after killing the filthy corporal. I know he says he loves me. But do I believe him? He can say it, but how do I know he means it? How can a man love me so quickly? He said it was, what?—a bigger force. Something larger than himself, larger than both of us, he said. It brought us together and made me his love is how he said it to me. He said it with sincerity. I yearn for him but I don't know if that means I love him."

She took the snake's skin and sliced it in half. "Enough for two belts, but the second will not be a belt, it will be the strap for his own quiver of arrows."

She folded the skin over lengthwise and admired the dark brown lines against the lighter brown. She sewed the seam tightly and secured each end. She held it up and snapped it hard. "This will hold a quiver with many arrows for a strong warrior," she said, and smiled. Next came the belt, and she repeated her steps. "I will put this around his waist myself the first time. Even better," she smiled to herself and could not help but giggle, "I will untie it the first time and we will lie together again. We will lie together tomorrow night and we will ward off bad dreams together. I do not want bad dreams to stop his loving me. I want him to touch me. I can feel it over every inch of my own body. I ache for him to be close. I shiver inside when he gets close to me. Does that mean I am in love with him? Does that mean I want him for as long as my mother had my father? I do not know. And how do I find out?"

◈ CHAPTER 22 ◈

"She Does Not Follow the Old Rules"

Deh-wan-guh did not know what to say to his friend, Ban-er-man-jah, who grew up thinking Wah-say-lan would be betrothed to him. Now she was off hunting with a stranger, hunting with the blessings of the women's council.

"Women cannot hunt," he said to Deh-wan-guh. "Women cannot fight like a warrior."

"Yet, my friend, you say you saw her slay her father's slayer," said Deh-wan-guh. "Wah-say-lan always wished to hunt. Do you remember when she was only 10 summers and she stole your bow? And now she shows us she can fight like a warrior."

"She has always been outside. She does not follow the old rules," said Ban-er-man-jah. "I was ready to show her how to be a grown Seneca woman. I was ready to be her man, to show her how to be a good Seneca wife."

"Maybe the old rules are not enough anymore," said Deh-wan-guh. "Maybe the gods no longer favor the Iroquois and our rules do not have the meaning they always have had."

"You speak like a fool," Ban-er-man-jah angrily retorted. He rushed off. He did not want to talk about this.

The band of Canandaigua Seneca, despite its losses, went about building another village in the protected glen. Winter was coming and preparations had to be made. It was the return of the scouts Pundatha had sent out after the battle that caused the whole village to forget about Wah-say-lan and her hunting with the man of black skin. The warriors returned with three scalps, smiling with revenge.

"We had gone to the great river and warned Cornplanter and Red Jacket of Sullivan's approach," said the chief scout, Deer Tracker, a man of many summers. "We told them of our escape across the lake. We told them the Blue Coats have many more soldiers than we have warriors."

"The great war chief Cornplanter told us to thank Pundatha and to tell him those he lost now live in peace with our ancestors. He said to tell the Canandaigua Seneca that if Sullivan's army comes, Pundatha will know how to save his people," Deer Tracker said.

He then said to the gathered people of his village that he and his scouts came upon six Blue Coats guided by an Oneida Indian. "They were heading for the great river. They seemed no longer interested in finding where we had gone. We saw them first. But four ran and hid and somehow they escaped. We held the Oneida, Thaosagwat, and two others."

"Ken-ra-jam knew Thaosagwat. He was called Hunts Beavers. He was the brother of Wolf-on-the-run. Ken-ra-jam wrestled with Wolf-on-the-run at the last council fire and they smoked the pipe that day after the contest. Hunts Beavers then made speeches about not fighting the rebel Americans in their war with the British," Deer Tracker went on.

"Yesterday Ken-ra-jam went up to this Oneida who would fight against his brothers the Seneca. Ken-ra-jam split his head open with his tomahawk. The two Blue Coats pleaded for their lives. We made them say their names—Lt. Boyd and Parker. We slit the lieutenant's stomach open and pulled out his innards. His entrails unwound as we held them and he ran in circles, howling. I avenged our dead from our last battle. I took my knife and cut his throat and then I cut his hair and you see it here." Deer Tracker held up the scalp and the people hollered and danced.

Then he told how they tortured the other soldier, sliced the skin from his arms before a Seneca brave thrust his knife into the man's heart. "We made him scream so that his pain will relieve the suffering of our dead warriors as they go to the spirit world," said Deer Tracker.

◈ CHAPTER 23 ◈

Deer Hunting

Freeman Trentham was nervous as he and Wah-say-lan went out together to hunt food for the winter. She insisted on going back north toward the head of the lake. Sullivan's army, if it moved on the great river and Cornplanter's town, would have to trek around the lake. The slave, now a traitor, tried to persuade her it would be better to hunt together for the first time without the worry of continental soldiers descending upon them.

"Jamwesaw, we will see them first. We will be alert for the elusive white-tailed deer and at the same time know we will see any Blue Coats before they see us," she said and took his hand. "Tonight I will lie with you and I want it to be under the tall hemlock I climbed as a child. I want it to be in the same place where you slept with me for the first time. Tonight there will be no bad dreams."

She said this to convince him to head back toward the army. She wanted to know if and when it circled the north end of Canandaigua Lake. But she surprised herself with her argument. She had not realized she wanted to go back to the spot of their first night together. For some reason she could not quite grasp, she needed to be back under her hemlock tree.

Jamwesaw wore the belt of snakeskin and the moccasins she had made for him. They carried bows fashioned from the strong branches of the shagbark hickory. Wah-say-lan's long black hair hung in two braids. When he looked upon her, Jamwesaw could feel his heart pound harder.

He gave up his protestations and was silent for a long time as they walked through the forest. He thought of their first bed, the soft pine needles and how she had held him after his dream. He did not tell her that in his dream he saw the corporal rape her and was about to jam her own arrow into her heart. He shivered thinking of the dream and put it out of his mind, but he also remembered how Wah-say-lan had rolled on top of him and held him tight. She is capable of making nightmares vanish, he said to himself.

She saw Sullivan's scouting party first and pulled Jamwesaw behind an outcropping of large boulders. They could hear their voices. He put his hand firmly on his woman's shoulder and shook his head no. She put her bow down and nestled close against him. The soldiers were soon out of sight and hearing.

"Jamwesaw, I could have killed the first and probably the second with my next shot," she said, instinctively whispering even though the threat was gone.

"I know you could, and I would have gotten another, but still more would come. We are not here to fight. Pundatha sent us to bring food back for the new village. His Seneca warriors will deal with those men," he said.

"I hate them. I wanted to kill them for killing my father and destroying my village," she paused. "But you are right. Come, if we go toward the lake we may see deer drinking along the shore," she said.

Several doe and a large buck were on the beach. The brush gave way to the gray shale. Exposed in the open, animals, but for the bears, crossed it warily to get to the water's edge. Wah-say-lan inched forward, an arrow set in her bow. Jamwesaw marveled at her skill, watching as she slowly raised her weapon, sighted on the big buck and sent the arrow straight into his shoulder. The animal snorted and leaped. The does scattered. The buck, halfway to the woods, fell head first onto the shale.

Jamwesaw and Wah-say-lan gutted the deer. She talked to its spirit and explained that her people needed meat for the coming winter. She packed its heart, liver and stomach into a pouch. She patiently told the deer its heart will be sliced and ground up for special food for the youngest Seneca children to grow strong, that his liver will be medicine when a Seneca falls sick and his stomach will be made into a water pouch.

"We thank the spirit of the animals we kill and explain why we needed to take their lives," she said to Jamwesaw.

"I think you will be doing a lot of explaining before we get back to the village," he said.

They were about to lift the kill when she noticed some movement in the woods. She looked closer and said softly, "Come, quickly, Jamwesaw."

She did not run but was across the beach with her long strides in a moment. She crouched and hustled along a line of bushes. Then she saw it again and recognized Pundatha's prized chestnut brown stallion. She spoke to the horse soothingly, went up to it and patted its neck and behind its ears. The horse whinnied and nudged the young Seneca woman. Soon a mare, lighter brown than the stallion, appeared.

"What a good sign, Jamwesaw. Pundatha's horse escaped with his mate. The Blue Coats did not get them. There were many more, but Pundatha will see this as a good sign," she said. She led the horses to the water and let them take a long drink.

They put the buck on the stallion's back, tied it down and headed for their camp. Wah-say-lan knew the way.

As she carved venison and put it in strips on their fire, she thought back to when she was a little girl with her parents at this place in the forest. She wondered about later that night under the stars lying with Jamwesaw on the bed of pine needles. She carefully hung the last strip of meat over the spit, then pulled a blanket from the pouch and spread it across the pine bed under the darkening sky. Her mind jerked back to the island and the corporal on top of her.

She jumped up, walked briskly to the clearing a few feet away. Her mind bounced back and forth to this day, to the rape on her island, back to her childhood on this spot in the woods.

She breathed deeply and looked up through the tall hemlock. She made herself concentrate on the branches, remembering how her small feet a decade earlier had stepped on the layers of branches as she climbed to the top. As she studied her tree, the highest branches reached into the night sky and touched a star.

She prayed to the tree as she saw it holding the star, "Help me put that dirty soldier out of my memory. Show me the way to the man who came here from across the great sea, came here to me."

Wah-say-lan crossed her arms in front of her heart. She held herself and squeezed tighter. She wanted to conquer her thoughts or at least to understand them. Her mind saw Trentham sipping her soup while he was tethered to the pole, and then she saw him pulling her away from the battle at her village. From prisoner to savior in one night.

"I am almost 18 summers. Why have I not thought of having a man until now?" she asked.

◈ CHAPTER 24 ◈

How Do You Know Monticello?

As they ate, Jamwesaw thanked her for slaying the deer and providing dinner. They sat cross-legged in front of the fire and slowly chewed the sweet strips from the deer's flank.

"Your arrow was true. You are good with your bow," he said.

"I have had enough practice. You know the place in the tree on the island," she said.

"Yes, you said your weapon, your clothes you kept there, were meant for me. Do you really believe that?" the black man asked.

She smiled at him. "I do. That is the only answer. My father's father used to tell me the Earth Holder, our Ancient One who rules the Sky World, sends many things to the Seneca people, even when they do not know they seek it. There is a path to every person, he would say. You, Jamwesaw, came down my path."

"That is what my father told me, too, Wah-say-lan. He talked of a path to follow. On the ship across the big gawa I tried to listen to my father's words, but I heard them spill out to be lies. 'How could this be my path?' I said to myself. For many years in Connecticut I did not think of a path. I forgot his words. But here now with you, you bring his words back. There must be places where the path disappears, but then a man, a woman, can find it again," he said.

He paused and looked at her and tried to pick his words carefully.

"Wah-say-lan, I must stay on a path to find my mother. I am accepted into your tribe and for that I am thankful. I have found you, which to me is unbelievable. But do you understand I must try to find my mother? I believe she is with Thomas Jefferson in Virginia, a trip of many days and nights."

The young Seneca woman moved closer to him and said softly, "Monticello. Jefferson is a white chief who lives at a place called Monticello."

"How do you know this?" Trentham said excitedly.

"Pundatha told me, when I told him of how you were separated from your mother. He said Jefferson is one of the American rebel leaders. He built his home near the warriors' trail. Iroquois have used the trail since before memory. It is too late to go now, but in the spring I will go with you, Jamwesaw. We will find your mother, if this Jefferson has her. I want to meet your mother and I want to meet this Jefferson who makes her a slave."

Again the slave was astounded. "What an amazing woman. I have known her for only a few days and already she tells me where to find my mother," he thought. He did not know what to say, so he said, "Pundatha will let us go there?"

"Yes," she said, then got up and said, "Come with me. I want to see my lake."

They walked silently under the night sky to the shore. She felt right. She felt she was led back to the hemlock tree where her father told her of the wind kissing her face. She felt that even the stabbing recollection of the solider trying to rape her was sent back into her thoughts so that she could confront it, defeat it, and push it from her memory. She studied the hemlock and how it reaches to the stars. She thought of her father traveling in the Sky World and then she remembered his words and how she now was certain Jamwesaw was sent to her. Her feeling for a man, her first feelings for a man, made more sense to her now. No other men had come down her path with such love for her. Only this man from Africa came to her.

At the water's edge they disrobed and waded in. It was cool and soothing and they swam, stretching the muscles of their tired bodies. He pulled up to her and touched her shoulder. They kissed in the water. They glided toward shore and stood chest deep. They embraced and held each other tight. Their lips touched again. Wah-say-lan pressed her mouth against Jamwesaw's. She could feel a longing rise up inside of her.

She led him to the shore. They did not dress, but gathered up their clothes and walked to their waiting bed. First she put a few more branches on the fire. As the flames rose and the light glowed, Wah-say-lan and Jamwesaw lay next to each other on their blanket. They kissed again. They did not speak. Without thinking, simply and naturally, she slid over on top of him. She felt his long legs against hers. She felt her nipples against his chest. She rose up, exposing her breasts to him. He caressed them in his hands. She could feel him rising between her legs and she opened them to receive him. He was gentle. They swayed together as if they were meant to be one. Her lips went back down to his. They both held tightly as their bodies moved in unison.

She awoke as the sun's first light chased the moon from the sky. She was smiling and she remembered her dream. Her father and her mother stood with the two horses and he said to her, "My friend Pundatha will be happy. Our daughter and her man have brought him his prized horse. This is a good sign."

She looked at Freeman Trentham and marveled at his chest rising evenly with his breathing. "He is such a strong man. His arms bulge in tight muscles. Yet he is so gentle when he touches me," she thought.

In a day's walk, Jamwesaw and Wah-say-lan arrived back at the new village still being built. They led the two horses, which were hauling seven large deer on skids fashioned from young pine trees. Pundatha's village, before it was burned, had many horses. These two had run far enough into the woods and around the lake so they were not captured by the invading army. They were a gift for Pundatha he did not expect.

"I thought Washington's army took our horses and here Lan-lu-rah's daughter brings me back my own horse," said the chief. "You are a wonder to me," he said, putting his hand on her shoulder. "You and your man have also brought our people much meat for the winter. We thank you and the spirit of the white-tailed deer."

Wah-say-lan had hoped Pundatha would not linger on her role in the hunt, and he did not. But she moved quickly to the other issue. "I am proud Jamwesaw and I could bring you what we have. I must now find my mother and tell her of my intent to marry him," she said.

Pundatha smiled and let her go.

Wah-say-lan went to Mary Angel and her mother. "I am ready to marry this man. I want him to live in our longhouse," she said.

"Do you doubt it at all?" asked the elder.

"I do not doubt. I believe my father's father when he told me of paths. This man from Africa came down my path to be with me," she said.

That night the Seneca feasted and their chief offered a prayer to the Ancient One for the return of two of their horses. The next day he performed the wedding ceremony. Wah-say-lan, the daughter of his good friend Lan-lu-rah, now killed by Sullivan's army, was made one with Jamwesaw of Africa, now a tested hunter and warrior of the Seneca people. It was a cloudy morning. Pundatha decided to hold the ceremony at the falls in the glen. Jamwesaw and Wah-say-lan held hands as their chief spoke the words all Seneca chiefs had spoken to a new husband and wife. He added, "As surely as the water will always cascade over these falls forever feeding our sacred lake; as surely as these hemlocks, their roots deep in the ground, will always guard over this spot; this couple unites to travel together now and later in the Sky World. You are bound together. You will start your own family, to be one with the Haudenosaunee, the people of the longhouse, to carry our ways into our future."

He touched both their foreheads. As Jamwesaw turned to look at his wife, their eyes met. And at that moment, the clouds broke and sun shone down on the Seneca of Canandaigua. Wah-say-lan whispered to Jamwesaw, "It is a sign. The sun streams through the hemlocks and blesses us." She kissed her husband.

As was Iroquois custom, Wah-say-lan and Jamwesaw moved in with her family. In the old village on Canandaigua Lake, her mother and father lived in one of the biggest longhouses with her cousin Tun-weh's family and other close relatives. They were of the Wolf Clan and their fires were kept burning and welcomed Wolf Clan members from all the other Iroquois nations. Often there were visitors and pipe smoking and storytelling in the long winters when clan members arrived on their snow-shoes bringing fresh-killed rabbits and other game as their contribution during their visit.

◈ CHAPTER 25 ◈

Sullivan Leaves

Sullivan's army had reached the great river, but Cornplanter's Seneca were prepared and, to the general's surprise, he could find no Seneca in this far western village. They had taken their stores of food, the harvest of the three sisters: corn, beans and squash and the apples and pears from their orchards. They took everything they could across the great river, away from the invaders.

The trick worked. Gen. Sullivan saw the leaves beginning to change, October arriving and he decided he did not want his men caught out in this wilderness as winter approached. He pulled out his original orders from Gen. Washington and reread them: "Lay waste all the settlements, that they not be merely overrun, but destroyed." He wrote his assessment to his commander. More than 40 Iroquois villages were destroyed in the nearly two months of his campaign. The outnumbered Indians usually fled and offered little opposition but for the battle at Canandaigua, and a month earlier at Newtown, where he defeated the enemy badly, he told Washington. Sullivan decided this last band of Indians could march west to the British fort at Niagara and be of no harm to the Patriot cause.

In his letter to Washington, Sullivan went into great detail about the acres of orchards his men chopped down and the number of longhouses they burned to the ground and the number of braves killed and British Rangers taken prisoner in the last battle. He did not mention the horrible fate of Lt. Boyd and Parker. Nor did he say where the Seneca of Canandaigua vanished to. He truly did not know. It was time for him to get back to Philadelphia. He expected a commendation from the Continental Congress for subduing the savages of Western New-York.

◈ CHAPTER 26 ◈

Joseph Brant

In the weeks after Sullivan's army withdrew, the Iroquois assessed the damage. They named the white chief Washington Segan-they-ler, town destroyer. Up and down the woodlands where the Haudenosaunee lived around Cayuga Lake, Seneca Lake, Canandaigua Lake, the Genesee River and the myriad smaller lakes and streams, the Continental Army had razed more than 40 towns along with their crops. Soldiers had spent more time cutting down fruit trees in the Indians' vast orchards than they had fighting. All the apple, pear and cherry trees fell under the ax.

By no means, though, were the Indians defeated. In the face of such a large army, they first made a stand at Newtown, losing 14 braves. Cornplanter called for resistance again at Canandaigua, where Pundatha inflicted the heaviest damage on Sullivan's troops. Otherwise, the Indians simply vanished before the army's eyes. At the end of the campaign, the Seneca, the Cayuga, the Onondaga who joined them and the most fiercely pro-British nation, the Mohawk from the east, could still field a formidable force of upwards of 1,000 warriors.

Before the long winter set in, the Iroquois were hurriedly building new longhouses, as Pundatha was doing in the valley with the falls. The Canandaigua Seneca chief had sent several women back across the water to see if they could reclaim any of their carefully dried stores of venison, vegetables and fruit. Amid the charred remains of their homes, the women went to the covered square holes in the ground where food was preserved through winters. Most, however, had been discovered and either eaten by the army or thrown into the fires.

With tears in her eyes, Tun-weh carried a few baskets of corn, squash and nuts back to her canoe. She and the others paddled across the lake hardly noticing the beauty and splendor of the late autumn leaves. Most of what they had found would be saved for spring planting, some could be used sparingly for the babies and children.

The famed Mohawk war chief Joseph Brant, making his way among his brother Seneca and Cayuga, urged them to travel to the British fort at Niagara, far to the west, for the winter. Hundreds did, camping in makeshift homes outside the stockade, girding down for what they felt would be the strangest, if not the hardest, winter of their lives

Pundatha set a council fire with Brant. Cornplanter came from his Genesee town. They and several other war chiefs discussed what to do.

"Joseph Brant, you are a wise and fierce chief. You have been across the great water and met with the British chief they call the King," said Pundatha. "But I do not wish to send my people to Niagara. As you see, we have built sturdy longhouses. We will hunt the deer and catch the fish in our lake and we will stay where our people have always been, here on this lake, our Chosen Place."

Cornplanter spoke up: "Pundatha fought Washington's soldiers bravely. He lost many warriors, but so did the Blue Coats lose many. Pundatha lost the noble Lan-lu-rah, his closest friend. Yet the wise chief has led his people to this valley for the coming winter. He will stay and be ready to take up the hatchet next spring and avenge Lan-lu-rah and his other braves who now travel in the Sky World."

"So be it," said Brant. "Do not think this will be a good winter. You have seen twice the acorns from the oaks on the ground and the many more caterpillars making their way across the forest floor. It will be a harsh winter, but I am content Pundatha will care for his people."

"One more thing," said Cornplanter. "There can be no midwinter council fire. Since before memory, all the Six Nations have gathered at Onondaga where the Peacemaker first brought us all together. We do not have the food for this."

There was silence and a sadness filled the air. Finally Pundatha said, "We will have our ceremony here and we will tell all the stories that have always been told. It will not be the same, but still we will do it and all Iroquois must do it when the moon shines full in midwinter. We will not be together this time, but we will raise our voice in song and dance and in our storytelling we will raise our voices to all the nations and the wind will carry our voices together in the air and we will hear each other."

"Well said, brother," said Joseph Brant. "I will listen for Pundatha's voice when he tells of how the Seneca were born on the hill above this lake. It is as fine a story as the Iroquois have and your man Star Traveler always tells it well, Pundatha."

It started to snow then. The Seneca chiefs and men rose and bade farewell to their Mohawk brothers. "We will see you in the sun of springtime. We will have many braves and we will avenge Lan-lu-rah and the others," Brant told Pundatha. He and his warriors walked off into the forest, heading for their British allies on the western frontier.

As they walked, it snowed harder, but they pushed ahead until dark, when they made camp beneath giant oaks and hemlocks. Their campfire was large that night to fight off the coming cold.

◈ CHAPTER 27 ◈

Ban-er-man-jah's gift

Ban-er-man-jah left the lake carrying a dozen large bass in his basket. He was expert at carving the thin vertebrae spurs of the deer into sharp fishhooks, attaching the hooks to long sinews and a willow rod. Since childhood he had come back with as many fish caught with a worm dangling on his hooks as others had speared or taken with the bow and arrow. Canandaigua Lake had always supplied the Seneca with trout, bass, pickerel, perch and the large delicious white fish to supplement the venison and vegetables that were their staples.

The young brave walked across the snow on his new snowshoes. He stopped to give the largest fish to Wah-say-lan to celebrate her union with Jamwesaw. As he walked into the longhouse, Tun-weh was kneeling near the fire, pounding corn kernels into meal. Mixed with syrup boiled down from maple tree sap, it was gobbled up by the baby, who still had not grown his teeth. She had found a few precious capped earthen flasks of the syrup buried in the old village.

"Thank you for these snowshoes, Tun-weh. I could not have walked to the water without them. Please present this fish to Wah-say-lan and her husband as my gift to them," he said to the young woman.

Tun-weh looked up at the warrior who had been wounded in the battle. A scar was forming on his right shoulder where the Blue

Coat's sword had struck. She stood and touched it. "You are healing well," she said. "And, yes, Wah-say-lan will be pleased you have thought of her." She paused. "I was told we needed snowshoes and I will start to make more later today. But I am honored, Ban-er-man-jah, that my shoes could help you bring back such good food for the people."

"If the ice does not form too quickly, I will bring back more," he said. "Your mother's baby will find the meat of the fish is tasty and he can eat it now. Here," he said, and took two 15-inch bass from his basket and gave them to Tun-weh. Then he walked back into the falling snow to take the rest of his catch to his own longhouse.

Tun-weh watched him push aside the bearskin at the door as he walked out. She knelt back down to finish the cornmeal and syrup but took a moment to watch the smoke from the fire curl upward and out the circular hole some 20 feet above her head in the roof of the new longhouse. She could see the snow falling. In her 14 years she had always delighted in the new snow, but she was unsettled this day. She had never seen the snow fall for so long. It had snowed all day and all night and lay in a thick blanket on the ground.

Her mother startled Tun-weh out of her thoughts. "Tonight there will be stories, my daughter. It will be like every winter. We will listen to the stories of our people. But finish the corn now. Then go to Mary Angel's lodge. She has more rawhide strips and hickory. We will make more shoes for the snow."

"Do you remember this much snow before?" she asked her mother.

"Always there is a long winter with snow," she said and walked over to the beds at the south side of the longhouse. The baby was fussing and she warbled a tune softly until the child was back asleep.

◈ CHAPTER 28 ◈

Storytelling

Pundatha was pleased with how well his people had built the new longhouses. In this small valley they erected six of the structures as the Seneca had done for eons—cutting down the saplings, bending them together in arches with strong branches along the sides tying them together. Birch and elm bark stripped from larger trees formed the walls and roofs. Beds for each clan lined the inside walls in bunk style, one above the other. Under the bottom beds were storage spaces for blankets, furs, earthenware and cooking utensils. The Canandaigua chief had tested each structure as it was being built and now he knew his people were protected from harsh winter.

He was pleased, too, at all the deer meat that had been brought back to their new village, though he would be careful to make sure it was rationed, remembering Joseph Brant's observations on the larger-than-usual crop of acorns, which meant a hard winter. The women of Canandaigua spread through the woods and gathered bushels of acorns to supplement winter meals. Tonight, though, with everyone coming to his house for a feast and storytelling, he ordered two large deer flanks to be roasted, along with two turkeys taken just that morning.

Wah-say-lan sat between Tun-weh and Jamwesaw with the other Wolf Clan members. Ban-er-man-jah's Turtle Clan sat on the other side of the fire. All of Pundatha's people were crowded into his longhouse, sitting among their various clans, the heron, beaver, bear, and eagle clans. Nearly 200 men, women and children were feasting and waiting for the tales to begin.

"It is only in the winter that we can listen to our stories," Wah-say-lan told Jamwesaw. "It is only then that we have time to sit still. Storytelling is not allowed any other time. And we must listen carefully."

"Yes, and quietly," Tun-weh interjected. "No one can speak. Only if someone proclaims, 'Ho!' will the storyteller stop. And that means the teller will announce a break so everyone can relax for a moment, stretch their legs, go out and relieve themselves and get comfortable again for the story to continue. The stories go late into the night," she said.

Pundatha stood and called for Star Traveler, On-gobar-thay-gen, the oldest man in the village, to come forward. He had lived for 81 summers and along with Pundatha and Du-bay-se-hah, the healer, he was the most respected man among the Canandaigua Seneca.

Star Traveler stood, holding a stout walking stick as long as he was tall. His dark, black hair was streaked with silver and held two white and brown eagle feathers. His gnarled fingers gripped his staff tightly as he pounded it on the dirt floor in a slow rhythm. He began to speak of the round hill that rose above the lake on the eastern shore.

"When we stand on the shore where the sun sleeps and look back across our lake, our eyes see the hill that is bare. It stands above all else, dark green against the blue sky. The trees that cover our country, the great oaks, maple, hickory, the hemlocks and other pines, do not grow on our great Bare Hill. Why is that, my children?" is how On-gobar-thay-gen began his story, just as he began this story every time he told it as far back as Wah-say-lan could remember. Tun-weh grabbed her hand and squeezed it. They loved this story and were entranced by the old man's telling of it.

"I will tell you why the hill is bare. It begins long past memory.

Long ago, before your grandmother's and her grandmother's time," said Star Traveler. "The children of the village brought home a snake for a pet. They found it curled in the brush. They chose to raise it and fed it field mice, for there were far too many mice and the mice ate the corn growing in the field. Soon, though, the snake grew and needed more and the children found it rabbits. And the snake grew and one day it consumed one of the dogs of the village.

"Some people began to worry, but it was too late. The snake had grown and become powerful and it ate what it wanted. The serpent turned on those who brought him to their village and it ate children. Braves struck at it with their weapons but the weapons were useless and the serpent ate the warriors and their women. It was a ravenous animal.

"It happened that only a small boy and girl were left. They were frightened. They hid behind a longhouse and whispered to each other how they might escape. That day an eagle flew down and showed them where to look for the magic bow and arrows. The eagle told the boy and the girl where to strike the serpent.

"They found the bow and arrows in the woods and they decided they could not run, that they must face the horrid creature. The boy and girl went back to the village at nightfall. They slept in the sachem's longhouse. They held hands together all night, for they had decided that when the sun appeared in the sky they would face the serpent.

"The giant snake crawled through the village seeking food. It had been many days with nothing to feed its growing hunger. Then it saw the two children emerge from the longhouse. It rushed and raised its giant gluttonous head above the top of the longhouse.

"The girl spoke quickly, 'Remember, the eagle said to strike right behind its head.' The serpent's mouth was wide open. Its tongue lashed out. The boy took his magic bow and placed an arrow ready to shoot. He dashed a few steps to the side to get a better aim, then released the arrow. It struck the serpent behind its great head. The animal let out a noise so loud it frightened the birds from the trees and all the animals scampered for shelter. The snake's body writhed and whipped back and forth. It knocked down all the longhouses of the hilltop village. It screamed and belched and roiled the ground where the village had been.

"Blood was spurting from the wound. Its enormous tail slashed at everything in its path. All the trees fell with each whip of its body. The serpent, in agony, flailed as it fell down the hill. Trees, brush, crops, everything fell to the torments of the huge beast.

"The boy and the girl watched in amazement as the animal screeched in its death throes. It left destruction everywhere. Finally it was at the base of the hill. It slithered into the cool waters of the lake. It tried to swim, but still blood flowed from the wound of the arrow behind its great head. The boy and the girl from the hilltop saw the great snake floating on the waters of their lake, its body stilled, its head sinking into the depths. It took some time, but soon the last bit of its tail disappeared beneath the surface. The monster was gone.

"The two young children looked up in the sky and saw the eagle circling. It called to them and they heard it say, 'This hill, this Bare Hill is yours with its lake and all the lands around it.'

"Though all the vegetation was ruined, all the longhouses were destroyed, all their people had been eaten by a monster, the two began building a new longhouse at the top of the hill. As they grew, they had their own children and the family grew and the Seneca nation was born. Never again did the serpent appear. And the Seneca people multiplied and spread out from the lake, but always some Seneca stayed at this Chosen Place, Canandaigua. And today, we are here, many summers, many generations since the serpent was slain. But still on the hill above our lake, as you can see any day, there are no trees because of that faraway battle between a serpent and two children."

When Star Traveler had finished, the Seneca of Canandaigua rose. They chanted. The drummers' fast fingers and palms laid down a current of music. Warriors and women danced to the beat.

Wah-say-lan held Jamwesaw's hand as they danced with the others in the big longhouse. Ban-er-man-jah found himself in front of the young Tun-weh. She turned toward him. He took her hand and they kept time to the beat, their moccasins moving together. The voices and music of the people carried out on the wind over the woodlands of the Iroquois.

As she danced, Wah-say-lan thought of the eagle telling the boy and girl about the hidden magic bow. Ever since she first heard the story as a small girl, she took it a step further in her own mind. She knew you cannot question the stories, but she could not help it. She always made it in her own mind that the boy tripped and fell with the magic bow and, just before the serpent struck, the girl grabbed the weapon. It was her arrow that struck the beast. Except for that time long ago when her father caught her with a curved stick pretending to kill the serpent, Wah-say-lan had never told anybody her version of the story, just as she had never shown anybody her hidden bow and arrows on the island.

She was smiling as she danced, thinking of her father's gentle scolding. Her husband knew her well enough that she was enjoying the physical motion but her thoughts were far away. He wondered how that certain set smile, the way her lips tilted up but slightly to the left, how that smile hid her thoughts. It was private places he knew she had, but he did not ask. He felt she would tell him things when she was ready. Almost always when he saw her in that inner reverie he lingered and watched her think. Her big, dark eyes somehow got larger, her graceful movements were more graceful, and her ever-present resolve became more pronounced in the way she held her head. Even in the midst of a crowd while dancing, it was like they were in a bubble traveling down a stream together. He loved these moments and it inevitably sent his own thoughts off somewhere.

Then he heard Pundatha announce that it was time to eat. Jamwesaw told his wife to be seated with her cousin Tun-weh and Ban-er-man-jah. The black man returned with large wooden bowls filled with the simmering venison stew. He let his mind wind back to the dinner in Wallingford when he and Mrs. Willington served Washington's men. It was a lifetime ago, he thought to himself. But then that day farther back in his life when his mother was carted away from him felt like yesterday; the pain was still palpable to the young man. As he sat with Wah-say-lan, she smiled at him and his heart jumped. She was the first person who was ever able to sooth his pain.

The snow was falling in the night sky.

◈ CHAPTER 29 ◈

The Snow

At the time of the traditional Iroquois midwinter festival, when all six nations would meet at Onondaga, the snow was nearly as deep as a man. Snowdrifts twice that high surrounded the new longhouses in the valley west of Canandaigua Lake where Pundatha had led his people. Even if Sullivan's army had not come and destroyed all their food, the Iroquois could not have traveled the days it took to get to their festival.

Not even the elders of the Six Nations could remember a winter with so much snow covering their land. More than 2,000 had trekked earlier to the British fort at Niagara. Staying outside the wooden walls in makeshift wigwams, those Mohawk, Cayuga and Seneca, all sturdy British allies, benefited from army blankets and supplies.

But the Iroquois who were spread out over the Western New-York wilderness were facing a crisis as lethal as any they had ever faced. The lakes were frozen under six feet of snow, making ice fishing impossible. The rivers and larger streams still ran, but trudging to them even on snowshoes was an enormous task. Some fish could be taken with nets and spears, but the usual holes were clogged with ice floes and the take was minimal at each arduous attempt. Trapping the muskrats, otters and beavers along the riverbanks was a near impossibility, and so their fresh meat and furs were sorely missed.

The Seneca felt that Ha'tho,' the god of frost, was cruel this season, more so than ever before. Some spoke quietly that he was angry the Seneca could not oust Sullivan's army from the land.

One morning They-yo-un-guh, who had two-year-old twin boys, took his traps to the river where he had been getting muskrats since he was a child. At the top of the drift rising above the fast-moving water he peered down. He could not see the riverbank, so he started to climb down the steep mound of snow and ice, his traps in his pouch around his neck.

It was a desperate move. He lost his footing and slid into the frigid water. It carried him downstream. The usual roots and shoreline rocks to grab hold of were buried behind sheer, glistening ice. He looked everywhere for a place to escape, but he realized in moments that his life here was over. His legs could no longer move, but it did not matter; swimming was useless. He sang his death song and asked the Ancient One to receive him in the Sky World. They-yo-un-guh's last thought was of his two small boys and then the cold water took him under. Ha'tho's retribution is the way some spoke around their fires when the young father never returned.

The herds of deer were either starving or freezing to death. The last four hunting parties had not seen a live deer. One young brave was lucky to find under a twisted and bent-over hemlock the frozen carcasses of two small doe. After they had thawed out near the fire, they were skinned and cut into rations. The young man took a hindquarter to They-yo-un-guh's widow. He helped her mash up the most tender parts for the two hungry little boys.

It was even a chore to keep their fires fed. Each day hunters were told to find and bring back dry wood. Far to the south they finally came upon a huge, dead oak still standing with its snow-covered limbs reaching starkly up to gray skies. The tree offered a continual harvest as braves carried the wood back to the longhouses. Around their fires at night, the Seneca thanked the great oak, which in death supplied life-giving warmth for the village.

Also around their fires at night, the Seneca talked more and more of revenge against the white man for intruding into their lands, for bringing an army to destroy the Iroquois. They talked of joining Cornplanter, Red Jacket, Joseph Brant and the other war chiefs.

It is what Wah-say-lan wished for, to personally avenge her father's death. Even though she killed the soldier who killed her father, she promised herself that she was not done. But as she listened to the talk of revenge with the gathering of Iroquois warriors in the spring, she feared she would be made to stay and plant and cultivate new fields, and skin the hides of the animals after the hunting began again. She did not mind the hard work of planting and making clothes from skins. It is an honorable way to provide for her people. But she was restless for more.

She remembered her promise to Jamwesaw that they would make the long trip to Jefferson's home in Virginia. It excited her thinking about the journey. She had journeyed the three days with her family to the council fires and festivals at Onondaga Lake. Once, as a young girl, her father took her all the way to Saratoga along the river where the Mohawk lived. She loved being able to travel with her people wherever they pleased to go. She was sure Pundatha would free her from the cultivating and Jamwesaw from the war parties, even though he would be a knowledgeable warrior against the Blue Coats.

If this Jefferson was a chief, then Pundatha must know that striking against him to free Jamwesaw's mother could be an effective tactic in their war against the Americans. She had told her husband that Pundatha would not stand in their way, but the young woman took the time to organize her thoughts to persuade her chief.

Not only had she and Jamwesaw brought back many deer from their hunts during the moon of the harvests, but they also had returned with Pundatha's favorite horse and its mate. Anticipating the bitter winter, Wah-say-lan had spent many afternoons before the snow came gathering grasses, leafy ferns and oak leaves, baskets and baskets that she had stored in a special shelter she built to keep the two horses fed through the winter. More than once the chief had thanked her for her forethought.

"You are wise like my friend Lan-lu-rah. He taught you wisely in raising you to womanhood," he told her one day as she was sewing deerskins for Tun-weh's baby brother.

"My father gave me more than I could ever repay him for," she said. "He and my mother showed me all the good ways of our people. He whispered to me, Pundatha, in a dream from the Sky World, that I should go out and gather what I could find for your horses."

"Your dreams are good dreams," said the chief. "My horses have survived. Our youngest children have survived. But for the loss of They-yo-un-guh in the river, I believe our people will live through this time. I can sense that Daga'e'da comes with his warmth to end the hold of Ha'tho's deep snow upon our land.

"I can feel the end of the long cold nights, Pundatha," said Wah-say-lan.

"When Deh-wan-guh and Ban-er-man-jah came back with the black bear, that was a good day," said the chief. "They went out to hunt whatever they could find and they came upon the fierce bear who had probably just emerged from his slumber. Their arrows found their mark and the two braves have brought life to our people in this bad winter. I was worried that some of the young children might not make it, but the fresh bear meat will bring us through until the thaw."

"Genden'wit'ha, the Morning Star, was with them when they shot the bear. I have told this to Deh-wan-guh and Ban-er-man-jah and have offered to prepare the fur. It was a large bear and will make two big blankets for their families." She paused, reached out to her chief's hand and held it in hers.

"Let me ask you one thing, Pundatha. Jamwesaw knows he must go find his mother. He believes this man Jefferson keeps her as a slave. You told me the white chief lives in Virginia down the warriors' trail near Cherokee territory. I know you know he must do this, but he cannot go alone and we cannot spare braves to go with him. I must go with him, Pundatha, and strike against this Jefferson."

The chief smiled. "You are your father's daughter," is all he said, and went out to visit another longhouse. For the chief made sure to visit all his longhouses and to comfort and reassure the clans and all his people that they would get through this bad time.

That night the people feasted for the first time in a long time. The succulent meat, carved in steaks thick and juicy, was a joyful relief from their meager diet of small portions of dried venison. They thanked Nia'gwai', the bear in the night sky, and the seven brothers who slew the great bear in the time after Sky Woman created the earth. They passed the pipe in honor of Deh-wan-guh and Ban-er-man-jah, who slew the bear and brought the people out of the bad winter. The sweet scent of the cooking bear meat mingled with the tobacco smoke, bringing a warmth to the gathering. Deh-wan-guh told of how his friend first saw the great animal clawing the snow around a tree trunk, and how they came around slowly and approached it from the front so it would stand on its hind legs and open its arms, exposing its heart for an easier target. Their arrows were true and the beast fell without a gruesome fight. The people chanted for the two braves and thanked Nia'gwai' again for aiding in the hunt.

Later, when the children had been put in their beds and the women of the council and Pundatha's warriors were gathered close, he asked his wife to bring him one of the three long guns taken when his scouting party captured and killed the Oneida and two of Sullivan's scouts last fall.

"Soon the Seneca will regroup with our brothers the Mohawk, the Cayuga and Onondaga. We will gather many warriors and avenge our slain warriors," Pundatha said. "Washington sent an army to destroy us. They burned our homes and our crops, but they did not defeat us."

Pundatha's braves responded with great shouts and whoops. He held up the musket to quiet his men.

"I must tell you that I looked forward to the strong Jamwesaw joining our war parties, and he will. But first he must finish his personal journey. He knows he must find and free his mother from slavery at the hands of the white man. He must travel the warriors' trail like so many Seneca have done. There, on the trail far to the south, he feels he knows where to find his mother of Africa. I say to him now he should take his wife with him. She is good on a long journey and she has asked to go. And I give him this musket, which he was trained to use, and I wish them success in their mission," the chief said, and handed the gun to the black man.

But the musket in his hands felt foreign. He thought how to tell Pundatha that the weapon should stay.

"Pundatha, great chief of the Canandaigua Seneca, I am humbled by your gift and thankful that my wife can travel with me down our warriors' trail. I need her on this journey, but she is all that I need. Please keep the long gun. Our British friends will be impressed that you have them and they will show whoever you choose how to best use them in the coming battles," said Jamwesaw. He watched Pundatha carefully, for he did not want to offend. The chief sat silently.

Jamwesaw continued. "Let me tell you, chief of the Seneca, about another chief, the American sachem Benjamin Franklin."

Pundatha grew excited. "I know this man. I spoke with this Benjamin Franklin many summers ago."

"It does not surprise me that a great Iroquois chief would know of Benjamin Franklin," said Jamwesaw. "I do not know him, but I know this of him. When I first joined Washington's army, one of his generals spoke to my company of Franklin's message. The great American sachem wanted the Blue Coats to use bows and arrows. He said it like this: 'A man may shoot as truly with a bow as with a common musket. He can discharge four arrows in the time of charging and discharging one bullet. A flight of arrows, seen coming upon them, terrifies the enemy.' This is what the general told us from their great Franklin as he handed out bows. We trained with them for many months until finally muskets arrived and we changed, foolishly I think.

"Pundatha, I saw Wah-say-lan with her bow in the fight for your village and how she terrified the Blue Coats. When I hunted with her and brought back the seven deer, the bow felt natural to me. I ask you to let me travel with my bows and arrows and then I will feel better that I will succeed."

Pundatha, a big and naturally happy man, smiled broadly. He stood and said, "Jamwesaw is a wise and brave man. And he and Wah-say-lan will travel with bows and they will find his mother and strike against Thomas Jefferson, the white chief who built his Monticello near our warriors' trail.

"The wisest white chief is Benjamin Franklin. I have lived 50 summers. I met him 25 summers ago when I was a young brave and traveled with my father and a large party of Haudenosaunee to where the two great rivers meet, the place the whites call Albany, where the river of the Mohawks meets the long river the whites call Hudson. There this Benjamin Franklin spoke of the strength of the Iroquois Confederacy. Of how all other Indians feared the Six Nations.

"He spoke of how the Tuscarora people traveled from their homelands to join with the Iroquois and make our Confederacy stronger. We accepted the Tuscarora and they came to live with the Oneida. Benjamin Franklin made a speech that the whites must join together in a Confederacy. He said they must be strong like the Iroquois. He told them all other Indians knew the power of the Haudenosaunee and no other nations could defeat us. He told his brothers they must join together, they must do what the Haudenosaunee have shown them how to do.

"When his speech was done, he came over to my father and Benjamin Franklin shook my father's hand. He told him that he did not think his white brothers would listen to him and he said, 'Your chiefs are much wiser. You have learned how to be strong and united.'

My father told Benjamin Franklin, 'This is my son Pundatha. He will be the future of my people. He will guard the western door of our Six Nations with all his Seneca brothers.' Benjamin Franklin shook my hand and said he hoped to see me again. Later we learned that the other chiefs of the white man would not follow Benjamin Franklin's ideas. That they had their King across the great water, that they did not need to join together like savages in the wilderness.

"It was our joining together that kept the Haudenosaunee the most powerful since the time of Hiawatha. I worry today that for the first time in memory our Confederacy has broken, that the Oneida and the Tuscarora have joined the Americans against their brothers the Mohawk, the Cayuga, the Onondaga and the Seneca. If we cannot bring our brothers back to us, I worry, but not so much. Because I know it is time to raise the hatchet again and go out and fight against these whites who come into our lands and burn our homes. We will fight back and we will put fear in their hearts. And we will use our own name: Haudenosaunee, our people of the longhouse. Those French, who fight with the Americans, they call us Iroquois. It is not a bad name but we do not need a name from the white French. We are Haudenosaunee. We are the people of the longhouse."

The warriors of the Canandaigua Seneca, satisfied with a big meal of bear meat, moved by the eloquence of their chief, stood and danced and shouted. Ban-er-man-jah went to Wah-say-lan. He put his arms around her. He said, "Before you go, you and Jamwesaw come and sit with me. You know that two summers ago I traveled the trail with a war party down to where the Cherokee live. I will tell you of things I know."

"Before I go, I will finish the bear blanket for Ban-er-man-jah. Jamwesaw and I will sit with you and listen to what you know of the warriors' trail." She kissed him on the cheek and hugged him tightly.

That night she lay with her husband and told him of her excitement as a young girl when her father brought her along with the large party traveling to Saratoga. The Mohawks' river was to her an easy path through the forest. She had canoed her lake, but never had traveled so far, days in the canoe as braves paddled steadily along its waters.

"My father, Pundatha, Red Jacket, Corn Planter and also Cayuga and Onondaga sachems met with a council of white men. My mother and some other women came too. I had never been so far to where the sun rises, even beyond Onondaga. Jamwesaw, I was so excited. I can still feel how wonderful I felt then. I felt like the wolf who could go wherever he pleased, like the eagles and hawks soaring," she said softly as others about them in the longhouse were sleeping in their furs.

"When you talked of Benjamin Franklin and Pundatha remembered meeting him, it reminded me of my journey. It was not this Franklin, but there were many white leaders. A man named Schuyler was talking with our chiefs. I do not remember the talking, but I do remember Eliza Schuyler, the white chief's daughter. She saw me and came over. She smiled. I had my cornhusk doll. She asked if she could see it.

"I held it tight at first. I did not understand the English all that well. But she smiled again and said a few words in Seneca. It was my eighth summer. She said enough I could understand so I said to her in her language, 'Share. Share doll.' And I handed it to her. She sat down. We played with the doll. She told me her name was Eliza. And she could say Wah-say-lan after I told her.

"The next morning she came to our campfire. She had another doll. It was not cornhusks. It was cloth stretched over a stuffing and sewn up tight. We traded dolls. I remember the next day when we were leaving, Eliza Schuyler hugged me and I hugged her back."

Jamwesaw listened to all this, then whispered, "What were your father and the Indian leaders talking about? In your eighth summer means 1770, before this war. Why did the Seneca go so far east?"

"I did not know then, my husband. All I knew was that I was on an exciting adventure. When I was a little older, my father told me this Schuyler, Philip Schuyler, was the son and grandson of Schuylers and they wanted to make sure the Haudenosaunee would trade furs for many years to come. But I did not much care about that. It was both strange to play with a white girl and somehow it felt dangerous or like it was part of the adventure. But what I liked the most was traveling so far on such a large river," said Wah-say-lan.

Jamwesaw gathered her close to him. He kissed her lips and said, "Soon we will travel farther than you ever have and it makes me feel so good that you will be traveling with me."

Jamwesaw had let his wiry brown hair grow out through the winter. He pulled it back each morning and tied it in a ponytail. Most nights he released it and let it hang loose. His wife stroked her fingers through the long strands. Then she put her head in the nape of his neck, her long black hair falling into his. They fell asleep.

Part II

THE TREK SOUTH

◈ CHAPTER 30 ◈

Starting on the Warriors' Trail

Daga'e'da, the god that melts the snows to begin the planting season, had come again. Tun-weh's baby brother could now walk. He held her hand as she went to Wah-say-lan.

"This will be a long and dangerous journey, but I know you will come back to me," said Tun-weh, now a young woman, survivor of the battle and the long winter. Her brown eyes were worried.

"Yes, I will come back, but do not forget that the moon will cross the sky many times. Do your work, my cousin, my friend, but when you can, swim to our island. Skip stones and watch the circles ever spreading out over the water. Think of me on my journey with Jamwesaw. We are one of those circles. We will come back to you and to Canandaigua and your little brother will be able to talk to me," said Wah-say-lan.

She picked up the little boy and tossed him in the air. He giggled as she caught him and tossed him again and again.

"But Wah-say-lan, the stones make circles on the lake but the circles do not come back," puzzled Tun-weh.

"Circles always come back. Think of the stone that makes the ripples on the water and how those circles go out over the water but also lap up to our shore. It is the stones, Tun-weh, remember, that sink if they don't keep skipping over the water. When moving they make circles, and circles are forever. So Jamwesaw and I are moving south down our warriors' trail as our people have always done and they have always come back, just as Ban-er-man-jah did two summers ago, isn't that right?" She said in her calm, easy voice to her cousin.

Tun-weh held her little brother. "Just like Ban-er-man-jah, you will come back too," she repeated.

Jamwesaw arrived with the two horses. Deerskin blankets, bows and quivers of arrows, extra clothes and moccasins were packed on their backs. "Pundatha insisted," he said. "We must take the horses."

"I know," said Wah-say-lan. "We cannot say no. And we must go."

She turned to her mother and to Mary Angel and hugged them both.

"Come to me," said Mary Angel, "lean down a little. How did you grow so tall?"

Wah-say-lan bent forward as the older woman reached above her head and wrapped a necklace over her shoulders. "The teeth of a female wolf to protect you, daughter of the Wolf Clan. When you least expect danger, the necklace will keep you alert," she said.

The older woman handed her, too, a small deerskin pouch. "In here is help if you have a wound. I take the leaves, stems and bark of tobacco wood, the whites call it witch hazel, and grind them together. Wash any wound, then take what you need from here and make a paste with water and put it on where you bleed. It will help," said Mary.

Her mother handed Wah-say-lan her father's knife in a new sheath. "You will be safe with my husband's knife," she whispered and stepped back.

Wah-say-lan undid her belt and slipped on the knife. It felt natural against her hip. She fingered the white wolf teeth and remembered Mary working with them over the winter. They were cool against her neck and she wondered about their power. Mary Angel's powers were always mysterious to her.

She thanked them both, then took Pundatha's stallion and led him by the rawhide tether she had made during the winter. Jamwesaw followed with the other horse. He was thankful the chief had said to leave now before Joseph Brant, Cornplanter and the other chiefs arrived to raise the warriors for war once more. It would be difficult to keep Wah-say-lan back as braves went out to seek their revenge, he thought. She proved herself in battle last fall, but still Jamwesaw did not look forward to the idea that his wife so easily broke the rules of her own people. He had learned over the long months of winter that a lesser woman would not be allowed to get away with such things. But he also had learned that everyone respected his wife and most were in awe of her.

Soon the thick woods swallowed them and the people of the village could no longer see them as they started out southward to find Jamwesaw's mother. It was late in the day when they climbed the last hill at the end of the lake. The shore curved broadly on both sides of a small river that carried the lake's waters farther south. Its valley disappeared into the folds of one hill upon another and another. The bright green canopy of early spring stretched to the blue horizon.

Jamwesaw looked back over Canandaigua. "Your Bare Hill where the Seneca children slew the giant snake stands above all the other hills," he said to his wife.

Wah-say-lan looked back. She let go of the horse's reins and walked a few steps to a small ledge and sat down, looking back across her lake at the hill with no trees. Jamwesaw sat down beside her.

"I do not know why that hill does not have trees," she said. "The story is an exciting story but I do not think it happened that way."

Her husband was startled. "What do you mean? That is the Seneca way. That is how your people came to be," he said.

"It is a story. I love all of our stories and you know there are many that go back to ancient times. And I do not say in the village that I do not believe them, but I say to my husband right now that I do not think two little children killed a giant snake that had been eating all the people," she said.

"Where did the story come from, then?" he asked, thinking again that his wife is so different from any other woman or man among the Seneca he has met. No one questions the stories.

"I will tell you what I think. I have thought many times of this. I would sit on the shore of the island where you saved me. I sat on that shore and stared up at the Bare Hill. I am sure my people had a village at the top of that hill. Wherever they came from, that is where their chief decided to build their village. I have told myself ever since I was a little girl that the boy tripped and it was the girl in the story who really shot the arrow into the serpent. But that, too, is just a story.

"The hill is a place that could be defended, and back in those times we did not have the Six Nations, those times before Hiawatha and Dekanawidah, the Peacemaker, who brought us together.

"Who were those other people before the Seneca or our brothers the Cayuga, we do not know. But there were always wars, that is what our storytellers tell us, and that our Seneca Nation was born on that Bare Hill. I think what happened on the hill was a war party, not a big snake, attacked. Maybe those people called themselves the snake people. Maybe they attacked in the fashion that a snake attacks.

"I'm sure it was a long battle and many were killed. But in the end the people of the hilltop village defeated the snake people and ran them back down the hill. And those people never lived again. They were wiped out and the hilltop people became the first Seneca. Over time, as Seneca women bore more babies, the storytellers turned the defeated warriors into a giant serpent," said Wah-say-lan.

Her husband stared silently at her. The sun was setting over Canandaigua Lake. The water glistened gold. It was almost like a giant mirror on the earth. Jamwesaw put his arm around Wah-say-lan and said, "You think of things that I would not begin to think. But then you make me think about them. And the way you say your thoughts, I believe you, even though they go against what your elders, your sachems, your people have always believed."

She put her fingers to his lips and said, "Shh. I do not tell such things to my elders. I tell them to you only, to my husband."

He looked again at the hill barren of trees. He smiled. She is unique, mysterious, but sometimes, Jamwesaw was thinking, the man who saved her life, the man she sleeps with, the man she tells her deepest thoughts can't resist a little egging on: "But then tell me, my wife, why is the hill bare of trees? Why are all the other hillsides around Canandaigua covered with many kinds of trees? You say you don't know why the one hill is bare, but you must have thought of some ideas."

Wah-say-lan shrugged. "I do not have all the answers, Jamwesaw." She laughed. She knew his mood and she wasn't falling for it. She pushed her hand into his chest and started to get up. "Come, it is time to find a bed for the night. Let us find some pine trees with their soft needles beneath them."

He put his hand on her shoulder. She sat back down and turned toward him. Her eyes locked on his. She moved her lips to his and threw her arm around his neck. Wah-say-lan loved it when he kissed her. When his tongue parted her lips. First came the goose bumps on her arms, then the very roots of her hair tingled. As he held her tighter, her body grew warm.

Making love in the longhouse was good, but somehow she always held back. The people in the longhouses always had sex and privacy was not important to the Iroquois, who had lived together in their longhouses for eons. But here, alone with Jamwesaw under the sky, looking out over her lake, she felt free and she felt wild.

Wah-say-lan loosened her man's belt, the belt she had made from the snake he had killed and they had eaten together. She pulled off his buckskin pants. She smiled at him and began kissing his thighs and rubbing his hardening member. She stroked it up and down, marveling at its size and power. She kissed it and played her tongue around its girth. Her husband lay back and looked up at the dark blue sky. She slipped out of her own pants and mounted him, guiding him between her stretched thighs.

Slowly she moved back and forth as he went deeper into her. She smiled down at her husband's beautiful face. His hands went under her shirt and found her breasts swaying. He played deftly and softly with her nipples. It made her shiver. Wah-say-lan quickened the pace of her hips. Her legs tightened against his body. She looked out over her lake, at the large mound of Bare Hill. She was conscious of his hands caressing her breasts and in her mind the hill and her breast became one. His hand cupping her breast and his thumb and forefinger rubbing her nipple became the wind visibly hugging the top of Bare Hill. She saw the wind circling where her people were born at the crest of that hill, she felt Jamwesaw pinch her own hard nipple. She cried for him to hold tighter. She thrust her hips harder and harder against him. With each movement she could feel him throbbing inside of her.

"Ahhh!" He called out, "Ah, Wah-say-lan." He rose urgently against her and pushed and pushed. She pushed down hard against his gushing member. His seed filled her. She lingered above him, gyrating her pelvis gently until his throbbing stopped.

Then she stretched her long legs against his, brought her face down to his. She lay on top of him without moving but holding him tightly. She kissed his neck over and over.

"I always want to be with you," she said.

He rolled her over on her back. They both stared up at the first stars poking out of the night. He held her hand for a long time before he said they had to find the horses and make a campfire and a bed beneath a great pine for the night.

◈ CHAPTER 31 ◈

Leaving the Lake Behind

As the sun rose to its peak the next day, Wah-say-lan looked around as she rode the chestnut brown stallion. She and her husband had walked through the hills and valleys south of her lake, hills she had for years viewed in their different shades of green in the distance. As a young girl she would sit on the beach of her island and count the hilltops, one behind another, and wonder what lay beyond.

Though they both had been anxious to start their journey, she had convinced Jamwesaw to wait until she could help with the planting. Pundatha had miraculously been able to save enough corn and beans for the spring planting. And he had made sure squash seeds were stored in earthen bowls through the harsh winter. Of all the women's work, Wah-say-lan most enjoyed planting the crops. She loved the renewal, the growth and nourishment these vegetables provided her people. Fields were cleared near their new village, the planting was done and late spring was turning to early summer.

It was Wah-say-lan's 18th summer and she was now beyond the hills at the south end of Canandaigua Lake. The hills gave way to gentle slopes studded with large maples and oaks with bright green leaves. The familiar thick pine woods around Canandaigua yielded to open fields with patches of woods and crisscrossing streams. It was as if Sky Woman had opened her arms and said to her, "Here is my earth. Look as far as you can and know it is larger than the imagination of any one person."

Wah-say-lan was elated. She had taken the well-worn Iroquois path many times to the annual council fire at Onondaga and as a child took that memorable adventure to Saratoga. But now before her lay country she had never seen. She wanted to see it all, not miss a single eagle gliding high on the wind, or flock of crows descending, or herd of white-tailed deer as several doe and one large buck rushed across the bright green expanse. And yet she wanted to keep moving to see what was next.

It was Iroquois land, Six Nations territory. She was envious two years ago when Ban-er-man-jah went off with a hunting party. She wondered what he felt when he first saw this land now stretched out before her. She remembered upon his return how he had told her of the long river where the Susquehannocks held a council fire with them. This small tribe long ago paid homage to the Seneca, as did the Delaware, the Shawnee and the others along the warriors' trail. Only the Cherokee still dared defy the Iroquois. Even in the first summer of this white man's war, a large party of Seneca and Cayuga men headed south to inflict harm on their ages-old enemy far to the south. They brought back more than 20 Cherokee women and children and four braves as a war prize. One defiant brave was tortured and killed. The others now live as Cayuga, speak the Cayuga tongue and have left behind their Cherokee ways.

Wah-say-lan knew she and her husband had nothing to fear from any Indians they may meet until the very end of their journey. If Pundatha was right about where Jefferson built his home, it sits very near Cherokee Nation land. She wondered how this all would end. Would there be Blue Coats at this Monticello, or Cherokee to contend with too? If it was true Jefferson had many slaves, would Jamwesaw find his mother among them?

Her thoughts were interrupted by his voice. "There, over east, do you see it?" he was asking.

She looked to where he was pointing and saw the wide and gentle

Chemung, bigger than Ban-er-man-jah had explained. She had never seen a river winding gently through an expanse of meadow. Down this long slope where they rode, it flowed wide, as wide as the Mohawks' river through the forests, but this river stretched on to the eastern horizon, where it joined the great Susquehanna. Wah-say-lan kicked her stallion and galloped across the slope. Jamwesaw did the same.

The charging horse and Wah-say-lan melded to one. The man marveled once again at his wife's prowess. Is there anything she cannot do? he wondered. He slowed his horse. He could ride, but he could not handle a horse the way Wah-say-lan could. He saw her bend forward, almost hugging the stallion's neck. They were a streak across the landscape, heading straight for the river.

She brought the animal to a stop and jumped off its back. She undid her braids and let her long black hair cascade across her shoulders. She pulled her buckskin shirt over her head and slipped out of her pants. Jamwesaw slowed his mare and looked down at his naked woman, her body glistening in the afternoon sun.

"The leaves are new on the trees. The water will be cold," he said.

"I know cold water. I do not know this river, but I am about to meet it," she said and turned and waded in. She dove and came up, standing on its sandy bottom, a little more than waist deep in the frigid water.

"Ah, Jamwesaw, this is so good. Come in!" she yelled.

"My view is fine," he said.

"But it will cleanse you. Invigorate you." She threw her head back and stroked her fingers through her hair. Then she dove under and felt the strong tug of the current, unlike the calm waters of her lake. Wah-say-lan stretched out and let the river carry her downstream. She turned over and in long, graceful strokes with her arms, swam back, her legs kicking just below the surface. Her long body glided forward. Near the bank she stood up and walked to where the horses and her husband were waiting. She walked in the green grass then sat down, lay back and stretched out under the sun to dry.

"You are right, that is cold water, but already I feel the sun warming me up. I feel so clean, so alive!" she said.

It was then that he saw the riders with a wagon pulling a cannon along the top of the slope to the east. They wore blue coats.

◈ CHAPTER 32 ◈

Soldiers

"Wah-say-lan, get dressed," said Jamwesaw.

She sprang to her feet, immediately comprehending the edge in his voice. She saw him staring up the hill as she ducked under her grazing horse, grabbed her pants and tugged them on. Then she saw the cannon, the wagon and three riders pull away, trotting toward them. She checked to make sure her knife was in its sheath on her belt. A few yards away at the lip of the riverbank was her shirt.

She dashed over, reached down and pulled it over her head as a Continental Army lieutenant halted his mount directly in front of Jamwesaw, the deserter Freeman Trentham. His two men brandished muskets at their sides. The officer stared at the young Indian woman and the black man. He looked at one and then the other and seemed unsure what to say or whom to say it to.

Wah-say-lan raised her voice: "Ho, what brings you to the land of the Susquehannocks?"

"What is your name, woman?" the officer said.

"I am Pheasant Feather, daughter of Lame Deer. This is my husband, Kills Bear," she said. "Why do you come here?"

"We go where we please," the man retorted. "Why are you with a nigger?"

"Kills Bear is African. He joined our village many summers ago.

An Englishman traded him as a child for furs. He is brave and saved my mother from an attacking bear. That is why he is called Kills Bear," she said, finding it easy to deceive a white man.

"I was African. Now I am Susquehannock," said Jamwesaw.

"Where is your village?"

"Down the river, on the high ridges a day's ride," said Jamwesaw. He hesitated, "You are welcome to come."

"We do not have time. We go to Fort Pitt. Have you seen Iroquois? Are there any Iroquois hunting parties?" asked the lieutenant.

"It was two summers when we saw Cayuga and Seneca," said Wah-say-lan. "Fort Pitt is a long journey. You are too far north."

"We know where we are," snapped the officer. "After this river we are told the trees grow thick again. Is there a path?"

"For walking or for one rider we have always had our paths. Not for your guns on wheels. You will need to cut your own path," said Wah-say-lan.

"Maybe you will come and cut the path for us," said the lieutenant. "When we reach the Allegheny, it will take us to the fort."

"The sun will rise twice before you come to the great western river," said Wah-say-lan, fingering the sheath at her waist. She looked up at the wagon and saw three more soldiers, one driving, two standing.

Jamwesaw tried to defuse the building tension. "The Susquehannock do not fight the Americans. The Susquehannock do not serve the Americans, nor the British, nor the Iroquois. We live in peace on our river. Tonight we bring fresh game back to our village." He stepped closer to his young wife. He saw her muscles tensing. He could feel her adrenalin.

"When we reach the Allegheny you can return. Come now, savages, do what we say," said the lieutenant.

"Not this savage," yelled Wah-say-lan, who in two instantaneous steps jumped on the back of the officer's horse, pulled her knife, grabbed him from behind, and plunged its six-inch blade into his heart.

Jamwesaw lunged at the barrel of the closest man's musket and pulled it away. He cocked the long gun, turned and shot the other man, blowing him off his horse. The soldier hit the ground a dead man. The other pulled his horse away and raced for the wagon.

The officer spat, "You dirty sav . . . ." Gurgling blood stopped his words and spilled out of his mouth.

"Pig," said Wah-say-lan. She pulled her knife out of his chest and slit his throat, bringing his revolutionary military career to an end. She pushed him off his horse.

Jamwesaw was already on his. Pulling an arrow from his quiver, he placed it in his bow while galloping after the fleeing soldier. The man was halfway to the wagon. The others hoisted their muskets. Jamwesaw rode harder. He was closing on the rider, who kept looking back in fear.

He heard the volley and felt a musket ball whoosh past his head. He kept charging. The soldiers were reloading. The rider was nearly back with his companions. Jamwesaw stopped and from the back of his horse sent an arrow flying into the side of the horseman. He fell, writhing on the ground.

As Jamwesaw placed another arrow in his bow, Wah-say-lan galloped past, her bow set. She fired from her racing horse. Her arrow sliced through the neck of another soldier, severing an artery. Blood sprayed from the wound. The man slumped to the earth.

The last two threw down their muskets and lifted their arms in the air. Wah-say-lan slid off her horse, her knife drawn. The first soldier, with Jamwesaw's arrow in his side, was groaning. She calmly bent over him.

"Did you burn my village?" she whispered.

"Wha . . . " he said. She slashed his throat. He did not move again.

She walked over to the man she shot. His dead eyes stared blankly at the sky. She went toward the other two.

"No! No!" cried one.

Jamwesaw grabbed his wife by the arm. "Wait," he said.

"Arms up," he ordered the two last soldiers. "Unhitch those horses from the wagon."

They did not ask questions.

"Get on," said Jamwesaw. He gathered the long reins, took Wahsay-lan's knife from her hand, cut the leather to fit horseback riders.

"See the sun? Follow it west. Do not turn back this way. Go!" shouted the black man.

The two young Americans looked at him.

"Don't shoot us in the back," one protested.

"Ride," said Jamwesaw.

They trotted off. He watched them disappear on the western horizon.

"We could have killed them," his wife said.

"Fort Pitt is many days away. They will not come back," he said. He looked at the two bodies at their feet and at the other two lying dead at the river. "There has been enough killing today."

Jamwesaw stood still. He began to think that he could have been with this patrol on its way to Fort Pitt. He had planned to fight for his freedom and at the end of the war find his mother. He very easily could have been ordered to carry provisions and a cannon to a western outpost, he thought. He shook off the idea and said to himself, "I am a trusted Seneca warrior with my Seneca wife on our way now for my mother, with three new horses."

As he rummaged through the wagon with its boxes of cannonballs, he found new uniforms, boots, blankets, an anvil, a bag of flour, jerky, a cask of rum, musket balls and powder, and two Bibles. We need to travel light, but some of this could be useful along the way, he thought to himself. He bundled the uniforms and blankets, took the flour, the jerky, the balls and powder, and, he wasn't sure why, but he grabbed the Bibles too. He fashioned packs from one of the blankets and placed their booty on the back of one of the cavalry horses.

He saw his wife examining the dead lieutenant's sword. She had gathered the five muskets.

"I'm sure you could learn how to do serious damage with that," he said, "but you already are expert with a knife and bow and arrow."

"It is sharp. I wonder if he ever used it against the British or against our people?" she said almost to herself. "You should take one of these muskets for yourself."

"I have already explained to Pundatha that I like the bow better," replied Jamwesaw. "Let me put these things on the horse. Then I will bring you some dried meat I found."

She then realized how hungry she was. They sat on the hillside overlooking the Susquehanna River and chewed on the soldiers' food.

"If Ban-er-man-jah were with us, he would already have their scalps," said Wah-say-lan. "But I did not want to. I have no desire for scalps on my belt."

This surprised her husband. He said, "Had this worked out differently and those six had taken us . . .

"That would not have happened!" she insisted.

"I know, but just if, they would have our scalps now," said Jamwesaw.

"What is the use of it? When we kill a deer, I like saving the skin. I made your moccasins, your pants from the skin of a buck. No one makes anything from scalps," she said.

She fell silent. She thought about the three men she had just killed. That's what you must do in a war, kill your enemies. The first, the lieutenant, had no idea his life was about to end, but she knew. She knew the minute he said she would be cutting a path for him.

She enjoyed the rush she felt; jumping on his horse, sticking her knife in his chest was effortless, she thought to herself. But what else? There was something else about it. She remembered slitting the throat of the soldier who killed her father—the first man she had killed. Anger. She was angry then. She was angry now—that was it. And hate; she hated them.

Wah-say-lan thought to herself that her hatred, her anger stemmed from fear. She was afraid these white people were stealing her life. Already the village where she grew up was gone. Already they have slain her father and would have raped, if not killed, her mother. What can she do but hate them and kill them, as many of them as she can?

"Where did they come from, Jamwesaw? Why do they not stay on their side of the big gawa?" she asked.

Her husband weighed his answer. He had been watching her deep in thought. She was looking for answers, but he was worried there were times he could not help his wife.

"These men today were most likely born here," he began. "Where Noah Willington held me as his servant, his slave, the first whites came to that little river many summers ago—more than 100 summers ago. They had 40 white families; now that town has 2,000 people. Many still come across in large sailing ships and many more are born here."

He looked at her, waited for a reaction, but she stared back silently.

"I heard Benjamin Franklin—the man who said the bow is a better weapon, the man Pundatha said praised the Six Nations Confederacy many summers ago—I heard him tell a meeting of Washington's chiefs that 60,000 whites were born that year in the rebel colonies," said Jamwesaw.

"We just killed four of them," said his wife.

"Wah-say-lan, how many are there in the Six Nations?"

"The Seneca are the most of all the Iroquois. We have towns, many, many towns."

"Yes, and Washington's troops burned them all. Except for Cornplanter's town of Conawagus, Canandaigua is the biggest Seneca town. We have, what, 300 people? The Seneca have many towns, yes, perhaps adding up to 4,000 of our people," Jamwesaw told his wife.

She argued, "Just because there are more white men does not mean they are right. We rebuilt what they destroyed. You helped my people rebuild a good village. All the Seneca live in new villages and the Blue Coat troops retreated from our land and Pundatha has joined Cornplanter and the Mohawk and the Cayuga, the Onondaga—they will avenge. They will kill many more whites than we did today."

Still she had questions.

"But Jamwesaw, why did they come here to our land? Do they not have their own land?"

"My mother's people in Africa have their own land and have lived there since before memory. I do not know why the whites came here. Why did the Seneca come here? Why did the Seneca decide to live on that hill above Canandaigua Lake?" he said.

"That was a long time ago. We chose it for us. We share our lakes and rivers, our woods, with all the animals, and with our brothers the Cayuga and Onondaga. We have gone to fight our enemies like the Cherokee and we defeat them but we do not take their lands. The whites came to fight the Iroquois but they did not win. They burned my village but they did not defeat my people. Even now Pundatha leads our warriors against the whites who keep trying to come into our land. They put up their strange houses and build fences. They do not share. They take, they try to take. They are strange people," she said.

She turned and looked at the wagon and the great weapon on wheels behind it. "And they bring ugly things like that cannon. What do we do with it now that the men who brought it are dead or fleeing?"

"We will burn it and their bodies," said Jamwesaw. He got up, led a horse down the hillside, thinking that the young woman he loves needs more from him. "But she is so independent, so smart, I cannot think how to help," he thought.

He lifted the two dead men onto the horse's back and led it up the hill. He laid the men and the two others in the wagon, wheeled the gun next to it. He spilled the rum all around and started a fire. It was soon ablaze, black smoke rising into the blue sky.

Wah-say-lan and Jamwesaw walked away, leading five horses. She reached out for his hand and held it as they walked. She looked at his face, his deep dark eyes, and she asked, "Why did you choose me? You escaped. You could be with Washington and Franklin and their armies and all the whites who are so many. Why did you choose to be with me?"

He gazed at her long hair blowing in the breeze. He was sure it was her beauty that he first noticed. But that was not it. Wah-say-lan, the best he could understand, simply stole his heart. "I did not decide," he said. "It was not a decision. The oak leaves do not decide to join the oak. The lake does not decide to make waves. The sun does not decide to rise each morning, nor the moon decide to show its brightness each night. They just do."

"Had you not come to me with soup when I was tied to that stake, had I not seen you and had I still been able to escape, I probably would be back with that army. I would have attacked your village. I was a continental soldier. That was my duty. Think of this, Wah-say-lan. Maybe it could have been me who shot your father and then you would have slain me."

"No, I do not want to think that, my husband!"

"I do not want to think that either. I watched you walk into my life, I had no choice. You were there. And when I think of it, you were why I broke free. I was never going to be without you. And so then, I really could not have attacked your village. I do not know how I would have found you. I don't know how I would have gotten away from the corporal. Then I saw him attacking you on the island, I did the only thing I could—I protected you. I killed my comrade in arms, beast though he was, because he was harming you. And then I touched you, I held you, and I knew I would never let go. I did not know how, but I knew."

She was still holding his hand while he said all this. She stopped, squeezed it tight. She stepped in front of him, threw her arms around his neck and brought his mouth to hers. She kissed him and held him for a long, still moment. She pressed all of her body against his and she thought how perfectly they fit together.

After a while they reached the place where the Chemung flows into the Susquehanna. They were silent, watching the waters of the two rivers mix and swirl together. The Susquehanna flows south, and in the distance they could see a high gorge.

"Look, Wah-say-lan. The river runs through high country. The water will flow fast. It will not be for swimming. It will be a beautiful sight from the top of those high banks," said Jamwesaw. "Come, the sun is fading. We will sleep up there tonight."

They mounted and went off at a trot. Soon Wah-say-lan could hear the river. She had been in streams where they narrow and the water tumbles swiftly over stones. She was excited thinking of this great river rushing and roaring through a hillside.

They stood at the top of the gorge and looked down into the swirling water. Farther down it narrowed and she could see white water gushing and a mist rising above in the canyon, catching the last orange rays of the sun as it was setting.

◈ CHAPTER 33 ◈

Susquehannocks

They led the horses a little farther, looking for a place to camp. Where they stopped they could hear the great Susquehanna. After they had eaten some dried deer meat and the fire had died down, Wah-say-lan, in a rare admission, said she was exhausted. Jamwesaw had gathered a bed of pine needles. They spread their blankets and fell asleep to the roar of the moving water deep in the gorge below them.

Lan-lu-rah came to his daughter in a dream. He was standing by a tree. His arms were folded in front of him. He looked down at her holding his knife stained with blood.

"You have avenged me, my daughter. You do not have to kill every soldier you meet," he said.

"But father . . .

"Wah-say-lan, listen to me. You are on a journey. It is the journey that is the most important. Today you killed, and maybe you had to. But killing may get in the way of what you have set out to do," he said.

His voice was calm. She could see him clearly. He continued, "You have joined with a good man. A brave man. He thinks of you first before himself even. Listen to this man."

Wah-say-lan wanted to talk more to her father. She wanted to ask him if he is happy in the Sky World or is he lonely for his wife. But in her dream he was walking away now. He turned once more and said, "Remember the necklace Mary Angel gave you."

Then he was gone into the deep forest. She ran after him, but it felt like her legs were trudging through deep snow, even though it was summer in her dream. She could not make herself run fast. She called to her father, but she could not find him. Wah-say-lan collapsed to the ground, her face against the dirt.

She woke up sweating, lying on her belly, her face pressed into pine needles. She sat up and tried to remember everything her father said. The young Seneca woman felt reassured and secure knowing that her father knew of Jamwesaw and his goodness and bravery. She told herself she would try to remember their mission is to get to Virginia. She asked herself if she had acted too rashly when the lieutenant demanded they cut a wider path for his wagon and cannon. She didn't have an answer beyond the fact that they were not with the soldiers and their journey was not delayed. But then why did her father come to her with that message? She puzzled over it and she fingered the wolf teeth Mary had put around her neck.

The sky was lightening. Wah-say-lan caught a glimpse of the morning star, a good sign to the young Seneca. Genden'wit'ha is the last star of the night and is not always visible. She is a goddess sometimes of good tidings, other times of mischief, sending men off into bad marriages, then making them wander the earth in search of their missing wives. But that is not morning star's fate for Wah-say-lan, whose husband was lying by her side. Genden'wit'ha is also known as the provider for starving villages and Wah-say-lan felt the goddess was with her when she and Jamwesaw brought all the deer to Pundatha. As the young woman gazed up at the star just above the western horizon in the early moments before the sun arrived, she felt it would be a good day.

Her father coming to her with advice and seeing Genden'wit'ha as she awoke were good signs indeed. She stood up quietly, trying not to awaken Jamwesaw. She stretched, breathed deeply. The river's hushed roar beckoned. As she stood at the top of the deep canyon, the sun began to poke over the treetops. The river flowed and swirled around boulders far below, sparkling in the new day's sunlight. The air was fresh and sweet. Her eyes followed the river as far as she could see. The banks opened where the slope began to level off and it seemed to her she could see the river widen off in the distance. And yes, there was smoke rising. It must be a Susquehannock village, she thought.

Later that morning she and Jamwesaw rode into the small Indian camp, leading three pack horses.

A few older boys squatted around a campfire fitting flint stones onto arrows. A half-dozen small dwellings were scattered about. An elder was instructing the boys. He stood and greeted the visitors.

"I am Raven-in-the-Cloud. Who is it that comes to my village?"

"I am Wah-say-lan, daughter of Lan-lu-rah of the Seneca, with my husband Jamwesaw, who came across the great water," she said in her own language.

The man switched easily to the Iroquoian tongue, "My ancestors, like yours, revered the Peacemaker, and Hiawatha was a great sachem who always looked kindly on my people. Come sit with us and have some fish broth."

The two visitors dismounted and sat with the old man.

"Our river has been good to us," he said. "But it has been a bad winter. I cannot offer you any meat. Our men are out on a hunting party. Our women are tending the fields. Did you have big snow?"

"The biggest snow we had seen. Hunting was impossible. We could not fish in our lake," said Wah-say-lan. She took a second spoonful from the wooden bowl. "Your broth is good. You have skilled fishermen. And you add corn kernels and I think there is squash here too. It is a fine taste."

The old man nodded and smiled.

Jamwesaw spoke up. "We have brought gifts. We have much flour and dried jerky. I know your men will bring back new meat, but we would like you to have these. Also blankets and clothes made by the white man, and their horses."

Raven-in-the-Cloud thanked them and said, "I saw black smoke to the north yesterday. Perhaps it was your meeting with the white man?"

"Soldiers. They did not agree with us. We have their muskets too. I am sure your chief will be pleased to have muskets," said Wah-say-lan, "and horses."

"My chief, my oldest friend, Eagle Feather, used to make raids for horses. He will be much pleased. You honor us with gifts."

Jamwesaw unloaded the things from the horses. As he put the blankets and uniforms on the ground, the two Bibles fell out. Raven-in-the-Cloud frowned. He got up and inspected the muskets. He said the blankets and the clothes will help his people on cold nights.

"We don't need the white man's books," he said. "The white man's writing is all lies."

Jamwesaw put them in his pouch on his horse. "I did not mean them for you," he said. "The Susquehannocks and the Seneca have traded and lived together for many summers before the British came with their books," he said. "We are on a long journey and must go. Thank you for your hospitality."

"You and your wife should take a horse. We will accept two. It is good to have another horse in case one gets lame," the old man said.

Wah-say-lan was telling one of the boys that his flint was not inserted far enough onto his arrow. She took her knife and made the notch deeper. She showed him how the sharp stone was now more snug. "Wind the sinew here. The arrow will fly true," she said. The boy was startled first by Wah-say-lan's beautiful face, then by her instruction. He wondered why a woman was telling him how to make an arrow. But he said nothing, and gazed into her deep, dark eyes, transfixed.

"Raven-in-the-Cloud is a good teacher. I'm sure he has a strong bow," she said to the boy and handed him his arrow. She turned to the old man. "We leave three horses, two for your chief, one for you, Raven-in-the-Cloud. You can show these boys how to shoot an arrow from the back of your horse."

“Your river flows to the great water, I am told,” she added.

“Yes, but I do not follow it all the way anymore. Where it opens into a bay at the great water is a white man’s town called Baltimore. I do not go there,” he said.

Jamwesaw shivered, but remained mute. Baltimore, he knew, was the last place he saw his mother.

“We do not go that way. We will follow your river to where it forks. And there our warriors’ trail heads west and south. That is our path,” said Wah-say-lan, rising and touching the old man on his shoulder. She hopped on her horse.

He walked up to her and said, “Give me your hand.” He held it for a minute. “You have a long journey, yet you bring me a horse. These boys, I promise you, will learn much on that horse. The gods will be with you.”

She smiled down at him, squeezed his hand. She and her husband rode slowly out of the little village.

◈ CHAPTER 34 ◈

Sky Woman

Gregory Pendleton and his companion James Embler had been traveling for three days out of Philadelphia, heading for Iroquois country. Like many of their faith before them, Pendleton lived among the American natives to learn their ways but also to gently show them the peace and quietude of the Quaker way of life. Benjamin Franklin himself spent hours listening to the Friends describe the Iroquois. Pendleton was overjoyed when Franklin agreed to print his observations on the workings of the Seneca women's council. The Quaker elder was mulling over his last conversation with the great man when he spotted two figures on horseback coming their way.

"We have company, James. Beware, but be calm," said Pendleton. He often worried about his young charge. Embler had been his project. He seemed a reluctant Quaker, too brash and impulsive for the Society of Friends. Pendleton hoped this trip west would help solidify the fellow's commitment to the teachings of his church.

The young man tensed. He felt his throat tighten. He wondered about his people's refusal to carry weapons, then tried to steady himself knowing that Gregory Pendleton knew his way around the wilderness.

Pendleton had spent most of 1775 with the western Seneca on the Genesee River. He lived in a large village of about 400, learned their language, their faith, and marveled at how easily they adopted others. Delaware, Shawnee, Ohio and other natives joined the village and became Seneca, as did two white girls captured in a fight and spared, unlike their parents.

But this was the first time he had encountered an Indian woman and a Negro.

It was a hot day for early summer in central Pennsylvania. The air was still. No leaves rustled. The sun shone brightly on the verdant wilderness. Wah-say-lan and Jamwesaw were letting the horses walk as they emerged from the woods into a clearing. A red-tailed hawk circled overhead. The young Indian woman stopped and watched. Whenever she saw the red-tailed hawk, something usually happened. Hawks to Wah-say-lan meant she should pay attention to whatever kind of message comes next. She heard the familiar screech near sundown one day last summer. That night a wolf came to her in her dream and told her to practice more with her bow and arrow on the island. Another day she watched a hawk swoop down on a low branch just a few feet from Tun-weh the day before her little brother was born. Wah-say-lan never ignored an appearance of the great bird.

It was Jamwesaw who saw the two riders approaching. As his wife gazed upward, the black man raised his hand in greeting. Gregory Pendleton did the same. As the bird screeched and flew south, Wah-say-lan instinctively checked to make sure her knife was in its sheath on her waist.

"We are Quakers and come in peace," said Pendleton as he slowed his horse.

"We take the warriors' path to the south," responded Jamwesaw, "as our people have done since time began. We carry weapons, but greet you in peace, Quaker. We were about to stop for the mid-day meal. Would you join us?"

"We would and we have bread to share," said the Quaker. He dismounted and his companion did the same. "I am Gregory Pendleton. This is my friend James Embler."

"I am Jamwesaw of the Seneca Nation. This is my wife Wah-say-lan."

They shook hands. Embler, barely a year older than Wah-say-lan, stood before her, gazing at her beautiful face. He blushed, whispered "uh, hello" and gently took her hand. A strapping, handsome young man, with curly black hair, dark eyes and a disarming smile, he felt his knees weaken as her fingers touched his.

"We have deer meat and cool water from the Susquehanna River," she said and moved away gracefully, taking the water pouch from her pack.

As Jamwesaw unpacked some good hunks of venison, the cavalrymen's two Bibles slipped to the ground as they had before with Raven-in-the-Cloud. Pendleton, however, did not frown.

"I see you read the Good Book," he said.

Jamwesaw said nothing. He picked them up and brought them along with the meat, following his wife to the shade of a large oak. The young Embler carried two loaves of wheat bread and could not take his eyes from the winsome Wah-say-lan. They sat on a lush carpet of green grass. He found himself slouching as he watched her fold her long legs and sit erect as if, he thought, she were a statue of Aphrodite. Embler straightened his back.

"Please," he said, breaking the bread and handing her a fresh piece. She smiled and poured some cool water into earthenware cups, passing them to the three men.

Pendleton tried again. "I find Genesis to be a story of truth and beauty."

Jamwesaw turned to his wife. "He talks of Adam and Eve."

Wah-say-lan said, "You believe a snake persuaded a woman to eat an apple?" She did not wait for a reply. "Two days ago we killed the soldiers who read those Bibles. They tried to make us go with them, show them the way to Fort Pitt. We are heading south. Those men will read no more of snakes and women, or anything else."

Pendleton took some water. "James and I do not need guides. I know the way to the great Genesee, where I lived among your people five summers ago. I will pray for the slain soldiers, but I understand you are at war."

Wah-say-lan said, "Yes, we are, and I know Quakers do not make war. I was only a young girl when you were at Cornplanter's town. Mary Angel was there and told us of your visit and of your reading what you call the Good Book."

"I remember Mary. A white woman who became a Seneca," said Pendleton. "She is a spe . . .

"Mary Angel chose to be with us. She is a leader on our council. She sees when others do not. She gave me this necklace." Wah-say-lan touched the wolf teeth. "And I will say that Mary Angel says the Eve in your book is a mere shadow to Sky Woman. Your book, the soldiers' book, says your god made the earth in seven days. You must write it all down or you whites forget.

"The Seneca, all the Iroquois, do not have to write what we believe, what we know. We always have known and always will remember that Sky Woman fell through the hole when her husband uprooted the tree of peace in the Sky World. The geese guided her to land on the turtle's back. It was muskrat who dove down into the deep water to bring soil to place on the turtle's back. The saving turtle, its shell and the brave muskrat's soil became the earth, and the Ancient One, the Holder of the Heavens, gave Sky Woman a daughter. And our people and the earth were born."

James Embler was awestruck at the force and persuasive powers of the young woman. Jamwesaw knew his wife was warming for a fight, if just in words. He suggested, "Why don't we all eat. Thank you for the bread, it is delicious."

Wah-say-lan did not stop. Chewing venison, she continued: "The West Wind impregnated Sky Woman's daughter with twins. But one was evil and he cut his way out of her body and killed his mother as they were born. Her good son grew and helped the Holder of the Heavens make all that we use, the lakes and streams and rivers, he showed the birds how to sing and brought soft rains for trees and plants to grow. The evil twin went behind and turned his brother's good works into harsh things. The rain became hurricanes and tornadoes. He made dangerous rapids and waterfalls in our rivers. The good twin fought his evil brother. For many days they struggled. Sky Woman, their grandmother, showed the good twin how to use deer antlers to defeat his brother and he was finally banished to the depths below the earth."

"This you believe?" the elder Quaker asked gently. "Yet a snake cannot tempt Eve? Did you hear of Cain and Abel in our Good Book?"

Wah-say-lan was not there for a debate and she didn't care to tell this white man any more of what she believed. She told him the story, a story that Iroquois storytellers take hours to unfold, the story that goes back to the beginning of time. She had said enough, she thought.

"Gregory Pendleton, thank you for your bread. I need to take a walk." She got up and started off in her graceful gait toward a copse of trees. An eager Embler pardoned himself. "If you don't mind, gentlemen, perhaps she could use a little company," and he hurried off to catch up with her.

Jamwesaw loved watching and hearing his wife when she had something she wanted to say. She is so deep yet can be so impatient, he thought. As he listened to her lecture the Quaker, his thoughts over the different beliefs he had encountered in his life piled up and needed some sorting out. He was never as secure inside as Wah-say-lan always seemed to be.

He scarcely noticed the young man chasing after his wife. He turned to Pendleton and said, "They will be fine. Tell me, what do you think of Cain and Abel and the good twin and evil twin? Why are the two stories so much alike?"

The Quaker elder let his young charge follow the intriguing young woman on this calm and clear day. He wondered about the black man's knowledge of the Bible, but decided to keep the conversation on track. "That is a good question. And what of the West Wind god planting his seed in Sky Woman's daughter. Is it not like God having the Virgin Mary give birth to a savior?"

The two men sat there, both surprised in their meeting and pleased for a chance to explore these questions. At times, the black man did not know what to believe. He had vague memories of his parents' lessons on tribal gods. Noah Willington taught him to read and made him study the Bible. And now the woman he loves and the people who adopted him have different beliefs. He had embraced them because he chose to be with her. Christianity was behind him and he knew he would give this Quaker the two Bibles. Jamwesaw, if he ever had, no longer had any use for them.

Wah-say-lan also needed to sort things out in her mind. "These white men always think they are right, they are better," she said to herself. "They bring a book full of lies and say it is the word of God and tell us to believe it. They bring whiskey that turns our braves into fools. They bring guns—ha! Even their Franklin says their guns are not as good as our bows and arrows."

These were her thoughts when she sensed someone following her. A quick step behind a tree and an unnoticeable glance backward revealed James Embler hurrying to catch up. "What a pretty man," she thought, and surprised herself at the notion.

"He is a white man. I have killed white men. Men who come with guns. But this one and his friend say they come in peace. And this one won't stop looking at me. His dark eyes see into mine. His arms are strong. He came up our trail and we met. Is this the hawk's message?" she wondered.

"I let them talk. I, too, need to stretch my legs. Can I join you?" said Embler as he caught up to her at the edge of the woods.

"Sometimes it is good to talk long. This is not one of those times for me," she said.

Just watching her walk from behind excited him. He had taken his time catching up so he could watch her move the way she does. She stomped off, he thought, but she cannot stomp. She stood erect, her long black hair swaying down the middle of her back as she moved.

She was nearly as tall as he. She has great poise and confidence, he thought. He was stunned to find a savage Indian so enticing.

He wanted to touch her again. He could hardly believe what he heard himself say. "Can I hold your hand?" He took her left hand in his right.

Her big brown eyes looked at him. She looked down at their hands. She did not pull hers away. They walked under a canopy of oaks and pines on the soft earth. His hand felt warm and large, clasping hers. She let him intertwine their fingers. As he did, she smiled and pulled his hand closer to her. She did not know why, except for a twinge of excitement.

After a little way he stopped and turned in front of her. "I came here with Gregory. I did not know what to expect or who I would meet. And so here I am with you, Wah-say-lan."

"And I am with you, James Embler," she heard herself say.

He inched closer to her. They stood in silence. He leaned into her and found her lips. He kissed her for a long time.

Wah-say-lan was excited at the taste of his lips. He put his other hand around her back and drew her to him. She liked his body pressed against hers. Then she pulled away. She stepped back.

Iroquois are physical people and Wah-say-lan had never been bashful in her 18 summers. True, it took a black man to bring out her sexual longings. Just then she said, "But you are a white man. You read a Good Book I do not believe."

Embler had never felt so bold, and he astonished himself when he said nothing but reached at her waist and pushed his hand under her buckskin blouse. She felt his hand embrace her bare back and she felt him pull her to him again. She did not resist. Her long thighs pressed against his and she felt his hardness rise. She reached down and pulled his hands up under her blouse. He grasped her full and firm breasts as she leaned back and let him caress them. She pulled her long hair from her back. It cascaded in front of her breasts undulating with the movement of his hands. She could feel her nipples harden. Her strong legs were feeling weak in the knees.

Embler stopped quickly and threw off his shirt. He tugged at hers and she helped him pull it over her head. She laughed, almost giggled. He moved her thick hair to the side and then brought her back to him, his bare chest tight against hers. She kissed him again and pressed her right thigh into the hardening in his groin. She reached down and caressed the bulge in his pants.

Then she gently pulled away and knelt down. But suddenly her playfulness was interrupted by a voice inside—"dirty white man"—and she reached over for her shirt.

"I will not hurt you," Embler whispered.

"I believe you. I do not know why, but I do. But my husband is just over the rise talking to your friend. I think I want you, James, but I am confused right now. I do not like being confused. Are you Cain or Abel, are you the evil twin? I cannot hold you right now, even though it feels good."

She paused and looked straight at him. "I think we will meet again and maybe it will be a better time for lying with me," she said, and pulled her blouse back over her head. She swooped her hair back with her hand.

He listened to every word. Her voice was like a song. Her lips that had just been pressed to his were full and lovely and the words that come out of them were entrancing. Still, he found himself pressing. "This is a good moment. Who knows if there will be another?" he insisted.

"I see you are a good and strong man. I can tell I would enjoy being with you, but this is not the time. These are confusing times, and who knows what will happen? But I think you will see me again another time," she said. She touched his shoulder and kept her hand there. She rubbed his neck, his cheek. She smiled, leaned and kissed the white man once more, then walked back toward Jamwesaw.

Embler sat on the ground and contemplated what had just happened. He was shocked. He had never kissed a stranger—an Indian, no less! He found himself incredibly disappointed. How he would have loved to lie with her right here on this spot in the middle of the wilderness. On his way to convert the heathen he was going to make love with one. He feared God's judgment. But, like the young woman, he was a man of certain confidence and strength. He wondered how she could think they would meet again. He saw her in the distance walking back to the others. His heart pounded and he hoped she was right.

As she walked back, she remembered her father's words in her dream that there is purpose in their journey. "We must go," she said to her husband, "Virginia is still to the south."

The two men stood. "I know. It is time." Jamwesaw shook the hand of the Quaker elder and thanked him for their discussion. The younger man arrived. He shook the black man's hand. Then he turned and took Wah-say-lan's hand and held it for as long as he dared.

"Be safe in your journey," he said. The four parted, mounted their horses and started off at a walk in opposite directions. Only a few minutes had passed when she saw the movement out of the corner of her eye. A white blur flew by just above their heads. The red-tailed hawk extended it talons and swooped to the ground. With a rush its powerful wings sent it skyward with a rabbit stunned, bleeding and dying in its grip.

Wah-say-lan instinctively reached for her bow and pulled an arrow from her quiver. Where there is one rabbit, there could be more. She saw it scurry, then stop, frozen. She pulled the string back, aimed, sending the arrow through the animal's shoulder. It took one hop and fell. She looped her leg over the back of her horse, jumped to the ground and looked up. The hawk was gone. Dinner was a few yards away.

"How did you know there would be two?" asked Jamwesaw.

"I didn't. But the red-tail tells me things," she said.

They rode several more hours that day, heading south on the path. After dinner of fresh rabbit, the two young Seneca sat close to their campfire. Wah-say-lan thought back to the worst winter of her life and how, lying with Jamwesaw each night, she could feel his strength in his taut body and it made her stronger. Through those cold and dangerous months, his presence gave her reassurance and at the same time awakened her desires.

Now, this night, she thought of the afternoon with James Embler. She leaned toward her husband, saying it was time for bed.

"Would you like to take off my shirt," she said.

He grinned, first removing his clothes, then lifting her blouse and pulling off her pants. He lay back as she climbed on him and clutched him tightly.

◈ CHAPTER 35 ◈

Jefferson and the Kaskaskias

Thomas Jefferson and his wife Martha had lost their infant daughter Lucy that spring. The grief-stricken father had made it known he would not seek another term as Virginia's governor. His woes were more than personal.

The Marquis de Lafayette was not yet on his way with 1,200 regulars to defend Virginia. Pennsylvania's Gen. Anthony Wayne with 2,000 more men still had not been ordered south. But Cornwallis from the south and the traitor Benedict Arnold from the coast were moving toward another victory with more than 7,000 soldiers. Jefferson moved his government west to Charlottesville.

As Wah-say-lan and Jamwesaw followed the ancient Iroquois warriors' trail, a small band of western Indians was also traveling to Monticello. These pro-American Kaskaskias, leaders of the Illinois Confederacy and old enemies of the powerful Iroquois, were bearing gifts of buffalo skins painted with figures signifying their long alliance with Virginians. They trusted the governor so much that the mixed-blood chief Jean Baptiste du Coigne had named his son Jefferson du Coigne.

Even as his government scurried for safety and Jefferson himself knew his capture could result in immediate execution, he ordered a medal for the Indian chief to be rushed from a Fredericksburg silversmith.

It had been five long years of war since he wrote the Declaration of Independence, thought Jefferson, and it did not look good for the Revolution against King George III. As the King's armies pushed him westward, he feared for his beloved Monticello and feared for his cause of liberty and equality. He had decided with Washington, Franklin, Adams and the others to overthrow tyranny, and here he was looking for options as the British overran Virginia.

The Kaskaskias set up their council fire on the grounds of Monticello. Jefferson and a few nervous assemblymen met them and sat down for the ritual of the peace pipe. The governor looked at du Coigne and said, "I have joined with you sincerely in smoking the pipe of peace. It is a good old custom handed down by your ancestors, and as such I respect and join in it with reverence. I hope we shall long continue to smoke in friendship."

Jefferson paused, as he often did in speech, before offering his next thought. He held up the buffalo skins and said, "The figures represented on the skins symbolize friendship. I shall always keep these skins, these works of art, hanging on the walls here at Monticello in remembrance of you and your nation."

It was late May. His term would expire June 2, and, Revolution aside, Jefferson knew he had to spend some time on his hilltop plantation with his deeply grieving wife. But he also knew the British were everywhere, and as he sat with these friendly Indians he wanted to explain why this visit could not be long and why, too, the Americans were fighting England, the land of their own ancestors.

"You find us, brothers, engaged in a war with a powerful nation. Our forefathers were Englishmen, inhabitants of a little island beyond the great water, and, being distressed for land, they came and settled here. As long as we were young and weak, the Englishmen whom we had left behind made us carry all our wealth to their country, to enrich them; and, not satisfied with this, they at length began to say that we were their slaves and should do whatever they ordered us. We were now grown up and felt ourselves strong; we knew we were free as they were, that we came here of our own accord and not at their biddance and were determined to be free as long as we should exist."

Chief du Coigne answered: "I know the British are a strong nation and have friends in the Iroquois and other red men. Our Confederacy has fought the warlike Iroquois for many generations and now we fight them again alongside our American brothers. As the paintings on the skins foretell, our alliance shall remain strong."

At that point Jefferson presented the chief with the silver medal and they signed a treaty of life-long peace between Virginia and the Illinois Indian Confederacy. The governor and the chief stood and embraced and then du Coigne gathered his delegation and headed west.

It was Jefferson's last official act as governor of Virginia beyond signing a few requisition forms for more muskets and bayonets and one last letter to Gen. Washington imploring him to send reinforcements.

◈ CHAPTER 36 ◈

Col. Banastre Tarleton, British Cavalry

Wah-say-lan held the reins of her horse at the bank of the Anna River. She and Jamwesaw had been traveling for six days since leaving Canandaigua Lake. Across the river and up a slow rise they could see the Red Coat encampment. She looked at the brave black man who was letting his horse drink at the river in the hot summer climate in the largest of the southern rebellious colonies.

"It was not that long ago," she thought, "when this man warred against Red Coats. And now he is with me. I do not trust Red Coats just as I do not trust the Americans who burned my village and killed my father. Yet it is the Red Coats who can lead us to his mother and to Thomas Jefferson."

Jamwesaw pointed to the lines of tents on the sloping field. "The only thing to do is ride up there," he said.

"Yes, slowly," she said, mounting her horse and walking him into the river. It flowed east in a gentle current. The Indian woman and the runaway slave knew what they would say and that she would say it. Mounted sentries approached as they rode out of the water. They were escorted into camp, told to dismount and wait.

Col. Banastre Tarleton, the young commander of British cavalry, could not squelch a smile as he said to the two buckskin-clad figures, "I'm told you are looking for Thomas Jefferson?"

"We are," said Wah-say-lan. "If you know where he is, you can help. He holds many slaves and we go to free them. My people are of the Seneca Nation and have fought side by side with our British brothers against these rebels. I am Wah-say-lan and I travel with Jamwesaw, whose mother is held by Jefferson."

"So you don't plan to free all the slaves, just one?" asked the colonel.

"Just as my people welcomed this man to be among us, we will welcome as many of Jefferson's slaves who want to join us," said Wah-say-lan.

The colonel's curiosity was aroused. A young woman recruiting slaves to join the Iroquois Confederacy. And where did she find this one? And why all the way from New-York to come here? Ah, his mother. Still, a journey of several hundred miles?

"But what if the poor slaves decide to join my army? We have already freed 10,000 slaves who now take up arms against their former masters," said Tarleton.

It was then that Wah-say-lan knew she was in the right place.

"It does not matter if they fight the rebels here or with my people in the North," she told Tarleton. "We have come for Jamwesaw's mother. Jefferson took her from him when he was only a small boy. He and I will find her and she will come with us. If others want to come with her, my British brother should let them return with us to fight the Americans in my country," said Wah-say-lan.

"And who leads your British brothers in your country?" demanded the colonel.

"Maj. Butler fought with my father against the Americans. Maj. Butler fought with the Mohawk and the Onondaga, the Cayuga and the Seneca. He is a brave officer. He knows the strength of the Six Nations," said Wah-say-lan.

With this the colonel was satisfied.

"If you mean Maj. John Butler, he is a fine gentleman. And I know the way to Monticello. Lord Cornwallis with orders from the Great Father King George has sent me to capture Jefferson and his rebel government. You will meet this man who it is said scribbled the drivel in their so-called Declaration of Independence. We march now. It is less than two days' ride," said Col. Tarleton.

Jamwesaw caught his breath. For the first time since his wife brought it up on the shore at Canandaigua last fall, he was ready to believe he could be with his mother again. "I last saw her on the pier in Baltimore in 1769. It is now 1781. I am a grown man. Will she know me? I know her face, her broad smile, her deep eyes, her high cheekbones. I have seen her face every day. I could never forget it. But in 12 years could she have changed?" he wondered.

He had never forgotten the vision of her being carted off, chained in a wagon with other captured Africans, her eyes looking back at her little boy crying for her on the dock. He did not understand the burly man speaking of his mother as a wench and shoving her onto the wagon for a young plantation owner, but he remembered that one peculiar word he heard that day: "Jefferson."

Wah-say-lan coaxed her horse alongside her husband's. She loved it when they rode together. She could feel his bravery, but she saw now the far-away look in his eyes. She reached over and touched his hand.

"We are close. It won't be long now," she whispered.

He entwined his fingers in hers and held tight. They stayed there, locked together, as British cavalry fell in around them and headed west toward Charlottesville. After a while Wah-say-lan and Jamwesaw eased their mounts into the moving line. Tarleton was commanding only 250 troops—180 dragoons and 70 mounted infantry. His orders were to move fast against the political leaders while Cornwallis circled his army back toward Richmond and the coast to crush the outnumbered American forces.

As dusk approached they reached Louisa, some 40 miles from Charlottesville, and pulled up outside a tavern called the Cuckoo. They had been at an almost constant trot throughout the day.

Tarleton ordered the column to halt, water the horses and make camp for the night. He led his officers inside.

A few older men in clerks' clothes sipped ale at the long, rough-hewn pine bar. The British men of rank pushed two tables together and sat on benches.

"Ale all around here," the colonel motioned to the barkeep. "Make it quick, man."

The balding proprietor shot a glance into the back room, where Jack Jouett put his fingers to his lips. A large man and a patriot, surely he would be detained and questioned by the British. What was a young, strong man doing hanging around a tavern during a war? In fact, he was reconnoitering to keep the Americans apprised of British troop movements. He positioned himself out of sight but as close to the door to the barroom as he dared.

The barkeep served up his draughts as Tarleton laid out the plan for the final approach.

"Gentlemen," he said raising his mug, "to the King."

"Hear! Hear!" his officers shouted.

"Gentlemen, we believe the Virginia Assembly is scheduled to convene in the morning. We shall be there to greet them. Capt. McLeod, your detachment will rush up the mountain road to Monticello, just in case Mr. Jefferson is dallying. You are not to harm anything or anyone, unless there is resistance. Bring the governor into town and we will deal with him there."

That is all Jouett needed to hear. He slipped out the back door and made for his horse, tied in some trees.

Wah-say-lan nudged Trentham as she saw the young man make for the trees. They watched as he walked his horse away from the tavern. He disappeared in the dark, but Wah-say-lan heard the horse gallop off.

"We must catch him. What if he is off to warn Jefferson?" she said.

Jamwesaw tried to calm her. "One lone rider will not lead slaves away," he said.

She was not sure why, but she let it go. Probably it was better to stay with the cavalry. In the dark she was not sure she could catch up with the rider. She also knew Jamwesaw's first thought was of his mother, but she needed to remind him of her need to see Jefferson.

"Jamwesaw, you know we are here to find your mother, and we will not fail. But don't forget about her master. We need to try to find him before the British do," she said. She spoke with the resolve he had come to respect. It was one of the reasons his love grew deeper for her the more he got to know her. He held out little hope they could actually get to the American leader, but he had seen her accomplish things others only dreamed of.

He gently challenged her: "Tomorrow this cavalry will capture rebel leaders. Do you think they will let us near the governor of Virginia?"

She thought of the night rider and was worried, but then whispered, "Something will happen. When this troop moves, I want to be as far up their column near their officers as possible."

She went to get their blankets and led him under a tall pine. Pine needles always made a more comfortable bed. The stars were out on the warm, cloudless night and the American deserter fell asleep with his wife's body pressing against him and his mother's smiling face in his thoughts.

◈ CHAPTER 37 ◈

Jouett Warns Jefferson

Jack Jouett galloped through the Virginia countryside all night. At dawn he made a dash up the steep road to Monticello and banged on the front door. A tall house slave let him in. Gov. Jefferson was beckoned. Jouett informed him that British dragoons were on their way. His guests, Patrick Henry, the two house speakers John Tyler and Benjamin Harrison and a few other assemblymen, thought the British were at least a half-day's ride away. They were sure the enemy could not possibly travel the distance as quickly as young Jouett had. They decided to have breakfast with their host and ordered up some prime Madeira wine for their night rider. Jouett joined them but nervously nudged the guests down the mountain.

When they left, the master of Monticello turned his thoughts and actions toward his family. He did not want them anywhere near if the British forward units were closing in. He gathered his wife and children into a carriage and sent them off to Blenheim, a friend's home a few miles away. "I will join you for dinner," Jefferson calmly told Martha and kissed her on the cheek. As the carriage drove off, he was not sure he would see her again.

Tarleton had allowed his troops only three hours' rest. His mounted forces charged into town, capturing seven members of the Virginia Assembly while the others dashed every which way. Patrick Henry barely evaded capture.

"McLeod, up to Monticello!" bellowed Tarleton.

Wah-say-lan nodded to her husband and they rode with McLeod's troops. As they rushed up the road, she veered into the woods. Jamwesaw asked no questions and followed. Expertly, as she had all her life, the young Seneca guided her horse swiftly over the tree-studded terrain, galloping up Jefferson's mountain.

It was only minutes earlier that Jefferson, his favorite chestnut gelding saddled and ready, had walked to a promontory and looked down on the town through his field telescope. He saw only peace and quiet and decided to go to his study for a couple of books. He wasn't sure how long he would have to stay away. As he walked he noticed his small ceremonial sword was not around his waist. He re-traced his steps and found it lying on the ground where he had knelt down to peer into the valley. He attached the weapon and took out his glass once more. It was a different scene. British cavalry filled the streets of Charlottesville.

He hurried back to where a slave held his horse. "Protect what you can, Martin," he told the black man. "I will be back."

He started down the road away from town and then decided it would be better to ride through the woods.

Jamwesaw and Wah-say-lan caught glimpses of the grand brick structure that was Monticello. With the British thundering up the road, the young Seneca knew that if the American leader was at home, chances are he would be rushing out the back way by now. She pushed her horse harder up the steep grade, ducking under low branches.

It was a clear morning. The sun's rays streaked through the trees and fell in bright splashes on the ground. As the land began to flatten, she saw what was little more than a deer path. It led away from the plantation. She instinctively took it and nudged the horse into an all-out gallop. Soon she saw the single rider ahead. Her father's knife was sheathed on her waist. She always had it with her. Jamwesaw carried his bow and quiver of arrows. They swiftly caught up with the tall, handsome man on his horse.

◈ CHAPTER 38 ◈

The Capture of Jefferson

Thomas Jefferson, always a clear-thinking man, was relieved he did not see dragoons but was perplexed at the sight of who approached, somehow out of nowhere. He drew his horse up at a small clearing. Jamwesaw was amazed when he saw the jutting chin, the high brow, the reddish hair. Could it really be Jefferson? he wondered. Wah-say-lan was sure they had found their quarry. The deserter from the Continental Army, the escaped slave, placed an arrow in his bow and said, "Mr. Jefferson, sir, please dismount."

Wah-say-lan pulled in front and blocked any quick escape. She jumped from her horse as he dismounted. She reached for his sword and pulled it from him. They were deep in the woods on Carter's Mountain, far beyond sight or sound of what was happening as Capt. McLeod burst into the front lobby at Monticello.

Twelve-year-old Sally Hemings didn't move as the captain pulled out his pistol, stuck it in her brother Martin's chest and demanded, "Where is Jefferson. Tell me or I'll shoot."

The house slave, who had just shoved silver under floorboards, said, "Then fire away."

Young Sally squeezed her eyes shut. The British officer hesitated, lowered his weapon and yelled to his men, "Search the mansion!"

In the woods the young Indian touched the sharp point of

Jefferson's sword to his chest and said, "I am Wah-say-lan of the Seneca Nation. Your soldiers, Thomas Jefferson, burned my home, my fields, and killed my father. My mother and my friend, Tun-weh, with her baby brother, escaped in a canoe with your soldiers shooting at them as they paddled as fast as they could. Why should I not burn your house? Why should I not put this sword through your heart?"

Jefferson had envisaged a British military court hanging him in Charlottesville. He had not foreseen an encounter with a Seneca Indian woman.

"I expect my home will be burned. And you could slay me right now, but you have come a long way . . .

Wah-say-lan silently rejoiced: "It is him!"

"I have come a long way, Thomas Jefferson, and I will say when you can speak!" she snarled. She surprised herself with her anger and she was ready to run him through. She had thought and planned for this moment for months, but now she needed help to calm herself.

"Jamwesaw, is this the man who wrote in his Declaration that we are merciless savages?" she blurted out.

"Mr. Jefferson wrote that in the Declaration," he said. "He wrote that the King 'excited the merciless Indian savages' against the Americans."

She wanted him to keep speaking. She wanted to hear his voice, but silence started to fill the woods. She put her face close to her captive and made herself speak slowly: "Who are the savages, Thomas Jefferson, who burned my village and tried to kill our babies? You are standing before a merciless Indian savage and I warn you be careful what you say."

Jefferson did not fear death. He had served his cause. He knew he had not served Virginia well as a war governor, but he had served the American Revolution against tyranny from England. He wanted to see victory, but he did not fear his own fate. At that moment his natural curiosity overcame his fear. He wanted to know more about these two. The black man looked so familiar. Who is this man? What is he doing here with this bold and beautiful—her beauty did not go unnoticed by Jefferson—young woman?

He began slowly, "Wah-say-lan, Jamwesaw, you know who you have before you. We live together on this earth at the same time, yet we are against each other. What is it that put us on opposite paths? What is it that brought us here together at this instant?"

"His mother," Wah-say-lan responded instantly, still holding his sword against his heart. "Why do you think you can own his mother?"

Jefferson turned to the African before him and knew immediately. His thoughts raced. "The regal Betsy. The house slave who always stands erect. The resemblance is clear. This man must be her son. But how is he free? My God, they have come for his mother," Jefferson said to himself.

"I know your mother," he said. "I can tell you about her."

"Where is she?" demanded Jamwesaw.

"She is at Monticello," responded the governor of Virginia.

Wah-say-lan felt a great relief. She felt like an eagle, wings spread, gliding high over her lake. She felt that their long trek south was worth it. She wanted to see her husband touch his mother again. She wanted his mother with them at Canandaigua Lake. She wanted to show her the island where he saved her life. She did not need Thomas Jefferson. British dragoons controlled Monticello. She thought of delivering him to Capt. McLeod.

"Sit down, Thomas Jefferson," said Wah-say-lan. She lowered his sword. He crossed his legs as he eased his towering frame to the forest floor. She and Jamwesaw did the same. She stared at Jefferson and put his sword at her side.

"You think you sit on your land. This is not your land. You cannot own land just as you cannot own human beings," Wah-say-lan said to the revolutionary leader.

Jefferson remembered changing Locke's "life, liberty and property" to the Declaration's "life, liberty and the pursuit of happiness." Americans in all ways made things better than the British, he thought. Property was one means to happiness. He bought this land and he bought the black man's mother for his own future and well being. He owned them both. In fact, on three plantations, two of them inherited, he owned more than 200 slaves. He admitted to himself for the first time that he had not considered, when he sent men to buy slave women, whether they lost their children.

"Why do you think you can own people?" asked Wah-say-lan. "The Earth Holder gave this land to my people, long before the coming of the white man. The white man thinks he can own the fields and the rivers and the mountains and that he can own black people and make them do all their work."

"The Iroquois take slaves from their enemies," began Jefferson.

Wah-say-lan wanted to listen to him, but she could not help interrupting. "We are a powerful nation. We have always defeated our enemies. Our enemies fear us. But we do not make them slaves. We take prisoners and we adopt them and they become Seneca. When they are Seneca, they share in the tasks. They are not slaves," she said.

"But you kill them if they won't be adopted," said Jefferson.

"Many braves go to the Sky World. We do not keep people in chains. We ask them to be with us. If they are captured and want to go instead to be with the Ancient One in the Sky World, they go," she said. "The Haudenosaunee do not own people." She paused. "Jamwesaw decided to be with me. Did his mother decide to be with you?"

Jefferson was astounded at Wah-say-lan. He had dealt with Indians all his adult life. He marveled at the oratory of many of their chiefs. But he had never spoken to an Indian woman. He knew Iroquois women had power in their tradition, that women selected their chiefs and had a clear voice in the decisions of their people. But he was amazed at her diplomatic skills. He realized she could out-negotiate many of the political leaders he had known for years.

He rolled her question over in his mind, "Did his mother decide to be with you?" and plumbed deep for a response. He remembered Betsy's arrival in 1769, the year he started building Monticello. He needed slaves in order to build it and sent a man to Baltimore who came back with several young men and the one stately black wench. He also remembered her first escape.

"I was building my home. You are right; we use black men to do much of our manual labor. I named Jamwesaw's mother Betsy and she has been with me all these 12 years since then. My people's laws do not allow me to free slaves. That same year when she came to me with others, I was elected to Virginia's council. I proposed that any white man could free any of his slaves without the council's permission. I was young, said the council, and it rejected my idea," said Jefferson.

Jamwesaw said, "There are many free Negroes in Connecticut."

"This is Virginia," said Jefferson, and added, "How are you a free Negro?"

"That does not matter," said Wah-say-lan. No one need know he is an army deserter. "He is free, as free as any Seneca. White men in the north free slaves. You are a white man. Yet you do not free slaves. We know white men torture slaves who run and try to be free."

When Betsy ran, a month after they started building Monticello, she stole a white horse. Jefferson's ad in the Virginia Gazette offered 10 pounds reward for the capture of the slave and horse, 4 pounds if only the slave was returned. He did not order her whipped when she was taken on the banks of the Anna River, but his overseer gave her 10 lashes to her bare back. Jefferson decided not to bring this up. He tried to change the subject.

"Only two days ago I sat with the Kaskaskias and smoked the pipe of peace and friendship. They gave me a buffalo skin to symbolize our treaty. The white man and the red man, both Americans, can live together in peace," he said.

"The Kaskaskias and their Illinois brothers are weak," said Wah-say-lan. "The Seneca are the keepers of the western door for our confederacy. The Illinois know we are their leaders."

"Still, their chief, Jean Baptiste du Coigne—who married a French woman just as you are with an African man—named his son

Jefferson du Coigne. My name is now carried by the next generation of the western Indians. We Americans fight with the French against the British. The Illinois Indians marry the French. I say we can live together in peace," said Jefferson.

"What of your brother Washington, who sent Sullivan's army to destroy Seneca and Cayuga towns? They destroyed our orchards, our fields of corn. They could not defeat us in battle, so they tried to starve even our children. That is not living in peace," she said.

"Why did you choose to fight with the British?" asked Jefferson. "Your brothers the Oneida and the Tuscarora fight with us."

"The white man is devious. He offers false promises. The Tuscarora came from here to join us for their own protection from white men. The Seneca have come here to what you call Virginia since before memory. We have had the warriors' trail for generations so that the Haudenosaunee can protect the land of our forefathers. Our braves have walked this land long before Thomas Jefferson built his home, long before Thomas Jefferson's father, or his father, built their homes on Iroquois lands," said Wah-say-lan.

To Jefferson her anger was palpable. He began to realize it was the anger not of a young woman who had come a long way to free a slave. It was the cry of a people who are witnessing the eclipse of their centuries-old civilization at the hands of an enemy they do not understand.

It is the antithesis, thought Jefferson, of his hope for victory over British tyranny and the beginning of a new American nation based on liberty and equality. His way was dawning. Her way was ending. Even if he could not resolve the fate of black slaves, he hoped that the native Americans could live with the new Americans, the red race with the white.

"I can tell you that your brothers the Oneida and the Tuscarora see that we will defeat the King's armies. I can tell you too that, in 1722 and again in 1744, your sachems signed treaties with the leaders of Virginia and that the land we sit upon was given by your people to mine. I built my home here after my grandfathers and yours reached agreement that in this part of America the white man and the red man could live in peace," he told Wah-say-lan.

"You speak falsely, Thomas Jefferson. I have seen the maps of the treaties. And I have just ridden the warriors' trail that had been the trail of my people long before your grandfathers came here. I do not trust the white man with treaties and the Kaskaskias have been warned not to trust your treaties. This ground we sit on is the ground of Sky Woman, wife of the Earth Holder, given to us to protect. We cannot 'give' you land. You take land and try to convince us with your words on treaties. My people never wrote words. My people know the truths of the earth. We know the beaver and the mountain lion and the bear and the deer live on the land. We know they live together on the land and sometimes must die so that all the earth can continue. We know the deer is slain by the wolf for food. We know the deer of the land and the fish of the lakes give the Indian food and our clothes. We give thanks to the Earth Holder and to the souls of each deer we take. The white man's treaties have no souls and are filled with lies. This is not your land. You may have come and built your houses and your towns. You have killed my people ever since you came here. You trample on our ways, the ways my people have lived forever. I say to you if your house is burned to the ground the forest will grow up again over its ruins and the land will be better that your house is gone. And if your house is not there, you do not need slaves to build it. If we take Thomas Jefferson's life today, your wife will mourn. Your children will ask where you are, just as so many Seneca children ask where their fathers are after Sullivan came and destroyed my village and killed my father. You say we can live together, yet you send armies to destroy us," she said and then stared into his blue eyes.

Jefferson was certain he would not see Martha for dinner—or ever again—as he promised when he kissed her cheek just a couple of hours ago. But he decided to ask this: "Why, Wah-say-lan, do the Seneca side with the British? Have they made promises to you that you think they can keep? Do you think your future is better with men who are ruled by a King far away over the great ocean?"

"My grandmother remembered when she was a small child the French came and burned her village on our lake," said Wah-say-lan. "The British fought the French and won. Now the French fight with you. The British have not burned my village. You have."

"Mr. Jefferson," said Jamwesaw, "You took my mother from me. You fight for the ideas of freedom and equality but you do not mean them when it comes to me and my mother. I do not care right now if you live or not, if George Washington lives or not. I came to free my mother from the chains you have put her in. Now it is time for us to go find my mother at your plantation and our British friends will make sure I can take her with me. If I came to you and asked for her, you would have put me in chains too."

Jefferson almost whispered, "I do not know, Jamwesaw. Our way would be to sell her to you."

Wah-say-lan sensed that Jefferson was trying to be honest. She thought the rebel leader meant what he said about Americans and Indians living together. She wondered if an honest leader with such thinking could someday be helpful.

"Thomas Jefferson. You believe your words," she said. She had never trusted white men. Only a very few—she thought of Maj. Butler, who defended her village—proved to be honorable. It is honorable men who will be needed in this time of upheaval when no one knows how it will come out.

"Maybe your people and mine will someday learn to share this land," she said. "You and I have met and maybe we will never meet again. But maybe you will remember meeting me and my husband. Maybe the time you spent here this day will mean something to you as a leader of your people. Maybe when this war ends you and I will meet again, Thomas Jefferson."

She paused, then said, "My husband and I are now going to your Monticello. Here is your sword."

Jefferson slid it into the scabbard on his waist. He waited for her to stand. Then he did and walked to his horse, pulling his telescope from the satchel.

"Wah-say-lan, Jamwesaw. I will never forget our meeting. I was not prepared, I have nothing to give you to honor our meeting but this, and so I present you with it. It can help you see faraway things more clearly," he said.

Wah-say-lan balked.

"Take it, my wife. He offers it sincerely. It is of value to him," said Jamwesaw.

She went over to Jefferson's chestnut gelding and led it to him. "What we offer you, Thomas Jefferson, is your life," she said and accepted the telescope.

He mounted the horse and rode off through the woods. As the path over the mountain turned, he stopped and watched them ride toward his home. Jefferson sat in his saddle trying to reflect on what just happened. The details were clear: her voice, her posture, her beauty and her sense of herself. Jefferson thought the big, strong black man would defend her to his death. But he could not, in that moment of escape, capture the full meaning of this meeting. He felt there was more, but he couldn't immediately collect and sort out all of his thoughts.

"Somehow," he said out loud, "I think I will meet them again," then turned the horse and rode away from his home.

The Seneca and the runaway slave trotted toward Monticello. Jamwesaw thought of how long he had waited for this day. He thought of all the plans he had had to find his mother. He thought of the thousands of times he had tried to imagine how it would be when he found her. He was sweating. He did not know what to do or how he would react. He could see the mammoth home and, as they approached, he saw Capt. McLeod's men gathering together more than 100 slaves.

Jamwesaw slowed his mount to a walk. He saw two small boys holding tight to his mother. He was startled to see her in a cotton dress down to her ankles. But she stood straight and tall as she always had. Her head high, almost defiant. Her high forehead, the sweep of her hair brushing past her sturdy shoulders. He swung down and strode toward her. When she saw him, her hand went to her mouth. She ran, her arms outstretched, and clasped him to her. She kissed his face over and over.

◈ CHAPTER 39 ◈

The Slaves of Monticello

Jamwesaw could barely believe he was embracing his mother. The last time he hugged her, he was 10 years old. He could wrap his arms around her waist. Now he towered over her and felt her body heaving against his. Tears flowed down their cheeks.

"It is you. It is you," she said over and over.

He held her tightly and whispered to her, "Yes, it is me, it is Jamwesaw." His mind was reeling back to West Africa, to the day they were captured, to the awful ship and the way the white sailors dragged her up to the deck, and to the last time he saw her as she sat chained to a wagon, riding out of sight.

Anger grew inside him, but he shoved it down, letting her touch and her words soothe him. But it also seemed odd to hear her speak English. Over the years he had lost much of his Hitu language, but he had never heard his mother speak English. He tried to sort things out, to steady himself. He brushed the tears from his face. "It's the clothes," too, he said to himself. "My mother in a dress is odd, just as her speech is not my mother's speech." He had prepared for years for this moment but found himself unprepared and confused. He kept trying to settle down. He made his mind think of how he was holding her, touching her.

They stood in a chaotic courtyard with British cavalry officers shouting orders, a frenzied search for the master and his family, and soldiers gathering the slaves together.

Capt. McLeod pulled Martin Hemings out of the crowd of slaves. He demanded to know from the well-dressed house slave, "Is Thomas Jefferson somewhere on this plantation, or has he fled? Where are his wife and daughters?"

Martin calmly lied, "Mrs. Jefferson and the children left in a coach two days ago. Mr. Jefferson left early this morning, sir. He is, by now, far from here."

Wah-say-lan caught Jamwesaw's glance. She shook her head imperceptibly and he knew they should say nothing.

"Where did he go!" McLeod demanded of Martin.

"The master does not tell me where he goes. Often it is to Philadelphia," the slave said.

McLeod told Martin to line up all the slaves, men in one line, women and children in the other.

Jamwesaw held his mother's hand and said, "Andoogagow, my mother, are these your children, are these my brothers?"

"I have not heard that name in many years, my son, my firstborn." She wiped tears from her cheek with her sleeve. "You are such a man now. Your father would be proud. I have a thousand questions, but I will tell you, yes, these are your little brothers. My name now is Betsy, all the people who know me call me Betsy. It is a good name for a good woman, my son," she said.

She was a slave, but she was proud. She did not stoop. She stood erect and held her pretty face up. She could sense her son's tensions. She had given up hope of ever seeing him again. But here he was and she told herself she would be good for him.

"This is Jonathan Trentham," she said, pulling the biggest boy over to her. "He is about the age you were when we were parted. He is a smart and brave boy, just as you were."

Jamwesaw went weak in the knees. "Trentham?" he choked.

"Yes, the sea captain. He is the father. They named me Betsy Trentham, and so Jonathan is Trentham."

"I remember the men taking you up out of the bottom of that awful ship. When they brought you back, you wouldn't look at anybody," said Jamwesaw.

"I was humiliated. I was powerless, but we all were. What could anyone do? I will tell you, Jamwesaw, the captain had me many times, but he was not a brute. He was, if you will believe me, he was gentle. And he gave me a son," said his mother.

"My master, Noah Willington, gave me the same name. I was Freeman Trentham. But I am now Jamwesaw. My wife wanted to know my real name, not my slave name. She has never called me my slave name. The first time she talked with me, she called me Jamwesaw," he said earnestly of the dark-haired woman standing at his side. "This is my wife, Wah-say-lan of the Seneca of Canandaigua Lake, daughter of Wah-say-han and Lan-lu-rah, who died fighting Washington's and Jefferson's rebels," said Jamwesaw.

The two proud women stood looking at each other, mother and wife. Wah-say-lan stepped forward and hugged the older black woman. Wah-say-lan kissed her on the forehead and said, "Betsy Trentham, if that is how you want to be called, Betsy Trentham, your son has been searching for you, searching for a way to find you ever since the white men took you away. And now he has found you. We have come a long way and I can see my husband is very happy to be with you."

Betsy smiled, turned to her son and said, "You have a good wife."

The commotion was growing around them. The British captain wanted to address the slaves of Monticello. A cavalryman came over and told Betsy to take her children with the other women.

"I am her oldest son and she will stay with me," Jamwesaw said, stepping in front of his mother. The soldier was stunned, confused.

"Who do you . . . " he began.

"I am Jamwesaw of the Seneca Nation, fighting with His Majesty's troops. Col. Tarleton knows I am here," he said with firmness and decided to explain no more. "This woman and my little brothers stand with me."

The day was getting hot as the sun rose toward noon. Capt. McLeod was telling an aide, "We missed Thomas Jefferson by only minutes, I am sure. But we have his plantation. We have his slaves. Lord knows if they can fight. But we shall find out."

"Men of Monticello!" he shouted. "Stand and listen!"

The mulling crowd quieted. McLeod's dragoons lined up in front of the some 100 black men. They stood uneasily but quietly, many shooting glances to the bevy of women and children off to the side.

"You have been slaves of the rebel leader Thomas Jefferson. His Majesty King George of Great Britain will grant you freedom if you serve in his army. We offer you the chance to defeat those who would keep you in the chains of slavery."

"Any man here who joins us will be trained to shoot a musket, you will receive new uniforms and healthy meals. At the end of these hostilities, when we have captured these rebels and crushed their revolt, you will be free men with grants of acreage for your own farms. Come with us and help defeat those who enslave you," the captain implored. His words carried. His officers and men stood proudly, some inwardly impressed with the eloquence of his speech.

The black slaves were silent until an old and bent-over man among them stepped forward and said, "Sah, Sah, excuse me, sah, but if'n we joins ya, what of our wives and chiddren?"

"My good fellow, you are a true man to worry about your off-spring, your families. We have captured this town, this plantation, and we will hold Jefferson's mansion for the military use of General Lord Cornwallis' army. The general has 8,000 soldiers in Virginia. He has just taken the Carolinas from the rebels and now we will secure this colony. Your wives and children can continue to live here and, when we are victorious, you will come back, receive your grant of land and begin your life anew as free men and free women under the good graces of King George."

"Thanks ya, sah. I's a bit old to shoots a musket but der are many fines mens heah who is ready to fights for der freedom," the old man said.

"Well said. And let me add, if there are men here who do not join our army, they will be treated as prisoners, humanely treated. But they will be viewed as collaborators with the rebels, and will not gain their freedom. And so now, my fine fellows, 'tis mid-day and we shall all have our mid-day meal. When my company moves out, we expect you to join our force. Please now rejoin your families. Enjoy a good meal and relax. Tomorrow we will be ready to go," said Capt. McLeod.

Martin Hemings made his way to his younger brothers and sister Sally and quietly told them, "I will stay. I will wait for Mr. Jefferson to return, which I know he will. They may call me a prisoner, but I will show them they need me here."

He stepped over to Betsy, touched her hand and said, "Do not worry. Mr. Jefferson will return."

"Martin, this is my firstborn son, Jamwesaw. He was taken from me on the docks at Baltimore so many years ago. He has come for me. He has joined the Indians of the North. This is his wife, Wah-say-lan of the Seneca of Canandaigua. They fight with the British," said Betsy.

At that moment coming around the corner of the mansion, two dragoons were scuffling with a barrel-chested white man. He was swearing loudly at the two, who pushed him forward toward the gathered slaves.

"It is Johnson, the overseer," Martin whispered to Betsy's son.

The soldiers shoved him in front of Capt. McLeod.

"Be still!" McCloud shouted at Johnson. "Has this man treated you well?" he asked those before him.

There was a murmuring, but no one spoke up. The slaves were silent.

Jamwesaw asked his mother, "Did he ever harm you, my mother?"

Betsy Trentham remembered back to her first escape and the lashing he gave her. She did not answer. She turned her head, but slowly walked toward Johnson. She was not certain what she was going to do, but in a few more steps she would confront the only thing at Monticello that truly unnerved her.

Martin whispered, "This man sometimes did things that Mr. Jefferson did not know of."

Jamwesaw could feel his anger rise. "Was this one of the men in Baltimore who tore my mother away from me?" he pondered. Years of worry and frustration and the raw hurt of missing his mother welled up within him.

And then Johnson wrenched loose from his captors, snatched the sabre from one, and in a blur grabbed Betsy. He pulled her backward, holding the sword at her neck. He let out a shuddering warning for everyone to stay back. McLeod ordered his dragoons to aim their muskets. What did he care if the wench died? He certainly would not allow a prisoner to get the upper hand.

Jamwesaw didn't think. Instinct took over. He reached over and grabbed Wah-say-lan's knife from her belt. In two bounding leaps he dove at his mother. His left hand gripped the base of the sabre. As the three crashed to the ground, Jamwesaw wrenched the man's arm backward and heard it crack against a rock. He sliced at his wrist and Johnson cried out in agony, his weapon useless in the grass.

The young black man lifted his mother aside and whispered, "Stay back."

He turned to the overseer and demanded, "You were in Baltimore 12 years ago, weren't you! You took Betsy and shoved her on your wagon, didn't you!"

The big white man spat in the black man's face. "How dare you challenge me!" snarled Johnson.

"It's not daring, you pig, you bastard," Jamwesaw replied drily. "You stole my mother."

He raised the knife and plunged it into the man's heart. Johnson groaned. Dragoons rushed forward; so did Wah-say-lan and Betsy. Wah-say-lan pulled her husband to her and tried to take her knife back. Jamwesaw held it away, leaned down and wiped the blade clean on the man's shirtsleeve. The overseer went limp and then lifeless on the ground. One hundred slaves cheered.

The old man raised his voice: "See, Captain, we is ready to fights wid you!" More cheers.

McLeod allowed Wah-say-lan to pull Jamwesaw away. They headed for the shade of a large oak.

The captain sensed that nothing would escalate. "Corporal, get this body out of here." He faced the crowd. His voice rose: "Justice has been done. Now, as I was saying, it is time for the mid-day meal."

◈ CHAPTER 40 ◈

Slave or Free

Jamwesaw looked at his mother and said quietly, "He hurt you, didn't he?"

"He won't anymore, my son," is all she said. She took his hand and they stood silently for several minutes. Wah-say-lan was at once stunned by her husband's sudden action, and proud. And yet she was worried. She had seen Jamwesaw's bravery in battle, but she had never seen this instant fury in him. She was glad that Betsy Trentham stepped in right then.

The beautiful black woman said calmly, but with authority, "Sally Hemings, you watch my boys," to the girl a couple of years older than her sons. "Martin, I must be with my son and his wife," and she sat down on a bench in the shade of the oak tree. She asked Wah-say-lan to sit with her. "Bring that chair over here and sit in front of me," she told her son. Jamwesaw carried over a stout chair fashioned from curved cedar branches.

"Now, my son, that day long ago when I was taken from you. You have carried that memory for 12 long years. Now you have avenged that theft of mother from son. I tried twice in desperation to get back to you, and each time that man whipped me. And now you have found me, how I don't know, but you did. Jamwesaw, I do not trust these Red Coats and so, please, you must not do anything foolish," she said.

He sat down, leaned forward and said quietly, "I have killed a Blue Coat who was attacking Wah-say-lan and others in battle and still others who rode up to us and ordered us to obey them. When I was before the man who stole you from me, there was only one thing I could do. I did it. But do not worry. My killing is over today.

"Now let me say to you that you must come with us to Canandaigua. It is a beautiful place to live and your young sons will grow up free. They will hunt the deer and catch the fish of the lake and go where they please."

"Jamwesaw, when I was a young woman and they brought me here in chains, the only thing I could think of was how to get back to you. I tried to watch the way the wagon traveled so I could run back to you. I knew you would also be taken somewhere. I hoped a wagon would bring you here. But when more slaves came and you didn't, I was losing my mind. I ran. I stole Mr. Jefferson's white horse. I did not know how to ride a horse, but I could see they could go faster than I could. I thought if I got back to that place, that harbor where I left you, I thought you might be there. I ran for you, my son," she said.

"I lost the horse, but I kept running. I ate berries and corn in fields. I hid and then I ran more. But they caught me and they put a rope around my neck and walked me back here. Mr. Jefferson told them to put me in a shed and lock it. He told them to be kind, but the next day his head man took me out, stripped off my shirt and whipped me on my back. All I tried to do was find my son."

"My mother, you must come with us. You will never be whipped again," said her son.

"The man who whipped me is dead. My oldest son has returned and taken revenge and that gives me pride. I was always proud of you, Jamwesaw. Even as a boy you were the bravest. You feared nothing. But then they took you from me a long time ago. Mr. Jefferson was young. He came here and built this big house. He brought many slaves here. He made Martin his head slave in the house and Martin told Mr. Jefferson I would be a good house slave. He told him I would be wasted in the fields and that Martin needed me to help run the house and help Mrs. Jefferson with her children. Except that I never stopped missing you, I have had a good life here. Mr. Jefferson and his wife rely on me. This is my home, my son."

Jamwesaw was silent. He looked around the expansive and manicured grounds, at the gardens, the orchards, the giant mansion on this mountain top called Monticello. He was trying to fathom why his mother would choose to stay here rather than be with him. Then she asked him where he was taken, how he met an Indian and how he got here.

"It is a long story, my mother. I was taken north, where a man raised me and made sure I learned to read and write the white man's language so I could help with his business and tutor his daughter. Then the Revolution began and I heard George Washington say Jefferson of Virginia. Jefferson was the only word I remembered when the white men stole you from me. They let slaves join the army, and I thought it might help me get to Virginia. In a way, it did. I am here.

"But I was in a battle and was captured by the Seneca. That is when Wah-say-lan saved me. Isn't she beautiful? I love her, my mother. I need to be with her. I can't not be with her. Her people accepted me. Her village chief knew the white leader Jefferson lived at Monticello near the warriors' path. He let Wah-say-lan come with me to find you and to bring you back to live with us," said Jamwesaw.

Wah-say-lan worried that Jamwesaw was trying to get everything out all at once and that his mother could not absorb all of what had happened. The young Seneca was still worried about the sudden stabbing. Rarely did she see her young husband lash out in such violent anger. She knew the overseer deserved his fate, but she knew how momentous this meeting was in Jamwesaw's life. In fact, she had not prepared herself for how he would be in accomplishing his life's pursuit. He didn't know it, but he needed her right then to provide some equilibrium. She interrupted her husband.

"Betsy Trentham," said Wah-say-lan, seated right next to her, "It was Jamwesaw who saved my life. He is a brave man, a fierce warrior. We have come a long way. It has taken him a long time. But he found you."

Jamwesaw could not stop his train of thought. He talked over his wife's words: "My mother, we captured this Jefferson as he galloped away from his home. We sat down and talked to him. I understand why he is a leader of the rebels. He is the one who wrote their Declaration of Independence. But, my mother, he writes of freedom and keeps you in slavery. I am not sure why we let him go. Today he is not the master of this plantation. The British Army has this place. The British Army is stronger than these rebels," said Jamwesaw.

"You captured Thomas Jefferson?" she asked.

"We should not talk of this," Wah-say-lan said with a tone of finality. "We do not want our British friends to know," said Wah-say-lan. "But if he was good to you, he cannot be good to you now. Jefferson told me he would not let you leave here freely unless we bought you. We did not come here to buy you. The British said they will give you and your man your own land, but you can have that with Jamwesaw in the North, too. Will the father of your young sons fight for the British?"

"No. As you know, Wah-say-lan, the father of Jonathan is the ship captain." She halted a moment. "His little brother . . . I am a house slave . . . I do not have a slave husband, a black husband. The boy's father is Mr. Jefferson's nephew, Mr. Carr. He visits and is with me some nights. My boys do not know. I do not know why I tell you this." She put her head down.

"My mother, you do not have your own man? You bed with a visiting white man . . . "

"He is gentle. Always gentle . . . "

"My mother, how can you be happy here? A slave. A white man's wench. Forgive me, my mother. What would your husband, my father in Africa, say?"

"Jamwesaw! Where was your father that day!" she raised her voice.

"Why could he not save us, he and the other men of our village? How did they let us be carried away? Across the great ocean. To this place we did not know. To these strange people who have all power over us. Where was your father? You and I will never see him again. I have had to make my life whatever I can. You are a brave young man. A grown man. You have made decisions and have found your way. If I can understand what you have done in these years, my heart fills with pride. You have found a beautiful wife. I hope you have many children. I have done what I could. I have two little boys. I love them."

"My mother, then let them be free," said Jamwesaw.

"They will be. They will be. That captain just told everyone. Their King will free us slaves," she said.

"If you will not come with us, my mother, then let Jonathan come. He is already getting big. Let him follow his own life. He will be with me. He will live free with the powerful Iroquois Nation on a beautiful lake," said Jamwesaw.

"Freeman Trentham and Jonathan Trentham together. My Jamwesaw, please, my oldest son, please. I lost you, until now. I lost you. They took you from me. It broke my heart. I tried to find you but they put a rope around my neck and whipped my back. My son, my son, please do not take away any more of my sons. I could not bear it," Jamwesaw's mother pleaded.

Jamwesaw fell silent. Wah-say-lan saw the hurt in his eyes. She reached over and touched his knee. Martin and Sally Hemings arrived with food and Betsy's young sons. Wah-say-lan stood up. She looked at her mother-in-law and said, "We will sit and eat with you, but first I will take my husband for a walk. He needs to stretch his legs."

"Come, Jamwesaw," she held out her hand. He took it and they walked away from the mansion. They walked silently. She held his hand tightly. She leaned her head on his shoulder. They took a path that curved around to a promontory. They could look down on Charlottesville. The streets were filled with British troops.

Jamwesaw did not see them. He looked out at the expanse of

wilderness. He thought how he and his wife could go anywhere. No one could stop them. And he thought how his mother is tethered to this place called Monticello.

Wah-say-lan stepped in front of him. She put her hand on the back of his neck. She leaned up on her toes and brought her lips to his. She kissed him gently for a long time. Then she hugged him and they stood like that together. She could feel his chest move with his breathing.

"My Jamwesaw. My brave, brave Jamwesaw. You are a good son. Are you all right? You have found your mother and you know she is well." She paused, "You, with my father's knife, my knife, you killed the one man here who would harm your mother. It is like when you killed the dirty corporal who was on top of me. You are a fine man, a good man, Jamwesaw."

He said, "Yes, just as the first night I was with you, with the same knife, I cut off the head of a snake—and we found sustenance. This ugly man here, this whipper of women, if I could have cut off his head I would have. But he is no more. His death does not bring sustenance in the form of food. But his death means just that his evil is gone, his whip is gone. All these black people cheered. I wonder how many he whipped, Wah-say-lan. But my mother does not see she can be free. He does not matter; I would kill him again. It is my mother that matters and my two little brothers."

Wah-say-lan was relieved. She had thought her man was outside himself, losing who he is. She was concerned, maybe even a little frightened. But as she listened, she understood that he was thinking clearly, that his own mother's welfare was on his mind.

She took his hand again and they walked back to his mother and her children. They ate and Jamwesaw told them how he joined Washington's army, and of Wah-say-lan's island in her lake and how he shot the corporal with her bow and arrow and how the Seneca women's council accepted him into their village. And he told them of their marriage.

That night Wah-say-lan took her husband back out on that high point of ground. It was precisely the place where Thomas Jefferson had seen the dragoons invade his town. Wah-say-lan started a small campfire. She fixed their blankets and lay with Jamwesaw, looking up at the stars.

They made love. And then they made love again, and again. She would not let him stop. She kept bringing him to her. She rose up to meet him. He filled her with his seed deeply, and many times. She held him tightly to her each time.

When they finally fell asleep, she slept fitfully. Her dreams were not connected. She woke early and saw the morning star and she remembered that in a dream she was heading back to Canandaigua alone. She lay still, gazing at the star, watching the sky begin to turn gray. A tear came down her cheek. She lay there silently and let more tears come. She turned and put her arm and leg over her Jamwesaw as he slept. She had met him less than a year ago but she felt she had known him her whole life. She did not let go of her husband as her eyes closed and she finally fell back to sleep.

◈ CHAPTER 41 ◈

Jamwesaw's Choice

Col. Tarleton was up early and walking the main street of Charlottesville. He looked up at the small mountain shrouded in mist and frowned that Jefferson had slipped away a day ago, if that slave was to be believed. He doubted it. His men had captured at least six members of the Virginia Assembly. Gov. Jefferson had brought his government here fleeing from Cornwallis, who was encircling Richmond. Jefferson would not have run while his legislators were exposed to an invading army. McLeod's men had missed Thomas Jefferson by hours at most, Tarleton was sure.

He had hoped to net both the man who, it was said, wrote their Declaration as well as the firebrand Patrick Henry and one or two other leaders, but they ran, like their governor, in the nick of time. Who warned them? Tarleton wondered, though he was satisfied that Virginia's government was in disarray. Lord Cornwallis would soon be accepting the surrender of the militia, the royal colonel believed.

He had ordered McLeod to rejoin him today, leaving a lieutenant with a squad to secure Monticello. The dragoons were to bring half of any of Jefferson's livestock and as many slaves as he could muster for His Majesty's service. Any local militia intent on harassment will certainly be surprised to see armed black men coming at them, Tarleton mused.

Up on the mountaintop Jamwesaw awoke to Wah-say-lan wrapped around him. He tried not to move but to just gaze at her beauty, feel her warmth and let her sweet scent envelop him. He had been with her nearly every day and every night since he was held prisoner of the Seneca Nation, tied to a post.

How could he part now? he thought. He can't, but he must, he told himself and gently moved her arm and leg. His wife stirred but she let him put the blanket over her as he got up to refresh their campfire. He warmed venison and some water and dropped in maple sugar carried all this way in his pack but used sparingly as a treat.

He preferred the wooden mugs the Seneca carved out of thick maple and oak limbs. He sipped the sweet drink and looked out at the mist rising in the valley. "If I stay in Virginia, how will that help? How can I convince her to come with me? If she stays with her own piece of land, without a man and her sons so young, how will she work it?" Jamwesaw wrestled with these questions and the bigger one: "How can I leave Wah-say-lan?"

He did not worry about her traveling alone back north. She knew all there is to know about the forests and meadows and the animal life all around. If she encountered the enemy, she would see them long before they saw her, he thought. But how would he tell her that he cannot go back just yet?

"I know you must stay," he heard her say and turned to see his wife walking toward him with just the blanket wrapped around her waist. He loved it when her breasts were exposed. It was often the way of Iroquois women and rarely carried sexual connotations. But after half his life with the white people in New England and their stiff ways, Jamwesaw exulted in Wah-say-lan's beauty, and doubly so when her raven hair cascaded down to her lovely breasts.

She knelt in front of him and hugged him. They kissed and she said, "I will miss you. I cannot stay. My lake beckons. I need to swim to my island. I need to know how my people are doing. I want to know if Pundatha and Cornplanter are avenging my father and the others who died. But you must help your mother through this. Maybe you will convince her to come live with the Seneca. If she comes, that will be good. If she stays, then you will always know you found her. You have done an amazing thing that not many men could do. You will know when it is time for you to return to me, and I will wait for you to come back."

"How did you know . . . " he began.

"My dreams last night told me, but I knew when I saw you with your mother. I knew that you will have to be sure she is all right," she said.

He laid her down on her back and kissed her lips, her cheeks, her neck, her breasts. He hugged her until they heard people stirring.

Wah-say-lan got dressed and braided her hair. As they walked he told her he was going to volunteer to lead Jefferson's slaves in their army. "They will not let me stay here, I am sure. But they will gladly have an experienced soldier in their ranks," said Jamwesaw. "When they defeat Jefferson's militia, I will bring these men back here and see to their land grants. I will have time with my mother, time to persuade her to come north. If I cannot, I can make sure she and her sons have their own land."

They found the British officers eating breakfast on Jefferson's porch. Wah-say-lan spoke up: "Capt. McLeod, my husband is a Seneca warrior who has fought skillfully against American troops. He is an expert marksman with the musket and he has a proposal for you."

"And what might that be?" asked the captain.

"Yes sir, I want to volunteer to lead these black men in your army. I can help train them and I can lead them into battle. I will serve whichever British officer they are assigned to and I will help make them effective soldiers."

McLeod was a man of action. A man on the rise under Col. Tarleton's command. He recognized immediately the benefits of this plan and said, "Mr. Jamwesaw, that is a fine idea. As of now consider yourself a corporal in His Majesty's service. Lieut. Bentley here will provide you with a uniform. Be here in two hours for muster. We leave before noon."

Betsy Trentham walked out to their table carrying a pitcher of tea. Wah-say-lan told McLeod that the house slave must join them. "She is Jamwesaw's mother and we must make our travel preparations," she said matter-of-factly, as if there could be no disagreement.

"Pour the tea, Betsy, and be off with you," said the captain.

She filled their cups and carefully put Martha Jefferson's porcelain pitcher on a side table. She took her son's hand and led him toward her quarters around in back of the mansion. A few steps from the main house a low-ceilinged structure was dug into the hillside. Not much more than a cellar door led to a small room with a bed, two wooden chairs with a rough-hewn table and a room to the left with a bunk bed where her sons slept. On the other side of the wall, with its own entrance, was Martin Hemings' room. A third room held two other house slaves, who with Martin and Betsy kept the Jefferson mansion clean and running smoothly.

Wah-say-lan thought of her family's longhouse and felt cramped inside this little hovel. Betsy asked them to sit in the chairs. She sat on her bed. "Every day I would wonder about you, Jamwesaw. I wondered how far away you were, whether you tried to run away, whether you were alive or not. Somehow I knew you were alive, but it would hurt to think of you and so I would get busy and try to concentrate. It was a little better when Jonathan was born and then when his little brother came. As the years passed, except for missing you, I cannot say I have been unhappy here. Master Jefferson has been very kind to me," she said.

"My mother, let me tell you something. Wah-say-lan and I have decided that I will stay in Virginia, that I will join the British Army here and help it defeat these rebels. When that is accomplished, I will be here to see that you receive your own piece of land as the colonel has promised," said Jamwesaw.

Betsy was startled. She immediately saw danger in this plan, danger for her oldest son. She tried not to show her concern. "You need not do that, my son. My heart is rested now that I know you are alive. That you have a fine wife. You must follow your own life now," she said.

"And that means right now seeing that you will be all right when this revolt is over. That is what I know I must do," he said.

Betsy stared at her son. She was proud of him and filled with love for him and was worried. For a decade she had watched through the eyes of a slave as these Virginians built their society in a wilderness. She knew the Americans would not fall easily to British might. She knew their power and knew they did not intend to lose this fight. She began, "Just yesterday morning I served breakfast on the portico not to British officers, but to Thomas Jefferson and the leaders of his government. Patrick Henry was one, and Benjamin Harrison, Richard Henry Lee and Thomas Nelson. After an evening of discussions with Gov. Jefferson, they spent the night. They were warned in the early morning of the approach of the cavalry but calmly ate what I served for breakfast. These are tough men. They talked of how they all signed their Declaration of Independence. Though they run from capture now, they believe in their Revolution, as they call it. Patrick Henry talks of liberty or death. These men intend to win their war."

"My mother, what of your liberty? What do they say of your liberty?" her son asked.

"Jamwesaw, you told me the Americans will give you liberty when they win. Isn't that the same the British offer here to my friends? Jamwesaw, you make a brave offer to join the British Army, but what will happen if they lose in this fight for Virginia? What will the American rebels do to slaves who are caught on the losing side?" she said.

Jamwesaw paused. He looked at Wah-say-lan. He put his hand on his mother's shoulder and said, "I know I must do this."

Wah-say-lan spoke up: "You heard the British captain say they have an army of 8,000 men. The British King is a great man. My people have been allied with the British against the French and other enemies. The British are the most powerful white men on earth.

Jamwesaw promised me he will return to Seneca country. But first he must be sure his mother is all right. You seem, Betsy Trentham, sure that Jefferson will win and that you will remain happy as you are. You are a wise woman and you are a caring mother to warn your son of the danger you see. Now he can make plans to take care if your Virginians somehow defeat the enormous British Army."

"Why don't you stay here with me, Wah-say-lan?" said Betsy.

The young Seneca woman was surprised at the thought, at the offer. She smiled, walked over to the bed and sat next to her mother-in-law. "Betsy Trentham, thank you. I am honored that you would have me stay here. I do not know what I would do if Jefferson returned. I am not ready to meet him again so soon. I do not expect that he will ever be back, though. I think these British soldiers will decide the fate of this place. And your son will be here to see you get your land," said Wah-say-lan.

"I will go back to my people, who continue the war. I believe I am needed to defend the land where the Seneca have lived since before memory. And I again extend to you my people's welcome. If you see fit to come north with Jamwesaw and to bring your two young sons and any number of your black friends, my people will welcome you into our village. If you come, you will have a good life, and your sons will grow up free in the ways of my people, who have always been free. If you choose to stay, I ask you to send me my husband. I know he must stay here now, but I will miss him and so he must come as soon as he can."

Betsy Trentham hugged Wah-say-lan. "I see that my son has made up his mind. He will go off with these British and when he returns I will send him north to you."

Her hand touched Wah-say-lan's necklace. "Did you make this?" the older woman asked.

Wah-say-lan fingered the wolf's teeth. "A woman much like you made this for me. Her name is Mary Angel. She is a white woman who came to the Seneca when she was young. She chose to be with the Seneca. She sees things before they happen, she knows of things. She tells me the necklace will protect me."

"Mary sees things because she is a woman who knows what she wants," said Betsy Trentham. "She made her choice to be with your people. Some choices are hard. My choice is to be here with my sons. I know this is right. If Mary Angel told you the wolf teeth will protect you, be aware of them on your neck."

A bugle sounded. Jamwesaw jumped up. "I need to gather the men of Monticello. I am here with the two women I most love. I feel the Ancient One has helped me find you both. I will return to you both. Wah-say-lan, my wife, in your young life you have seen and done many things. You are smart and you are brave but you have never been alone. This is only your 18th summer, yet you are ready to travel the warriors' trail alone back to Canandaigua. You know the way. Now I need you to listen to me."

He paused for a moment. Then he said firmly, in his quiet voice, "Do not attack soldiers alone. Do not jump a man on his horse who has a musket at the ready. I am not there with you. Together we beat many soldiers. Alone you must be careful."

Wah-say-lan smiled at her husband. She had not thought at all of being alone. She had no fear of her journey back. She hugged him and kissed him and said, "Jamwesaw, I will not jump on any soldiers. I will see them before they see me. I know how to be careful. I go back to my people and you come back to me as soon as you can."

She kissed him once more for a long time. Already there was a kind of emptiness inside. She was not afraid. But she knew she would miss him.

Jamwesaw touched his mother's cheek and walked out the door.

◈ CHAPTER 42 ◈

A Letter to Dr. Franklin

Lord Cornwallis had driven Thomas Jefferson's government from Richmond to Charlottesville. With the state militia dispersed into defensive pockets, a dejected Jefferson wrote to George Washington pleading for assistance. His letter went by courier just days before Tarleton's troops captured the town. The British devastation of Virginia could "lead the minds of the people to acquiescence under those events which they see no human power prepared to ward off," he wrote. He also told the commander of the Continental Army that he was retiring as governor and leaving it "to abler hands."

Released by his two unlikely captors, Jefferson raced nine miles northwest over Carter's Mountain and was reunited with his wife and children at his old friend's plantation. Embarrassed that once again his government had fled in disarray, that he himself had narrowly avoided capture by the British, Jefferson worried that the enemy would soon descend again. His host reassured the tall, regal Virginian that the British had no way of knowing in which direction to look for the governor.

Uncharacteristically befuddled, he was at the same time so astounded at his encounter with an Indian and a Negro that he could not bring himself to speak of it. He politely excused himself and requested solitude in Carter's study. He had to sort out his thoughts and always found writing a help. He decided to write to Benjamin Franklin in France. The letter would take weeks, months perhaps, to reach him, but Thomas Jefferson simply had to tell someone. Franklin, he thought, would be the proper recipient of such news.

Dear Dr. Franklin,

It has been nearly four years since you so ably edited my words in Philadelphia. "We hold these truths to be sacred and undeniable" was a true thought in my mind, but I believe you made the phrase for the ages with your clarity: "We hold these truths to be self evident."

You, sir, have been my master, my guidepost since our first meeting and I remain indebted to you for your ever generous advice and friendship. The words of the Declaration are so noble and so wise and, as we have solemnly pledged to ourselves and our honor, they represent the future of mankind. We wrote and we believe that "all men are created equal."

And so now I write not to tell you of Virginia's near collapse at the hands of Lord Cornwallis. Mr. Washington is well aware of our dire situation and I am still hopeful he will send relief. Our cause depends on his military leadership. I write not to tell you of my ignominious escape from the clutches of a brigade of dragoons, for mine own enemies will be telling of the governor's cowardice at every opportunity they find, I have no doubt.

I write to tell you of a private moment in this disastrous escapade that I hope, dear friend, you will keep in confidence. I feel the two other participants will not communicate publicly their remarkable "capture" of the governor of Virginia, else they would come in for punishment by their superiors for letting their prey loose.

Before I espied the dragoons down in the village, but after the young Jack Jouett, a Virginia patriot, rode through the night to warn of their coming, my man Martin had dispatched my family in the coach. He then readied my fastest horse. I was making my escape through a back trail known only to a few denizens of our little town and felt I was safely out of the hands of the enemy, when from nowhere came two riders. My steed is fast and sure, and yet was no match for these two in pursuit.

I was stopped by a large Negro in native garb and a Seneca princess of striking beauty. Lest you think me mad, or confessing a dream, I assure you that what I am about to say is astounding, yet every word the truth, dear sir. I was certain I would never see my Martha again.

The Negro pointed an arrow in a taut bow at my chest. As I dismounted under his orders, the young woman, tall and muscular, again, sir, I say in all truth, as beautiful as any you gaze upon at the French Court, she pulled my own sword from its scabbard and touched its point to my heart.

What ensued was a discussion of the points of our Declaration wider than we held in that summer of 1776, challenges to the very foundation of the document upon which we fight this contest against the oppressor in England. Also, a negotiation with this savage woman equal to your counterparts on the Continent, I assure you.

She said she is Wah-say-lan of the Seneca Nation of the Six Nations. I know southern Indians who are fearful of these Iroquois. She spoke to me, Dr. Franklin, in this wise: "You think you sit on your land. This is not your land. You cannot own land, just as you cannot own human beings."

Then she asked why I thought I can own people. She told me her Earth Holder gave the land to her people, "who protected it through generations back before memory, long before the coming of the white man. The white man thinks he can own the fields and the rivers and the mountains and that he can own black people and make them do all their work."

I know, sir, you oppose slavery and I say to you what a remarkable conversation you could have with this woman and her blackamoor husband. Southern economies do not allow me to agree with your philosophical stance, as you know, kind sir. What is most amazing in all this, wherever they happened to meet, they are married and came down their warriors' trail to Monticello and found his mother at my home! When I return, and I hope I am there even before you are in receipt of this missive, perhaps the house I built myself will have been burned by the British, but I am certain my house servant Betsy, his mother, will no longer be in my service. And so, Dr. Franklin, your philosophy was served before my eyes by an angry son in search of his mother. I discovered from these two that my practice has been to steal mothers, or at least buy mothers, a thing I had never before contemplated.

Why they let me go I am not certain. They gave me pause about the equality of man. Their wits, their depth of thought, I have seen in other native Indians but had never seen in a Negro. This man, this Jamwesaw, was her equal in arguing for human rights.

Dr. Franklin, I share this wilderness conversation with you and I hope, my friend, that somehow you will believe me. Wah-say-lan, with my gift of my spyglass, said her gift was my life. I left feeling strangely, hoping, perhaps, that we might meet again. Oh if you could be there if and when that happens! These things I tell you because I cannot say them to any other, but I must say it and confide it to you.

I close now, dear Dr. Franklin, once again in your debt for convincing Louis XVI to send his armies to our aid.

I remain,
Yr. Mst Obdt. Srvt.
Thos. Jefferson

Thomas Jefferson sealed the envelope and then moved to an expansive sofa. He propped up a red, felt pillow and stared at the high ceiling. He closed his eyes, exhausted, and fell to sleep.

◈ CHAPTER 43 ◈

Heading North

Up north, the British still occupied New-York with more than 14,000 soldiers and Washington dearly wanted to recapture the city from which he had so ignominiously fled five years earlier. Even with Sullivan's ravishing of the Iroquois, it was a backwater victory at most, and Washington sensed a weariness among the people over this long conflict. He needed a decisive turn of events.

Thanks largely to Benjamin Franklin, the French had joined their cause. The Comte de Rochambeau was in Rhode Island with 7,000 men and Washington was trying to persuade him that together they could retake New-York. He had already sent one of his most daring and intelligent officers to Jefferson's aid.

The Marquis de Lafayette left his wife and wealth in France when he was 19 to volunteer in America's Revolution. A captain in the French Army, he received a commission under Washington as a major general. The fearless young Frenchman was wounded at Brandywine and had proven his mettle countless times. Four years into his service, with only one trip home to Paris, Washington sent him south to Virginia with 1,200 regulars and orders to hook up with militia along the way.

The marquis did anything Washington asked, but he particularly relished this southern assignment once he heard that Gen. William

Phillips was with Cornwallis. It was Phillips' artillery that had killed Lafayette's father at the Battle of Minden in the Seven Years' War when the marquis was only two years old.

With only a small force, he kept on the move. After crossing the Rappahannock and meeting a company of Virginia militia one day, the young major general asked where Phillips was camped. Jack Jouett, who had warned Jefferson of the British drive to Monticello, spoke up that he knew of an abandoned roadway two miles to the west. With some brush clearing, it could be a shortcut to Mechunk Creek, where Phillips' detachment was last seen, he said.

"I myself watched Tarleton's dragoons ride into his camp. I counted two dozen 16-pound cannon deployed around the encampment," said Jouett.

It was late in the day, but Lafayette wanted to see this road. Jouett had saved Jefferson's life and now rode side by side with the French marquis to save Jefferson's Virginia. Upon reaching the road, Lafayette was curious. He took Jouett and two scouts to see where it led.

Wah-say-lan had been walking north leading her horse for most the day. She was not hurrying. She wanted the pace and exertion of a steady walk. The young Seneca also had decided she wanted a closer look at the white man's villages. She had never been in a white man's village. On her trip to Albany as a child, she was at the edge of the forest playing dolls with Eliza Schuyler. So this day she left the warriors' trail and was letting her horse drink at a small creek when she saw in the distance what looked like a scar in the tree line.

She remembered that in her pack was the small telescope Jefferson had presented her. She pulled it out and put it to her eye. She held it out and looked at the inscription on its gold plate. She felt the engraved letters of the man's name and remembered how Jamwesaw told her she must accept the gift. She held it to her eye again and focused on the tree line. Yes, there was an opening that seemed to lead into the woods. She marveled at the power of the instrument, that it could bring faraway things so close. She examined it again, then put it carefully back in her pack. She joined the horse for a drink, splashed cool water in her face and walked toward the small opening. The day was late, but there was still time to see what was there. It looked like a good place to camp for the night.

As she tethered her horse, she thought how Pundatha had so generously presented it to her as a gift for their journey. She thought of how the Seneca chief had directed the building of new longhouses on the west side of the lake and how comfortable they were even in the long, hard winter. When she saw for the first time Jefferson's Monticello, she could not understand why anyone needed such a large structure. The white man is wasteful, she thought, and spends too much time erecting structures they do not need and building roadways through the forest, disturbing nature's way.

Here they built a road making a scar on the land and then forgot about it, she thought, walking along what was then little more than a widened path still with the telltale signs of wagon wheels that had cut through the ground. Wah-say-lan gathered wood and dry leaves for her campfire. It sparked easily with her flints and caught as she leaned down and blew the flames to life. She pulled a blanket from her pack and some bread Betsy had giver her. She leaned against a log and stared into the fire. It was not yet dusk, but Wah-say-lan felt tired. Traveling alone, she had made good progress on the first day of her journey back home. She chewed her food and let her thoughts drift.

Her mind settled on Jamwesaw, such a good man, a good son. He meant to find his lost mother one day, and finally, after years of wondering, hoping, catching snippets of conversation, small clues and hunches as to her whereabouts and traveling hundreds of miles, he did it, he found his mother. And when she wouldn't leave with him, he stayed, putting his own life in danger to make sure she would be safe, or perhaps in the hope that she would change her mind and come back north with him to live as a free and proud Seneca Indian. Her husband had shown his skill to all the braves. They saw how devoted he was to me and accepted him fully as a Seneca warrior, she thought.

She wondered about her mother-in-law. How could a woman choose to remain a slave? Especially such a beautiful and strong woman as Betsy Trentham. A slave who did not or could not choose her own man. She lies with Jefferson's nephew, who is the father of her youngest boy. The oldest is the son of the slave ship's captain? A woman should be able to choose whom she will lie with, whom she will live with.

The young Quaker they met on the trail popped into her thoughts. She smiled. The man was so eager. "I was curious. What was that about?" she thought. "I have my man and I love Jamwesaw as I love my life, but this young white man followed me, and wanted me, and I was open to him. Jamwesaw was the only man I wanted, the only man who aroused me, the first I gave myself to. Betsy Trentham is a slave, she did not choose this nephew to bed with; he chose her. And so this Quaker chose me and I was, what, interested? But it was my choice and my choice was to tell him no."

The fire was warm. Wah-say-lan pulled her shirt off and rolled it up. She placed it behind her head against the log and lay back and imagined herself in the eyes of someone looking at her. She did not know why her mind went there, but she found herself gazing at her half-naked body, her long dark hair, her firm breasts. She knew she was a pretty woman and she felt that was a good thing. She always took care of herself as she would take care of her cousin, or of her village. She was protective of herself and was comfortable with the knowledge that she was valuable in a physical sense. And so she began to understand why a man would be attracted to her.

Away from the tensions at Monticello, on her own even hundreds of miles from home, she felt safe, released and entirely independent. Wah-say-lan felt whole and one with all around her. She felt her long legs against the blanket on the earth and allowed herself to relax. She closed her eyes, easing into sleep at dusk.

Jouett and Lafayette had seen the gleam from her campfire, left their mounts and crept forward. When they saw Wah-say-lan stretched out on the ground, they looked at each other and looked back, not quite believing the scene.

"She is alone," Jouett finally whispered.

"Yes, and so am I," the Marquis de Lafayette whispered back. "I will deal with this. I am going to ask her a few questions. Take the scouts back, I will rejoin you later."

"Uh, yes, sir," responded Jouett, casting another look at the sleeping Indian woman. "Are you sure, sir?"

"Jouett, I can handle one young woman," said the major general. Jouett backed out reluctantly and silently, leaving the marquis to his prey. Lafayette knelt on one knee behind a tree, peering at Wah-say-lan. In the glow of the fire he could see her face and was struck by her beauty. He thought of a painting hanging in his Paris home of the lovely Aphrodite reclined on a fine sofa, exposing all.

"A savage alone? A young woman alone?" he thought. "What is this who lies in my path? Why now, why here?"

She stirred. Wah-say-lan felt a strange pressure at her neck. She touched the wolf tooth necklace. Instantly she sprang up, grabbed her knife from its sheath at her waist and jumped behind the log, crouching.

Lafayette made an instant choice. He stepped from behind the tree, held up his hand and said, "I come in peace."

Wah-say-lan felt an urge to run and had learned to let her instincts lead. But she hesitated, then stood to her full height, holding the weapon out straight. She stepped over the log and took four paces toward the Frenchman.

The marquis gasped at what he saw. "Am I dreaming?" he thought as this bare-breasted and strikingly beautiful woman came toward him with a large knife that she obviously knew how to wield. He said again, "I come in peace. Do you understand?"

Wah-say-lan stopped. She said nothing, but let him take a few steps forward. The marquis stretched his palms in front of him. "I do not arm myself. But I could," slowly touching with his right hand the pistol in his belt. "I mean no harm."

The young Seneca heard her husband's voice: "Do not attack

soldiers alone. Be careful." Clearly the man in front of her was a soldier, and of some rank. She heard him say, "I was coming this way and you were here. I am Marie-Joseph-Paul-Yves-Roch-Gilbert du Motier, Marquis de Lafayette. I come in peace."

Wah-say-lan studied him. She kept her eyes on his hands. She did not offer her usual greeting, but only "I am Wah-say-lan. Why would a soldier come in peace."

The marquis smiled. "I fight my enemies. I come in peace to a woman."

"Who are your enemies?" she said.

"Those who oppose freedom," he said.

"I am free. I am free to go where I choose. I am free to be here," she said.

"Indeed. You seem absolutely free," he said.

She knew his French accent. She knew he fought with the Americans. She knew he was the enemy. She supposed he was an important officer. Not as important as Thomas Jefferson, but an officer with an army, no doubt.

"Why are you here?" she said to him.

He wanted to know more, much more. He shouldn't trifle with a single savage, pretty though she may be. But he couldn't bring himself to leave. Is she indigenous? Could she tell him things of this area? But he was kidding himself, he knew. He quite simply wanted to spend some time with this mysterious creature before him, still holding out a large hunting knife.

"I am on my way south. This is the path I am taking. Why are you here?" he said.

She thought a moment. "I am on my way north. This is the path I am on."

"And so our paths have crossed," said the marquis. "I am alone. I have troops not far away, but I am alone here on this spot. I would like to sit with you at your campfire for a few moments. I will not harm you."

"I will harm you, Marquis de Lafayette, if you are not careful."

He was surprised hearing his name from her lips. Who did she say she was? He tried "Wah-lay-mans, we now know each other's names . . . "

"Wah-say-lan, I am Wah-say-lan."

"Yes, Wah-say-lan, please call me marquis." He took a risk. "Look, I am putting my pistol here on this rock." He gently lifted it from his belt and placed it down.

"Your sabre."

"Ah, yes." He pulled it from its long sheath and put it next to his pistol. He felt more naked than she, but he sensed he had deflected danger. He couldn't help but stare at her breasts.

Wah-say-lan noticed his gaze, but it did not faze her. Seneca women often wore only a dress and pants to the waist. She held her knife, but lowered it to her side.

"Come. You may sit at my fire."

He removed his tricorne. He had shed his coat in the afternoon sun and was traveling in a shirt open at the neck. She tossed on a few gathered sticks to boost the flames and pulled from her pouch some dried deer meat. With her father's knife at her side on the ground in full view of her visitor, she handed him some nourishment.

"Merci, thank you," he said. "Tell me, why are you here alone on this path?"

She ignored his question and asked, "Why do the French fight in this war?"

He was amused at her pluck and said, "Wars are fought for many reasons. This is a war for liberty and I fight for liberty."

"You come across the big gawa to fight. It is not the first time the French have fought here. The French burned the village of my grandmother's grandmother. They burned the crops. They left nothing. My people fought, but the French had many more soldiers. They burned our villages. Your armies left us nothing."

This was off to a bad start, thought the marquis. "That would be a long time ago, your grandmother's grandmother," he said. Then it occurred to him: Denonville, the Marquis de Denonville's raid against the Seneca, who were riling up the western Indians late in the last century and flirting with an alliance with the British. Louis XIV, intent on keeping his North American empire, decorated Denonville for punishing the Seneca. He grew up on tales of the great Denonville's leadership in the new world.

"My God, she is a Seneca," he thought.

"Why are you so far from home, why are you in Virginia?" he asked.

"So you know of what your people did to mine. Tell me, why are you so far from home in Virginia?"

"General Denonville was trying to preserve our friendship with the Iroquois, the Haudenosaunee. We did not want the devious British to interfere, but that was nearly 100 years ago. And I am here today, as I told you, to fight on the side of liberty," he said.

"One hundred years in white man's time. Your people hurt my people. Time does not stop that. Now you march with Washington. He sent an army. It destroyed my home, burned my crops, killed my people. Blue Coats killed my father," said Wah-say-lan.

"The Seneca are fighting with the British. The British, the Red Coats, killed my father. The battalion that killed him is in Virginia, maybe not far from here. I was only two, but now I can take my revenge," the marquis heard himself say. He immediately knew the conversation was not going where he wanted it to go. But at least he knew he was sitting with the enemy, a delightfully half-dressed enemy.

He started again: "My father is dead, your father is dead. I am sorry your father died. I am sure he died honorably, as mine did, fighting for what he believed in."

"Believed in? My father, Lan-lu-rah of the Seneca Nation, died defending his people, his land, his home."

"Tell me, Wah-say-lan, what is a Seneca woman doing in Virginia, alone."

"You say it is Virginia. I am on my people's warriors' trail that we have traveled since before memory. My people are respected by all other people in the hills and forests along our trail. Only the Cherokee people do not accept our power, but we have defeated them many, many times. Maybe I am not alone. If you say this is Virginia, maybe I will tell you we captured Thomas Jefferson. Maybe we will hurt Washington's army as we have hurt the powerful Cherokee Nation."

"What do you mean you captured Thomas Jefferson?"

She got up and pulled the spyglass from her pack and handed it to the marquis. He saw Jefferson's inscription. He was astonished.

"Where did you find this?" he asked.

"Thomas Jefferson gave it to me. The glass helped me get to this spot."

The marquis was confused. On a personal level, he wanted to know this fascinating woman. As a general in Washington's army, how could he let her leave? The first stars were out. He looked around, but realized if there were others, he could not see them.

"You said you were alone. Now you say 'we' captured Jefferson."

"Yes. Do not worry, Marquis de Lafayette, I am alone, except I have my father's knife. I killed the soldiers who killed my father. And I believe you would want to kill those who killed your father. But we let Jefferson live. He gave me this glass. The British have his home and his slaves, you who believe in freedom."

The marquis could not believe this young woman held Jefferson, but he needed to know more. "You mean Jefferson is safe?"

"We let him go. He rode off. His house is taken, but he rode off."

"Is it Phillips, General Phillips, who has Monticello?" he asked.

"I do not know this Phillips. It is Col. Tarleton in Charlottesville."

"Banastre Tarleton! He took Monticello! He would not let Jefferson go free."

"I told you, Marquis de Lafayette, it is I who let Jefferson go."

"No, you said 'we,' " he said.

Wah-say-lan did not want to speak of her husband to this officer in the American army.

"I will not say who 'we' are. I will tell you I decided to let Jefferson go. I feel he and I will meet again."

Lafayette was not entirely satisfied, but he had Phillips on his mind. "You avenged your father's death. Yes, I want to avenge my father's. It is Gen. Phillips' troops who killed my father. Do you know where he is?"

"I do not know of this Phillips," she said.

The marquis was silent. He believed she did not know of Phillips' whereabouts. He would find him and deal with him. And he sensed that he would not learn more of this Jefferson business. As the flames flickered, he looked at her for a long moment. She held his stare. She smiled slightly at him. He asked, "Do you think we will meet again?"

"I think I will meet Thomas Jefferson again. You are a war chief fighting against my people," she said.

"Not all your people. Your brothers the Oneida and the Tuscarora joined me—more than 50 Iroquois warriors joined my men. They helped us outwit and defy the British troops at a battle on Barren Hill in 1778 in Pennsylvania. The British have always tried to trick your people. It is my King, my country of France, that has always befriended the great Six Nations. It was British trickery that caused our French General Denonville to punish the Seneca in the last century."

"Marquis de Lafayette, it is British Red Coats who helped defend my village when Washington sent his army against us," she responded. She did not understand how the Oneida joined the Americans, and she was tiring of this debate. She wanted to know more of this young Frenchman seated before her. Who is he? she thought.

"How many summers are you?" she asked softly.

"I am 24 years," he said. "How many summers are you, Wah-say-lan?"

"I am in my 18th summer," she said. Then she felt an urge. He was the enemy, she knew, but she did not want him to go. Her taking soup to Jamwesaw tied at a stake flashed through her mind. She saw the young Quaker James Embler pulling her shirt off. Now, here, with another more dashing white man, her shirt was already off and he was fixated on her breasts. Something stirred inside her. He fought on the wrong side of this war, but she was moved by him, by his honesty, his strong good looks. She knew that she wanted him.

"I do not know if we will meet again," she said, and rose to her knees. She bent down on her hands and prowled over to the marquis. He noticed the knife was still over on the ground. Her face was close to his. She put her hand on his chest and pushed him to the ground. He went willingly on his back. She straddled him, her fingers played with the buttons on his shirt. She laughed and spread her fingers through the dark hair on his chest.

The marquis moved his hands along her long thighs. He held her hips as Wah-say-lan moved them back and forth. She felt his growing hardness between her legs and pushed her pelvis to meet it. His hands reached up to her breasts. He massaged them gently.

Lafayette groaned and pulled her down to him. He kissed her and ran his hands through her thick black hair. He said to himself that he knows pretty ladies at the royal court in Paris who preen and promenade for the gentlemen, but there are no women like this one. No woman had ever crawled to him in the forest, nor been so forceful as to push him back on the bare ground. He was excited beyond his own belief.

Wah-say-lan could not sort out why she wanted this Frenchman. Another day she would have fought him and killed him if she could, she thought. "Now I am kissing him and wanting him," she said to herself. She tugged at his pants, pulling them down to his boots. She whisked hers off and jumped back on him, guiding it to her. She kept up her rhythmic motion and he pushed upward. Her long hair fell and flowed with their motion. Wah-say-lan pushed harder and harder, she was reaching, reaching.

The marquis, in a great motion, rolled her over. He was panting and plunged back between her thighs spread wide and waiting. She told him she wanted more and harder. She pulled him to her and raised her hips to his motion. More, more, she said and she was there. She yelled out "OOhhhhh, oohhhh! She held him tight and could feel him strong and hard in her.

Then he roared, but at the last second he pulled out. He spurted on her in great gushes. He wanted so much to be in her, but the marquis, even in his frenzy, said silently to himself that he did not want a son raised as a savage. He was at once ashamed to pull from this incredible, this beautiful daughter of Aphrodite. Yet he knew he could not live knowing his own small boy, the gift of his passion, could one day be running near naked on the western frontier among a people destined for defeat.

As he had these images, he grabbed Wah-say-lan and held her. She touched where he had splashed on her hard, flat stomach. She rubbed it into her skin and smiled at him.

"You missed," she laughed. "I hope you are a better shot with your pistol."

He buried his head in the nape of her neck, kissing it gently, whispering in her ear, "Wah-say-lan, you are an unbelievable woman. How I came to meet you here I will never know. I hope we never meet on opposite sides of this war, for I could never try to harm you. This was a moment of peace—fantastic peace—between two warring people. I hope you will not forget this."

"Marquis, I will not forget this. I will not forget you. Now your troops are waiting and it is late. What if they come for you? You must go. If you bring your soldiers down this path tomorrow, I will not be here. Nor do I go to find my braves; they are far away. I am alone and tomorrow I will travel north as I did today. I have a long way to go before I get home."

His pants were still down at his boots. He struggled to his feet and pulled them up. He buttoned his shirt. She stood before him naked. The moon shone brightly. Standing next to each other he saw she was nearly his height. He looked at her again and marveled at the sight before him. He reached out and touched her neck and asked, "Where did you get this fine necklace?"

Wah-say-lan touched the wolf teeth and remembered how they

had pierced her hotly when the marquis was approaching. She fingered them and said, "A very wise woman gave them to me. They will help guide me home." She kissed him long on his lips, then walked to his pistol and sabre and handed them to him.

He touched her necklace, then her cheek, smiled and walked back up the abandoned road to where his 1,200 men were encamped two miles away.

◈ CHAPTER 44 ◈

The Morning After

Maj. Gen. Lafayette led his troops down the abandoned roadway. He approached the log and the small campfire where he knew Wah-say-lan would no longer be. But she wasn't far.

When she awoke at dawn, she poured water into her birch bark container, splashed her face and washed her thighs and her stomach. She wished she could jump into her lake and swim to the island, but this would do until she found a river or pond on her long journey back to Canandaigua. She did not take time for breakfast but chewed on some bread and dried venison as she led her horse into the forest. When she was out of sight, she found a patch of grass in a clearing and let the horse graze. She knew he would not go far. She took her bow and quiver of arrows and doubled back toward the pathway. She found a rise with boulders and fir trees and a clear view down to the spot where she and the marquis met. She waited.

She heard them before she saw them. A forward unit was slashing and cutting brush and limbs. Then came several officers astride mounts, with the young Frenchman at the head. The column of infantry stretched back nearly a mile—1,200 regulars along with Jack Jouett's 200 militia.

Wah-say-lan put an arrow in her bow. She watched the marquis ride up to where they lay last night. She thought she saw him smile.

She pulled the arrow to her chin and spotted down its rigid length. Lafayette's chest was an easy target. She thought of the buttons she undid last night, of the hair on his chest, of his words about a moment of peace between two warring people. She could kill him right now and she could probably get away. She kept him in her sights, then she let the bowstring ease back.

Wah-say-lan sighed. "My husband told me to be careful. I was not careful last night. But I will remember his words this morning. The marquis will live and we will see if he ever enters my life again," she said to herself.

Unseen, she watched his troops. She had never seen so many marching to war. Once she saw 300 Seneca braves gather for battle. Lafayette had five times that many. He led them against the British, maybe against the detachment that Jamwesaw was serving in. She shivered in the Virginia morning, worrying for his safety.

"But how can I shoot at these many soldiers? Jamwesaw made his choice; he is staying for his mother. Besides, he is an amazing fighter, and he joins 8,000 British troops. The marquis has many, but not that many," she thought.

But her thoughts didn't stop. "At Canandaigua, Sullivan's men kept coming and even our British allies were taken prisoner. Like my father, many Seneca men fought and died. How many more will?" she asked herself. "Should I go find Jamwesaw? No, he will survive and come to me. I need to go back and be with Tun-weh and my mother. And Pundatha knows I can fight as well as any brave."

She watched Lafayette's column head deeper into Virginia. She found her horse and started walking north, up the abandoned roadway the troops had just come down. As she came to where they had camped, small columns of smoke spiraled from the embers of their fires.

Suddenly a large red-tailed hawk swooped over her shoulder. She saw it dive, talons extended, and effortlessly grab a thick snake off the ground. The hawk flew off over the treetops with three feet of snake draped behind it.

Wah-say-lan thought back to how Jamwesaw had grabbed a snake and sliced its head off in seemingly the same motion, presenting her their first meal the day that Sullivan's army pushed her people from their village on the lake.

She wondered if the hawk was delivering the next meal to its mate. They are messengers, she knew, but what message did he bring? she asked herself. She felt very alone and wished her husband was with her. "What kind of mother would tell her son she would rather remain a slave? And so my husband stays to wait and to fight in hopes she would change her mind? In hopes that Jefferson will have to free his slaves? How long must I wait for his return to me?" All these questions filled her head as she looked at the land around her. The trees are different here. The air is heavier, without the crisp breezes off the lake, she thought. "My lake, it is time to get back to my lake." She hopped on Pundatha's horse and headed north.

◈ CHAPTER 45 ◈

Alone at night

Wah-say-lan decided she had seen enough white men, put off her idea of seeing their villages and made good time back up the warriors' trail. In fact, near nightfall she was due west of Baltimore, where more than a decade ago Jamwesaw and his mother had arrived as slaves.

The young Seneca woman may as well have been a thousand miles west. The Appalachian Mountains were the backbone of a wilderness so thick with great and ancient trees that a squirrel could travel for miles without ever touching the ground. Here and there, as if splashed down by a benevolent being from on high, were meadows with streams and lakes. Black bears, wolves and panthers staked out their territories with little to worry them but the small hunting parties of native Indians and occasional forays by pioneering whites.

The Iroquois did not hunt wolves, but honored them as protectors. As a member of the Wolf Clan, Wah-say-lan was taught from her earliest days that the wolf is sacred and that much could be learned from knowing the ways of a wolf pack. Slowing her horse to a walk, she felt the teeth around her neck presented by Mary Angel. She thought how her mother had told her there is nothing more ferocious than a she-wolf protecting her young. And she thought again of Betsy Trentham's decision to keep her young boys on Jefferson's plantation. "She does not see that coming to Canandaigua to live with the Seneca protects her family. How can I blame her? She is doing what she thinks is best for her sons," thought Wah-say-lan.

"And what of my children? Will Jamwesaw give me children? Ha, the marquis spilled his seed. I will not have his child. He is a beautiful man, but I would not want to carry the child of my enemy. Why has Jamwesaw's seed not grown within me? I will protect my children as my parents protected me. My father died protecting his family and his village. I would do the same."

These were her thoughts as Wah-say-lan stopped, unburdened her horse and made her campfire. She roasted a quail whose misfortune earlier in the day was to cross her path. She drank fresh water she carried from a stream several miles back. Wah-say-lan was satisfied, yet tired after a day of traveling at a fast pace. A day spent hurrying home. As she laid out her blanket it did not occur to her, as it had not occurred to her the night before, that she was alone, truly alone day and night, for the first time in her life.

She was fingering her necklace as she fell asleep. The dream came in full and vivid color. She was kneeling at a stream bed splashing water in her face and hair. A large panther with sleek golden fur was crouched and creeping toward her. In her dream she could sense the predator coming toward her, but she also saw in her dream that she knelt at the water not knowing of the danger.

Outside of her dream, on the edge of her dream, Wah-say-lan wanted to holler to herself, but she watched herself take the soapweed and crush it in her fingers to work up a lather for her long hair. It was cool and slick and felt good as she ran her hands through her dark hair. She tossed it back, but somehow a strand twisted in her necklace. She tried to work it free and felt a tooth press hard against her thumb. Then she felt the other teeth hot on her neck. In her dream she remembered Mary Angel saying to her to pay attention to her necklace when she least expected the need to. From the edge of her dream she warned herself of the approach of the panther.

Wah-say-lan lifted from her knees at the stream and locked into a defensive crouch, turning slowly. The animal, as big as she was, had reached the top of a boulder. One long leap and it would be upon her. She looked across the clearing to her bow and arrows leaning against a small tree. She did not take her eyes off the cat as she inched toward her weapon.

The panther growled. Its lips trembled. It bared its fangs in a defiant roar. Wah-say-lan stopped. She did not make any fast motions. She growled back and put out her hands as if they were claws. She did not know her next move. She knew a panther could snap her neck with one bite.

When she looked again, the panther's face blurred and the cat grew. It floated above and turned blue. The blue panther was a giant. Fire soared out of its tail. Wah-say-lan knew she needed tobacco, for this was the much feared death panther. If braves burned tobacco and the panther breathed it in, it was an offering that would make the animal leave, satisfied its deadly mission was for another place and time.

Wah-say-lan knew she did not have tobacco and could not satisfy the beast. She began to run for her weapon but in her dream her fine strong legs were sluggish, and though she tried to run she could not. "Gaa-siondiet-t-ha, the death panther, will take me," she said to herself in her dream. The panther crawled back down to the rock, huge and ready to pounce.

There was a screech from behind her. Wah-say-lan turned to see an enormous hawk; a red-tail, the biggest hawk she had ever seen, soared overhead. It screeched again as if to warn any and all. The blue panther tensed. The hawk dove, its wing span twice the size of the giant lion. Wah-say-lan could see the extended talons. It was ready to strike when the death panther vanished. And then the hawk was instantly gone.

The young Seneca ran and grabbed her bow. She swung around, but her foot twisted against a root and she fell. The panther, with short golden fur, was once again on top of the boulder. Wah-say-lan in her dream could feel her ankle in great pain. She couldn't seem to get an arrow set in her bowstring. She struggled with an action that had been second nature to her. The pain in her ankle grew. She tried to hurry with the arrow. It fell out of her hands. The cat was ready to pounce.

From behind her came a howl, then another. In a blur, the wolf pack charged at the boulder. The lead wolf howled and jumped, followed by the others. The panther hesitated, held its ground. Strong as the cat was, it was no match for the pack. Snarling wolves lunged at their prey. The cat fought, swiping its large claws, but the wolves kept at it. The leader of the pack gnashed a long wound across the panther's back. It screamed and jumped from the boulder. It ran with the wolves inches behind. A she-wolf stopped, turned and looked back at Wah-say-lan. It said to her, "Mary told us where you were." Then it trotted off.

Wah-say-lan awoke at dawn. Her ankle did not hurt. She looked over at the boulder. She walked to it, climbed to its top. Warm blood was on its surface. She jumped down and saw the cat's tracks with many wolf tracks all about. They led to the west and disappeared. Wah-say-lan picked up her bow, set an arrow and let it fly. She watched it arch to the west and out of sight. She touched her necklace. "Mary, what are you telling me?"

◈ CHAPTER 46 ◈

A Decision

Wah-say-lan found the horse and started walking along the warriors' trail. She tried to think about all the Seneca warriors who had traveled this way, victorious over ancient enemies. But she was shaken and confused. She did not see the beautiful landscape, the virtually untouched wilderness. The deep green of a deep, warm summer. It was always a time of solace and plenty. Tending the growing corn stalks, picking the ripening fruit from the orchards. Even thinking ahead to the storytelling times of winter evenings. She had always listened to the elders tell the stories, all the wonderful stories. But she never liked the stories of the death panther, the blue panther without a clear face.

She could examine some of the long-told tales, even question the validity of the great snake on Bare Hill, as she had confided to Jamwesaw. The death panther, though, had always scared her and it scared her in her dream last night.

"What does this mean?" she asked. "Am I to die? Am I ready to join my father in the Sky World? No, I am young. I will die, but not now. The wolves saved me in my dream. This morning I saw their prints in the dirt and the puma's prints too. So, was it a dream? Yes, it was a dream, but the footprints? All I could do was shoot my arrow as far as it would go. Mary's necklace was with me. The she-wolf told me so."

But her young heart was heavy. Her bravado, her bounce, her optimism were not with her. She thought, "My Wolf Clan necklace saved me. But my Jamwesaw does not have a necklace. He is Wolf Clan through me, but certainly the wolves will not go near an army. Is the dream about my husband? Did he see the blue panther?"

Wah-say-lan stopped. Her knees buckled. She found herself on the ground, sprawled. Tears filled her eyes. She thought, "They have killed my husband. No! No! He is too brave. He is too fine a fighter. He is not dead!"

She made herself think. She straightened up. She crossed her legs. She shut her eyes. Her hands pressed against her knees. She thought about wolves, about how Jamwesaw killed the corporal who was trying to rape her, about his bravery in pulling her from the battle. "He cannot be dead. The death panther, the blue panther. Ah, my Jamwesaw is with soldiers. They have tobacco. Jamwesaw knows the story, he would burn tobacco. He would burn tobacco, yes he would. And the panther would go away. My husband is alive. I know my husband is alive."

Wah-say-lan sat where she had collapsed. She sat for a very long time. Like a deer who dares not move before it flees danger, she sat there all day. She did not flee. She sat there as dusk fell. She saw the first stars in the sky. Only then, only when more stars appeared, did she stir. When she saw the seven brothers in the sky who had slain the giant bear, when she saw them clearly and shining brightly, only then did she move.

She found Pundatha's horse and tethered it to a tree limb. She pulled her blanket out. She put her father's knife at her side. And she fell asleep, exhausted. She slept well. She did not dream. She almost willed herself not to dream.

She awoke at first light, hungry and in need of a bath. "I need food, but I need to swim," she said to the horse as she untied the reins, hopped on and galloped north. Over a rise she saw a small lake at the bottom. She raced the horse down the hill. She whooped and whooped, "Ahhhyyeee, aahhhyyeee!" She ran the horse right into the water. It was cool. She dove off and swam deeper. The horse followed. Wah-say-lan swam back and forth, back and forth. She dove under the water and came back up over and over. Finally she swam to the shore and called the stallion. It trotted over to her. She grabbed everything off its back. She unpacked it all and laid it in the sun.

She undressed and laid her clothes on the grass. She pulled dried venison from her sack and sat naked and ate. The meat was tough, stringy and bland. It was not taste she was seeking. She was hungry and ate many pieces. "Later I will take a quail or a rabbit for a decent meal," she thought. Right now the cool water revived her, made her skin tingle. She lay back in the grass and let the sun soak into her body. "There is nothing like a good swim," she thought, feeling again the freedom she always felt as her legs and arms stretched through water, embracing her yet allowing full movement in any direction she chose.

Her mind wandered. She wondered where on the trail she was. "I am halfway home," she thought. "I have met soldiers both rebels and British, and Susquehannocks, and Quakers, and Thomas Jefferson, and the French marquis and Betsy Trentham. I have seen Jefferson's home."

There were no sounds, not even waves lapping on the shore of the little lake. The leaves on the trees were still as even the wind rested. The stillness was reflected in the clear blue sky. Then she saw it soaring high, drifting with hardly a flap of its wings. Wah-say-lan loved when the red-tail turned up. She always listened, always paid heed.

The great bird dove, banked toward her and let out its screech; "kree-eee-ar, kree-eee-ar," it called. The hawk swooped lower and flew past the lone Indian woman. It screeched once more and then with a few pumps of its powerful wings it turned east, northeast, and she watched it disappear in the horizon.

"It flies toward the white man's towns. I have seen Jefferson's home. And now I will see the white man's towns," she decided.

At the shore of this small, calm lake she noticed her reflection on the water. Still naked, she moved closer and peered at the surface of the water. Her long dark hair framed her face. She could see her big brown eyes looking back at her. She smiled and saw her smile. Her high cheekbones accented her pretty face. She looked at the wolf-tooth necklace on her long neck. Her hair reached to her full breasts. She was pleased with what she saw. "I do believe I please my husband," she thought. She knelt and bowed her head, letting her hair cascade in front of her face. She parted it and then took the time to make two braids. She remembered the older women scolding her for noticing her reflection. Seneca women are not supposed to be vain or spend time gazing at themselves. "I am bad. I know. I like looking at my face in the water," she thought. "I like the way I look. What is wrong with knowing that? Our ways do not always make sense. I like knowing who I am." She stood and saw her whole self reflected in the lake water. It made her feel strong and confident. "I am here alone. I know my way," she said out loud. "I know my way."

Wah-say-lan gathered up her belongings and packed them on her horse. She pulled on her clothes warmed by the sun. Then she mounted the horse and headed north and east. "I will see how these white men live. I have seen white men in my land. But I have never seen their towns. It is time."

CHAPTER 47

A Cabin

Leaving the warriors' trail, she meant to keep traveling north but also to keep the sun behind her more as she headed northeast, where she knew the white man lived. She recognized the Susquehanna and was pulled by its familiarity. She stopped and watched the flow of its water, but turned away through a forest, intent on her chosen path. It was slow going.

Still, she loved the smells and the sunlight breaking through in places, making highly defined shafts of light against the dark tree trunks. She saw a black bear with cubs. She watched as the mother guarded her young romping in blueberry shrubs, nuzzling them and showing them how to lick and bite the sweet purple fruit from the leafy green bushes.

Wah-say-lan nudged her horse along a ridge. Chipmunks scampered. A doe and a fawn trotted into the underbrush and disappeared. She could sense that her path was taking her down to lower ground. The ancient Appalachian Mountains had sustained her people even before they had formed tribes, for thousands of years dating back to the last ice age. Just as Wah-say-lan traveled alone, small bands of human beings had walked these lands following herds and rivers. The land had always provided an abundance of food and the people eventually learned to grow corn and its sisters, beans and squash. As the people settled in villages, they planted the seeds of apples and peaches, pears and cherries, growing the trees into orchards. The people became the nations of the woodlands.

Coming down out of the mountains reminded Wah-say-lan of the many times she had climbed to the top of Bare Hill above her village, the hill that legend held was the birthplace of the Seneca Nation. She would walk down through the greenery of the hill to where it sloped gently into her Canandaigua Lake, the Chosen Place of her ancestors.

This day, Wah-say-lan rode down a slope as the ground leveled and she wondered how many native people had traveled the same way. The Delaware, the Shawnee, the Susquehannock all have hunted these lands, she thought. Did the Tuscarora come this way to join the Iroquois Confederacy so many summers ago, long before she was born? she wondered.

Then she saw the smoke rising. It was a bright day and the trail of smoke made a rising gray line against the blue sky. "It is bigger than a campfire, but it is not a large fire," she said to herself, nudging the horse in that direction.

As the sun approached its noontime zenith, Wah-say-lan came to a clearing, a field with corn growing. She could see the cabin beyond, smoke rising from its chimney. She left the horse in a thicket and walked silently, checking her father's knife in her belt. She walked along the side of the cornstalks and saw a woman in a long skirt and calico blouse bent over, hoeing a small garden. A boy was with her on his hands and knees. A small girl was playing with a doll.

Wah-say-lan crept over to a stand of birch trees sprouting out of an expanse of blackberry bushes. She could hear them talking.

"Ma, Dad has been gone a long time. When will he be back?" the boy said.

"Oh, Robert, I miss him too. I wish he were here to help. But you are doing a man's job keeping the weeds from our vegetables," she said to her son. "You know he's off fighting the British for our independence. Remember he said he and the lieutenant and a couple of others were delivering supplies and a cannon to Fort Pitt? That's a long and dangerous assignment, but your father is a brave and strong man."

"Yes he is, Mommy," said the little girl.

"Oh, I know, darlin'. Your dad is a good man and he will come home to us as soon as he can."

Wah-say-lan looked on this scene and couldn't help but think of her mother working in the cornfield. She thought, "White women, Seneca women, we do the same things." And she thought that she probably killed this little girl's father. "Or maybe he was one of the two that Jamwesaw scared off, that he let go as they raced away without any weapons, into the west. If they did not meet any Shawnee, or they didn't starve, maybe they got to their fort," she said to herself. "I hope not."

Where did these white people come from? Why are they invading our land? Why are they building strange homes of logs on the land Sky Woman created and gave to us to keep safe? My people have been on this land since before memory. The Seneca, all the Iroquois have roamed over the mountains, the lakes, the forests forever. Who do these white people think they are, coming across the big gawa and moving onto our land? Wah-say-lan had worried about the white man for half her life. And then she saw them burn her village and kill her father and many others of her people.

She had the urge to jump out with her knife and watch this woman beg for her life and for her children's lives. "Maybe I should burn this corn as Washington's army did to my cornfield," she thought.

Revenge lodged deeply in Wah-say-lan's soul. If the man had been in his field, she would have rushed and slit his throat. She would have scalped him in front of his wife. But she could not bring herself to disrupt this small, peaceful scene; this family hoping the father will return, not knowing that he probably never will. "Maybe he is the one I shot in the neck with my arrow. Or maybe he is the one on the ground with Jamwesaw's arrow in his side. The one who died with my knife slicing through his white neck," she thought of the detachment of Blue Coats they had met on the Susquehanna.

If Jamwesaw were with her, they would take this woman to Canandaigua with her children and they would either die or join the village. Wah-say-lan contented herself with stealing some ears of corn as she made her way back to her horse. She packed some ears and offered three to her companion. The stallion munched them hungrily.

As she waited, Wah-say-lan remembered how Mary Angel told her, just once, of her capture when she was a girl of only 12 summers. Her family had a cabin and fields like this family. Her father had even built a barn. The French and Shawnee came one morning and took them, her mother and father, the baby, her two brothers and her. They burned the cabin and the barn. They marched the family for two days with ropes around their necks.

She begged her father to protect them, but it was her mother who soothed her, spoke to her to quiet her fears. Mary and her brothers were taken away by some Shawnee braves and she heard the screams as the rest of her family were murdered. Later in the day the Shawnee gave her to two Seneca sisters, who put her in their canoe. As they paddled around a curve in a river, she saw her family's burned bodies leaning grotesquely against stakes in the ground.

"Mary told me of this, and of how frightened she was but also angry that her father could not protect her or her mother and the baby. Mary decided to live with my people. She was there when I was born, she told me. She became a Seneca woman with her own Seneca children. Mary learned our ways and became a wise medicine woman on the council of the Canandaigua village," Wah-say-lan reminded herself.

The sun was high. There was no breeze. Wah-say-lan was sweating. She felt hot and uncomfortable. The young Indian woman lifted her deerskin shirt over her head. She sifted through her bags and pulled out a smaller, sleeveless buckskin top, open at the neck. She took her water pouch and splashed water on her shoulders, her breasts, her arms. She smoothed the coolness into her skin, took a long drink, then slipped into her new top. She stretched and felt a new freedom, touched her wolf-tooth necklace that hung above the v-shaped vest exposing what the Marquis de Lafayette would call an enticing bit of cleavage. If a portrait artist could spend some time with Wah-say-lan, any gentleman would hang the painting in his library. "American Savage," a French marquis would label it and show it off to his guests as a remarkable example of the wild and striking beauty that could be found in the North American wilderness.

Wah-say-lan hopped on her horse and made a wide circle around the cabin. She kicked the horse into a trot. She did not want to be tempted to use her knife. She wanted to put distance quickly between herself and the woman and her children.

◈ CHAPTER 48 ◈

Philadelphia

The next morning on Market Street in the important and busy city of Philadelphia, Gen. Philip Schuyler was talking not war, but business, with a small group of investors. They chatted casually on the field-stone sidewalk outside the three-story, brick structure built only six years earlier as the growing municipality's City Hall.

Commander of the Continental Army's Northern Department, Schuyler had been ordered to monitor British movements out of New-York City as Washington and Rochambeau plotted a southern strategy. Schuyler's grandfather was a pioneering Dutchman who made an early fortune trading with the Mohawk and building saw-mills and other businesses in the Hudson River Valley.

Philip Schuyler was a wealthy and influential patriot to the American cause who looked westward and saw clearly the American future. This morning, after a delightful breakfast with bankers in the roomy, comfortable Algonquin Tavern, he observed the bustle of two newspapers being delivered along the street, wagons of grain, vegetables and other produce going by to the outdoor markets three blocks down, and squads of young continental soldiers marching to the outskirts for drilling and training.

In just a generation Philadelphia, with its deep port on the Delaware River and short distance to Chesapeake Bay and the

Atlantic, had joined Boston and New-York as America's premier cities. Gen. Schuyler was in the right place to find investors in his business development plans. This day he had brought along his 19-year-old daughter, Elizabeth, known as Eliza, a petite, pretty brunette with lively dark eyes and an unusually inquisitive nature. She often perplexed her famous father with her questions and her opinions on everything from the war to the pricing of their just-cut lumber for the growing shipping trade in New-York.

Last fall she had met the dashing Army Col. Alexander Hamilton in Albany. Though her suitors were many, Hamilton was the first man who also held her attention. She found him to be not only handsome but intelligent with an imposing, yet not off-putting, intensity about ideas and life. Some would call it charisma. To Eliza Schuyler, it was charm.

She was delighted to learn that Washington had ordered his young aide-de-camp to meet with Schuyler in Philadelphia. Young ladies of scions were expected to see and know the finer offerings of America's new urban centers and, for Eliza, Philadelphia's finest offering was Col. Hamilton.

Eliza knew Albany well. She found New-York too noisy, too large and boisterous. Here, after just a few days in Philadelphia with its rectangular street patterns and pleasant green parks in the city's center, she found its 40,000 citizens friendly and helpful. Dinner last night with Mr. Hamilton had been one of the most exciting evenings in her young life. He was ever so polite, but at the same time fascinating.

This morning she was only half listening as her father told of his plans for a canal from the Mohawk River to the large Lake Oneida in central New-York State. "And other mighty canals can link to Seneca Lake. Not just furs, gentlemen, but we have found great salt deposits in the area. Canal boats from the interior will carry it to Albany, then down the Hudson to New-York."

"But Philip, my good man, what of those horrid savages, what do you call them—Iroquois? Trading furs is one thing, but certainly they will not take kindly to canals pushing into their lands?" said Jedediah Fisher, president of Merchants Bank & Trust Co.

Eliza picked up on the banker's reference to the Six Nations. She recalled a young Indian girl she had met near the frontier village of Saratoga several years earlier. They had exchanged dolls. She was intrigued with how corn husks, stalks and cobs could be fashioned into a doll. "She learned to say my name. She had a pleasant voice and sweet smile. And she taught me some Seneca words," thought Eliza Schuyler. "What was her name? Wah something. Wah-say. Ah yes, Wah-say-lan. Tall, regal for a girl."

Deep in her thoughts, Eliza had not noticed the lone Indian astride the chestnut stallion right in front of her. As the figure sitting straight and proud gazed down from her mount, Eliza started. She gasped, "How could it be? No . . . "

Wah-say-lan's dark and shiny black braids ran to below her shoulders. Her wolf tooth necklace sparkled in the morning sun, accenting the open neck of her sleeveless buckskin blouse. She wore her quiver of arrows on her back.

It was just then that Gen. Schuyler reassured his new friend that canals could be built and reminded the banker that Gen. Sullivan had severely punished the Six Nations last year. "They will not be a big problem," Schuyler emphasized on the street corner. "As our settlements approach their country, they must from the scarcity of game, which our approach will induce, retire farther back. The Iroquois will dwindle comparatively to nothing, as all savages have done, who reside in the vicinity of civilized people, and leave us the country without the expense, trifling as it may be, to purchase."

Wah-say-lan had entered the city only minutes earlier. She had cautiously drawn her horse to a slow walk and stopped at the sight of Eliza. Though it had been 10 summers, she had recognized her immediately, and instinctively Wah-say-lan had moved to greet an old friend. But then she heard Gen. Schuyler confidently predict the disappearance of the "savages." The last time a soldier called her a savage, the soldier died, she said to herself.

She had approached Philadelphia with some trepidation. The country path she had been traveling widened. As she waded her horse across the shallow tributary flowing into the majestic Delaware, she could see the city. It was as if, she thought, a great hand had come down from the sky and pushed aside the forest and instead set down great unnatural blocks side by side in straight rows.

Just past the river, a few Delaware Indians were walking her way: A couple of old men, two mothers with children and a young man carrying a jug and sipping from it. He stumbled as he walked and Wah-say-lan knew he was drinking the white man's fire water.

"Be careful in this town," one of the old men said to her. "There are many who say they love the Indian. But they do not. They take furs and give us their whiskey. The whiskey does not make our braves strong, it gives our braves false and foolish courage."

The stumbling man had sad eyes. A woman wrapped her arm around him and tried to steady his gait. Wah-say-lan nodded to the group, but said nothing.

"Are you Susquehanna?" asked the old man in his own language.

"I am not. I am Seneca," she said in her tongue.

"Seneca? Here? Be careful in this white man's town. You do not want to say you are Seneca. They speak of fighting your people and destroying your towns."

"Their soldiers did not defeat us. They left. We rebuilt our towns," she said. "But I thank you for your warning. How many whites live here?"

"We thought the Delaware people were many," he said. "We are few. There are many, many white people here. Their homes are huge, made of flat red stones all the same size, or of timbers cut from all the trees of the forests. Their paths are wide for their wagons on wheels. There are many white people everywhere in their city."

She thanked them again and soon found herself riding her horse on a wide street with two- and three-story buildings stretching as far as she could see. It unnerved her. She saw sidewalks and wondered why the white man must put down flat stone for a path. Women in long dresses and black boots hurried along the stones. Wagons were passing noisily back and forth on the street so that Wah-say-lan had to move out of the way. Their large wheels creaked, the men on these wagons shouted. Others crowded around piles of pumpkins and pears, waving their arms and talking over each other's words.

It wasn't just all these monstrous structures that dwarfed the elm bark longhouses of Canandaigua; it was all the people, white people, everywhere she looked. More than she had ever seen, going in and out of these buildings, standing and talking loudly in groups. The cacophony assaulted her ears. It was overwhelming, and she wondered why she had thought she had to see their villages. But village is the wrong word. This is nothing like Seneca villages built into the forest, with the gardens and orchards blending with the earth. The white man is separate from all around him. He pushes all away and all is changed into, into what? These large structures with no fields, few trees. Wide dirt paths next to small paths with stones.

Even the sun is angry with this, she thought. It shines, but its light bounces off these buildings and hurts her eyes. It is like the sun is saying that it is captured and there is no purpose in shining on this village. Nothing grows. The sunlight itself is trying to escape, and Wah-say-lan was ready to bolt from this place too. A little to the south she saw a red building with a white domed tower rising above the few trees around it. She was horrified. But she rode on slowly. As she looked up at a second-story window, she could not have known that five years earlier Thomas Jefferson had sat in that room writing the Declaration of Independence, writing that King George had incited the merciless savages against the Americans.

Then she came upon Eliza Schuyler and, in a strange way, it settled Wah-say-lan's mind. Here was someone familiar. She smiled, instantly remembering the young Eliza and their trading of dolls when they met as young girls. These easy thoughts came quickly, then just as swiftly disappeared as Schuyler boasted of vanquished "savages."

That pathetic group of Delaware she had met at the edge of the city flashed in her mind. "Be careful," the old man had warned.

She dismounted. She slowly removed her quiver of arrows and secured it to her pack. She turned to the young white woman who was standing with her right hand to her mouth. Wah-say-lan stood a head taller. She spoke softly and said, in English, "Greetings, Eliza Schuyler."

Philip Schuyler saw the men gaping in wonder. He turned and said, "What? Who are you? Did she greet you, my dear?"

"Father, yes. Um this is . . . Father, wait." Eliza was in a rare moment of utter confusion, trying to return a greeting from what seemed to her a vision emerging from her own thoughts and at the same time explain to her father who was before them.

"Wah-say-lan, I was just thinking of you and . . . Father, this is Wah-say-lan from Saratoga. Do you remember, Father? You introduced me to her long ago at the Six Nations conference. She is of the Seneca Nation," she said.

Wah-say-lan stood motionless at the mention of her people. Her hand touched the handle of her father's large knife, always in her belt.

"A Seneca Indian? What is she doing here?" asked one of the Philadelphians. "Are there others with her?" The man could not take his eyes off the beautiful Wah-say-lan. "Philip, she is, uh, uh, a savage?"

"Mr. Wilson, please watch your words," Eliza spoke up. Still startled by Wah-say-lan's sudden appearance, she calmed herself and took a bold step forward, holding out her hand. Looking up to Wah-say-lan, she said, "I remember our days together. I did not think we would ever meet again. I am happy to see you."

Wah-say-lan took Eliza's hand in hers. "Eliza Schuyler, I remember our time together."

Almost protectively, the general moved closer to his daughter. "I say, you are a long way from your people. And you are alone?" he said.

Wah-say-lan looked the general in the eye. She responded calmly. "I am on a journey. I travel alone."

"A Seneca Indian woman traveling alone. I have never heard of such a thing. What is the purpose of your journey?" the general insisted.

"It is my journey for my purpose," she said.

Eliza saw no good coming from this knot of men and her father's bravado. She turned to him and told him she was taking her old friend to the park. "Father, we will sit in the pavilion and we will talk. Then we will join you for lunch on the hotel porch at noontime," Eliza said.

"But Elizabeth . . . "

"Father, you need to conclude your business with these gentlemen." She took Wah-say-lan by the hand. "Please come with me."

Wah-say-lan stood still. She looked at the pretty young white woman. She looked at the group of men, Schuyler in Continental Army uniform, the others staring at her.

Eliza started to worry. "Please, Wah-say-lan. I have much to tell you." Still holding hands, she started walking down the street.

Wah-say-lan held firm. "Eliza Schuyler, I will speak to your father." She looked right at him and said, "I am on my journey and I will take my horse and go with your daughter and I will listen to what she has to say. My father, Lan-lu-rah, took me to Saratoga as a child, where I met your daughter and you met my father and his friend Pundatha."

The general did not remember the two men, but decided not to say so. He said, "The good Cornplanter came with the western Seneca. Lan-lu-rah and Pundatha and many others came with Cornplanter and we talked in friendship at the council fire. It was a good talk. Now, many years later, the daughters will talk in friendship. My daughter wishes to speak with you and I know where you will be."

He addressed his daughter: "Eliza, the pavilion, no farther. Be at the hotel at noon."

Wah-say-lan looked at the uniformed general and knew they

were not friends. But she had talked enough with this man. As Eliza said, "Yes father," Wah-say-lan led her horse down the street.

Eliza Schuyler was a little dizzy. She steadied herself and caught up. They walked side by side. Wah-say-lan wanted to look back to see if any men followed, but she kept walking ahead. She thought of the young Delaware man staggering with a jug. She walked straight and with purpose.

"What is this pavilion you speak of?" she asked Eliza.

◈ CHAPTER 49 ◈

The Park

Eliza Schuyler actually had goose bumps. She was walking down Market Street in Philadelphia with a Seneca Indian, the fierce enemies of the insurrection. The little girl she met years ago is a big, strong woman with, Eliza couldn't help but notice, a large knife in her belt. She was unsure what her father might have done, had she not gotten Wah-say-lan out of that bevy of men. Had she been a man, a Seneca brave, the militia would have captured and imprisoned him. Yet here was a woman with a knife and a bow and arrows. Eliza was fascinated. Curious by nature, she could hardly believe that Wah-say-lan had arrived apparently out of nowhere. And, why, why did the two reunite here and now? There were things she needed to find out.

Wah-say-lan was worried but somehow remained, if not confident, then secure in knowing she at least was leading a fast horse. She was here out of curiosity, not to renew old acquaintances. Still, she was intrigued that in the midst of a teeming city of white people she had run into a girl from her childhood. Aside from that puzzling happenstance, the young Seneca's curiosity about the white man's village was met. What she wanted to do was get out of the stifling place. But what coincidence of time had put her together again with this child now a woman? Wah-say-lan wondered.

"This is the park, Wah-say-lan. Isn't it pretty with the pines and the maple trees and the green grass, here in the middle of the city?" she said.

Wah-say-lan looked around at the bustling streets and then back at the expanse of greenery. The park is pretty, she agreed, but it is surrounded by ugly buildings, some of them higher than the trees.

"The white man has it backwards," she said. "People should build places to live among the trees, surrounded by trees, not the other way around. Why do you do this, Eliza Schuyler?"

Eliza laughed, then stopped at seeing Wah-say-lan's furrowed brow. She looked into Wah-say-lan's deep brown eyes. She picked her words carefully. "A park to me is a peaceful place. But oh, Wah-say-lan, it is of no matter. I am trying to understand why you and I are here, right now. We left each other as young girls with dolls and now here we are again as grown women. Come sit down with me."

Wah-say-lan tethered the horse to the pavilion, walked under the roof with Eliza and sat on a bench looking out on a couple of acres of open space. Several large tree stumps dotted the land.

"Do you remember your chief gave me a Seneca name? He came to us when we were playing. He called your father over and said to him in English, 'Look at Wah-say-lan, how she is good with this girl. We will give this girl a Seneca name.' They called me Un-da-gaa'o. They said it means 'one of us.' Your father liked me, Wah-say-lan. Your chief gave me an Indian name."

"Eliza Schuyler, I remember they named you Un-da-gaa'o. I did not think you were one of us, but I was happy for you and I was glad my father and chief Pundatha noticed you then.

"I do not know why you and I are here in this place. The red-tailed hawk helps show me the way. She flew in the sky a few days ago. She helped guide me on my journey to see the white man's village. She did not tell me of you. You are a surprise. I have never seen where you whites live together. When we were young, we did not meet in your village. Now I am ready to go back to my people, our longhouses on the lake, our Chosen Place of Canandaigua. But

I met you again and maybe it would be good to know you again. You are a long way from your home on the great river. I see you travel with your father."

"Wah-say-lan, I rarely travel with my father, but he decided to bring me here. Did you travel with your father?"

"I was traveling with my husband, but he stayed where we had gone. He will join me later. My father died fighting continental soldiers. Was your father with this Gen. Sullivan whose army attacked my village and killed my friends and my father? Your father is an American soldier, a leader, a chief, I see. Did he fight with Sullivan against the Haudenosaunee?" asked Wah-say-lan.

"Wah-say-lan, there is a war for our freedom and independence. My father hoped the Six Nations would join us against the British. My father was on another mission when Gen. Sullivan was sent west. The Mohawk chief Joseph Brant led the Iroquois to kill and capture white settlers, burn their homes."

"Sullivan burned my home after his men killed my father, Lan-lu-rah. I killed the soldier who killed my father. I slit his throat with this knife, my father's knife." Wah-say-lan lifted the knife from her belt.

Though these were hard and divisive subjects, the two women had no trouble at all conversing even as it unnerved Eliza to hear that Wah-say-lan had slit someone's throat. She looked at the knife in her hand. She said softly, "I am sorry, Wah-say-lan. I am sorry for your home and for your father." She touched the taller woman on her forearm. She reached up and touched her shoulder and held her hand there.

Wah-say-lan put the knife back in her belt. She took Eliza's hand from her shoulder. She squeezed it and placed it in Eliza's lap and said, "I heard your father tell those men that the 'savages will dwindle.' Am I a savage, Eliza? He says 'dwindle to nothing.' Does he mean I will not have children, a family? Am I nothing, Eliza?"

The daughter of Philip Schuyler, the most powerful white man in New-York State, did not know what to say.

"You say you fight for your freedom. You fight your brothers the

British. It is a white man's war. I have had enough of the British. I have had enough of Blue Coats fighting the British and attacking my people. I do not know why you war with each other.

"The Haudenosaunee, our people of the longhouse, our Six Nations, have lived in peace together since before memory. We defeated other nations and became powerful so that we can stay at peace. Before my time we fought the white man who speaks the French tongue, and now we fight more white men. On my journey I met a Frenchman, he led many soldiers and now fights with the Blue Coats. On my journey I met this Thomas Jefferson who talked of freedom. I could have killed both of these men. Instead, I have a gift from this Jefferson and I lay at night with this Lafayette as if we were of the same people in friendship.

"My people, since the time of Hiawatha and the Peacemaker, we have lived in peace together—five nations, then six into one. Now your father speaks of my people being nothing, dwindling to nothing. There are many whites, Eliza, but my people know the land and have protected the land and we are strong. I think Thomas Jefferson and this Lafayette do not feel I am nothing."

Eliza was fascinated, stunned, confused. What does she mean she met Jefferson and lay with the Marquis de Lafayette?

"You have a gift from Gov. Jefferson?" She asked.

Wah-say-lan went to the pack on her horse, pulled out the spyglass and handed it to Eliza. She held it in wonder, the fine gold piece with the inscription, "Thomas Jefferson."

"Wah-say-lan, Thomas Jefferson honors you greatly with this gift. You must tell me about being with him," said Eliza. "But let me say I listen to you with great interest. I like being with you. I know you were my friend and I want always to be your friend. I do not know why your chiefs fight on the side of the British. We fight our 'brothers,' as you say, because they have treated us unfairly, badly.

"My father's father came to America from another land so his family could have a better life. And now three generations later I sit here with you and I wonder if you and I can be friends, if you and I can meet seemingly by chance after so many years and remember our friendship and keep it, then I hope we will always be friends.

"Wah-say-lan, here is your spyglass. Keep it always . . . Wah-say-lan, I want to know how you met Gov. Jefferson. Did you go to Virginia? But um, Wah-say-lan, with Lafayette, you, um, met him too?"

"At my campfire, Eliza. He came to me. He wanted to talk with me and soon he wanted to lie with me. He spilled his seed on me. It was strange. The next morning he led his troops, many troops, past where we lay. I hid in the rocks and trees. I had my arrow aimed at his heart, but I remember my husband telling me to be careful. So Lafayette still lives."

"And so do you live, Wah-say-lan. And I am so glad," said the young New-Yorker, who was brought up properly and could hardly believe what she was hearing. At the same time, she knew the Seneca woman was speaking honestly. Eliza Schuyler was simply in awe. She could have sat there all day listening. She wanted to know everything. How did she meet Thomas Jefferson? Who and where is her husband? And Eliza could not help but wonder, if Wah-say-lan has a husband, why she lies with another man. Is Wah-say-lan a savage? was the thought that entered Eliza Schuyler's mind, but was abruptly interrupted when a platoon of militia marched two abreast into the park.

Wah-say-lan jumped up and quickly untethered her horse.

"Do not worry, they drill here all the time," said Eliza, but a lieutenant was leading the men toward the two women.

"Where I met you on the wide path, does it lead out of this village?" said Wah-say-lan.

"Yes it does, but Wah-say-lan, you are with me. No harm . . ."

"Mornin', Miss Schuyler. We're here to escort you and your friend . . ."

Wah-say-lan vaulted onto the horse. The lieutenant lunged at her, but horse and rider were already at a gallop to the street.

"No, don't shoot!" yelled Eliza as soldiers raised their muskets.

She ran against the nearest man and shoved him as he got a shot off. More shots were fired as Wah-say-lan raced down Market Street. Suddenly she stopped, grabbed an arrow and her bow, turned and trotted back to the edge of the park. She quickly aimed and an arrow flew past the officer into an upright of the pavilion.

She shouted in Seneca, "We are keepers of our land. We will not dwindle. Un-da-gaa'o, you are good, but I fear you are really not Un-da-gaa'o."

The militia ran at the Indian. She pulled another arrow. It flew into the leg of the closest soldier, who collapsed writhing on the ground. Another fired back and Wah-say-lan felt a burning in her left forearm. The musket ball scorched her skin, a near miss.

"Be careful," she heard the voice of Jamwesaw. She turned her horse and raced down the street, past wagons laden with wheat, past a church with its bell ringing, past store fronts with windows reflecting the sun. She sped and soon there were fewer buildings. She saw the river and a wooden bridge. There she stopped and looked back. No one was following.

Eliza was running back up Market Street toward the hotel and her father. Tears flowed down her cheeks. Wah-say-lan imagined Eliza sitting with the lieutenant. She nudged her horse, crossed the bridge and trotted north as the road narrowed.

◈ CHAPTER 50 ◈

Homeward

She followed the sun all that afternoon, heading north and west. She needed to find the warriors' trail. She needed the familiarity of Indian country. She felt dirty and needed to swim, but she pushed on because she wanted to put that city behind her, far behind her. At dusk, she thought she heard the rapids of a river, the Susquehanna she was sure, and then she would know she was back on her path home.

At least she was in forestland with the tree limbs reaching up and inviting sunlight. She breathed in the scents of wildflowers and pinecones on a gentle breeze. As the sun fell from sight but still lit the sky, Wah-say-lan came upon a clearing and saw the first evening star high above the trees. At a small brook she knelt and splashed water on her face and her arms. The clear water cleansed her flesh wound, but blood still oozed. She remembered the pouch of ground witch hazel Mary Angel had given her. She found it and pinched some into her palm. She dipped the fingers of her other hand into the stream and let a few drops of water mix with it. She poked the concoction around her palm to the right consistency, then applied the salve to where the musket ball had sliced her skin. It felt cool and Wah-say-lan knew Mary's medicine would heal the wound. She sat for several minutes pressing the poultice on her arm.

She filled her water pouch and gathered wood for a fire. A handful of pine needles caught the flint spark. She sat on her blanket and chewed venison strips. Soon she lay down and pulled the blanket around her. She fingered her necklace. The smooth, sharp wolf teeth made her feel safe. As the moon rose, an exhausted young Seneca woman, alone in the wildness of the forest, the kind of place she knew intimately, fell easily into a deep sleep.

Her dreams were easy, happy dreams of her childhood on Canandaigua Lake. She and her cousin Tun-weh played on the gray shale shores. They climbed up gullies together, found blueberries to munch on hikes that would last whole afternoons. And often the boys would appear, carrying long sticks they pretended were spears. And they pretended they were chasing bears when Wah-say-lan knew they were following her and her cousin.

The dream shifted to high above the lake with her husband, Bare Hill in the distance, she on her back and he holding her breast and licking her nipple, kissing her mouth. Wah-say-lan stirred in her sleep as she dreamt of Jamwesaw taking her as she gazed into the blue sky.

In the morning star time, before dawn, she awoke, refreshed. She sat up and smiled to herself, "My husband is a good lover." She wondered where he was, exactly, with the British Army. "He is also a good and brave fighter. He will help those British put an end to this war. And then he will come back to me at our Chosen Place, at our home on our lake," she thought.

The Marquis de Lafayette jumped into her mind's eye, she beneath him, accepting him. "Why did I not shoot my arrow into his heart? Ah! This is too much to think of right now." She listened in the early morning air. She could hear the rush of a river. "Yes, that must be the Susquehanna and I will be back on our warriors' trail." Wah-say-lan jumped up, wrapped her blanket into her pack and led the horse north and west. As the sun rose, she saw a bend in the river and white water rushing down a slope and falling into the pool of the oxbow. She hurried to the water, disrobed and waded into the cool current. As she went deeper, she dove in. She stretched her fingers, her arms, pointed her toes and kicked her legs wide. She wanted to have her body receive the gift of the river's freshness. She ducked under, then stood and loosed her braided hair. She threw her head back, tossing her long dark hair into the air. Then she dove again and felt the water swirl through it. She opened her eyes so the water could flush the dirt and dust of her travels. She relieved herself and let the river carry away what her body gives back to nature. She eased out to the middle, found the pace of the river's pull and then drew her arms and legs and feet against it in long steady strokes in the way she had swum since she was a small child.

As she reached a large boulder, the current hurrying around its grooved sides, she went limp and let her body float. She turned over on her back and stared into the morning sky. Then she flipped over and stroked back upstream. She did this many times, feeling her muscles strengthen, her whole body melding into the rhythms of the river. She felt so much a part of all around her, under her and above. Wah-say-lan was familiar with this sensation and loved pushing thoughts from her mind and simply being conscious of water, sunshine, tree lines, rocks, the air she breathed. She saw the fish in the water with her, saw in her mind's eye the deer, the raccoon, the bear, the panthers and wolves of the forest. She was one with it all. She was on her back, stroking her long arms through the current, gazing skyward as a red-tailed hawk soared above. She watched it float on the wind as she floated on the water. She watched the regal bird pump its wings twice and climb higher and soar again. She called to it joyfully and she called again, "Akee, Akee!" she called. The bird dipped. It dove like a streak, sailed along the treetops and alighted on a branch. Wah-say-lan sank her feet to the pebbly bottom. She stood in the river and said loudly in her native tongue, "Oh hawk, what message do you bring?" Aside from the rush of the water, her voice was the only sound. Then the great bird screeched, leaped from the tree and dove at the river. It swooped low, hung its great talons and touched the water's surface. It pumped its wings, pulled a fat fish from the river and flew north out of sight.

The young Seneca woman waded to the shore. She sat on a boulder and let the sun dry her skin. In the pool below, a deep notch in the shoreline, she saw a shadow move in. She dashed to her horse, pulled out her bow, readied an arrow and crept, naked, back to the big rock. She waited. She peered over the rock, the shadow moved again. She waited some more, hoping the fish would surface. Then the water swirled and she saw the concentric circles spread out. The fish's back broke the surface again. If things were right, just ahead of the swirl, she thought. She pulled the arrow back and let it fly. Instantly a large splash and another. She sprang to the river and grabbed the shaft, pulling a fine, large trout from the water.

"Ban-er-man-jah could not have done better," she said to herself. As her horse grazed and lapped at the water's edge, Wah-say-lan enjoyed her breakfast, toasted perfectly over her open fire. She thought of Tun-weh and Ban-er-man-jah while she ate the pink meat, the gift of the river. Wah-say-lan thanked the river's spirit and she thanked the fish for her sustenance. She dressed, braided her hair and walked north, leading her horse and following the river.

◈ CHAPTER 51 ◈

Haudenosaunee Country

Wah-say-lan walked the whole day and slept restfully again on her folded-over blanket near the embers of her campfire. The next morning she reached the place where the Chemung, flowing from the west, joins the Susquehanna meandering down from the northeast. It seemed a long time ago that she and Jamwesaw had stood at the confluence of the two rivers. It is as if time greets itself where rivers meet.

They arrived here together on their trek south, but to Wah-say-lan at this moment, it was she who came down the Chemung from Seneca country and Jamwesaw who came down the Susquehanna out of nowhere, out of Connecticut, out of slavery, to be her husband. The confluence of their lives was like the meeting of these two rivers, separate but destined to meet and be bound together, two into one. She thought of the two streams that, once joined, were much more powerful. Gurgling, plunging, moving water from two directions forging a bigger force. One river carrying two and heading south just as the Seneca had done for centuries.

She shivered and wished Jamwesaw was with her. She wanted to hold him as she did here before and to feel his body press perfectly against hers. "But he is not with me. He is fighting with the British. He is in Virginia to protect his mother. I do not deny him the chance to be with her. He searched half his life, but in the search he found me. Now he stays and tells me to be careful traveling alone. It was his choice, not mine."

"And so I went alone. I do not need to hear him say be careful. I do not need to be careful. What would he have done when Lafayette stopped at my campfire? What would he have done in Philadelphia? He would not have gone to Philadelphia. I would have missed Eliza Schuyler. I would not have lain with the Frenchman. The Frenchman will never forget lying with me. And I am glad I was not careful with him that night. The oaf spilled his seed, but it was a good night.

"Eliza is not Un-da-gaa'o, but she is good. She is truthful. Did she not shove that soldier? Perhaps she saved my life? She moved instinctively and I was only grazed in my arm. I held my arrow at Lafayette's heart. I could have sent that arrow just as I could have slain Thomas Jefferson. Why did I not? Why did I not slay the Frenchman? I talked with that Jefferson. It was a good talk. I lay with that Lafayette. That, too, was good."

"It is good that I am traveling alone. It is good to find your own way, to listen to your messengers in the sky, to have your totem protect you in bad dreams."

As she stood where the Chemung met the Susquehanna, she wondered how many Seneca braves had stood at this spot, going back far beyond memory. Wah-say-lan looked for a flat rock, like the shale on her beach at the lake. But there were none. She picked up a stone, rounded and smooth, and threw it into the current. It splashed and sent out its circular wake, which soon vanished in the river's current. On her lake, she could watch the circles spread over the surface. On the Susquehanna, circles on the surface disappeared into the flowing water. Wah-say-lan was traveling the other way.

"Many Seneca braves did this, came by this place in all of my 18 summers and in all of the summers before that. Not many Seneca women have. Maybe I am the only Seneca woman who has walked this trail alone. I hope Pundatha will listen to my stories. I hope he will have me speak to our people of my travels. I want him to know I captured Thomas Jefferson and I can show him the eyeglass."

She decided to take it out and look at it. She remembered how it helped her find the old road—just a scratch in the tree line until the glass showed it might be an inviting spot—where she met Lafayette. She put the small telescope to her eye and looked up the Chemung river valley. "How does the white man make such things?" she found herself asking. "We do not need such things, but it is useful."

Wah-say-lan laid it back in her bag and for some reason reached down for her father's knife. It was almost a part of her. She had used it in many ways, to slay enemies, to slice food. She had sat and sharpened its blade. But as she held it she examined it closely. The handle was a thick piece of buck's antler. The blade was of thick, lethal metal. She sat down and felt the cool iron blade and said to herself, really for the first time, "This is not Iroquois. This is a white man's weapon. Where did my father get this? . . . I know he told me once . . ."

The thought unsettled her, but she reached back further in her mind. "That is it. After I met Eliza and we traded dolls. I showed my father as I sat in front of him in the canoe on the Mohawks' river. I showed him her doll and told him I gave her mine. He set down his paddle and let the canoe drift. He pulled out his knife from his belt. 'My father, too, made a trade with the white man, my little Wah-say-lan. My father, your grandfather, gave many beaver pelts to this Schuyler's father. And in return he received this knife.' "

Wah-say-lan amazed herself that she had forgotten all about that. Her knife, her father's knife that she grabbed from the longhouse the day of the battle, belonged to a Schuyler. "It is a white man's knife. A Schuyler knife, Schuyler who said we will dwindle to nothing. It is a good weapon. Just like Jefferson's glass is good for seeing. How does the white man make such things?" she asked. Her mind was racing. Her thoughts jumbled. "But the Iroquois Confederacy is strong. Pundatha and Cornplanter are out with warriors avenging the deaths brought by Sullivan's army. And Sullivan's army brought me my husband," she thought. She breathed deeply. She smoothed the stirrings in her mind. She concentrated. She stared at the weapon. "I have killed white men with this knife," she said to herself and put it back in its sheath in her belt, her snakeskin belt. She ran her fingers along the belt. "The white man could not make a belt like this. The white man does not even know how to trap the beaver for furs."

She let her mind wander back to being the only Iroquois woman to travel the warriors' trail. "I am Wah-say-lan. I know my way," she said, taking the reins and hopping on her horse's back. She nudged him into a trot, heading home. She was now anxious to see her mother and Tun-weh. She wanted to swim to her island and lie naked on the beach as the sun warmed her body. It would not be long now and she would be in the high hills above her lake. She would look down on the shining jewel, Canandaigua Lake, birthplace of the Seneca Nation.

As she trotted along the large expanse of meadow heading northwest, she saw over to the northeast smoke on the horizon, more than a village's campfires, much more.

◈ CHAPTER 52 ◈

Revenge

Reluctantly, Wah-say-lan swung her horse away from home. The tug to return to her people was strong, but her curiosity propelled her toward the rising gray smoke against the cloudless blue sky. "Is this the work of more continentals?" she thought, and pulled an arrow into her bow.

After Jamwesaw and Wah-say-lan had left the village last spring and headed south, Pundatha took his warriors and joined Cornplanter, Joseph Brant and British Maj. John Butler with 200 Rangers from Fort Niagara. Nearly 800 Iroquois braves—Mohawk, Cayuga, Onondaga and Seneca—were poised for attack. After the long, hard winter they sought revenge for Sullivan's wake of destruction the previous fall. His army was gone. The people of the longhouse headed out with their British allies to strike back. Their target was any patriot town or homestead encroaching into Iroquois territory. If Washington had sent an army to subdue the savages, it had burned villages, destroyed crops, brought near starvation for many through the terrible snows, but it had failed. The Iroquois were not defeated. They struck everywhere, burned homes and barns, stole cattle, sent white families fleeing eastward as fast as they could.

As she made her way through the woods, Wah-say-lan searched her memory for what village was here, Tuscarora? Oneida? She wondered. Or one of the white man's settlements? She rode up a hillside studded with hemlocks and birch. At the top she could see a small stream and what she knew were deer paths, barely perceptible, leading into the woods beyond. They were close enough to smell the smoke. The stallion was getting nervous. She let him stop and drink at the stream, then led him along.

She heard voices but could not make out the words. Wah-say-lan left the horse, readied an arrow in the bow and ran ahead. She saw about a dozen figures and knew immediately it was a Seneca brave in the lead. He turned and she heard him shout sternly in English, "If you do not keep up, your scalp is as valuable as you are back at Fort Niagara!"

An old man was stumbling and crying. A brave said, "Dah-gay-a-doh, this Yankee is too much trouble." The brave took his hatchet and, with one swing to his forehead, the man slumped to the ground. "No! No!" a woman cried as the brave took his scalp. Wah-say-lan had yet to take a scalp, which she knew was a human sacrifice, a substitute for a relative killed in battle. She and Jamwesaw could have taken scalps when they killed the soldiers with the wagon and the cannon. "I have not seen the need to scalp someone," she mused. "I kill my enemy, I avenged my father's death. Maybe I will take a scalp, we shall see."

The small party kept marching, Indians prodding two weeping white women, several children and, oddly, thought Wah-say-lan, a young Mohawk woman being led by a Seneca brave.

"I know you, Dah-gay-a-doh," Wah-say-lan said in her language as she stepped forward. "My chief fights with Cornplanter, your uncle."

The startled young brave hunched instinctively and raised his hatchet.

"Save us! Save us!" hollered one of the captive women. Wah-say-lan ignored her and raised her left hand to Dah-gay-a-doh. "You are Wolf Clan, as am I. My chief Pundatha and Cornplanter have known each other many summers. When you were younger, you danced with me at the harvest festival at Onondaga."

The young brave smiled. He turned to two braves and told them to watch the group. He walked to the young Seneca woman and said, "I do not forget, Wah-say-lan. Even when you were young, all the boys wanted to dance with Wah-say-lan." He grasped her hands. "I had heard you journeyed down the warriors' trail with your husband. And here you are, alone, and find me in the woods. You look well."

"What are you doing with these people?" she asked.

"There is a clearing ahead with a stream. We will sit and eat and we will talk," he said.

After finding her horse, Wah-say-lan joined the group. A fire had already been started. A young brave was placing strips of red meat on a spit above the flames. It sizzled and filled the air with a dusky, delicious aroma.

"It is good. The meat of a cow we killed at their homes," said Dah-gay-a-doh, pointing at his cowering captives. Three young girls in long skirts huddled with the two women. Two boys of about 10 years sat silently and stared at the ground. "Many, many warriors are with Cornplanter, and with your chief of the Canandaigua Seneca, and Joseph Brant of the Mohawk, our brothers the Cayuga and even many Onondaga braves. They have been attacking the white man's towns. Washington sent an army against us, and now we fight back. These prisoners we keep and Cornplanter entrusted me to take them back. But tell me, Wah-say-lan, of your journey. Where is your husband? Here you are, alone, and you find me?"

"Dah-gay-a-doh, do they call you Blacksnake?"

"No, only an elder will call me that. I must earn that name."

"You will. But if you wish, I will call you Dah-gay-a-doh. My husband stays in the land of Virginia. He fights there with the great British Gen. Cornwallis. It is a long story. I will tell it at my village council fire and you are welcome to join us," she said. "But tell me of this woman, is she Mohawk?"

"Sarah, come here," he said.

The woman came over to them and sat down cross-legged. "Tell

Wah-say-lan of the Seneca Nation why you are here. Tell her of Philip Schuyler."

Wah-say-lan's heart jumped, but she suppressed any outward reaction. "Gen. Schuyler? The American general?" she asked.

"Yes, this Mohawk was his spy. It is said she would lie with Schuyler. She would tell him of our plans. She is our prisoner now. We take her to Fort Niagara. Her mother died in the winter. No one knows what happened to her father."

The woman looked hardly older than Wah-say-lan herself. But she slouched, her eyes cast down.

"I do not want to hear of this right now. I am hungry, Dah-gay-a-doh. Let us eat."

She took the Mohawk woman by her arm and sat her down with the other prisoners. Wah-say-lan took her chin and lifted her head. "We will talk later," she said, and went back to the young brave.

"Blacksna . . . I mean Dah-gay-a-doh, is Pundatha well? Are Deh-wan-guh and Ban-er-man-jah with him?"

"My uncle tells me Pundatha and his warriors fight bravely. I have not seen them. There are many braves spread all over our lands. This Washington, this Town Destroyer, is having his own towns destroyed. I know your Canandaigua people took many prisoners at Fort Schuyler. The general was not there. Perhaps this Mohawk woman warned him. But we must go now. It is many days to Niagara with these people."

"Dah-gay-a-doh, I will come with you for a day. I must return to my village, but I can help. I will take this Sarah on my horse. Your braves will not have to worry about her while I am with you," Wah-say-lan ventured.

The young brave thought a moment. "That will be good, Wah-say-lan, but stay close."

As they headed west through the forest, the Mohawk spy sat in front of Wah-say-lan on the horse. They at first rode in silence. Wah-say-lan sorted out her thoughts. She wanted to know more about the Schuylers.

"Sarah, your name is Sarah, right? Tell me of Philip Schuyler."

"I am Sarah. My mother was Mohawk, Maya-un-go-dah of the Wolf Clan. She married a white man. They named me Sarah. My father, John Steeple, worked in Gen. Schuyler's sawmill."

"I am Wolf Clan," said Wah-say-lan.

"I know. I saw your necklace. My mother had one, but she gave it to her sister," said Sarah.

"Is the saw mill near where the two great rivers meet?" asked Wah-say-lan.

"Yes, there. My father cut logs into lumber. It was put on ships and went down the great river the whites call Hudson to New-York."

"Why did you lie with this Schuyler?"

"You do not say no to Philip Schuyler."

"Is it good lying with a white man?" asked Wah-say-lan, letting her mind wind back to her campfire the night Lafayette arrived.

"My mother lay with a white man every night. My mother gave birth to me from my father's seed. My mother was proud of John Steeple."

Remembering that the French officer spilled his seed, Wah-say-lan felt relief. "The oaf," she thought. "He was good to lie with, but I am glad I did not take his seed. He is nothing like my Jamwesaw."

It was tight on the horse's back. It was odd listening to the woman talk but not seeing her face. In the Philadelphia pavilion she had sat face to face with a Schuyler.

"Tell me of Eliza Schuyler," said Wah-say-lan.

Sarah turned her head. "You know Eliza?" she asked, startled.

"Yes, I met her many summers ago at a council fire near where the two great rivers meet."

"Ah, it is you! You were the Seneca girl with the dolls. You and Eliza played with the dolls."

"Yes, we did. You were there too?"

"Yes, I saw you. I was too old for dolls. But I was envious. Eliza never paid me any attention. It does not matter. A few summers later her father paid attention to me."

Wah-say-lan found herself saying, "But you are not his wife. Your father stayed with his Indian woman."

"Gen. Schuyler fights Indians, but only because we have sided with the British. He has tried to persuade the Mohawk and the Seneca not to take up the hatchet. He has tried to tell us this is a fight between white men, the British and the Americans. He says the Americans will win and then the Six Nations will wish they had not fought with the British."

"I have heard this Philip Schuyler call us savages who will dwindle to nothing," said Wah-say-lan. "Do you lie with a man who thinks you are a savage?"

"He does not think I am a savage. No, I will not be his wife, but I might have his child. Then he will protect me. I have tried to tell my Mohawk brothers and sisters to bury the hatchet and give up this war. Instead I am taken prisoner and called a traitor."

Wah-say-lan stopped the horse and jumped to the ground. "Get down," she said to Sarah. "Look at me. I have seen this Schuyler tell other white men that he will build what he calls canals into our country. And he will put boats onto these canals into our country. And the canals will bring more whites and they will build more towns in our country. Do not tell me befriending Schuyler is wise for the Six Nations. Now Sarah, I must go. I hope you have many babies, many children, and that they grow up to be like your chief Joseph Brant. If Brant and Schuyler met, who do you think would win? I know who."

She called to Dah-gay-a-doh. "My brother, your path is different than mine. I must go this way. I must go to my village."

"I understand, Wah-say-lan. Thank you for your help. May Sky Woman guide your journey and the morning star greet you as you awake." He walked to her and fingered her necklace. "Whoever gave you this knows the strength of the Wolf Clan. Keep it with you, Wah-say-lan. I hope to hear the tales of your journey. I hope to see you at the harvest festival. Even in a war, the Six Nations need the harvest festival." He hugged her tightly.

Wah-say-lan let his grip wash over her. She held onto it even as she led her horse away. She did not like hearing Sarah talk of the Americans. She wanted to be alone before she got back to Canandaigua.

◈ CHAPTER 53 ◈

The Lake

Two days later, in the early afternoon, she stood high above Canandaigua Lake. Its calm blue water glittered in the sunlight. A mile wide, the lake stretched to the horizon, cupped by the green hills on either side and canopied by a blue sky with pure white clouds. Bare Hill, a lighter green of grass and shrubs where no trees grew, the legendary birthplace of her people, stood out above the eastern shore.

A tear surprised Wah-say-lan as it trickled from her eye. Her knees felt weak. She sat on the ground, and allowed more tears to come. Her vision blurred. Green and blue merged, water and hillside spilled into each other. She envisioned Philadelphia and saw it momentarily, its wide streets and wooden structures spread across her Bare Hill. She shouted, "No! No!" Her personal protest wafted out over the landscape. She wiped her tears off her cheeks and stood. She spread her arms and her hands to the sky and she hollered as loudly as she could, "This is Seneca land! Since before memory we have shared this land with the deer and the wolf, the bear, the panther, the fish, the trees, the eagles and the hawks! We are of this land, of this lake!"

"We have grown apple and cherry trees, we grow the three sisters of corn, beans and squash. We build our longhouses as we always have. This is our land. Do you hear me, Philip Schuyler, father of Eliza? Do you hear me, Marquis de Lafayette? Do you hear me, Thomas Jefferson? Pursuit of happiness. Pursuit of happiness. Your happiness is not our happiness.

"You do not know what happiness is. You do not know of silence. You do not know of living with the trees and the birds and the animals. You do not know of swimming to my island. My island. My island . . . " She whispered it again: "My island."

Wah-say-lan grabbed the reins of the horse and headed down the hill. When they reached the water they both drank deeply. The young Seneca woman bent down and cupped her hand, sweeping her lake's water to her mouth. How sweet it tasted, she thought. A few more mouthfuls and then she jumped on the stallion and jerked him into a quick trot along the beach. She raced north, urging the horse on faster. The lake stretched north to south for 18 miles and her island was near the north end.

She neither saw nor heard anyone. It was just she, the horse and her lake. She steered him along the water's edge, splashing as his hooves pounded the small waves lapping at the shale beach. Horse and rider jumped felled tree trunks with branches reaching into the depths, sped past lakeside cliffs cut with deep gullies where water spilled from the heights on its way to join the lake. She slowed her mount in a cove as she saw several deer where the shore curved into a long point jutting into the lake. The deer drank. Two fawns, their spots fading, jostled into the water. Wah-say-lan stopped and watched. One large buck stood knee deep in the water. "What a prize he would be," she thought.

A flock of ducks suddenly and noisily took to wing from the surface of the lake. The deer sprang back up the hill and into the woods, a doe nosing a fawn along. Wah-say-lan rode out to the edge of the point. All was quiet save for the waves reaching the shore in a whispered shushing. She looked south from where she had just come, and then north. She could see her island out in the middle of the lake a few miles ahead. She whooped aloud and kicked the horse into a run. The wind blew through her long black hair. She could feel her heart beating to the horse's gait. She felt one with the animal and bent low, kicking him again with her heels as they sped faster up the lake.

Once she was opposite her island, she stopped, slipped off the horse and decided to remove his halter and the packs. The horse was free, unburdened. Wah-say-lan stepped out of her moccasins and her deerskin pants. She lifted her shirt off and waded naked into Canandaigua Lake. She dove in, stretching her long body out fully. She stroked her arms, kicked her long legs and felt the cool water surround her. She dove and stroked and kicked down, twenty feet down, and opened her eyes to bottom grasses and a school of perch, the sunlight slanting into the water in bright golden streaks.

She stayed down longer and saw a large bass glide by, and then another. She surfaced, flipped over on her back, stroking her arms, and watched a white cloud go by. Wah-say-lan was not thinking. She was seeing and feeling and tasting. As she reached the island's shore she bent to find a smooth, round piece of shale perfect for skipping. She waited for her own wake to dissipate. When the water was calmed she tossed her piece of shale. It skipped several times across the surface. She watched the circles expand across the water.

Then she sat down. She stretched out. The beach was warm, the sun, nearing the end of the day, still sent its warmth. She lay there, shut her eyes and smiled. "I am home," she said to herself.

She basked. She let her mind go blank. Her body was part of all that was around her. After awhile she decided she'd spend the night here. She dove back into the water and swam to the shore. She found the trusty horse, stroked its head, its mane, and told it, "You have brought me back. We have come a long way, but here we are. Now we are going to sleep on my island." She hugged it around the neck, put the packs high on its back, the halter over its head and led it into the water. They swam easily together to the island. She led the horse ashore and took it to a grassy place. She gathered wood, struck a fire on the beach, ate some dried venison. She sat on her blanket watching the stars come out. Directly overhead were the bright lights of the Big Dipper, the seven brothers who slew the bear Nia'gwai'. She lay back down—still naked, one with nature—and let her eyes close.

She saw herself as a child in the village on the lakeshore. She thought back, as far back as her mind would take her, a naked girl, toddling at the water's edge. Is that me? she said to herself.

Lying under the stars, Wah-say-lan felt her hands rubbing her tummy. Her fingers reached down to the soft dark triangle of hair between her thighs. She thought of Jamwesaw and she thought of Lafayette, the two men who had taken her. She thought of how other men look at her, how she knows they want her. But she chooses. Her hand clamped between her legs and she held her mound tightly. "Why has not Jamwesaw given me a child?" she wondered. "Will we bring our baby into this world? Our world that the white man wants. And what if the father of my baby is black-skinned? What if he is French, white-skinned? What if I let a savage take me? Two savages mating to bring more savages here to fight back the white man. How many women of the Haudenosaunee will bring more Haudenosaunee into the world to grow to be warriors to protect our country? Why did I not let my arrow fly into the heart of the marquis? My Jamwesaw told me to be careful . . ." Her thoughts slowed and she fell asleep.

◈ CHAPTER 54 ◈

Home

The next day Wah-say-lan lingered on her island. She stared across the lake to the eastern shore where her village once was, the village where she grew up, the village that Sullivan's army destroyed. Then she looked westward, over the green hills to where Pundatha decided to build the new village. It was the village where Jamwesaw was accepted into her life, where they married. It was not to the longhouses that she always went for solitude. It was the island that she swam to each morning and where Jamwesaw saved her life as the vile corporal was about to rape her.

She walked to the hollow tree in the island's forest where she had hidden her bow and arrow. She trotted to the outcropping on the shore, dove in and came up in her secret cave where she and Jamwesaw hid as Seneca warriors searched for him, an escaped prisoner. She sat in the cool dampness watching the daylight filter down through the small opening in the great rocks. She could almost feel him sitting next to her. Since that day when he freed himself from the post he was tethered to, Wah-say-lan had been with him nearly every day and every night. Except now. Except for the time during her long trek north when he had told her to be careful.

"Is he being careful?" she wondered.

She stayed one more night on her island. She slept fitfully and dreamt of Philip Schuyler with other men in a large boat heading for its shore. She threw stones at them. In her dream she heard him say again that "the Iroquois will dwindle comparatively to nothing, as all savages have done, who reside in the vicinity of civilized people . . . " In her dream she searched for her bow while her stones landed harmlessly in the water. When they came ashore, Eliza Schuyler stepped out from behind her father to say, "My friend Wah-say-lan. Do not resist. We come to pay you for your island. I will build my home here and I hope you can come and visit."

"No!" Wah-say-lan shouted. She sat up wide awake and shaking as the embers of her campfire burned low and died out. The moon was low in the sky. The spires of the tallest hemlocks stood black against the moon glow, shadowy sentinels over the ancient Seneca homeland.

She gathered her belongings, found the horse and led him into the water. On the western shore she dressed, hopped on the stallion's back and walked him slowly inland as the first light of dawn awakened the birds. She rode slowly. She found the spot where she spent her first night with Jamwesaw after the battle. She remembered it was also the place where her parents brought her as a child and, encouraged by her father to go higher, she climbed to the top of the tall hemlock. She silently marveled that she and Jamwesaw, in their escape from the battle, would sleep together under the very same tree. She dismounted and walked to where she had lain for the first time with him. She sat down and touched the soft earth, the layer of pine needles. She smelled the sweet fragrance of a place in the forest where twice in her young life she saw and heard and felt things for the first time.

In the early afternoon Wah-say-lan rode into the village. Tunweh ran to her and hugged her tightly. "You are home. You are home," she said over and over.

Her mother, Wah-say-han, walked toward her. She held out her arms and Wah-say-lan ran to her. The returning daughter wrapped her long arms around her aging mother.

"I was thinking just this morning that you would be home soon. I was thinking that Mary's Wolf Clan necklace would guide you. I needed you home. I lost my husband, I could not stand losing my only child," Wah-say-han said to her daughter in calm, measured language. "And your husband, Wah-say-lan, is he with you?"

"My mother, I am glad to see you. I have missed you. Jamwesaw stayed. He found his mother and he is trying to convince her to come here . . ."

Everyone wanted to speak to her. Wah-say-lan turned to her mother: "I will tell you everything, my mother. I came back alone. It was a good journey. I am here. I am home."

Pundatha and the warriors were still out fighting, but the women prepared a good dinner that night to honor Wah-say-lan and hear of her travels. She told them of Jamwesaw finally finding his mother and of how they had captured Thomas Jefferson. She showed them all his spyglass and said, "I feel I will meet Thomas Jefferson again."

Tun-weh at first did not dare speak, but then asked, "You captured this rebel leader and you let him go free?"

Wah-say-lan was surprised at the question from her younger cousin. She paused, then said, "Yes, Tun-weh. We let him go. We were there to find Jamwesaw's mother. We had a long talk with this Jefferson. He told us where my husband's mother was. He gave me a gift of this spyglass. Jamwesaw said I must accept it. So I told Jefferson that our gift to him was his life."

Around the bright campfire many women nodded, and so Wah-say-lan continued her story. She thanked Mary Angel for her wolf tooth necklace and told her of her dream of the blue panther and how wolves had saved her from the panther's clutches. She told them that Jamwesaw led slaves from Monticello in Col. Tarleton's forces. She did not speak of her encounter with the Marquis de Lafayette. But she told them of meeting Eliza Schuyler, the girl from her childhood, and of her escape from Philadelphia. She said that north of the Susquehanna she had met Blacksnake and the others taking prisoners to Niagara. She spoke of how she was proud of

Seneca warriors for avenging her father's death. "The Seneca Nation remains undefeated," she said.

Wah-say-han rose and said, "My daughter, in all my long years I have never heard of a Seneca woman traveling the warriors' trail alone. Lan-lu-rah's spirit was with you, I am sure, but you journeyed alone, a brave Seneca woman." She called for her daughter's election to the women's council and later that night the women happily brought her to their council fire. Wah-say-lan sat next to her mother and said to her that her father's spirit was with her, but so was his knife, and it protected her from danger. "More than once, my mother, your husband's knife kept me from danger," she said.

As time passed and the fall harvest came, the people were thankful that Pundatha had led them to this valley where life went on. Wah-say-lan helped bring in the corn, beans and squash and she felt secure knowing there would be stores of food for the winter. She contented herself with the traditional women's work and did not go out hunting with Ban-er-man-jah and the other men of the village.

Wah-say-lan came home to the good news that Tun-weh had wed Ban-er-man-jah.

She and Tun-weh walked to the lake shore and netted fish together, bringing back supper for the many families of the Canandaigua Seneca. Tun-weh was with child, but still the two cousins swam to the island. "I hope it is a boy," she said. "My husband wants to show him how to hunt and how to fight."

"Ban-er-man-jah is a good man, Tun-weh, and I think more of him that he chose you to be his wife and the mother of his children. We must have more babies. The whites multiply and multiply and the Haudenosaunee must too," she told her cousin.

Part III

SURRENDER

◈ CHAPTER 55 ◈

Yorktown

Jamwesaw was not happy. He missed his wife. He was fighting on the side of Benedict Arnold, the traitor. Not that he and the slaves he "commanded" from Monticello were doing any fighting. They were digging trenches and making earthwork fortifications for Lord Cornwallis and his army of 8,000 men deployed to crush the rebellion in Virginia.

In the Continental Army the Connecticut slave Freeman Trentham had been a soldier, fighting not so much for independence but for his own personal freedom. Though he had switched sides in this war, like Arnold, Jamwesaw did not feel at all like a traitor. He had fallen in love with a beautiful woman and decided to be at her side. He had saved her life at the Battle of Canandaigua. She had changed his life forever.

But he wasn't at her side. Without Wah-say-lan, he was not sure he could have achieved his improbable life goal of finding his mother on this vast continent. Then, in the hardest decision of his young life, he let his wife go back home alone. He stayed so that somehow he could buy time and convince Betsy Trentham to escape from slavery, as he had, and live free with the powerful Iroquois Confederacy. He was giving her time, but he did not know how that would change his mother's mind.

He thought that by joining the British and helping to finish this business in Virginia of subduing the rebels, he could at least establish a farm for his mother and her sons, his little half brothers, but he held out hope of bringing them back to the beautiful lake. With Gov. Jefferson himself running for his life, Jamwesaw was confident of a British victory. Though the noble Tarleton had spared Monticello, Lord Cornwallis had burned Jefferson's Elkhill plantation to the ground, destroyed the corn and tobacco crops, carried off most of his slaves and virtually all of his livestock. Arnold had arrived by sea with 2,000 more British regulars. Cornwallis, fresh from victories in the Carolinas, had his armies swarming all over Virginia in what looked like another sure victory and the total defeat of the rebels in the South.

Jamwesaw had heard of a Frenchman named Lafayette commanding some one thousand American regulars and a few hundred militia. In fact, the one time he joined in the fray he was leaving Monticello with Tarleton's dragoons and marching along a creek in the rear guard. They were hit with a fusillade from behind. Several dragoons fell from their horses.

An officer ordered a rush against the ambush. As two dozen cavalry rode into the forest, Jamwesaw grabbed a wounded man's musket, hopped on a horse and joined the pursuit. It was a short skirmish, as they ran into more Blue Coats waiting on a ridge. Jamwesaw took aim at a continental officer on a brown steed. His shot missed and the man disappeared in the trees. He wondered if he had shot at this Frenchman he had heard of, the Marquis de Lafayette. The American light infantry vanished in the deep woods and the British continued on their way to occupy Richmond.

But that seemed a long time ago. Now the platoon of black men was kept busy with shovels, not weapons. The rousing words to the Monticello slaves of joining the fight with the King against the Americans who enslaved them were ringing hollow to Jamwesaw as he stood in a trench tossing dirt into piles for the defense of Cornwallis's army at a coastal place called Yorktown.

Why the renowned general had led his troops to this place, Jamwesaw could not understand. As he looked over the parapet he could see more and more American soldiers gathering daily. Word had spread that Washington himself had marched south with a French count named Rochambeau. As Jamwesaw dug and positioned rows of sharpened stakes pointing menacingly from the embankments, he wondered if the French and the Americans were like the Seneca and the Mohawk—joined together for friendship in peacetime and for strength in time of war.

The Seneca had joined with the Mohawk and the other nations of the Iroquois generations ago to form their Confederacy. And now they had joined with Great Britain, the most powerful nation on earth, as Jamwesaw had heard over and over in his lifetime. Could these rebels, joining with these French, breach the ramparts and overrun this huge British army? Jamwesaw asked himself. Bombardment from the rebel artillery was unceasing. Day and night the shells roared and fell while Jamwesaw and his Monticello slaves dug the trenches.

Col. Alexander Hamilton waited impatiently 600 yards away for the day he could lead an attack. "My Dearest Eliza," he wrote one evening, "Gen. Washington has just honored me with the command of a battalion being readied to breach these ramparts. My honorable friend the Marquis de Lafayette insists on a joint attack, French and American. I accede to his idea so long as we Americans can lead the way to glorious victory.

"The other night Ld. Cornwallis made a valiant attempt to save his army in a retreat by sea, but a ferocious storm descended from the heavens, making his escape impossible. Our siege, I know, has broken their spirit and a good strike at their outer breastworks will hasten their surrender. The time is soon. We will receive the British as prisoners and secure Virginia for our new country. Then, my dear, I will give my leave to my leader Gen. Washington and fly to be by your side.

"My good and dear Eliza, I think I could have you in my embrace within the month, as that is my fondest wish and desire.

"Your Most Beloved Serv't, Alexander Hamilton."

The young officer dispatched the letter with others heading north by courier and he thought that surely he and Lafayette will have accomplished their assigned missions long before his missive arrives in Albany. He could hardly wait to lead his men in the attack. "This is my moment," he said to himself. "This is where I will lead hundreds of soldiers bravely into the fray and serve my country with all my might. We rise up against Great Britain, against her most decorated general, and we will bring him to his knees!"

The next day a brigade of British regulars moved into the two outermost redoubts Jamwesaw and the slaves had just finished building. Officers deployed their men, bayonets fixed, along the fortifications defending Cornwallis at Yorktown. As night fell, the bombardment began anew and men hunkered down as the shells thudded and exploded all around.

Several consecutive shells fired into the air illuminated the sky, the signal for Hamilton. He raised his sword and led the charge, racing the 600 yards against the defenses. The Americans stormed to the left, the French to the right. They whooped and hollered as they ran, nearly overtaking the sappers sent to cut off the points of emplaced stakes, opening a breach.

Hamilton hopped on the shoulder of a kneeling soldier, sprang onto the parapet and led his men into the battle. A volley of shots from the defenders felled a few of the Americans, but they kept rushing in and overwhelmed the British. A few British officers rallied their men, but far more were retreating, running from the Americans' bayonets. Hamilton himself was surprised at how quickly he had taken the enemy. He saw a captain about to run his bayonet through a British officer with his hands in the air. "Stop!" hollered the American colonel. "We will take prisoners. We do not imitate barbarity."

"I thank you, sir, and I surrender my platoon to your mercy," the Englishman said.

Jamwesaw had already decided he was not surrendering. He told his men to fall back with the troops who were doing the same, moving deeper into the huge encampment.

He pulled Isaac, Big Joe, Samuel and the other Monticello slaves to the side and whispered in the dark, "This does not look right. If Cornwallis surrenders, we will be delivered to the slave masters. We need to get out of here and we need to leave tonight."

"But, Jamwesaw, what of the land, the farms the British promised us?" said one.

"The war is not done. But here it looks like this siege has beaten this army. If Cornwallis surrenders, the rebels will punish any black men who joined in the fight," said Jamwesaw. "We will fight again, but I think not here."

"But sah, they promised us freedom . . . "

"They can't give it to us if they don't have it to give," Jamwesaw whispered. "Come with me now, before the dawn. We will go through the woods, we will get back to Monticello and your families. Then we will go north and join my wife's people. We will fight these slaveholders with the powerful Indian nations. There you and your families will be free. If you stay, you will be slaves of the Americans again."

There was murmuring. One older man sat down and hung his head. His eyes welled with tears. "I cants go no more, Jamwesaw. You are young and strong. You knows whats you can do. You mens go wid him. Takes your wives, your younguns, and go north where I hears they don't have no plantations. Jamwesaw says live wid da Indians, his woman is a Indian. Jamwesaw says he knows how to gets up there, dat right Jamwesaw?"

His mind was racing. With a British victory in this war, he knew he could set his mother up on her own plot of ground. He could always find her and journey to see her. With a defeat, she and his young half brothers would remain Thomas Jefferson's slaves. Even as a Seneca, he would risk enslavement should he try to see them. He had to persuade her to come north.

"I am going to save my mother from life as a slave. We go to the first set of tents and grab muskets and shot and we leave now before the day breaks. Who is coming?"

Jamwesaw strutted off. Six men followed. The other Monticello slaves sat down. They did not know who he was, but they could hear Alexander Hamilton ordering men to send the captured British troops back to the American lines. They hunkered together in the dark as Jamwesaw led his men to where a wagon and three tents stood. Several muskets were stacked outside the closed tent flaps.

He whispered commands: "Quickly, each of you take a musket. I will find ammunition." He went to the wagon and found horns of powder. He grabbed two pouches of musket balls. Young Samuel handed him a musket. The seven of them ran for the woods.

The next day, Lord Cornwallis surrendered to the strains of "The World Turned Upside Down." Washington ordered Virginia militia to capture fleeing slaves.

◈ CHAPTER 56 ◈

A Messenger

It was Red Jacket, Sagoyewatha, who arrived with the news that the British had surrendered in Virginia and there was talk of peace. Wah-say-lan had grown up knowing Red Jacket from afar. He could travel swiftly through the forest. When he was young, a British officer gave him a jacket for being a good messenger. When he began to wear the jacket all the time, Wah-say-lan would have little to do with him. And now he announces that his British friends are surrendering to the Americans.

Pundatha wanted to hear from Cornplanter and dispatched Red Jacket and a few others to find the Seneca war chief. He sent others to find Joseph Brant of the Mohawk.

Wah-say-lan was filled with worry for her husband. The British, she thought, had been so confident of victory when they were happily eating lunch on Jefferson's porch. They had promised freedom to any slaves who joined them. Her husband had marched off and now he was part of a surrendering army. "I know Jamwesaw will find a way out of there and return to me," she told herself.

Days later, Red Jacket returned with Cornplanter. He addressed the village council. All the people gathered around to hear him tell that the King of England had made peace with the Americans. "He keeps Canada north of the great lakes, but the British say the

American colonies are free and independent. The Americans, Gen. Washington who sent his army against our people, have buried the hatchet with the British and now they will make a treaty with the Six Nations," said Cornplanter.

"We will travel to Fort Schuyler, near our brothers the Oneida, and we will make a treaty with the Americans."

"The Oneidas were once our brothers," said Pundatha, "but they took up the hatchet with the Americans. They fought their brothers the Mohawk, the Cayuga, the Onondaga and the Seneca."

"I know, my friend. It is the only time since before memory that the Six Nations have been divided. Now we must reunite," said Cornplanter. "We will make peace remembering that we did not lose. The Americans burned our villages, but they did not defeat us. We will see what the Americans have to say. The British have lost their colonies, but they keep their vast lands to the north. In this treaty the Six Nations must keep our lands. The Americans know how we fight. They know how we protect the lands of our ancestors. We will travel to Fort Schuyler and listen to what they have to say."

◈ CHAPTER 57 ◈

To the Fort

The Congress of the new United States, the body that gave Washington command of the Continental Army, now had to govern. But the formerly separate 13 colonies had their own traditions and leaders. It was immediately clear to the men who won the American Revolution that it would not be easy to turn a revolt into a functioning nation. Virginia and Massachusetts fought together for independence, but to forge a new republic was another matter.

When it came to the Treaty of Paris, the new United States claimed victory. But when it came time to deal with the Iroquois, who had been deliberately shut out of any role in Paris, both Pennsylvania and New-York State sent emissaries to Fort Schuyler. The Americans were unsure of who would be the diplomats to deal with the Indian nations, envoys from the Congress or men like Philip Schuyler of New-York, who had put their generals' uniforms aside and could now plan their dreams of land and roads and canals. They rushed to make the states pre-eminent in any negotiations.

The Six Nations of the Iroquois had been the most enduring and powerful Confederacy in North America for centuries. They clung to the idea that they had not been subdued. Unlike the British at Yorktown, the Haudenosaunee had not surrendered.

Pundatha picked which Canandaigua Seneca would go to the treaty negotiations. Several warriors, including Ban-er-man-jah and Deh-wan-guh, and a few women, Wah-say-lan among them, were told to prepare for the journey. Tun-weh begged to go with her cousin, but her child was due, so she stayed with Mary Angel, Wah-say-han and the others finishing the harvesting and storage of beans and squash.

The small party set out in canoes, crossing their lake as the sun rose over the forested hills. Wah-say-lan stared up at Bare Hill. They paddled past the island but she set her gaze to the south, down the length of the great lake. The hills folded into each other all the way to the mists on the horizon. "Somewhere down there, down the warriors' trail, my Jamwesaw is heading home, I am certain," she said to herself. "Be careful, my husband, come with your mother and your little brothers, or come alone, but come home to me soon."

They pulled the elm bark canoes ashore at the site of their old village, now grown over with grass, bushes and the tiniest of sapling oaks and maples just pushing out of the earth. They followed ancient paths through the woodlands, walking swiftly and silently in single file. The paths had linked the Six Nations for eons. The leaves were crimson, yellow and brown with the turning of the season as Pundatha's party traveled to the north end of Seneca Lake, 20 miles east. The next day they reached the headwaters of Cayuga Lake, another 20 miles eastward; and the next to the southern tip of Onondaga Lake, where generations earlier, far in the legendary past, Hiawatha and Dekanawidah, the Peacemaker, first forged the Haudenosaunee Confederacy. An old Onondaga sachem greeted the Seneca. He shared strips of venison fresh from a hunting party just returned. The groups ate around campfires and smoked the elder's pipe with him. They thanked him and said they must go to the treaty talks at Fort Schuyler.

"I have been there many times near Oneida Lake, a large, stormy lake. I was there catching the lake pike before a white man's fort was put there. Our Oneida brothers fought with the white man in this war, but they were our brothers for many, many summers before that. We, too, fought with the white man—those British from across the big water. In this treaty we must speak as one nation," he told them. Pundatha thanked him for his food and for his thoughts.

That night, before the sun set, they arrived and built their campfires among dozens of other Haudenosaunee. The Seneca from many villages west of Canandaigua—from the tiny Squawky Hill and from Jen-uch-sha-da-go and Honeoye along the great Genesee River and farther west to Tonawanda and Buffalo Creek—had already arrived with Cornplanter. The Cayuga, Onondaga, Mohawk greeted one another. The Oneida and Tuscarora camped together, fully aware they had broken from their brothers but anxious to help provide a united front in the negotiations. All told, nearly 400 Indians had gathered for this treaty that would set, like none before, the fate of their people.

Congress dispatched a formal delegation to the treaty signing. Two promising young men, James Madison and James Monroe, were sent as observers. Also the Marquis de Lafayette, who, as he traveled to Fort Schuyler, wrote to Thomas Jefferson that "it was thought my presence, and even my personal influence with the Indians, could be of some public utility." In fact, Madison was so impressed with Lafayette as Indians and whites converged, he wrote to Jefferson that "the commissioners are eclipsed. The marquis is the only conspicuous figure. The sachems hold him in the highest reverence."

Thomas Jefferson was pleased to receive these letters. He had taken the young Madison, a fellow Virginian, under his tutelage even before the Declaration of Independence pronounced the Revolution. And his respect for Franklin in bringing France into the war, thereby making victory possible, had endeared him to all things French and most especially to the proud and dashing Marquis de Lafayette.

What surprised Jefferson, though, about the marquis' missive was his reference to a beautiful Seneca Indian woman. "I am wondering if I will see her again at Fort Schuyler, a striking young woman clearly defiant of any entreaties against her people," he wrote to Jefferson. "I must tell you, my dear sir, that one night while bivouacked in Virginia I had met her in the most unusual of circumstances. While

I sat with her at her campfire, she alone there with no explanation of what she was doing so far from her Seneca homeland, she told me an outrageous story of how she captured you, she and someone else whom she refused to identify. When I doubted her, Wah-say-lan pulled from her sack a fine golden spyglass with your name engraved upon it.

"I bring this up, sir, in confidence and out of simple curiosity. She most assuredly is clear evidence of your view of the equality of the white and red races. She calls herself Wah-say-lan and I quite honestly find her a fascinating woman, as conversant and intellectually curious as any countess I have met at Louis XVI's court. She insisted that she knows she will meet you again. My friend, if you can elucidate for me anything about her, I surely would be in your debt. Your Obedient & Humble Srvt., Lafayette."

Though it made him uneasy, Jefferson found himself smiling as he read the marquis' letter. He, too, after that encounter during his escape from Tarleton's dragoons, had the feeling he would meet Wah-say-lan again. He had been fascinated with her ever since their strange encounter. But now the fact of his capture by her and her husband was more than a secret. He sat down in his easy chair to contemplate his reply to the Frenchman.

In the cleared forest around Fort Schuyler near Lake Oneida in the middle of what had been for centuries Haudenosaunee lands, Lafayette was walking among them. The Oneida chiefs stood to welcome him. Years earlier he had convinced them to fight with the American rebels. Oneida warriors had served directly under the marquis and they looked to him now to help their cause at this important council fire. The tall Frenchman wearing the uniform of a continental major general greeted many by name. And then he saw her. She was standing several yards away with the Canandaigua Seneca, who were wary of the Oneida and still embittered that the Confederacy had broken for the first time ever.

Wah-say-lan walked toward the marquis. He gulped. He did not know what to do next. Her beauty again bewitched him. In Virginia he had not seen her walk. Now she approached with a regal gait, her chin up, her dark hair dropping below her shoulders. Her mouth was set, not in a smile. What was that look she gave him? he wondered as their eyes met.

◈ CHAPTER 58 ◈

They Meet Again

"Marquis de Lafayette, the French war chief. I see you were right. We do meet again," said Wah-say-lan. "Do you come in peace?" She reached out her hand. He took it, calmed himself, and raised her fingers to his lips.

"Wah-say-lan, my Seneca princess, my friend. I worried we would never meet, but I hoped we would. For you, for your people, I come in peace." He kissed both her cheeks. He loved her scent. He was excited to touch her again. To hear her voice. To see her face, a face he knew he would never forget.

Wah-say-lan did not know what she could do at this council. She had spent the journey worrying what would happen to the Seneca. She dug deep into her thoughts to come up with some way she could help Pundatha, Cornplanter, Joseph Brant and the other tribal leaders find fair solutions in the treaty. She hoped to be able to urge Cornplanter to be strong in his stance with these Americans. And now, before her, she had her agent, her unlikely ally when the Haudenosaunee most needed one.

"Your lips are familiar, marquis," she said, squeezing his hand. "If I were meeting Thomas Jefferson again, I do not think he would kiss my cheeks. I will meet him and remind him that I spared his life. But today, here I am with you, again. I see you know the Oneida."

"I told you, Wah-say-lan,—don't you remember?—that many Oneida braves served with me in 1778 when we fooled the British at Barren Hill in Pennsylvania."

"Why are you here now, marquis? To fool my people?"

"It is the British who fooled your war chiefs, Wah-say-lan. The British surrendered. Now your people must also accept the terms of peace."

"Marquis, when you were with me on the warriors' trail in Virginia, you said you wanted to fight the general who killed your father. Did you?"

"I led the attack with Col. Hamilton on Cornwallis and, when he surrendered, I was so looking forward to seeing Gen. Philips surrender personally to me. I found he had died of fever. How I wish he had died at my hand, my sabre. But I feel I honored my father. I defeated Philips and his commanders."

"Marquis, I honored my father. I killed the American soldier who killed him. I must now honor my father's memory at this peace council. I know you understand this. But I also have another question for you, Lafayette. When the British Army surrendered, what happened to the American slaves who had joined them for their freedom?"

"Why do you ask?"

"I have my reasons. Thomas Jefferson spoke of freedom and equality. Yet he kept slaves."

"Wah-say-lan, this is the great contradiction in the American Revolution. I have argued this with Gen. Washington and Gov. Jefferson. But I do not have time to discuss this right now."

"Marquis, tell me about the black men with Cornwallis."

"They ran. They ran into the woods. Continental soldiers were sent to round them up and return them to their masters' plantations."

Wah-say-lan was relieved. She knew Jamwesaw could avoid capture, but she knew, too, that he would try to get back to his mother. Still, he would be smart about that inevitable rendezvous. "He will come to me," she told herself. Then she reached for the young

Frenchman's hand. She pulled him close. "I know you have duties, marquis, and tomorrow the talks begin," she whispered. "Later tonight I will be under that large hemlock. Do you see it? It stands taller than the rest. I will wait for you. I will be alone."

He put both hands over hers and said, "My princess, if I can I will meet you there when the moon has risen high above the forest."

Wah-say-lan smiled at him and said to herself, "I am not your princess."

◈ CHAPTER 59 ◈

Wah-say-lan's Plan

Ban-er-man-jah went up to Wah-say-lan after the marquis walked into the fort. "How did the tall Frenchman know you? You talked for many minutes. He kissed your cheek."

Wah-say-lan never told untruths to another Seneca. She looked straight into his eyes and said quietly, "Ban-er-man-jah, my oldest friend. When I was alone on the warriors' trail, I met this marquis. I did not tell our people. I do not tell everything about myself. I think, I hope, this Frenchman can now help our people."

"Wah-say-lan, you have always confused me. I know you but I don't know you. I love you like my sister. My wife Tun-weh adores you. Many saw you with this marquis. What do I say?"

"Tell them this, you whom I love like a brother: Tell them he came to me and said I am a beautiful woman and he greeted me like a Frenchman greets a woman. Tell them I asked him to be helpful to our people. You do not have to say more. All that I just said is true," she assured the young brave.

"I say I love you like a sister, but I have always wanted to kiss your cheek, and now this Frenchman has in front of me," he said.

"You are Tun-weh's man. She will have your child. You two were meant for each other. You are here to help Pundatha protect our people, protect Tun-weh and your baby, who will be in this world when we return to Canandaigua. You will know what to do here at this council fire. I know what I must do."

Ban-er-man-jah walked away, puzzled and amazed yet again at this girl he grew up with whom he never quite understood and who was always just out of his grasp. As she walked away she saw the marquis pass through the stockade gate and greet another white chief. Arthur Lee, chief negotiator for Congress, was put out at the Indians' obvious affection for the Frenchman. "Well, Marquis, you certainly have your way with the savages," said the envoy.

"Mr. Lee, it is good to see you. I appreciate the invitation to be of assistance. Let me tell you what I plan to say tomorrow. I hope you approve. Then I cannot, regrettably, stay another day. But the treaty is in your capable hands."

The two men walked into the officers' quarters. As they sat down, Lee said, "Who was that Indian woman you spoke with?"

"She says her name is Wah-say-lan of the Canandaigua Seneca. That Gen. Sullivan burned her village and her father was killed in the battle. She said her people deserve a fair agreement. If I could bring a native to show the court of Louis XVI, I would bring her, a strikingly beautiful savage, wouldn't you say?"

Lee nodded.

"Now here is my plan, sir. I will address the Indians and remind them who are the victors . . . "

Arthur Lee listened and made a point of saying he would inform Congress that he approves of the marquis' address. He was privately satisfied that the Frenchman would be leaving. After all, this was now the new United States. It was appropriate to have France at the table in the treaty with Great Britain. But the Americans now must decide how to deal with the savages.

"I am joining Oliver Phelps, Nathaniel Gorham and Gen. Schuyler for dinner, Marquis. Please join us," Lee offered half-heartedly.

"Ah, thank you, kind sir, but Mr. Madison and Mr. Monroe have kindly asked me to join them. I will see the general in the morn.

Please give him my regards," he said, heading for the observers' cottage just outside the stockade.

Madison and Monroe were already seated, sipping Bordeaux. "Gen. Lafayette, please, we have fine French wine shipped north by Mr. Jefferson. He will be pleased to know you could enjoy his gift," said Madison.

An army chef brought a wooden mug and poured for the marquis. "We have a first course of chowder, sirs. The fish were caught this morning in Oneida Lake—pike, bass, perch. The mixture is a tasty blend. I'll bring it directly."

"Gentlemen, my pleasure," said the marquis, lifting his mug. "A toast to Thomas Jefferson, who wrote a magnificent document underscoring the liberties for which we fought and won."

"Hear! Hear!" the two young Virginians retorted.

"I believe Mr. Lee and Gen. Schuyler are dining with Phelps and Gorham," said Monroe.

"Yes, he asked me to join them. As much as I respect the general, I can tell Mr. Lee is a bit addled by my presence here. If Gen. Washington had not personally asked me to be here, I could now be on my way back to Paris, my wife and my newly born son. Might I tell you, gentlemen, we have christened him George Washington Lafayette?"

"Hoorah!" said Monroe, raising his wine to toast a new son. "Mr. Washington must be proud."

"I believe he is, sir," smiled Lafayette. "Tell me, who are these gentlemen Mr. Phelps and Mr. Gorham?"

The two men looked at each other. Madison spoke up. "They are business partners of Philip Schuyler. Land speculators. Once the treaty is signed, they are ready to offer fair prices to the various tribes for land."

The marquis sighed. "It is inevitable, is it not? I must say I hope these hapless people find a way to coexist. They are a brave and noble people. Many are very intelligent. They also have considerable diplomatic skill."

"Yes, Marquis, Mr. Jefferson has written how the Indians could live peacefully with us if they take up agriculture, schooling and some light industry such as grist milling," said Madison.

"Oh, they know agriculture. Their orchards before Sullivan destroyed them back in 1779 were astounding. Their crops spread over vast acreage. That is largely the work of their women. The men, the braves, they will not know what to do if they cannot hunt, trap and fish. I do not know if they can adjust," said Lafayette.

Conversation continued for hours. The Frenchman found Jefferson's two young friends to be fascinating. They discussed the new government, the new nation, how France and Britain will get along in this new world. How menacing, in fact, are the British just north in Canada? And what of the western Indian tribes and French lands and trade along the Mississippi River? The marquis enjoyed his evening immensely, but he also was anxious to meet someone under a tall hemlock tree.

"Gentlemen, thank you. This has been grand. But my speech comes early tomorrow and I must retire," he said. They shook hands and the Marquis de Lafayette, a famous American war hero and confidant of George Washington, walked into the moon shine.

The young marquis could hardly wait. His wife had given him two children back in Paris. In bed she is a frisky young woman. The ladies of the French court, no matter how grand, were available to a marquis as saucy bedroom wenches. But they are nothing compared to the wild Wah-say-lan, he thought as he approached her beneath the tall hemlock. No woman at the royal court in a plush bed could match the sexual power of this Seneca Indian woman on the forest floor.

And then, oddly, a letter Washington had written to him popped ominously into his mind. He remembered it was dated the Fourth of July and described Gen. Sullivan's expedition against the Six Nations. In particular, the marquis recalled, Washington wrote that he expected the army to "destroy their settlements and extirpate them from the country."

The marquis slowed his pace and considered the word: "extirpate," and a great sadness washed over him.

Wah-say-lan had laid her blanket over a soft bed of pine needles. The tree was several yards into the woods. Her bed was protected by large, low-reaching branches. She had struck a small campfire, keeping the flame low, a glow just enough to show a French marquis the way.

She was nervous and wondered why. "I have had this man before," she told herself. "This time, though, he needs to know. He needs to understand he can lie with me, but only for a reason. But will he? Surely he did without hesitation before. Ah, how he looks at me. He will lie with me. He will. He must." She slipped out of her blouse, sat back against the large log she had put there earlier and said, "I believe he will find this to be a good place." Wah-say-lan was beginning to feel proud of herself. Her plan, she felt, could only help her people.

The moon showed half, reflecting its yellow glow across the night sky. She looked up through the woodlands. A passing cloud, gold around its edges, momentarily hid the moon until the breezes carried the cloud away.

"I am the half-moon tonight. I show only one side of me. I am the breeze that can send a cloud to hide all of me and then shove it aside to reveal me to whoever will gaze upon my warmth and my inviting light," Wah-say-lan found herself musing, whispering to her inner self. "This man will enjoy me, but I will not give him all of me. I save all of myself; my full moon glow is for my Jamwesaw."

She saw the marquis approaching. Suddenly she was lonely. But then she sat up and readied herself. He did not speak, but removed his coat and then his shirt. He sat down next to her and took off his boots.

He said quietly, "You are exactly as I remember you, Wah-say-lan. You are still that young, beautiful, defiant woman. I see you still carry your father's knife."

"I do, Marquis de Lafayette. It is always with me. I see you come without a weapon."

"Wah-say-lan, this is a peace conference. I do not need a weapon and neither do you."

"We shall see how the talks go, Marquis. My people are ready to fight again. The continentals never defeated the Seneca and our brothers. These talks must be honest and fair," she said.

"Did you invite me here tonight to talk of war and peace, or did you invite me here for another reason?"

"I invited you here because I believe you are honorable. And I invited you because you are good, good at lying with a woman and taking her, taking me. I thought if I met you again it would happen again," she said.

"As I recall, it was you who took me," he said.

"I did. You aroused me. Then we took each other. But, Marquis, you did not finish last time. Tonight you must finish."

"What do you mean, my Seneca princess?"

"I am not a princess."

"You are to me."

"Marquis, if I am, then you must not spill your seed on me or waste it on the ground. I want your seed in me."

Wah-say-lan kissed him. He leaned her down and touched her cheek, kissed her neck and pressed against her. She pulled his pants off, then hers, and pressed her naked body against his. She rolled over on her back and spread her long thighs. He mounted and slid in. Her pelvis rose to meet his thrusts.

"The French ladies must want you," she hummed. "You are good, Marquis. Oh, you are good."

He was lost in her—in her arms, her legs, her mouth, her whispers. She was too amazing to believe, he thought. She was wild. She was pinching his nipple hard. She was whispering to him—her soft voice, her tough fingers. She wrapped her legs around him and wrapped her arms around his neck, pulling him in and in deeper.

He wanted to pull out but he didn't want to. No savage children, he heard himself say. Aloud? No, not aloud. His secret. But he was reaching, reaching. What a woman. My lord, what a woman. He moaned. He sang out. He gushed and gushed. She pulled him deeper. She pushed her pelvis against him, thrust her hips up and up. Her legs wouldn't let him stop. He pumped and pumped and then collapsed on top of her.

"Oh my God, I must see you again, Wah-say-lan. I must."

"You will, Marquis. You will." She kissed him. Their lips locked. Her tongue played with his. Then she whispered, "Thank you for your seed. I could feel it. It is deep in me. You will give me a son, I am sure." She hesitated. "My people will be your people, Marquis de Lafayette."

He looked at her for a long minute, then said, "If you have my son, then you must let me take him to France. He must learn French things, Wah-say-lan, and I want you to come too."

"You will come and see him, Marquis, in my Seneca village. He will know Seneca ways. But he should know his father. Go across the big gawa to France? We will see. I would like to see your home. I could not live there. I must live where my people have always lived. But I could see your country with your son. Marquis, you must protect your son. He will be born here. He will grow here. His mother's people need to be able to protect him and the other children of our longhouses. They must grow as I have and my parents did and their parents back before memory. The Haudenosaunee have always lived here, ruled here. Tomorrow you must speak these things and protect what will be yours in your own son."

The marquis realized she had it planned, but he did not feel tricked. He admitted he might even love Wah-say-lan. There were moments he had longed for her. He wanted to know much more about her. He doubted one night would give him a son. But maybe. If so, then he would find a way to civilize him. To educate him. But he also sincerely felt his boy, any boy, could benefit from living with her. All this flashed through his mind as he knew she was looking for assurances.

"Wah-say-lan, you know I speak tomorrow. I will try to be wise and ask your sachems to be wise. I believe in the new American nation and that its ideals will make the world better. I ask you to listen to what I say and I will tell you I speak for your son and my son—if that is to be. The Americans and the Indians can live together, Mr. Jefferson himself believes this."

She breathed deeply. She put her hand on his shoulder. She almost trusted him. And she was sure his seed would give her his son. She enjoyed it—he is good. But she did not love him, she knew. She did this for her people. What else could she do? She could not think of anything else, so she did this.

CHAPTER 60

The Treaty

There was a chill in the morning mist as the white men and the Iroquois woke to begin the negotiations that would bring peace to the people of the longhouse. The Americans and their crucial allies the French had signed the treaty with the British in Paris. Britain's ally, most of the long-lived Iroquois Confederacy, now stood alone at this fort on the edge of a frontier that American settlers were pushing westward. The British had surrendered their colonies to the new American nation. This morning no British dragoons, no Rangers, no British diplomats were present for this process of making peace with the Six Nations.

Red Jacket sat with Pundatha at a campfire as others gathered. "These Americans are cunning people, my friend," said the younger man to his chief. "They speak a lie that Haudenosaunee lands are part of their country now that they have pushed the British back to Canada. Our lands lie between the Americans and the British. These Americans are not to be trusted."

Pundatha stirred his cornmeal in hot water. He ate slowly and told the young man he must eat a good meal. "This will be a long day, my young friend. I hear the Mohawk are already moving to Niagara and the St. Lawrence to be with the British. Joseph Brant is not here. We will rely on Cornplanter to speak for us."

"Pundatha, Cornplanter is a great war chief, but he is not a Peacemaker. You know I have a gift for this. Maybe I am not the Seneca's greatest warrior, but the Great Spirit has given me the gift of speaking for his people."

"I know, Red Jacket, and I will talk with Cornplanter and tell him you must be given a time to address these Americans and this tall Frenchman, this Lafayette. The Oneida followed him. The Oneida and with them the Tuscarora, split our Six Nations for the first time since before memory. And now we face this treaty. They stand with us again, but the wounds have not healed. This Frenchman, I hear, is a war chief with Washington, who beat the great army of the King in Virginia. I saw him yesterday with Wah-say-lan. Do you know of that, Red Jacket?"

"No, Pundatha. I know only that Wah-say-lan went down the warriors' trail and left her husband in Virginia to fight with the British. You know she is a brazen woman and I would not doubt she went to this marquis to ask if he knew about Jamwesaw. She is a strong woman, but she is lonely without him."

"That is true. I see Cornplanter. I will go speak to him now."

Inside the stockade, Arthur Lee and the other Congressional commissioners were making final preparations for the day. "So it is agreed the Marquis de Lafayette shall speak to the savages first. His message is clear: they must surrender. He is admired by at least some of them. He can be persuasive. Then we must listen to them respond, I understand."

The Americans were surprised that nearly 400 Indians were present. Fort Schuyler housed 250 continental soldiers. General Schuyler himself brought a hundred cavalry with him. New-York State and Pennsylvania both had emissaries, though Congress was making it clear this was a federal treaty. A group of a dozen Quakers, many who lived among the Iroquois, were also in attendance.

"Congress expects a settlement here," Lee said as Lafayette joined the breakfast meeting. "Ah, Marquis, here you are. Please have a seat. Corporal, bring some fresh tea. Are you ready, Marquis, to set the proper tone, to begin this historic negotiation? We hear some of the savages are saying they have not been beaten and they are ready to keep fighting."

"Good morning, Mr. Lee. Yes, that is true. The Seneca and the Cayuga in particular know they were not beaten on the battlefield. But their Mohawk ally Joseph Brant is not here. They are also diminished by the split with the Oneida. Still, they have protected their country for centuries successfully. At the very least we must speak in terms of fair prices to them for their forestlands. I shall do my best, Mr. Lee, to talk sense into them."

"Thank you, Marquis. I suppose we should get this thing started. Lieutenant, are the grounds ready and secured?"

"Yes, sir. We have men stationed on three sides. The Indians are gathered and say their speakers are ready."

The morning mist was dissipating. The several war chiefs and sachems of the Six Nations sat at the front of their gathered people. Wah-say-lan had slept under the tree in the forest. She found Ban-er-man-jah sitting with Red Jacket. She sat with them near the front. She was comforted at the sight of so many of her people—a formidable force, she thought. The air was still. The leaves did not rustle. The very birds were silent. Wah-say-lan looked up and saw a bird, wings spread, soaring high above. A red-tail, the messenger, she hoped. But then another and another came into view, circling. Turkey vultures. Something was lying dead on the ground, she thought, and shivered.

When the Marquis de Lafayette stepped forward, she did not betray any feelings. But she was close enough to look into his eyes. She felt him holding her stare. The clearing outside the fort was sloped. He stood on high ground with the Congressional delegation, raised his hand and spoke in a clear voice:

"My friends and brothers the Haudenosaunee, I give thanks to the heavens that led me into this place of peace where you are smoking the pipe of friendship together. I come to thank the faithful brothers, the chiefs of the nations, the warriors for coming to meet with the

leaders of the Americans in peace and to renew a friendship that will benefit both nations. To begin this great council fire, my friends the Americans have asked me to speak the truth to you so that we can look forward to a future of mutual understanding.

"If my memory did not forget the evil sooner than the good, I could punish those who while opening their ears have closed their hearts; who, blindly raising their hatchets, risked striking those who would be their brothers."

Wah-say-lan's thoughts raced back to the abandoned roadway, the marquis leading 1,500 continentals, her arrow aimed truly at his heart. She did not let it fly, but "I did not blindly raise my hatchet," she said to herself. "I choose when to fight." She turned back to the marquis, who spread both arms high and continued:

"The American cause is just. It is the cause of humanity. Under the great war chief Washington, peace is accomplished. You know the terms of it, and I shall oblige some among you by abstaining, out of pity, from repeating them. Listen to the advice I offer you. Do not forget that the Americans are close friends of your long-lasting friends, the French. Past mistakes require amends. The Americans intend to live in their new nation in peace with you. In selling lands, do not consult a barrel of rum to give them up to the first who come, but let the American chiefs, and yours, join together around the fire and conclude reasonable bargains.

"Until the day we shall join pipes, when we shall lie down again under the same bark, under the same tall tree in the forest, I wish you good health, good hunting, unity and abundance, and the success of all the dreams that promise you happiness."

With that he ended. He paused and found Wah-say-lan's eyes. She held his gaze. He smiled and walked back to the commissioners.

It had been decided that the Seneca war chief Cornplanter would be the first to respond. He held his head high. It was topped with a beaded band holding two long brown and white hawk feathers. The tanned and muscular leader stood at the front of the 400 Indians and raised his voice to the delegation of Americans. He addressed the marquis directly by his given Indian name:

"Kayeheanla, brother to the Oneida and the Tuscarora of the Six Nations, war chief of the French King, open your ears to the words I am about to speak. At the beginning of your speech you acknowledge the guidance of the Great Spirit on high, who leads you to this place where you find your brothers in peace. You then give us some lessons and advice in which you declare that affection forgets mistakes sooner than good actions. You also remind us of the words you spoke to us at our first meeting seven years ago at Fort Johnson. You told us then that you knew the basis of the quarrel between America and Great Britain and that the great King of your people would form a link with America that would live forever. You called upon our memory of it for the fulfillment of your prediction.

"My brother, open once more your ears. It is very true that no nation is free from error, and we have been led into very great mistakes, at Great Britain's instigation, in uniting against the American states. We were vanquished, but it is fitting for all nations to be concerned about each other in misfortune, and it especially becomes the victors to show this compassion to those who are vanquished. Our hopes, our trust, are concentrated in this treaty negotiation at this council fire. If the Americans speak to us kindly, all will go well and peace will spread over all the nations. My brother, take this belt with you, and do not forget our words."

Cornplanter stepped forward with a long blue and white belt signifying peace. Lafayette accepted it and joined hands with Cornplanter, who turned and spoke up: "Now we wish my brother Red Jacket to speak his thoughts of this day. The young brave is recognized by our sachems as an orator of rare gifts. We will listen."

Red Jacket, not as tall as most Seneca men, pulled at his coat, stretched his neck and stood erect. He took a deep breath and, in a near baritone belying his small frame, he began:

"You white people have increased very fast on this land which was given to us Indians by the Great Spirit; we are now become a small

people, and you are cutting off our lands piece after piece—you are a hard-hearted people, seeking your own advantages. Our brothers the Mohawk are already being pushed from their valley.

"There was a time when our forefathers owned this great land. Their seats extended from the rising to the setting sun. The Great Spirit had made it for the use of Indians. He had created the deer and other animals for food. He had made the bear and the beaver. Their skins served us for clothing. He had scattered them over the country and taught us how to take them. He had caused the earth to produce corn for bread. All this he had done for his red children because he loved them. But an evil day came upon us. Your forefathers crossed the great water and landed in this country. Their numbers were small. They found friends and not enemies. They asked for a small seat. We took pity on them, granted their request, and they sat down amongst us. We gave them corn and meat, they gave us poison liquor in return.

"More white people came amongst us. Yet we did not fear them. We took you to be friends. You called us brothers. We believed you and gave you a larger seat. At length your numbers have greatly increased. You want more land. You want our country.

"Long ago the white man with sweet voices and smiling faces told us they loved us and that they would not cheat us, but that the English King's children on the other side of the lake would cheat us. When we go on the other side of the lake, the King's children tell us your people will cheat us, but with sweet voices and smiling faces assured us of their love and they will not cheat us. These things puzzle our heads, and we believe that the Indians must take care of ourselves, and not trust either in your people or in the King's children.

"Our eyes were opened and our minds became uneasy. Wars took place. Many of our people were destroyed. You have now become a great people and you want our country. We will not sell our lands. We hope you clearly understand the words we have spoken. This is all we have to say."

Red Jacket turned and walked back. He sat with Ban-er-man-jah and Wah-say-lan. She touched his shoulder, smiled at him and said,

"Red Jacket, a friend of my friend Ban-er-man-jah, today you spoke our truth. We cannot sell our lands and you spoke that truth."

"Yes, I spoke the words, Wah-say-lan, but they are only words. These white people say they are here to make a treaty, but what they mean is that they are here to take our lands. The only real question, my friend, is how much we will give them. We will sell them land, we will take their American money, but we will lose our hunting territory. The places to build our longhouses and plant our corn will dwindle."

He said these things quietly. She whispered back, "But we are still strong. Here today we have more warriors than there are Blue Coats with muskets."

"More will come, Wah-say-lan. We must today see what we can keep in this treaty," the young man said.

She noticed the Marquis de Lafayette mounting his horse with several cavalry riders. She grabbed Ban-er-man-jah's hand. "Come, quickly," she said. They walked boldly toward the departing Frenchman.

"Marquis, we listened to your words of friendship. Did I hear you right that in that friendship you mean that your people are mine and my people are yours?"

The marquis looked down from his horse. "You are a brave young Seneca woman. I am hopeful the future will bring friendship among us. If your people are mine in peace, if the wars between us are over, you will let me know if a Frenchman and a Seneca are friends and that our people are one."

"We shall see, Frenchman, what will be," she said.

He rode over to Arthur Lee, to James Monroe and James Madison and gave his farewell. Then he and his entourage headed out.

Wah-say-lan took Ban-er-man-jah's hand and walked back to sit with the Seneca delegation. Cornplanter and others were congratulating Red Jacket on his speech.

"It is time to sit together and smoke the pipe," said Arthur Lee. Sachems of the Six Nations came forward. The congressional emissaries met them. A dozen white men sat with the same number of Iroquois. An Onondaga elder spoke up: "We are the keepers of the council fire since the Haudenosaunee joined together before memory. I say, in the name of the people of the longhouse, what do you propose in this treaty of peace?"

With Lafayette gone, Arthur Lee made it clear he was in charge. "I am sent here by Gen. Washington and the Congress to inform you, first, we want all prisoners released. And until all prisoners are released, including slaves who may have abandoned their posts with the Continental Army, we shall hold hostages. I demand, here and now, six braves as hostages. When all of our men, and even some women you have taken, are returned, then we will release the hostages."

Before any of the sachems could respond, a squad of soldiers, bayonets fixed, marched to the fore. "Take six," ordered a captain, and the men marched forward and prodded at Indian braves.

"Wait!" hollered Cornplanter. "We will tell you who you may have." Cornplanter huddled with a sachem from each nation. One brave from each was selected, including Ban-er-man-jah of the Seneca.

"No!" yelled Wah-say-lan. "He must return with us. His wife is with child. He will be a father when we get back to Canandaigua."

"This is fine, Wah-say-lan. I am helping how I can. This will lead to peace. We will return any we have captured and who choose to return," the young man said.

"It is so, Wah-say-lan," said Pundatha. "Let Ban-er-man-jah serve his purpose."

He and the five other braves went back into the fort with the soldiers, who placed them in a one-room hut with a dirt floor and one window.

"We now propose separate negotiations. The Oneida and Tuscarora please follow Commissioner Thompson and his group. The Onondaga, Cayuga and if there are any Mohawk, follow Commissioner Cunningham. The Seneca will meet here with me and Mr. Phelps and Mr. Gorham," Lee announced.

This was not going well and it was not the kind of council fire the Six Nations understood. But the sachems could do little but agree and all but the Seneca went off to other parts of the grounds. The soldiers were gruff. The atmosphere grew tense.

"Now you listen to me," said Lee. "As Cornplanter acknowledged, you are a vanquished tribe. Here is the peace we offer. Mr. Phelps and Mr. Gorham are businessmen and they pay fair prices. We will start with the demarcation line of 1768, which, as you know, begins here at Fort Schuyler and goes directly south to the Pennsylvania border. These men are prepared to offer you a handsome sum for the land that stretches to the west to Buffalo Creek."

Pundatha looked at Cornplanter. That is essentially all of the traditional Seneca lands. The keepers of the western door to the Confederacy would be reduced to small tracts at the very western edge of their ancestral lands. The legendary Seneca Nation birthplace on Bare Hill above Canandaigua Lake would be sold under this proposal.

Pundatha spoke. "That we cannot do. We will not do. Our ancestors looking down from the Sky World are shedding tears. We will take up the hatchet again, Arthur Lee."

"Be careful, my good fellow," said Lee.

Cornplanter said, "We will consider selling you lands up to the great Genesee River. That is half of what you ask for. It is still a substantial expanse of open land. What do you offer for this land?"

Oliver Phelps spoke up. "We will pay you $10,000 and offer an annuity of $500 each year. This will give your people riches they had never known before."

The Seneca leaders knew they were beaten. They knew what they could do right now is save the western half of their lands. They sadly put their marks to the papers offered by Lee and they gave a peace belt to formalize the agreement in the traditional Iroquois way. Cornplanter and Pundatha gathered their people together for the trek westward.

Wah-say-lan was stunned. She could not move. She would not

move. Pundatha went to her. "My best friend's daughter, come. Come now, we have much to do this fall to prepare our people."

"Pundatha, you know I love you and I have always obeyed your wishes. I cannot go right now. We have just sold our lake to these miserable white men. My island. I cannot swim to my island?"

"My Wah-say-lan, you have traveled far, you know there is vast land. We will go west, west of the Genesee. There are lakes there. You will see there is still a good life."

"Pundatha, my chief, my father's best friend. I will come, but I cannot go today. I cannot leave Ban-er-man-jah. I will stay here, nearby in the forest. No one will know I am here. When our braves bring the prisoners they want back, I will be here and will come back with Ban-er-man-jah. At least one of us must stay to make sure they treat him right."

"You are Lan-lu-rah's daughter," is all the tired old chief said. He kissed her forehead and touched the knife in her belt. "I know this knife. I know your father's knife will keep you safe."

He and Cornplanter led the Seneca men and women back westward. Soon the forest swallowed them up.

Wah-say-lan went back to her small camp under the large pine. She sat down and put her head on her knees. Tears fell from her eyes. She tried not to think. She wanted to make her mind blank. She sat silently without moving for hours. The sun was falling low in the sky. Dusk was coming when she heard a commotion in the fort. She walked carefully in the direction of the noise.

Several white men, not soldiers, not commissioners, rough-hewn men, were arguing and swearing. They had just brought some wagons with provisions from Albany and they had been drinking rum. One was pushing another, several others were egging them on.

"Goddamn savages. They kilt my cousin in Cherry Valley," she heard one say.

"So let's git 'em," said another.

"Gimme a swig a that jug," still another said.

She watched as they drank more and got louder. A couple of

soldiers had joined in. Two Quakers walked over and tried to calm the bunch, but they picked up knives and chased them away.

The commissioners and observers, the officers, were at the far end of the fort in the large dining hall. They were celebrating the signed peace agreements. Each was telling how they had fared and how much the separate tribes had to give up in land. It was a celebratory mood and they were unaware of any hooligans over near where the hostages were held.

"C'mon, I hear there's only six Indians in that hut. We got twice as many. Let's go string 'em up, dirty rotten savages."

"Yeah, let's get the murderin' bastards."

And then they ran at the hut. They slammed down the door and dragged out the hostages. Two pushed and slipped away. They ran for the forest. Ban-er-man-jah was swinging his fists and kicking the armed men away. He slapped one to the ground, two others jumped on him.

Wah-say-lan looked on in horror. She screamed, "No! No!" and ran at the angry knot of men. One slapped her in the face, a direct hit, and sent her reeling. She hit her head on a stump and felt herself losing consciousness. Another Indian hostage broke loose and ran through the gate into the forest. Three men were holding Ban-er-man-jah down. They tied his hands behind his back. They grabbed the Cayuga brave and tied his hands. Ropes went around their necks and the mob pulled the two Indians out to the nearest tree. They threw the ropes over a limb.

Ban-er-man-jah kicked, struggled the best he could. Then he stopped. He knew he would never see Tun-weh again. He would never see his baby. He chanted his death song as he felt the rope tighten around his neck. His last vision was of his lovely Tun-weh holding a small bundle in her arms and smiling.

It was dark when Wah-say-lan awoke. Two Quakers were cleaning a bloodied gash on the side of her head. "Whoa, calm there," one said quietly.

"Ban-er-man-jah, where is he? Where is he?"

"It will be all right. You are all right," said the gentle man applying a cool cloth to her temple.

Then she saw the two bodies hanging in a tree. She knew immediately one was her friend. She bolted up and ran. She jumped up into the tree, onto the limb and cut the ropes. She jumped back down and ran to Ban-er-man-jah. He was lifeless. She slashed the ropes at his hands and held him tightly to her breast. She swayed back and forth, tears welling. Then she carried him to the tall pine of the night before. She laid him down, went back and carried the Cayuga man, too, and laid him next to her friend.

She pulled out her knife and walked back toward the fort. She found the ruffians, drunk and snoring on the ground near their wagons. Silently she went up to one and slit his throat. His snore turned to a gurgle. Then she went to the next one and nearly severed his head with the thrust of her father's knife. One stirred and she plunged the knife into his heart.

He screamed and staggered and fell on another man, who pushed the lifeless body off only to face a tall figure coming at him with a large bloody knife. "No, nooo," he groaned. He stumbled. She was on him, pulled his hair back and slashed the knife through the front of his neck. Others were waking from their stupor.

"Hey, what the . . . Hey, wake up, you bastards!" The startled man knew something was wrong and ran toward the gate, yelling.

Wah-say-lan did not care. She was avenging her oldest friend's murder. She wasn't sure how many of the murderers she had killed, but she was looking for more. They were now awake and suddenly two dashed at her from behind. They grabbed her, she cut one on his hand, he yelped. The other held tighter and pulled a pistol from his belt. He cocked it and pointed it at her head, but just then went limp and thudded to the ground.

A large hand grabbed Wah-say-lan's wrist. She held her knife tightly and tried to swing. "Stop," he said. "Stop." He kicked away a man coming at him. "Come, come, now. Now, Wah-say-lan!" He held her wrist and pulled her hard.

Four or five men were cautiously approaching.

The voice pulled her: "Wah-say-lan, quick. This way. Now."

She obeyed. She did not know why. She was not thinking. But she heard the command and she went with it. Into some brush, deeper into the woods, behind two boulders. They stopped. He held her.

She fell against him. "Jamwesaw, my Jamwesaw," she whispered. Her knees went weak. He brought her gently to the ground. They were there for several silent minutes. He caressed her hair. He held her face close to his chest. And he listened.

"Come now, my wife. Quietly. Come." He took her knife and put it in his belt. He held her hand and they went farther into the forest, away from Fort Schuyler.

◈ CHAPTER 61 ◈

Flight

They walked quickly and silently. Jamwesaw held her hand, pulled her along. She started to say things, but he warned her to be quiet. "A little longer, my Wah-say-lan. A little farther. We need to go a little farther. Then we will stop," he whispered.

He found the worn trail. The night was cloudy, with little moonlight. He urged her to run with him. He needed to make sure no one was pursuing. He knew she had killed at least one white man, and so had he. He thanked the Great Spirit for helping him get to the fort on time. Even a few minutes later and it could have been too late.

The running was pulling Wah-say-lan out of her stupor. She began to breathe steadily. She understood she was on the path that had brought her to the fort and that she was now escaping from men who were after her. Her heart ached for her friend Ban-er-man-jah but she felt her strength returning as she recalled avenging his murder.

"Jamwesaw, we are far enough. They are not following. They were louts, drunks. We can stop. I need to talk to you. I need to know how you came here now," she said.

He stopped. "Listen," he said. They stood still for a long moment. They heard nothing. "All right, my wife. We will find a spot," and they walked off the trail, holding hands. In a while they came to clearing under an oak tree. The night was cool and they had no blankets, but they did not risk starting a campfire. They sat down side by side and leaned back against the great trunk. Wah-say-lan leaned over and found his lips. She kissed him long and tenderly. Then kissed his cheeks, his forehead, his eyes. She pulled his shoulders to her and hugged him tightly.

"How did you do it? How did you find me, Jamwesaw? I heard about the British Army surrendering. How did you get away? How did you get back? Did you bring your mother, her little sons? Tell me, tell me."

"My Wah-say-lan, I want to know how you got back. I will tell you all in good time. I will tell you this now—that I got to our village and your mother told me of the treaty negotiations and how to follow the trail to Fort Schuyler. Tun-weh showed me her baby, a son, a handsome son. I told them I must run to the fort. I ran all day and came upon Pundatha and the people returning. He said he was glad I came because you were foolish and stayed to be with Ban-er-man-jah and the other hostages. He told me I should hurry and convince you to come home."

"Jamwesaw, it is not home. They sold it. And Ban-er-man-jah is dead."

"He is dead? That is what you were fighting about. Pundatha told me to hurry to you because he was worried something would happen. He was right."

"I killed them, Jamwesaw. I slit their throats, the pigs. But there were too many. And then you pulled me away."

Jamwesaw hugged her tightly. He kissed her forehead. He stroked her long black hair and found it clotted with dried blood.

"Jamwesaw, I want you to take me. I ache for you. I have ached for you since I left Monticello for my journey back. I want to take you. But not tonight. I want to be clean for you. I want to go to a place. I know the place. I will take you there in the morning. I am tired, my Jamwesaw. I am very tired."

She curled down and pulled him with her. She pushed her back into his chest. He held her and she fell asleep in his arms. Jamwesaw could hardly believe he was holding his wife after so long, after escaping from the surrender at Yorktown and his long trek back to Seneca country. He wanted to tell her how he got back. He wanted to know about her own journey alone back up the warriors' trail. But he held her and felt her heart beat. He breathed in her scent. That alone was enough. He shuddered to think what would have happened if he had not rushed to Fort Schuyler. Then Jamwesaw closed his eyes and fell asleep with her.

◈ CHAPTER 62 ◈

Home

In the morning, Wah-say-lan saw the blood on her hands and her arms. She remembered slitting throats. She wanted to go back for her friend's body. Jamwesaw convinced her that Ban-er-man-jah was safely in the Sky World with her father and they could not risk going back for his body.

"I should wash, but I will wait until we get to where I am taking you," she said. "We should go. Who knows about these Americans? Maybe they have soldiers coming right now."

In fact, Philip Schuyler that morning, upon being informed of the carnage the night before, decided no one should pursue westward. "We have made our treaties. We have purchased much of their lands. We will go forth when we are good and ready," he told the fort's commander.

Wah-say-lan and Jamwesaw found blueberry bushes and stopped to eat. They were luscious and sweet. There was an abundance and they ate handfuls.

"The small blueberry bush supplies so much," she said, smiling. "The Great Spirit was kind to his people to provide such a good taste. But come, I want to take you to Onondaga Lake before we go back to Canandaigua."

She found the trail and walked westward. "Tell me about—what is it? Yorktown?" she said.

He told her how he led a few slaves out of the enormous British encampment. Continental soldiers with dogs started hunting for runaway slaves. "We made very little progress during the day and tried to travel at night. The second day out, we heard the dogs. When they were almost on us, I had three of the men fire first. They killed two dogs and wounded another. Then the Continentals rushed in and my other three men fired. Two of them fell. The others pulled back. We got out of there. We were able to get back to Monticello the next night.

"I found my mother's room. I was glad that she was alone. She hugged me. She asked me to stay but said she knew I wouldn't. She would not come with me and she asked, 'My son, your British friends have lost. What will the Seneca do now?' I told her the Seneca have lived on their lands for centuries and they will know what to do. She told me to love you and raise a family in freedom. Then she asked me to look in on my little brothers. They were sleeping quietly. She gave me cornbread and kissed my cheek and told me she loved me and always would. She told me someday, somehow, we will see each other again."

Jamwesaw walked with his wife in silence for several minutes.

"I went for the others, but they all decided to stay with their women. Even if they were whipped, they wanted to be with their loved ones," Jamwesaw told Wah-say-lan. "I came to you as fast as I could."

"It is a long way to travel in a hurry. I did not make the journey in a hurry, my husband. I will tell you of my trip, but not today. Today I want to wash my body and my hair in the lake where the Peacemaker brought the Haudenosaunee together," she said.

In half a day they reached Onondaga Lake. Smaller than Canandaigua, it glistened like a diamond under the deep blue sky. Wah-say-lan led her husband to the shore. She undressed and waded in. She turned and waited for him. They dove in together and swam to where she could stand, shoulder-deep in the cool water.

"Rub me, Jamwesaw, rub the white man's blood from me."

"It is in your hair, too. Go under."

She dropped down and kicked away. She dove under, letting the water course through her long hair. She ran her fingers through it, loosening knots and clots. She came back up and dove back down. Soon she felt her hair had been cleansed in Onondaga's waters. She swam back and Jamwesaw caressed her arms and her shoulders. He rubbed where red stains still stuck to her skin. The water was calm. The lake shore was peaceful. No one was around.

"Come," she said, holding his hand. They waded ashore. "Here on the southeast beach is where the Peacemaker, Dekanawidah, and Hiawatha forged the Iroquois Confederacy, many generations ago, long before my grandmother's memory."

Wah-say-lan ran her fingers through her wet hair as she talked. She tossed her dirty clothes in the lake, bent over and rustled them in the water, scraping the dried blood away. She twisted the water out, shook them and placed them gently on the shore in the sunshine. She walked a little way down the beach, her husband marveling at her beautiful movements. No one moved like Wah-say-lan, he thought as beads of water shone on her dark skin.

"Right here on this spot long ago, my husband, is where it began. Our stories say Dekanawidah was born of a virgin. Our children will not be born of a virgin, Jamwesaw. Long ago you took care of that. I have not had you in too long, Jamwesaw."

She sat down. Then she stretched out and beckoned him. "I need you inside me. I need to feel you deep inside me," she said.

Jamwesaw looked down upon his wife, the most beautiful woman in all the Six Nations, he thought, and the most dangerous—or at least the most adventurous. Here she was, the day after slaying white men, her long legs stretched on the shore, asking him to come to her. Her face, it seemed to him, was at once sorrowful and yearning, beckoning him. She held out her arms as he walked toward her.

It seemed to Jamwesaw like an eternity since he had been with his wife. He knelt down between her spread legs. He gently rubbed her long, muscular thighs. He leaned over and kissed her, moving his mouth across her cheek, lightly kissing down her neck, down to her breasts. She rubbed his shoulders, his back, and pulled him to her breasts. He put his head in the welcoming valley between them. She held him there. He petted her hips, down again to her thighs, rubbing up and down, up and down. She could feel him getting hard against her inner thigh. She pressed against it.

They did not talk. She pulled him up. She was ready. It had been too long. She was open to him. They made love softly at first. Then he went deeper in long strokes. He held her ever more tightly. They throbbed one against the other. Their lips locked sweetly. She loved tasting him. Their bodies moved together as one. When she knew it was his time, she thrust upwards and hugged him, pulling him in and in. She wrapped her legs around his middle. She groaned and thrust up and up as he exploded inside her. Jamwesaw was gasping and pounding her hard. She arched her back and cried out, "My Jamwesaw, my Jamwesaw! Oh, oh, my Jamwesaw!"

Then she lay back, he sprawled on top. She held him and thought back through time, to long ago when the five nations came together here to form their strong Confederacy.

"It was here where the people of the longhouse, the original five nations, joined as one," she whispered. "We were born here on this spot, Jamwesaw. And it is here where you have given me your seed again for the first time in so many turns of the moon. We have both traveled far, first together and then alone. And now we are together. It is time to have our family, a Haudenosaunee family, with this first child," she said.

"I do not know why you have not been with child before, my Wah-say-lan. But I think you are right. I think this morning we are one and we have created our son, or maybe our daughter."

He started to get up. She held him. "Don't move, Jamwesaw. Not yet. I want you like this. I need you like this." She stared straight up into the deep blue sky. She stared into his large dark eyes. She kissed his lips and ran her hand through his hair, across his broad shoulders. She pulled his groin to her and held him for a long time.

She did not speak of her encounter with the Frenchman. She hoped that somehow Jamwesaw's seed was the more powerful. She wanted his seed, no one else's. "What was I thinking?" she thought to herself. "That a marquis would protect my family?"

"Jamwesaw, I know, I just know you are the father of my child," she said.

"I am your husband and I will be our child's father," he said. "I could lie like this all day, my wife, but I think we should go to the village and see Pundatha and listen to his plans," he said.

"I told you, my husband, Cornplanter and the other chiefs, they sold our land. They sold Bare Hill. They sold Canandaigua Lake, the Chosen Place of the Seneca people. Pundatha is taking our people westward to the other side of the great Genesee River. I will not go, my husband. I do not need to listen to Pundatha. I will not leave my people's home."

"Come," said Jamwesaw. "We will travel to the Chosen Place and we will talk."

When they reached Bare Hill they climbed to the top and looked down on Canandaigua Lake. "So this is where the boy killed the serpent?" he said.

"That is our story, but do you remember I told you as a child I would shoot my little bow until my father told me to stop? 'But father, I am killing the serpent!' I said. And he told me only a boy can kill the serpent."

"My Wah-say-lan, whoever killed the serpent and brought peace to Bare Hill gave the people a beautiful view of our lake," said Jamwesaw. They walked down the hill, down to the shore, to where her village had been before Washington sent the army. They took off their clothes, bundled them, and swam together to the island. Jamwesaw shivered in the cool water of early fall, but it seemed to him that Wah-say-lan was born to swim, and he would follow her anywhere, any time.

She walked across the beach and got dressed. She said, "This is where I will have our child, Jamwesaw. We will make our home here.

We will fish and we will build a canoe and go hunting on the shores. If Phelps and Gorham come and tell us to leave, I will tell them we are buying my island—think of that, Jamwesaw: that somehow a white man can say he owns the land and sell it for money. We will pay in deer skins. You and I will live here. Tun-weh, too, if she wants to come here with her baby. Jamwesaw, it is I who should tell Tun-weh of Ban-er-man-jah, but I cannot. I cannot leave this island right now. Will you go to the village and tell her and say to her she must come with you back to our island? Tell my mother and tell Pundatha this is where Wah-say-lan and Jamwesaw will start their family."

"I will tell them. And Tun-weh will grieve deeply. But I will tell her you want to grieve with her and remind her that her husband is with his ancestors in the Sky World. She will want to be with you, Wah-say-lan." He stepped over and hugged his wife. He kissed her, then swam to the west shore and walked toward the village.

Wah-say-lan went to the edge of her island. She looked north and saw the tall tree, taller than the others in the forest. Under it was where she first slept with Jamwesaw. As a young girl with her parents, she had climbed to the top at her father's urging. Everywhere she looked was Seneca country. It always had been.

Wah-say-lan found a flat, round piece of shale and skipped it across the surface of the lake. She watched the concentric circles grow and then fade. She sat down on the beach and watched the sunlight sparkle on her lake. She did not move for a long time. Her head was on her knees. Tears welled in her deep brown eyes and rolled down her cheek.

THE END

WORKS CONSULTED

Abler, Thomas, ed. 1989. Chainbreaker, The Revolutionary War Memories of Governor Blacksnake, As told to Benjamin Williams. Lincoln: University of Nebraska Press.

Adler, Jeanne Winston, ed. 2002. Chainbreaker's War, A Seneca Chief Remembers the American Revolution. Hensonville: Black Dome Press Corp.

Adams, James Truslow. 1936. The Living Jefferson. New York: Charles Scribner's.

Blake, Nelson. A History of American Life and Thought. McGraw-Hill, New York, 1963.

Bleeker, Leonard, ed. 1865. Order Book of Capt. Leonard Bleeker, 1779, Major of Brigade . . . Under Gen. James Clinton Against the Indian Settlements of Western New York in the Campaign of 1779. New York: Joseph Sabin.

Boardman, Fon W., Jr. 1978. Against the Iroquois, The Sullivan Campaign of 1779 in New York State. New York: David McKay Co.

Bowers, Claude G. 1936. Jefferson in Power, The Death Struggle of the Federalists. Boston: Houghton Mifflin.

Bowers, Claude G. 1945. The Young Jefferson, 1743–1789. Boston: Houghton Mifflin.

Brodie, Fawn M. 1974. Thomas Jefferson, An Intimate History. New York: W.W. Norton.

Brown, Dee. 1970. Bury My Heart at Wounded Knee, An Indian History of the American West. New York: Holt, Rinehart, & Winston.

Brown, Dee. 1994. The American West. New York: Charles Scribner's.

Brown, Ralph Adams, ed. 1842. Notices of Sullivan's Campaign or

Revolutionary Warfare in Western New York . . . Port Washington: Kennikat Press.

Bruchac, Joseph. 1996. Children of the Longhouse. New York: Dial Books.

Callahan, North. 1972. George Washington, Soldier and Man. New York: William Morrow & Co.

Calloway, Colin G. 1997. New Worlds for All, Indians, Europeans and the Remaking of Early America. Baltimore: The Johns Hopkins University Press.

Chomsky, Noam. 2004. Hegemony or Survival, America's Quest for Global Dominance. New York: MacMillan.

Courlander, Harold. 1967. The African. New York: Henry Holt.

Densmore, Richard. 1999. Red Jacket, Iroquois Diplomat and Orator. Syracuse: Syracuse University Press.

Dos Passos, John. 1954.The Head and Heart of Thomas Jefferson. New York: Doubleday.

Eccles, W.J. 1998. The French in North America, 1500–1783. East Lansing: Michigan State University Press.

Farrow, Anne; Lang, Joel; Frank, Jenifer. 2005. Complicity, How the North Promoted, Prolonged, and Profited from Slavery. New York: Ballantine Books.

Ferling, John A. 1988. The First of Men, A Life of George Washington. Knoxville: The University of Tennessee Press.

Fischer, Joseph R. 1997. A Well-Executed Failure, The Sullivan Campaign Against the Iroquois, July-September, 1779. Columbia: University of South Carolina Press.

Fleming, Thomas. 1969. The Man from Monticello, An Intimate Life of Thomas Jefferson. New York: William Morrow.

Francis, Daniel. 1992. The Imaginary Indian. The Image of the Indian in Canadian Culture. Vancouver: Arsenal Pulp Press.

Franklin, Benjamin. 1986. The Autobiography. New York: Penguin Books.

Gangi, Rayna. 1996. Mary Jemison, White Woman of the Seneca. Santa Fe: Clear Light Publishers.

Gillespie, C. Bancroft, and George M. Curtis, eds. 1906. A Century of Meriden. Meriden: Journal Publishing.

Graymont, Barbara. 1972. The Iroquois in the American Revolution. Syracuse: Syracuse University Press.

Grinde, Donald A., and Griffin, Robert. 1997. Apocalypse of Chiokoyhikoy, Chief of the Iroquois. Quebec: Les Presses de l'Université Laval.

Ha-yen-doh-nees (Leo Cooper). 1995. Seneca Indian Stories. Greenfield Center, NY: Greenfield Review Press.

Harrington, M.R. 1965. The Iroquois Trail, Dickon Among the Onondaga and Seneca. New Brunswick: Rutgers University Press.

Hauptman, Laurence M. 1999. Conspiracy of Interests, Iroquois Dispossession and the Rise of New York State. Syracuse: Syracuse University Press.

Hauptman, Laurence M., and McLester, Gordon L., eds. 1999. The Oneida Indian Journey From New York to Wisconsin 1784–1860. Madison: The University of Wisconsin Press.

Idzerda, Stanley J., ed. 1979. Lafayette in the Age of the American Revolution, Selected Letters and Papers. Ithaca: Cornell University Press.

Jean, Terri. 1995. 365 Days of Walking the Red Road. Avon, MA: Adams Media Corp.

Jemison, G. Peter, and Schein, Anna M. eds. 2000. Treaty of Canandaigua 1794. Santa Fe: Clear Light Publishers.

Jennings, Francis. 1984. The Ambiguous Iroquois Empire. New York: W.W. Norton.

Johansen, Bruce E. 1982. Forgotten Founders, Benjamin Franklin, the Iroquois and the Rationale for the American Revolution. Ipswich: Gambit Publishers.

Johansen, Bruce E. 1998. Debating Democracy, Native American Legacy of Freedom. Santa Fe: Clear Light Publishers.

Johansen, Bruce E.; Grinde, Donald A. 1997. The Encyclopedia of Native American Biography. New York: Da Capo Press.

Katz, Jane, ed. 1995. Messengers of the Wind, Native American Women Tell Their Life Stories. New York: Ballantine Books.

Kupperman, Karen Ordahl. 2000. Indians & English, Facing off in Early America. Ithaca: Cornell University Press.

Larsen, Deborah. 2002. The White. New York: Alfred A. Knopf.

Levine, Ellen. 1998. If You Lived With the Iroquois. New York: Scholastic.

Lyons, Oren, et. al. 1992. Exiled in the Land of the Free, Democracy, Indian Nations and the U.S. Constitution. Santa Fe: Clear Light Publishers.

Malone, Dumas. 1948. Jefferson the Virginian. Boston: Little, Brown.

Mann, Charles C. 2005. 1491, New Revelations of the Americas Before Columbus. New York: Alfred A. Knopf.

Martin, Rafe. 2002. The World Before This One. New York: Arthur A. Levine Books.

Merrill, Arch. 1949. Land of the Seneca. Interlaken, NY: Empire State Books.

Mintz, Max. 1999. Seeds of Empire, The American Revolutionary Conquest of the Iroquois. New York: New York University Press.

Morgan, Edmund S. 1975. American Slavery, American Freedom. New York: W.W. Norton.

Moscow, Henry. 1960. Thomas Jefferson and His World. New York: American Heritage Publishing Co.

Neihardt, John G. 1932. Black Hawk Speaks. New York: William Morrow.

Niemczycki, Mary Ann Palmer. 1984. The Origin and Development of the Seneca and Cayuga Tribes of New York State. Ph.D. dissertation. State University of New York at Buffalo.

Parker, Arthur C. 1929. The Indian Interpretation of the Sullivan-Clinton Campaign. Publication Fund Series. Vol. VIII. Rochester: Rochester Historical Society.

Parker, Arthur C. 1989. Seneca Myths & Folk Tales. Lincoln: University of Nebraska Press.

Parkman, Francis. 1851, 1994. The Conspiracy of Pontiac. Lincoln: Bison Book, University of Nebraska Press.

Parkman, Francis; Tebbel, John, ed. 1865–82, 1948. The Battle for North America. London: Phoenix Press.

Persons, Stowe. 1960. American Minds, A History of Ideas. New York: Holt, Rinehart & Winston.

Peterson, Merrill D. 1975. The Portable Thomas Jefferson. New York: Penguin Books.

Richter, Daniel K. 1992. The Ordeal of the Longhouse, The Peoples of the Iroquois League in the Era of European Colonization. Chapel Hill: University of North Carolina Press.

Ridington, Jillian and Robin. 1982. The People of the Longhouse. Buffalo: Firefly Books.

Schlesinger, Arthur M, Jr. 1992. The Disuniting of America, Reflections on a Multicultural Society. New York: W.W. Norton.

Seaver, James E., and Namais, June, eds. 1992. A Narrative of the Life of Mrs. Mary Jemison. Canandaigua: J.D. Bemis. 1824. University of Oklahoma Press.

Shenandoah, Joanne-Tekalibwa and George, Douglas M.-Kanentiio. 1998. Skywoman, Legends of the Iroquois. Santa Fe: Clear Light Publishers.

Sneve, Virginia Driving Hawk. 1995. The Iroquois. New York: Holiday House.

Snow, Dean R. 1994. The Iroquois. Oxford: Blackwell Publisher.

Trigger, Bruce G. 1985. Natives and Newcomers, Canada's "Heroic Age" Reconsidered. Montreal: McGill-Queens University Press.

Van DerBeets, Richard. 1973. Held Captive by Indians, Selected Narratives, 1642–1836. Knoxville: The University of Tennessee Press.

Van Doren, Carl. 1938. Benjamin Franklin. New York: The Viking Press.

Venables, Robert W., ed. 1995. The Six Nations of New York, The 1892 United States Extra Census Bulletin. Ithaca: Cornell University Press.

Vennum, Thomas, Jr. 1994. American Indian Lacrosse, Little Brother of War. Washington: Smithsonian Institution Press.

Wall, Steve. 1993. Wisdom's Daughters, Conversations with Women Elders of Native America. New York: Harper Perennial.

Wallace, Anthony, F.C. 1972. The Death and Rebirth of the Seneca. New York: Vintage Books.

Wallace, Anthony, F.C. 1999. Jefferson and the Indians, The Tragic Fate of the First Americans. Cambridge: Harvard University Press.

Welch, James. 1986. Fools Crow. New York: Penguin Books.

Wilson, Edmund. 1959. Apologies to the Iroquois. Syracuse: Syracuse University Press.

GOVERNMENT AND PRIVATE DOCUMENTS

New York State. 1999. Ganondagan, State Historic Site. Victor, NY. Office of Parks, Recreation and Historic Preservation.

Chemung County, NY. Undated. Newtown Battlefield Reservation, Home to Sullivan's Monument Park. Wellsburg, NY. Chemung Valley Living History Center.

Byrne, Thomas E., and Lawrence, E. Eyres, eds. 1999. The Sullivan-Clinton Expedition, 1779, In Pennsylvania and New York. Elmira: Chemung County Historical Society.

ARTICLES

The Rev. Samuel Andrews—One of Wallingford's Early Outspoken Clergymen. 1967. The Morning Record. Meriden, CT. 27 July.

Carter, Diana. 2001. Seneca rebury ancestors. Rochester (NY) Democrat & Chronicle. 11 September.

Chen, David W. 2000. Battle Over Iroquois Land Claims Escalates. The New York Times. 16 May.

Dabney, Virginius. 1928. Jouett Out Rides Tarleton and Saves Jefferson from Capture. Scribner's Magazine, Vol. 83. June. pp. 690–698.

ONLINE SOURCES

Constitution of the Iroquois Nations: The Great Binding Law, Gayanashagowa. Undated. The Constitution Society. Available from http://jmu.edu/madison/irocon.htm.

The Canandaigua Treaty of 1794. Undated. The Seneca Nation of Indians. Available from http://www.sni.org/treaty1794.htm.

A Short History of Pittsford, NY. Undated. Available from http://www.pg1.com/pittsford/short_history.html.